a Sid Rafferty Mystery

OLD GROWTH

by Matt Hughes

Old Growth
Copyright Matthew Hughes, 2014

Published by Matthew Hughes
ISBN: 978-1-927880-13-5

Cover and book design by Bradley W. Schenck

For Linda, still

Chapter 1

Stu Haglund was a tree-hugger's nightmare.

Squat, squinty-eyed and squirting tobacco juice from a constant lipful of Copenhagen snus, he dealt with trees in much the same way Bill Cody had treated buffalo. You didn't have to read what was painted on the doors of his pick-up — *HAGLUND AND SON, WE FALL AND HAUL* — to know he could have stepped out of a 'Know Your Enemy' poster on the washroom door at Greenpeace headquarters.

I watched him from my perch on the hood of my battered old AMC Concord, parked on a logging road not far from the Vancouver Island village of Cumberland. It was late June in 1993, one of those hot summer days when the bugs buzz like high-tension wires and the Forest Service's highway signs were warning the risk of wildfires had gone from high to *extreme.*

Haglund waded through sun-bleached grass across an old clearing, a long-bladed Husqvarna chainsaw bouncing off his hip with every other bandy-legged step. The forest near the road was second-growth, the land originally cleared in the first few decades of the twentieth century, but, farther back in, beyond the grass stood trees that were huge and ancient, the wide spaces between so dark the only things that could grow there were ferns and mushrooms.

Haglund snugged his ear protectors into place, smacked his orange hardhat firmly down onto his sweaty bald spot, and yanked the cord on the Husqvarna. The machine whooped into life with a sound like a cross between a naval destroyer's siren and a bad old Harley Davidson, then squawked as Haglund goosed the trigger a couple of times.

He rasped the grey stubble on his chin, craning his neck back to look up the length of the Douglas fir, six hundred years old and sixty metres from mossy roots to needled crown. He looked down, and I guessed he was marking the spot where he would make the main cut, lining it up how the tree would fall sideways across the edge of the clearing.

He spat a brown gobbet, then he swung the saw around like Yogi Berra in slow motion, and set its whining teeth to the bark. Sawdust made a sweet smelling cloud around the incision, chips flew like shrapnel into the undergrowth, and Haglund sliced into centuries.

Most of the way through the bole, he eased off the throttle and slid the saw out of the wood. Gingerly, he picked his way around the massive trunk, set his cork boots square for balance, and made two quick angled cuts. A wedge of wood dropped out of the tree, then the giant fir leaned resignedly into the pull of gravity, a tired old tree ready for its afternoon nap. There was a loud *snap* as the narrow isthmus of wood he had left between the cuts gave way.

The tree began to topple, at first achingly slowly, then gathering irrevocable speed. If it had been me holding the chainsaw, I would have stood there gaping, probably chewing over some lame metaphor that would have connected my brief lifespan with the demise of an organism that had first sprouted back when all of my ancestors were hewing and hauling for their medieval betters.

But Haglund was an experienced faller. He knew a dying tree often takes a man with it. As the fir began its final descent, he dropped the Husqvarna and legged it.

He probably planned to be twenty or thirty feet back

when the wood slammed into the ground. But plans have a way of not working out. Haglund took no more than two steps before he sprawled headlong onto a spreading fern. He jumped up immediately, but immediately was not soon enough.

The fir crashed into the clearing, but the sawn end kicked back over the stump: not very far, no more than a couple of metres, but far enough for a spear of splintered wood to catch Haglund from behind. The wood entered below the ball-and-socket joint of his right shoulder, sliced through flesh and cartilage, and removed the arm as neatly as Julia Child could take off a chicken's wing.

The impact knocked Haglund face down onto the grass. I saw his severed arm fly off to one side, pinwheeling lazily into a bush, where it landed upright, palm turned out. It looked as if the plant had taken up panhandling. The faller made a sound like a surprised snort, then collapsed.

They say emergencies separate people into two kinds: the movers and the freezers. I guess I'm a freezer. I sat there on the hood of my car, staring like a hick at a two-buck carny strip show.

Haglund's son was a mover. He'd been waiting by his old man's pick-up, ready with the two smaller saws they would use for trimming and bucking the tree. When the butt tore into his father, he dropped the gear and raced across the clearing. He knelt by Haglund, grabbed the armless shoulder and rolled him over, then turned to me and shouted, "Help me, goddammit!"

And suddenly I could move again. I was aware of racing to the young man's side, but it was as if I was taking forever to cross the clearing, and the only thing I could think about was how I couldn't remember the kid's name — it was Skitch or something — and then all at once there was Stu Haglund revealing life's big secret: that beneath our clothes and attitudes is a whole lot of vulnerable pink meat and pale fragile bone.

There wasn't much blood, just seepage from the wound, and at first I thought that was strange. Then I realized although arteries were open to the air, Haglund's heart wasn't pumping any more blood through them. He was dead.

The faller lay there gape-mouthed, and I could see his eyes were not taking one last look at the forest canopy. He had the oddly flattened look corpses get, all muscle tone gone. The only thing on him was a trickle of tobacco juice leaking from a corner of his mouth and ran down his cheek.

"He's gone," I said. "Musta been shock."

A big black fly bumbled in and landed on the dead face. Young Haglund waved it away, but it didn't go far. He stared at his father as if the old man was playing some incomprehensible trick on him.

My brain had begun to work again. I closed the dead man's eyes and said, "Listen. I'll get a tarp from the truck to cover him. Then I'll go for help while you stay here."

He nodded. His face was as grey as his father's. I knew any help I'd be bringing would be for the surviving member of the Haglunds.

I got the tarp, spread it over the body, and went back to the car. Luckily, it turned over first time, so Skitch or Mitch didn't have to listen to my starter motor singing its current new hit.

But turning the Concord around on the narrow logging road was a whole other chapter. The car had always had character, which was my thumbnail description of such minor defects as the electrical short-circuit that switched the headlights off and on at random, and the recent failure of the handle on the driver's door, which now meant I had to exit and enter from the passenger side.

The car's latest idiosyncrasy was a short circuit which caused the horn to beep fitfully whenever I cranked the steering wheel hard in either direction. Now, getting the machine turned around on the narrow road resulted in a minor chorus of toots, until I had it straightened out and pointed back at Cumberland. I tromped on the gas and spewed pea gravel behind me.

I hadn't gone a hundred metres before I saw something that made me stomp on the brake. The Concord's back end seemed to want to come around to confer with its front, but I spun the wheel this way and that — steer into a skid, I told myself, with no idea whether I was doing it or the opposite — until the old car shuddered to a stop.

Just off the road, a fancy four-by-four was backed into a small opening in the forest. It was the kind of vehicle favoured by folks who combined a recent win on the lottery with a long-standing enjoyment of country and western music. It was maroon in colour, with a tan pinstripe from headlight to tail, and blacked out windows. On the windshield was a sticker from a Vancouver FM station on which the singers all had Ozarkian accents, even though many of them came from places like New Jersey and Timmins, Ontario.

Normally, none of the vehicle's attributes would have stopped me even if I hadn't been on a mission of mercy, but the thought had flashed into my head that this was just the kind of ride whose driver would have a cell phone. I'd been meaning to get one, but I was hoping the prices would come down.

I left the Concord's engine running, and went to bang on the opaque driver's window. "Hey, in there!" I called. "Man's been hurt up the road! You got a phone?"

Nothing happened. I cupped my fingers around my eyes and tried to see through the tinted glass. If there had been daylight on the other side of the vehicle, I could probably have made out any shapes inside pretty clearly.

But the four-by-four was backed into second-growth fir that had got high enough to deny the sun to anything underneath its lower branches.

All I got was a sombre reflection of my own eyes. *Through a glass darkly*, offered the guy who lives in the back of my head, the one who actually composes the speeches and other commercial writing I peddle for a living. I squinted and put the edge of my palm to the glass, trying to find an angle that would let me see in. I had the odd feeling somebody was in there, looking back at me with cold eyes, but then I make that living I mentioned from having a working imagination.

I got back in the Concord and spun it down the road. I didn't have far to go. The twenty-hectare patch of old growth the Haglunds had contracted to cut stood on top of a low bluff above the old graveyard, little more than a kilometre from the village's main thoroughfare, Dunsmuir Avenue. The street was named for the rapacious Scots mining engineer who had founded Vancouver Island's coal and railroad dynasty back when Cumberland's port at Union Bay, a few klicks away on Georgia Strait, was a coaling stop for the British Empire's Pacific fleet.

It was a narrow street lined with three blocks of dilapidated one- and two-storey shops, old-style beer parlours, a blond brick post office and the village museum. In the middle of it all was an empty store that had been converted into the RCMP's local policing centre, after villagers complained about how long it took the cops to drive the seven miles from Courtenay whenever the local wild boys needed a little reining in.

Ordinarily, I tried to keep the Concord out of sight of the police, lest some safety-conscious gendarme decide to put me to a road worthiness test. But today I came down Dunsmuir with the hole in my muffler in full voice, did a u-turn that raised a few cheerful toots from the horn, and stopped right outside the storefront cop shop.

I let the engine idle, slid over to the passenger side and got out. A young Mountie looked up from papers spread over a folding table just inside the store's open door. He eyed me, he looked at the Concord, and then he started to get up.

I stuck my head in the door, and shouted over the gurgle of the car's engine. "A man's been killed. Logging accident."

"Where?" he said.

I told him, and he reached for a hand-held radio, called for an ambulance, and gave directions. Then he took out a pen and notebook. "Who are you?" he wanted to know.

I told him I was Sid Rafferty, a freelance writer from the town of Comox across the harbour.

"What were you doing at the logging site?"

"I was supposed to meet a client there. He didn't show up."

Of course he wanted to know who my client was, and of course I told him. Detectives and lawyers may have rules about keeping their clients' names out of conversations with the constabulary, but if there was any such code for freelance writers nobody had ever sent me a copy.

I had gone to the logging site to meet Rod Bilder, a real estate developer who planned to construct some two hundred townhouses and condos on the land he had hired Haglund to clear. The cop had heard of Bilder. Everybody in the Comox Valley knew about Cumberland's home-grown real estate tycoon who aimed to take this sleepy little community left over from the nineteenth century and turn it into a twenty-first century up-market enclave for retirees and yuppy downshifters fleeing the big bad cities.

Having lived in the Comox Valley for a year now, I

could complain about the influx of newcomers with only the faintest hint of a blush.

"Is Mr. Bilder at the site?" the Mountie asked.

"No," I said. "He didn't show up. I was waiting for him when the accident happened."

The constable took down the particulars. Then he locked up and got into the blue and white Chevy with the bison head on the doors. But before he pulled away, he climbed out of the cruiser and took out his notebook again. He made a note of the Concord's licence plate, swept me and the car with one long look that needed no interpretation, then drove off.

I said one short word, got into the offending vehicle, and puttered up the street to the Cumberland museum. The museum was a deceptively small building, clad in brown-stained vertical siding, with a bogey-wheeled piece of coal-mining equipment I couldn't identify parked on the front lawn.

Inside was a trove of bygone village life from the time when the world ran on steam boilers powered by the black stuff that ran in rich seams under the hills above Cumby, as the locals called it. The museum preserved relics like the wickets from the old mine office where the miners came for their pay: $3.50 a day for an experienced white man; $1.70 for an equally skilled Chinese. There were trophy cups won by village sports teams a hundred years ago, odds and ends of household utensils, and the warped sheet-metal sign — with empty sockets where the 40-watt bulbs went — that used to hang in front of Campbell's general store until the big fire in the thirties.

There was plenty more, I'd heard, including a life size mock-up of an underground mine tunnel in the basement. But I'd never done more than glance around the place, and the only attraction that drew me to the museum this afternoon was to be found in the little office to the left of the front door. She was Maureen Migliorini, although she preferred to be called Mo. She owned a wild mane of red hair, a magnificent smile and all of my affections, and she had volunteered to help organize an exhibit of 'women's work' from the 1860s to the present.

I poked my head into the office. Mo was bent over a long wooden table beside a middle-aged woman with frosted blonde hair. They were arranging cut-out paper shapes on a floor plan diagram of the exhibition space.

"If we angle the loom like so," said Mo, rotating an oblong piece of paper ninety degrees, "we can open up some room for the tub and washboard to be displayed in the round."

The other woman nodded agreement. That was Sally McMahon, a strong featured, quiet woman whose great-grandfather had come to Cumberland to help dig the first pit. She was a licensed physiotherapist with a small practice in Courtenay, and also the estranged wife of the man I had gone to meet at Hockney's Woods. The connection was no coincidence: Rod Bilder had learned that I was a writer for hire through Sally's growing friendship with Mo. Mo had got to know Sally when she'd needed a course of ultrasound for an old tennis elbow condition that occasionally flared up when Mo spent too many hours working the trackball on her PowerBook laptop.

Major real estate developments need all kinds of written material, from presentations for zoning hearings, brochures for home buyers, even audio-visuals for prospective investors. I'd done this kind of work before, and I looked to Rod Bilder to keep my pantry stocked this summer.

The two women both became aware of me at the same time. Mo looked up, gave me one of those smiles that still hit me like a burst of sunlight ravishing a dark room. By contrast, Sally McMahon's gaze seemed more darkly intense than ever. I'd noticed from the first time I'd met her her face seemed preternaturally still and her eyes scarcely ever moved, just bored into whatever or whomever she was looking at like a pair of gun loops set in an armored vehicle.

"Hey," I said.

"Hey, yourself," said Mo. "What are you doing here?"

"Weren't you supposed to meet Rod?" Sally asked.

"He didn't show. And then there was an accident." I told them Stu Haglund had been killed by a falling tree, but I didn't go into the gory details.

Sally went a little paler than usual. "Was Titch there?" she asked. I mentally slapped my forehead. That was the name I couldn't think of.

"He saw it," I said.

"My god," said Mo.

"Poor Stu," said Sally. "We were in kindergarten together." She took a deep breath, let it out slowly. "What happened? Was it quick? No, don't tell me. I don't really want to know." She shuddered. It was as if the news of her neighbour's death had taken a few seconds to travel from her ears to the inner part where she lived, and now it had suddenly arrived. "I don't feel too well," she whispered.

She didn't look it. Mo threw me a concerned glance, said, "Get a glass of water," and led Sally to a chair. I went down the hall to the washroom and came back with a paper cup. Sally drank the water and appeared to regain her spirits.

"I'd better go," she said. "Maeve Haglund's going to need some support."

"Are you up to it?" asked Mo.

"I think so." She stood up. "We can do this tomorrow, if you're free."

Mo said she'd be happy to come in again. We all walked out together, and soon Sally McMahon was tramping down Dunsmuir's worn sidewalks. Mo and I stood on the corner and watched the determined swing of the woman's little handbag match her firm steps.

"Are you sure she's okay?" I said.

Mo shrugged. "They're a tough breed up here. She was telling me about how when she was a little girl they'd send their men down into those filthy dangerous mines every day, never knowing if they'd ever come back to daylight again."

I had a sudden image of Haglund's face staring into nothing. "Jesus," I said. "People shouldn't have to risk dying just for a living."

"Was it bad, the accident?" Mo asked.

"Bad enough." I told her about the arm spinning through the air.

She winced. "Come on," she said. "Let's go home."

Her orange Hyundai was parked across the street. It was old and developing acne from rust, but next to the Concord it was high-class transportation. I got into the AMC, crossed my fingers, and keyed the ignition.

Nothing.

I took out the key, reinserted it, and tried again. I had no idea why it should make any difference, but it often did. The six-cylinder engine farted into life, and I revved it discreetly. I rolled the window down and called to Mo, "Follow me!" Then I put up the window, patted the car's dash and said, "Sorry, old love, it's time."

I drove the grumbling Concord down Dunsmuir to Fourth Street, turned left and found the road back to Courtenay. It was downhill and twisty in places, curving past the graveyard where the headstones were old enough to have settled and tilted. Then the two-lane blacktop looped around the gravel pit and cement plant and went into the woods.

It was all second growth now, fir and spruce mostly. In Sally McMahon's great-grandfather's time there had been big timber all over the coastal valley, from the sea right up into the foothills, including ancient cedars so massive ten men couldn't stretch their arms around one.

They'd taken them down at first to clear land for homes and farms, and to rough out props and joists for the mines. The men stood on boards jammed into the living wood, leaning in and out on two-handled saws, then finishing the job with double-bit axes.

By the turn of the century, they'd laid rail lines along Vancouver Island's valley bottoms, and pocket steam engines pulled logs to the sea, where they were shipped to lumber mills as far away as China.

In the forties, with the valley floors mostly stripped, the forest companies got trucks strong enough to take the strain of hauling big timber on rough-cut roads, and truck-loggers brave enough to drive them. They started cutting the slopes that rose towards the mountains.

Now, a hundred and twenty-five years after the first steel blade had bit into a Comox Valley tree, the old growth was only a memory — except for the twenty hectares that Rod Bilder was preparing to log and build on. It was the last stand of big timber in the valley. I wondered how much it was worth.

The two-laner came out of the woods on the outskirts of Courtenay. Instead of passing through the little city and heading home to Comox, I hung a left onto Willemar Street. The Concord beeped meditatively as I took the corner. In my rear-view mirror, I saw Mo take the corner and follow.

A half mile on, I came to Lake Trail Road, turned left at the junior high school — with yet more toots from under the hood to excite the wonder of passing pedestrians — and trundled up to Powerhouse Road, at the end of which was an auto wrecker's yard.

I parked beside the office. Mo put her Hyundai a discreet distance away and carefully avoided looking at me.

Five minutes later, I came out of the office with a borrowed screwdriver, removed the Concord's licence plates, took them back to the man inside, and emerged again carrying fifty dollars and a piece of paper that said the AMC was no longer mine.

I got into the passenger seat of Mo's car and said, "Home."

She pulled out without a word, and affected not to notice when I turned to the rear window and sneaked a last look at my faithful old companion. I knew how the kid felt in *Old Yeller*.

We drove through Courtenay, down Seventeenth Street to the swing bridge that would open to let fish boats come up the Puntledge River to the moorage at Green Slough, and took the dyke road along the east bank towards Comox.

High tide was just turning, so the mud flats and reed beds were submerged, but a couple of blue herons were working the shallows. I saw a dark spot out in mid-stream where the fresh water met the sea. It was moving against the current, probably a harbour seal chasing salmon fingerlings.

Mo steered us up the hill into Comox, and we turned onto Back Road. A couple of minutes later, we were in my driveway — technically, our driveway, now that Mo had moved in.

She reached to turn off the ignition. "Wait," I said. "Do you mind being my chauffeur a few more minutes?"

She shrugged and left the motor running. I went into the house and came out a minute later lugging my old fax machine. It was a five-year-old Savin, state of the art in its day, with all kinds of bells-and-whistles I'd never used. It was also a continuing annoyance to work with, because it printed out on rolled thermal paper. Whenever a client faxed me a lengthy document, the Savin would cover my floor with little facsimiles of the Dead Sea scrolls, which I had to uncurl, flatten out and put into order.

I stowed the fax machine on the back seat, got in beside Mo and gave her an address over on Lazo Road, north and east of the Comox town site. We were there in under ten minutes.

It was a white frame house on a five acre parcel at the end of a mud-and-gravel driveway. Somebody in a previous generation had ambitions in the direction of orchard-keeping, but the drive must have since leached out of the gene pool. The pear and apple trees had been left to run as wild as tame trees ever get, their roots shooting up a riot of suckers that would be draining their parents' energies before they could make fruit.

I wasn't interested in what might be on the trees; I had come for what was parked in the dappled shade beneath them, covered by a sheet of plastic held down by rocks and firewood.

The owner of the place was at his ease in a tubular steel and plastic chaise longue, the end of a long-necked brown bottle not far from his bottom lip. He was a little older than me, maybe forty, a former slab of muscle that was now mounding into paunch.

"That it?" he said, as I unloaded the Savin from Mo's back seat.

"Yep," I said. "Still want to deal?"

He up-ended the beer, then dropped the empty into a case by his side, rocked himself forward and stood. His belch made it a two-syllable word when he said, "Sure."

I humped the fax machine into his house, hooked it up to his phone line, then used the hand-set to phone a local friend who also had a fax. I told him I was going to fax him a page and asked him to retransmit right back to me at the number I gave him.

I hung up, sent the page — it was from an old manuscript — and within a minute it was back again, unrolling out of the fax machine. I flattened it out and showed it and the original to the owner of the beer belly.

"See," I said. "It sends and receives just fine. You can also use it to make photocopies."

He nodded. "Okay," he said. "I'll show you mine."

Outside, he hauled the plastic cover off, and there was the Concord's prospective replacement. It was the same colour and roughly the same size as a pocket battleship, but with four doors and fancy hubcaps. It was hard to believe they actually used to make cars this big.

"Nineteen-seventy-seven Ford Ell-Tee-Dee Two," said the beer belly. "Hundred and twenty thousand miles, don't know what that is in kilometres, but it runs okay. Got a leak in the power steering pressure hose, hole in the exhaust system, otherwise she's a beauty."

I shook my head as if pondering weighty matters.

"Look," he said. "Pressure hose is gonna cost you a hundred. Exhaust maybe a little more, time they bend the pipe and weld it in. But that's it."

I cleared my throat. Then I popped the hood, looked around the engine compartment for anything I could identify. The brake cylinder's brassy finish stood out. Since it was one of the few components I recognized, I thumbed up the wire that held down the lid and lifted it off. The hydraulic fuel inside might have been low, or it might have been fine; it was hard to tell since the cylinder sloped to one side.

"Hmmm," I said, and waited.

"All right, all right," he said. "It's a thirteen-year-old car for Chrissake! You're probably gonna have to look at the brakes."

"Well..." I said.

"Okay, look, I was saying the fax machine plus a hundred. Whattaya say we make it an even trade?"

I chewed my lip a little just to make it convincing, then said, "Deal," and shook his hammy hand. We went inside and filled in the government forms.

When I climbed back into Mo's car, she said, "You're not really going to drive that."

"It's a classic," I said.

She snorted. "You're going to need one of those wide load signs."

"Ho ho."

"And maybe a man with a red flag to walk ahead so you don't scare the horses."

I looked back at the LTD as we headed down the driveway to Lazo and off to transfer the vehicle's title. "They were pretty good cars."

"You know as much about cars as I know about..." But she couldn't think of anything she knew that little about.

"Come on," I said. "Think how much fun we'll have bringing back all the old jokes. Like, *I don't need a spare; I just keep a Honda in the trunk.*"

We tooled up Lazo, past the stony beach south of Point Holmes. A bald eagle was planing low over the beach like a special effect.

"How many cars do you see these days that can land small aircraft on the hood?" I said.

"Uh huh," she said. "Why not buy something a little more dependable?"

"I like cars with character," I said. "Besides, I'm cheap."

"No kidding," she said.

An hour later, I had the LTD re-registered, with new plates and insurance papers. I dropped them off at the Anchor Garage down at the foot of Church Street and arranged for them to tow the car in, check it over, and fix everything up to a limit of five hundred.

Mo and I went home. As we eased along Comox Avenue to Back Road, she reached into a bag on the floor behind the passenger seat. "Here," she said.

She dropped it into my lap. It was a nicely bound book, the dust jacket showing a portrait in pastels of a youngish man with a scarf tied around his neck. Above the face was the title: *Ginger — The Life and Death of Albert Goodwin.*

"We've done this," I said.

"It won't hurt you to read it."

"I don't want to write another movie."

"Tell me that after you've read the book."

I opened it, riffled the pages. There were photos in the middle, black and white snaps of Cumberland a hundred years or so ago. Shacks and mine works; mine owners, serious, prosperous and upright in stiff collars; and miners, hard faces under old-fashioned hats as they crowded up to the bar at a tiny saloon.

And a gravestone, rough hewn, and on it the words, *LEST WE FORGET, GINGER GOODWIN, SHOT JULY 26th 1918, A WORKERS' FRIEND.*

"Is this up in the Cumberland cemetery?" I asked.

"I've seen it," said Mo.

"I don't want to write any more movies," I said.

"You've got to do something."

"I thought I was."

She said nothing, but I knew her silences could be very well-spoken.

"I don't want to fight," I said.

"We're not fighting."

Not yet, I said to myself.

We had wound our way down Back Road to the turn-off to our house. A purple and white car was sitting in the driveway, and an RCMP corporal in the black and khaki working uniform was rapping on our front door.

He turned as we drove in and parked beside the police cruiser, waiting as we mounted the front steps. He was middle-aged with a military moustache, one of those career noncoms who live up to the image of the *we-always-get-our-man* Mounties. "Mr. Sid Rafferty?" he said.

"Yes,"

"Corporal Mikhailovsky. I wonder if I could ask you

about what you saw this afternoon in Cumberland."

I invited him in and we sat in the kitchen while Mo made tea. He put his hat on the table, then opened his notebook.

"How well did you know Mr. Haglund?"

"Not at all," I said.

"Why were you there?"

I explained about going to meet Bilder and his not showing up.

"Would you tell me what you saw?"

I told him. He interrupted occasionally to ask for amplification — how far away was I, did I see anyone else in the area — until there wasn't anything left unsaid. I could recognize a trained interviewer when I saw one.

"That's what happened," I finished. "It was a straight-out accident. He fell and the tree got him."

"It was no accident," he said.

"I saw it," I said.

"But you didn't see this," he said, and produced a coil of colourless nylon fish line. "There were lengths of this stuff strung all over the area. Trip wires. We're investigating Mr. Haglund's death as at least manslaughter, perhaps murder."

Chapter 2

There was a hole in the wall behind Rod Bilder's desk. Something fist-sized had crashed through the gyproc at shoulder height, causing a fine spray of white powder to sift down onto the papers and elevation drawings spread over the imitation oak.

There were more flecks of white dust on the right sleeve of his lightweight jacket and among the thick red hairs on the back of his right hand. I didn't have to be a forensic whiz-kid to put it together: Bilder had recently received news that didn't please him. I didn't have to guess what it was.

I stood in the doorway. He was on the phone when I arrived at his office, and he flashed two fingers like Winston Churchill in an old newsreel, to tell me how many minutes he expected the call to take. I looked around his office on the top floor of a small two-storey commercial block in what passed for the City of Courtenay's downtown core. Nothing fancy, no luxuries. A barebones place of business: desk, credenza, file cabinet, chairs, computer, fax and phone. Either Bilder was a man of spartan tastes, or he had little money to spare.

He waved me into the room, gestured to a steel-and-fabric chair in front of his desk. I sat down, folded my hands and waited. He was listening with increasing dissatisfaction to whatever he was getting over the phone. The tips of his fingers showed a deep pink from the pressure of his grip on the handset.

"No goddamn way," he told whoever was on the other

end of the line. "Bunch of eco-wackos, assholes, let 'em shit in their hats. We get some guys, we go in there with metal detectors. Any spikes or booby traps, we clear 'em out, get them trees down. Anybody wants to get in the way, they take their fuckin' chances."

He listened, and I saw a ring of white grow around his irises, and his mouth opened wider. "Well, Jesus Christ," he said, "get the stuff out of there. The hell you doin', plantin' in there the first place?" He listened some more, then said, "No, you had no right. You can't find Crown land, for chrissake?"

The voice on the other end of the line leaked past Bilder's ear and came to me as shrill rapid-fire, too faint to resolve into words. It was like overhearing a cartoon flea telling somebody off. The developer's face darkened as he listened. He put the phone receiver between his shoulder and his jawline and fumbled in a desk drawer, until he brought out a bottle of pills with a tamper-proof top.

The bottle chose the wrong moment to resist his efforts to open it. Bilder squeezed the cylinder in one big fist. The bottle said *crack!* and amber shards of plastic spilled onto the elevation drawings along with a rustle of flesh-coloured pills that made a break for the edge of the desk. The man corralled a couple of them and tossed them back, followed by a swig of something cold from a styrofoam cup.

The medicine had no discernible effect. He still looked like a man imitating a volcano that would just as soon get it over with and throw some lava around.

It can be embarrassing to watch a guy lose his temper. I looked around, searching for something other than Bilder to take my attention .

There was a sheet of paper on the corner of the desk nearest to me. It looked to be the ordinary eight-and-a-half-by-eleven, twenty-pound bond, the kind that fed through my laser printer on every job I did. It was partially covered by some blueprints and architect's sketches of the houses Bilder wanted to put up.

It was something I'd seen a score of times in movies and TV shows. Someone had laboriously clipped individual letters from a newspaper — by the green tinge of the paper, I knew that at least some of them had been cut from the local biweekly — and arranged them into words on the page.

The message was partially obscured by the stuff Bilder had piled on top of it, but I could make out some of the words. "...OF HOCKNEY'S WOODS...," said one line. "...L BE REAL TROUBLE," said the next.

There was even a signature, if you could call it that: "EARTHSTRIKE!"

Bilder had reached his all-fed-up level with whoever was on the phone. He shouted over the chittering voice, "I don't give a red-rimmed fuck! Get in there and cut 'em, or rip 'em out, or whatever the hell you do, and don't leave any trace. Jeez, it's not like there's no official interest!"

He listened some more. His wide shoulders hunched and he leaned forward to shout into the mouthpiece. "No, goddammit! Do it today, or I'll go in there with a can of gas!" He banged the handset into the cradle.

I could hear the air whistling through his nose. I watched him get hold of himself. It only took ten seconds, then he shrugged and closed his eyes, blew out a breath through his open mouth.

"Sorry, Raff," he said. "Guy gets on my nerves." He took another breath, and let it go. "Anyway, damn project's on hold. Just temporarily," he added. "But I don't know how long before I can get back in there."

He rubbed his face, noticed the dust on his hand, and wiped it off.

"Have the police sealed off the woods?" I asked.

He blinked. "Nah... well, yeah, but just that part where Stu Haglund got it. They may even be out of there by now. I'm gonna talk to them soon." He looked at the movie-style letter on the corner of his desk, saw me looking at it too, then moved both hands in the way that says, *Who gives a shit?*

"No," he continued, "somebody called Workers Compensation and said the place was too goddamn dangerous to work in. So then the WCB calls me and says, 'hold it, don't do nothin' until we check it out,' and I say, 'well, how long's that gonna be?' and they say, 'two weeks, maybe three .'"

He rubbed his face again. "I got to get that timber down. I have to, I'll cut it myself." He told me he had a contract for the wood with the local sawmill down on the Puntledge River. If he could deliver it on time, he'd get enough to get the housing project started. Once he got past that first step, there was an institutional investor — a pension fund, I thought — that would come in with the downstream money, and then he'd be rolling.

I told him I understood. And I did, from experience. I'd once had a potentially life-changing movie deal which had depended on being able to coax a whole lot of money from different sources into one pot at one time. When a key player pulled out, all the dominoes had toppled, and I'd had to abandon my dreams of six-figure Hollywood deals. I'd gone back to hacking out a freelancer's living — doing speeches, annual reports, and the kind of promotional bumpf Rod Bilder would need for his condo development if it ever came back on stream.

"So, there it is," he said. "Right now I can't use you. This thing comes back together, I'll still need a writer and I still want you to do the job."

He opened a desk drawer, took out an envelope and gave it to me. Inside were four pieces of orange, each with the face of a forgotten prime minister on them. "That's for your wasted time," he said. "I still want to use you, but...."

"Well, call me whenever," I said, and took the money. It was a pleasant surprise; I'd been expecting "tough luck and bye bye," but Bilder had a reputation as a straight arrow. His neighbours in Cumberland called him a rough diamond, but they'd trust the former barroom brawler turned real-estate entrepreneur to do the right thing.

"I'll bring back the material you gave me," I said. There was a small pile of paper — architect's sketches, a prospectus, some old newspaper articles about Bilder's previous projects and the history of Hockney's Woods — that he'd given me as background information. It was sitting on the desk next to my word-processor in my home office. "Tomorrow okay?"

I was also going to ask him about the threatening letter. But then the phone rang again and he reached for it. "Sure," he said, and waved goodbye.

I decided not to be nosy. As I left, he was telling whoever was calling that the setback was no big deal. "We'll be up and running soon as I find another faller."

Outside, the sun was shining up the blue-white ice of the Comox Glacier. The Beaufort Range still looked like a generic grouping of mountains from an amateur painter's stab at a landscape. I stood in front of Bilder's office and felt good about where I'd chosen to live. It was another one of those fine, high days that Vancouver Islanders like to keep private from the rest of the world.

Otherwise, the rest of the world might move here and ruin the place. As it was, the Island was undergoing a relentless population boom, helped along by developers like Rod Bilder — who were helped along, in turn, by people like me, if I cared to think about my small couple of pixels in the big picture.

But I didn't care to think about that right now. Instead, I looked toward the mountains, where a bald eagle was wheeling patiently and picturesquely on a thermal above the foothills, probably circling some steelhead fisherman who was cleaning his morning catch. For all their noble image, eagles liked nothing better than a pile of fish guts they didn't have to work for.

I couldn't criticize them. My old man had long ago explained to me that the real meaning of the expression, *the best things in life are free,* is that life's occasional freebies are the only real profit most working folk ever see.

Swapping a fax machine for the Ford LTD was almost a freebie. I'd traded something I couldn't use for something I could. My old man would have given me a boozy "goodonya" for making the deal. I felt good about it.

I crossed Eighth Street to where I'd left the behemoth parked out on a hill. It was nice having a car that could be trusted to resist the lure of gravity and remain where I'd put it; the old Concord had developed an irrepressible wanderlust once the hand-brake cable finally dissolved.

I was still getting used to driving a vehicle not much smaller than an escort aircraft carrier. Puttering about in Vancouver Island towns like Courtenay and Comox was a little like navigating the *Bismarck* around the Norwegian fjords, and I just wasn't going to think about how it would handle in downtown Vancouver.

I headed south on Eighth to the T- intersection with Cliffe, turned left and drove three blocks. I parked in front of the Courtenay branch of the regional library, housed in what used to be the offices and production plant of the *Comox District Free Press,* before the Bickle family had bought themselves a more commodious location at Fitzgerald and 17th .

The venerable bi-weekly had long been known for its fire-breathing, anti-union rants, an editorial tone first set by E.W. Bickle, a nineteenth century Cumberland miner who had become Courtenay's town clerk before prospering as an entrepreneur. Old E.W. had started the paper, still nicknamed the *Green Sheet* for the colour of its front page, back in the boom days of the Cumberland coal fields, and it had stayed in his family through the generations.

But now Bickle's heirs had allowed the paper to be swallowed whole by the Thomson chain. Any traces of its vitriolic, red-baiting origins were smoothed over by Bay Street blandness.

I had a very slight attachment to the *Green Sheet*. Fifteen years before, I had been a young journalist, editing a tabloid weekly in the mid-Island mill-town community of Port Alberni. The tab's competition — an independent daily — owned the only printing presses in town, and they weren't about to do any favours for the upstart rag that was trying to nibble them to death by undercutting rates for local ads. So every week my boss the publisher and I would slide a flat box full of pasted-up pages into the back of his van, and drive the ninety minutes over the Beauforts to Courtenay, where Bickle's big green Heidelbergs would print the Port Alberni news.

That was how I had discovered the Comox Valley, and decided it would be the perfect place to live. That was one of the few unquestionably right decisions I'd ever made.

The Alberni tabloid died young. Since then, I had segued through a series of career stages from journalist to political speechwriter to freelance commercial hack, while a failed marriage and a brief stumbling whirl through movie writing provided a counterpoint to a general theme of impermanence.

Put it this way: some people immerse themselves in existence as if they were captivated by a great book; others skim paragraphs and flip pages. I used to think I was one of the deep delvers. Lately, I was beginning to see myself as just another flipper.

Across from the library was the Comox Valley's original vegetarian restaurant, the Bar None Cafe, owned by the folks who ran the health food grocery next door. They had taken over a 1950s-vintage coffee shop, and surrounded the u-shaped counter with tables slightly larger than postage stamps. The menu was wholesome fare, lightly seasoned with moral triumph over cholesterol and salt.

At mid-morning, the place was better than half empty: a few postal workers and some staff from the library were taking their coffee break. The people I had come to see hadn't arrived yet, so I ordered a coffee and took a seat in the back corner.

People kept telling me about places where the coffee was excellent. I listened to them with the same bemused patience that came over me when my kids ran on about video games. To my way of thinking, the world's best cup of coffee stood about knee-high to a mediocre cup of tea. I drank coffee whenever I was away from home, because the chances of getting even that so-so cup of tea were pretty slim. Most restaurants made tea by filling a cup with hot water, and laying a tea bag on the saucer for the customer to dip.

If that was tea-making, then grape juice and alcohol made a grand cru Bordeaux. For me, tea wasn't drinkable without the full ritual: warmed pot, water at a rolling boil, and a fine blend of loose leaves — like Murchie's Uva Highland, the best strong tea in the world. Lately, though, I had down-stepped to another and lighter Murchie's tea, Brentwood Ceylon. The more heavily fermented Sri Lankan leaf was unfriendly to Mo's bladder .

Somebody had left a copy of the *Times Colonist*, another Thomson paper published seven days a week from Victoria, the provincial capital. It circulated all over the Island and was read by most people in the Comox Valley who kept up with the daily news.

Stu Haglund was the line story on page one. There was also a background piece on A3. I skimmed the news story first, saw a quote from Corporal Mikhailovsky but no mention of my name. The RCMP were being typically close-mouthed, and the corporal had given a standard "no comment" to the reporter's suggestion, no doubt breathlessly offered, that the death was the result of "environmental terrorism." But the paper had apparently made up its mind without police assistance, because whoever had slotted the story for page one had capped with a headline that read, *Boobytrap kills logger.*

I turned to the background piece. It was no great feat of journalistic analysis. Somebody had culled the *Times Colonist's* morgue for recent incidents on the Island. There had been an attempt to burn a bridge on a logging road in Clayoquot Sound. In the west coast community of Tofino someone had torched a boat that belonged to a local fisherman who was also on the town council and had spoken out against the anti-logging campaign.

At the spring opening of the provincial legislature, a mob of young greenies had smashed their way into the parliament buildings, knocking down an old security guard and breaking his hip. The reading of the Speech from the Throne by the Lieutenant Governor had to be suspended until the chanting mob could be driven away from the doors of the legislative chamber.

Then there were the crazies who tied themselves into the top branches of old-growth timber so that it couldn't be cut without endangering their lives. When the Mounties brought in skilled climbers to arrest them, the protesters coated themselves with their own excrement. I wasn't sure whether that actually counted as terrorism, though I had no doubts the cops did not relish making those arrests.

The most disturbing incident involved a young woman who had fallen from her protest perch and broken her pelvis. Her fellow activists had not come down from the trees to help her, but left it to first-aid attendants from the logging crews they were keeping from earning a day's pay.

I remembered Mo reading that one out to me over the breakfast table a few weeks back. It had bothered her.

"They're nuts," I said. "Have to be, or they wouldn't do what they're doing."

"Are they?" she said. "Or are they just totally committed?"

"You let a teenage girl — one of your own — lie there in that kind of pain and danger, you're nuts. You've lost sight of what's real."

We didn't take it any further. My opinions on environmental issues had been formed during my stint in the public relations department of West-Can, a fair-sized forest company a dozen years before. I knew that all the forest companies wanted to do was to cut trees, turn them into pulp, paper and building materials, and give the proceeds to its grateful shareholders. They would live up to the letter of environmental regulations most of the time, and to the spirit some of the time, as long as the Ministry of Forests kept a close professional eye on them.

But the idea that British Columbia was being deforested — as the most radical tree-huggers claimed — was just not true . The reality of life in B.C. was that the only way to stop the forests from growing back was to plough the land annually and put it into agricultural crops, or cover it with asphalt, lawns and houses. If you didn't work at turning the land into city or farm, trees would grow on it.

Ten, twelve thousand years ago, most of the province had been covered by an ice sheet a mile thick. There had not only been no trees, there had been no soil for trees to grow in. But, as soon as the ice went away, in came the trees. They took over every square centimetre of land that was not too dry or too cold. And once they had hold of it, they held it.

I remembered what an old forester had told me when I was learning the forest business. "The trees grow back," he said.

"Don't cut your lawn for a year, you'll get weeds waist high. Don't cut it for ten years, you have aspen, maple, alder saplings. Twenty years, it's a mixed forest, deciduous and conifer. Fifty years, it's mostly evergreens. A hundred years, the spruce and Douglas fir own the land. Your house, your blacktop driveway, your concrete swimming pool, you couldn't find 'em.

"You see those jungle places, the Yucatan, southeast Asia, where whole cities are broken up and buried by trees. Same thing happens here, just slower. If everybody walked away from Vancouver and didn't come back for a couple hundred years, you wouldn't be able to see it for the trees."

I finished my coffee and looked at my watch. As if right on cue, a green VW Westfalia nosed into the space in front of my behemoth. The driver got out, a heavyset man in his thirties, tall and round-shouldered, with lank blond hair and a droopy moustache. He looked like a Viking going to pudge. He hitched up the waistband of his jeans under a stretched grey sweatshirt, then waited for his passenger to come around from the curb side of the van, before they crossed Cliffe to the cafe.

The big guy was Benny Filiatrault, local environmental gadfly, all-round utopian, and rumoured to be a candidate for Councillor in the next Cumberland municipal election, which was only a couple of months away. Seeing him from close up, my first impression centred on sheer size. While he stood in the doorway of the Bar None, looking for me, nothing bigger than a small bird could have gotten through the unused space.

I lifted a hand, and he saw the gesture. It was only when he sloped forward into the room that I finally got a look at his companion, who had been totally eclipsed by Filiatrault's bulk as they crossed the road. He was the bigger man's opposite: scrawny, maybe twenty-two, his head and jaw covered in a week's growth of stubble, eyes pale behind rimless glasses. His skinny neck had an almost right-angled bend that made his Adam's apple stick out. His all-black clothes looked as if they needed a laundry.

I stood up and Filiatrault and I shook hands and said our names across the little table. "This is Davey Clemmer," he said, indicating the younger man.

Clemmer said nothing, but sat down and crossed his arms. His thin, white fingers wrapped themselves around his meagre biceps. I could see blue veins snaking under the hairs. He looked at me sideways.

The Bar None staff knew Benny Filiatrault, and didn't have to be told before bringing him a cappuccino. He asked his companion if he wanted anything, but the kid barely shook his head and said, "Uh uh."

The big man and I traded the usual ice-breaking small talk about weather and other inconsequentials. I figured I'd let him come to the point. He'd called me, after all.

When he was halfway through his cappuccino, he wiped the coffee foam from his moustache and said, "I got your name from Ted Fetris."

"Yes," I said. Fetris was a Victoria political consultant who was frequently involved in environmental causes. He had a connection to the British Columbia Round Table on the Environment and the Economy, and had arranged for me to do some writing jobs for that agency.

"I'm planning to run for council. He said you could be useful."

I nodded. "Do you mind if I ask a rude question?" I said.

He shrugged.

"Can you afford me?"

"How much do you cost?" he said.

"My standard rate is a hundred and twenty-five dollars an hour," I told him.

He blinked, but he recovered. "Money's not a

problem," he said.

"Good," I said. "And, as long as we're being candid, I've worked on a couple of campaigns where I was promised full rate, but when it was all over, somehow the budget had evaporated. So I will require an advance."

"Ted Fetris said I should bring money," Benny said. He took a folded envelope out of his hip pocket. "Is two thousand enough to get you started?"

"Yes, it is," I said, and took the envelope. I put it next to Rod Bilder's contribution. The day was getting better.

Clemmer was looking at me dead on now. It was not a warm and approving gaze. He seemed to have something against people giving other people large amounts of money. I ignored him.

"I'm not looking for a big-time political career," Filiatrault said.

"That's good," I said, "because anyone trying to build a political power base on environmental populism has all the staying power of a guppy floating into a shark feeding frenzy. Folks will cuddle you on the doorstep, but come election day they'll vote for whoever's most likely to fill their wallets or feed their prejudices. All the Greens ever do is split the left-wing vote."

I could tell that Filiatrault was ready to defend his philosophies and the basic decency of the Canadian electorate, but I held up both hands in that movement that says, "Why should we argue?" He shrugged and let it go.

The kid with the stubble-forested head sniffed and looked disgusted, but I guessed that was his standard reaction to most of the people and things he encountered from day to day.

"Look," I told Filiatrault, "you don't need to convert me and I don't get my jollies from treading on people's idealism. I'm a mercenary. You're hiring me, so I will work for you. I will do the best job I can. So why don't you tell me what you need, and I'll give you an idea of what it would cost you. If the end figure sounds scary, you can have the two grand back."

"I told you," he said, "money is not a problem." He leaned on the table and took a moment to order his thoughts. Then, in the next three minutes, he showed me that while the outside view of Benny Filiatrault might be rambly-shambly, the inside of his head was as organized as a Japanese company picnic. In a few brief words, he told me he wanted to get onto Cumberland council in order to put some checks on the village's rapidly accelerating growth. He dissected the incumbent councillors into two neat piles: the gotta-have-that-growth-at-any-cost boosters, business types who would all make money in one way or another from an expanding population; and the old-timers, folks whose great-grandparents had worked in the mines and who were almost guaranteed regular re-election to council because they *were* Cumberland.

"The old guys don't see what's happening to the village," he said. "All they know is Cumby. They all fell asleep in the fifties, when the mines started closing. They've never seen what happens when real estate developments snowball. Unless they do something now, unless they give themselves more power to control growth and zoning and land use, we're all going to wake up someday and find ourselves buried in ticky-tacky boxes."

"Pete Seeger," I said.

"Huh?" Filiatrault said.

"Pete Seeger," I repeated. "He wrote the song about suburbs made of ticky-tacky boxes. Back in the fifties."

"Oh," said Filiatrault, blinking. "Well, whatever." Clemmer somehow managed to look even more disgusted.

I apologized for interrupting, and he went on. "The thing is," he said, "Cumberland's forgotten what it's like to be a boom town, the stress and the strain, the damage to our quality of life. But it's going to be a boom town again, and nobody's ready."

"Don't you think you might be pushing the panic button a little early?" I asked him. "I mean, a few dozen yuppie downshifters and back-to-nature types don't constitute a population explosion."

"They're not the problem," he said. "It's the thousands of people who are going to come flooding in once they re-open the mines."

This time I was the one who blinked. Cumberland's coal pits had been sealed with massive concrete plugs back in the mid-fifties, when western Canadians were quickly weaning themselves of their taste for coal power and starting a forty-year binge on diesel, bunker-C oil and cheap hydro-electricity. "Why would they re-open those mines?" I said. "They were practically stone-age."

"Because coal is going to make a comeback in the early twenty-first century," he said. He ticked off the points on his outsize fingers. "Look, the oil is running out. Then you've got a continental market for our reserves of natural gas, with increasing demand driving up the wellhead price. Third, the cost of building major hydro dams keeps climbing, even if you can find any more river valleys to turn into reservoirs. Hydrogen is fifty years away. The economics all point to coal."

"Yeah, but the pollution," I said. "Acid rain. Remember the killer fogs in London?"

He ticked off his smallest finger. "Coal burning technology has improved so much that it's now as clean as natural gas. You got all these precombustion systems and reburn of emissions and scrubbers on the smokestacks." He spread his arms. "I've studied this. In ten to fifteen years, the whole Pacific Northwest, from B.C. down to northern California, is going to be horny for coal. And places like Cumby, with high-grade anthracite, a rail line already built, and a deep-sea harbour five klicks down the slope — places like that are going to be hot properties."

He was making me think. I'd done speechwriting jobs for the senior execs at BC Gas, the province's major gas utility. I'd heard them say that coal-seam methane was where the industry would be heading in the twenty-first century, once natural gas reserves peaked and began to shrink. I was willing to believe that coal could make a comeback, and that sleepy old Cumberland could be an economic hot spot again.

"Okay," I said, "Say I buy your argument. What exactly are you proposing to do about it?"

He started ticking off fingers again. "First, get on council. Second, get a modern community plan put together. Third, rewrite the zoning bylaws so that developers can't drive trucks through them. Fourth, try and stop the provincial government from riding over us if they decide to turn Cumberland into some kind of special development zone."

"So it would be a *trouble in River City* campaign," I said.

His nod said he got the reference.

I mulled it for a moment, getting the flavour of it, then shook my head. "Warning of potential trouble that's at least ten years down the road doesn't motivate many votes your way. You need an issue they can grab onto right now. Have you got one?"

"I've got one."

"So tell me."

"Save Hockney's Woods."

"Shit."

"What?"

"I may have a conflict of interest," I said. Hockney's Woods was those twenty hectares of old growth where Stu Haglund had been killed. I was waiting for the project to revive so I could go back to work for the developer Benny Filiatrault would be campaigning to stop.

I told him about my connection with Bilder, and the meeting I'd just come from. He listened attentively, but his scrawny sidekick let a sneer crawl onto his face. It knew its way around, I thought, probably having spent a lot of time there.

When I finished, Filiatrault shrugged. "So the project's on hold," he said, "and Rod thinks it's iffy whether it comes back to life?"

I didn't think I'd broken a confidence. "That's about it."

He thought it over, then said, "Look, I only really need you for the pre-campaign period — help me write a position paper, a speech, a brochure for the doorsteps, news release. Once we launch, there's no time for anything fancy. It's basically door-knocking and the all-candidates meeting, right?"

I agreed.

"Well, I don't have a problem if you don't," he said. "You won't be working for the two of us at the same time."

The sneer had ducked off the kid's face to make room for astonishment. "You're gonna trust this guy?" he asked Filiatrault.

"If he wasn't straight up, he would've just kept his mouth shut," my new client said.

Davey Clemmer rolled his eyes and blew out his cheeks. I was getting to see all his favourite facial expressions on first acquaintance.

Filiatrault drained his cappuccino and pushed back his chair. "You want a warm-up on that?" he asked. "Then we can get to work."

"Thanks," I said.

He took the cups over to the girl at the counter. I noticed he moved very softly for his size .

The kid had put his sneer back on. He was eyeing me as if I were something that might stick to the bottom of his shoe. "You do corporate work," he said.

It wasn't a question, so I didn't feel obligated to answer. I just looked at him.

"You do anything for MacMillan Bloedel?"

MacBlo was the biggest forest company in B.C. I had done some speechwriting for one of their marketing veeps back in the eighties. "Now and then," I said.

He sniffed and squared his bony shoulders. "We're gonna shut 'em down."

The last time I'd looked, M and B had about four billion dollars worth of assets; by now it might be five billion. The NDP provincial government had just bought a substantial block of the company's stock, as part of a scheme to reinvest taxpayer's money in the province. "I don't think so," I said.

There was a hard look in his pale eyes. "They got no right to destroy the rainforest. People are gonna come from all over the world to stop 'em."

"Sure," I said. I had the kid pegged now. I was familiar with the type.

"You're from back east, right?" I said. My speechwriter's ear picked up the flat tones and slightly nasal tone of southern Ontario.

"Dundas," he said.

I nodded. It was a suburb of Toronto. I knew I'd been through it in the 1970s, when I was communications aide to the federal Minister of Justice. I would accompany the boss to speaking engagements, to hand out copies of his remarks to reporters covering the speech. I would also show the TV news crews the particular passages in the text where they should definitely have the lens pointed at the speaker and the mic turned on. Back then, TV news still worked with 16-millimetre film cameras, and the cameraman never had enough film to waste on an entire speech.

Afterwards, the minister would go press the flesh at some Liberal Party function, and I would tag along to hold his coat and take notes.

"Dundas," I echoed, remembering rows of anonymous houses behind rectangular lawns. "No room for epiphanies amidst the asphalt and ticky-tacky boxes. So you come out here and find God in the ancient forest."

His face closed. I could see I'd made a real enemy now, but I didn't expect to stay up nights worrying about it. He got up and headed for the door.

Benny Filiatrault came back with the coffees as the kid left the Bar None. We watched him stalk past the big window, his jaw muscles working.

"What was that?" Filiatrault said, and sat down.

"Your buddy and I are philosophically incompatible," I said.

He shrugged. "Davey means well. Gets a little wound up, time to time. No big thing."

"Sure," I said. "He's not your campaign manager?"

My client laughed. "He couldn't manage a good crap. But he's willing. He'll run an errand."

"Sure," I said again, then let it drop. I got out my notebook and pad. "So let me get some background."

I interviewed him for the next forty-five minutes. It was the kind of work I'd often done twenty years before, a when I was a small-town newspaper editor putting together a profile on a local candidate. Filiatrault came across as a sincere, community minded citizen. He wasn't an anti-growth fanatic or a new-age tree worshiper. He was a fourth-generation Cumberland man who recognized that the village he had grown up in was in the path of change. He just wanted to make sure the coming development boom didn't hit Cumberland like a tornado touching down in a trailer park.

I sympathized with him, and when I had filled seven pages of notebook, I quoted him a sympathetic price for my labours. He agreed to it. It would only take a couple of days to write his material, and I told him I would get started on it before the end of the week.

"I'm sure we'll be finished before there's any possibility of a conflict of interest," I said.

His tongue poked a bulge in his cheek. "You got that right," he said.

I heard a message behind the words. "Something I should know?" I said.

He eyed me for a moment, making up his mind, then leaned forward across the table and spoke quietly. "Word is," he said, "a lot of Rod Bilder's backing is coming from the Ketterich brothers."

It meant nothing to me. I raised my eyebrows and waited for more.

"Dodd and Colin Ketterich. Except everybody calls them Trick and Butch. They're Cumby guys, like Rod, like me. We all went to school together. We know each other, you know what I mean?"

"Uh huh."

"Ketteriches never had two beans till the past few years. Suddenly, they're driving four-by-fours, all the options. They're putting a new roof on their mom's place."

"And the money comes from where?"

"The number one crop in B.C. agriculture." He put his thumb and index finger together, brought them up to pursed lips, and sucked in a little whisper of air.

"They're growing marijuana," I said.

"Yep," he said. "So if the Mounties are nosing around, you won't see the Ketteriches for dust. I'd say Rod's going to have to look for another source of money."

"Too bad."

"Yeah," he said. "It would help the campaign to have a live project to work against. But we can do almost as much good with a potential threat as a real one."

Not for the first time, I recognized there was a genuinely savvy politician behind Benny Filiatrault's jeans-and-sweatshirt facade.

I was on the clock now, so I said what a good mercenary political hack is supposed to say. "Is there any mileage to be gained from the doper connection?"

Filiatrault shook his head. "If they were out-of-towners, we could play it up. But nobody blames the Ketteriches for making a buck. Their grand-daddy used to have a still up the back end of the lake. Family tradition."

I put my notebook away, and we both stood up. Then something occurred to me. "What do you know about Ginger Goodwin?" I asked.

The change of subject took him by surprise. "Everything," he said. "I'm from Cumby. Why?"

"My girlfriend wants me to write a movie script about him." I said it in that tone men use when they tell other men about the ridiculous things their womenfolk are trying to get them to do.

Filiatrault must have missed the tone, because he didn't bat Mo's idea back over the net with the traditional manly commiserative shrug.

"Good idea," he said. "Somebody should make a movie about Ginger." Then he offered his hand and said, "I got to go."

"I'll call you when I have a draft of your material."

"Fine," he said. He turned to leave, then turned back. "Have you been to the grave?" he asked.

"What?"

"Ginger Goodwin's grave."

"No."

"Take the time," he said. "Then you should check out that big leather book in the museum. The story's all there."

"What book?"

He told me that all the raw material of the Goodwin story had been compiled by a local writer a dozen years before. The author had brought together official records of testimony before the coroner's inquiry, along with transcribed interviews with old-timers who remembered Goodwin and the manner of his death. It was pasted up on the black pages of a giant photo album, bound in tooled leather under the title *The Shooting of Ginger Goodwin*.

"Maybe I will," I said. But I was thinking, *No thanks.*

Chapter 3

Mo wasn't home when I got back to the house we shared on a slope above Back Road, with the big picture window overlooking Farquharson's farm and the bird-rich wetlands of the Puntledge River delta.

The sun was tickling points of light out of the water, down among the distant reeds. I stood in the living room for a moment and watched. The only birds I could see right now were the little gaggle of domestic geese that belonged to someone on the dyke road, following each other like a trail of white smoke puffs along a sand bar just out from the near bank. By Christmas, the water and the fields would be polka-dotted with trumpeter swans, tearing up the forage crops the farm planted specially for them.

I'd been here four years now, and loved the house. It was the only place I'd ever lived that was genuinely my home, my calm sanctuary from the world. I'd put a down payment on it with the advance I'd received for a movie script, back when I thought I was going to break into movies. Then I'd had to scrabble hard to keep from losing it when the deal fell apart.

While that was going on, I'd met Mo and fallen for her in a helpless, hopeless rush. Then, almost immediately, I'd come close to losing her: a client who specialized in shady manoeuvres around the Vancouver Stock Exchange got us mixed up with mobsters and worse. After the shock faded, and she accepted I wasn't a lightning rod for violent criminals, we'd steadily built something wonderful between us.

It had started as one of those long-distance romances. I was in Comox and she was in Sechelt, across Georgia Strait on the Sunshine Coast, where she was helping her brother set up and operate a rehabilitation camp for kids who had lost limbs or at least the use of them. We'd done a lot of long, getting-to-know-you phone calls and faxed each other little things clipped out of papers or copied from whatever books we were reading — she leaned toward John Ralston Saul and David Halberstam; I was more into Elmore Leonard and Reginald Hill.

Occasionally she would come over for a week-end of walks on the beach, dinners at local restaurants, and at-home breakfasts over the Saturday editions of the *Globe and Mail* and the *Vancouver Sun* — intercut with lovemaking that ranged from the fierce to the leisurely, depending on how long it had been since the last time. I couldn't get enough of her; I still couldn't.

I didn't visit her in Sechelt. Her brother, Miggs, had never quite gotten over the upset I had put Mo through when we first met. She said to give it time, and he'd come around.

For the past seven months, we'd been living together, sharing expenses fifty-fifty. I was freelancing speeches and other configurations of corporate writing for the suits in downtown Vancouver again. I'd have got more work and made more money if I'd moved back to the city, but I'd rather have had my skin peeled off with needle-nose pliers.

Vancouver was like a compulsive eater on a permanent binge, stuffing itself sick with all the crime and congestion that come with being a world class city." Comox was small and beautiful, clean and quiet, the kind of place where people actually smiled and said "Good morning" to each other as they passed in the street.

Money wasn't a problem. I made enough to get by, and Mo was doing lucrative odd jobs as a self-employed management consultant. She showed big, indifferently run businesses how to tighten themselves up and become efficient.

"Actually," she told me once, when I asked how she did what she did, "the guys in the executive suites usually know already what has to be cut — or to be blunt, who gets fired. They just don't want all that messy unpleasantness on their hands. So they bring me in as a glorified charwoman, and I sweep out and mop up."

"Doesn't it bother you?" I asked.

"Uh uh," she said. "They generally get a good severance package. And, most of these companies, if they don't do what I tell them, they're going under anyway in two, three, five years. Then everybody's out in the rain."

"Still," I said, "must be hard finding out you're deadwood."

She looked at me with those vast sea-green eyes that still astonished me. "You're a sweet guy, Raff," she said. "But sometimes life is about making hard choices. You don't make them, life will make them for you."

It was early afternoon and I had nothing else to do, so I thought I'd get started on Benny Filiatrault's campaign literature. I took my notes into the small room I'd fitted out as an office. I'd upgraded to a new IBM PC the year before, buying a 386 just as they went off the market. I still used the same old HP LaserJet II I'd bought when I thought I was going to be a big-time movie writer.

Mo's PowerBook was missing from the small table under the window where she liked to work. In its place was a stack of paper underneath a note telling me she had been called to a meeting at Elk Falls, forty minutes north of Comox on the Island Highway, just past the fishing resort mecca of Campbell River. A New Zealand conglomerate called Fletcher Challenge had a pulp mill up there, and Mo was helping to redesign its management information services group. The note also asked me to deliver a small stack of pages to Sally McMahon at the Cumberland Museum, if I had nothing better to do.

"All roads lead to Cumby," I said to the empty room. I leafed through the pages. Mo had done her usual detailed, comprehensive job on the women's work exhibit, then thrown in a few hundred dollars worth of free consulting advice regarding the museum's other operations.

I decided that the Filiatrault job could wait. It was a beautiful summer day, and would be better spent taking a run up into the hills around Comox Lake than hunching over a computer to write political propaganda — even for a candidate I liked . Also, I liked pleasing the woman I loved — when I could.

I was almost out the door when the phone rang. It was my ex-wife, Karen, who had left me back in 1980 for a man who offered her all the things I couldn't: power, mostly, and the company of those who held and wielded it.

I didn't blame her anymore. We'd married after what some would have called a whirlwind romance. Looking back on it, I could see that it was more like a dense fog in which we had accidentally bumped into each other and clung, tightly as limpets, unable to see anything beyond our mutual attraction.

We'd been fools for each other, drunk on hormones and romantic notions. After a year or so, Karen had sobered up. I'd gone on being a fool: I used to carry my wedding ring in my pocket, like a talisman, ten years after we split up. Then along came Mo Migliorini, to reach down into the pit I'd dug for myself, grab me by the hair and haul me back into daylight .

"Sid?" Karen's voice was almost as silky as the designer suits she wore, although my speechwriter's ear caught a little roughening of the vocal cords that was accompanying her power glide into middle age. The backroom machinery of politics is perpetually lubricated by fine whisky.

"How you doing?" I said.

"Fine." She was always fine. There might have been a picture aging harshly in some attic, but the years seemed evenly good to Karen. "The boys want to know when they can come over."

"I was thinking the B.C. Day weekend," I said. "They can be here for Nautical Days then stay for the air show at the base. The Americans are sending up a Stealth fighter."

"They'll like that," she said.

I agreed they would. Bill and Dick had come to the air show at Canadian Forces Base Comox the year before. They had tramped around the apron out front of the military hangars, walked through a giant Hercules transport and sat in the cockpit of a CF-18 fighter. They had ducked just a little when a visiting USAF F-16 Strike Eagle had roared in over the crowd, low and fast, then climbed straight up to become a tiny sliver suspended in the high blue.

"This rules!" they had said, in the unison that you come to expect from twins. They'd always been very bright kids, talked early and polysyllabically almost from the start. Now, as they entered their teens, they seemed to have learned a much simpler language — one that divided the world into two contrasting categories: things that ruled and things that sucked.

"In the novel *1984*," I'd told them the last time we'd talked, "George Orwell invented a form of English so completely stripped down that it divorced speaking from thinking. Complex thought was impossible. There were no words for abstract concepts."

But the language of "sucks" and "rules" made *Newspeak* sound like the ornate prose of Fielding or Thackeray. "Neither of whom you've ever heard of, right?"

"*1984* kicks ass," was Dick's response.

"It totally rules," put in Bill. "Big Brother."

"You read the book?" I said.

"We saw the video," they said together .

I told Karen, "Tell them this year there's also going to be a flying boat from the German Navy and one of those humongous water bombers from Port Alberni,"

We settled details of dates and arrival times. Then, the parenting responsibilities done, she said, "So how's it going with you?"

"Good," I said.

"It's working out, you and Mo?"

"It's working."

"I'm glad," she said. I knew it was true. She hadn't wanted to cripple me thirteen years before. She just hadn't been prepared to settle for less than she felt she deserved.

I didn't ask how things were going with her husband, Lyle Pastorel, still the most powerful federal Liberal operative on the west coast. I knew that life for the two of them was everything they wanted it to be.

We said goodbye and I picked up Mo's papers and went out into the world I had managed to build without Karen. It was not bad, if I could keep hold of it. I drove through the quiet little streets of Comox, down the hill to the Dyke Road which passed between the Indian reserve and the Puntledge River delta. Five minutes after leaving home, I was across the 17th Street Bridge into Comox and heading for the junction with the Cumberland Road.

Two minutes before the village, the Behemoth wallowing around dips and curves in the road, I passed the little cemetery below the big old trees. The graves were clustered in two clumps — one bigger than the other — at either end of the small space. I looked for Ginger Goodwin's odd-shaped stone, but couldn't take my eyes off the road long enough to pick it out if I wanted to avoid drifting into the oncoming traffic.

Sally McMahon was not at the museum.

"She'll be here pretty soon," said the teenage girl in the office.

I gave her Mo's pages, and glanced at the nearby displays. "Mind if I look around?"

"Sure," said the girl, at the same time shyly indicating the hand-made sign that said *ADULT ADMISSION — $3*. I dug out a two-dollar bill and a loonie and handed them over. She rang them into the cash register — itself a big crank-handled antique — and went back into the office.

The biggest thing in the main display area was a long counter of polished wood, with iron-grilled wickets set above it. It looked like the kind of thing that would hide a ticket seller in a Victoria train station, but it turned out to be a relic of the old customs office that had once occupied one half of the Cumberland post office. It dated from the time when the little coaling dock at Union Bay was one of the thousands of entry ports of the British Empire, where goods from as close as Seattle or as far away as China might be landed with duties to be paid.

I ran my hand along the smoothness of the counter's rolled wooden lip. Chinese miners, American mule drivers and Italian bakers had stood before this length of oak — if oak was what it was — their work-worn fingers counting out coins with the old Queen's head on them, to pay the Dominion's tax on their parcels from home. I half closed my eyes, and for a moment the past touched me with its odd smelling fingers, carrying that strange sharp odour of polish and age that clings to old wood.

I opened my eyes and looked to my right, and there was the man I wanted to avoid: Ginger Goodwin, about half life-size, in a blow-up of the full figure photograph that I'd seen in Susan Mayse's book. I'd read most of it the night before, drinking tea at the kitchen table, while Mo was working on the pages I'd brought for Sally.

The poster was in a tall, wood and glass display case against the wall. I went and had a look at it, my feet dragging a little.

The poster was clearer than the reproduction in the book. It showed a young man, now halfway through his twenties, standing on the wooden steps of a shiplap-sided building. He wore a black jacket — it was too long for him — and a buttoned-up waistcoat. He had no tie, but had tied a miner's sweat rag crossways over his throat. There was some kind of pin in one lapel; it caught the sunlight that streamed past him from his right.

Mayse's book had given me a good picture of Albert 'Ginger' Goodwin. He'd come to Canada before the First World War, sailing steerage from class-ridden northern England, where a working man never made more than just enough, and many made less. It was the same place my family had crossed the Atlantic to get clear, two generations later. My old man would have been proud to shake Ginger Goodwin's hand, would have stood him a pint.

In the mining towns of old-time Canada, Ginger found the same deep social divisions he'd left behind. He jumped into the class war with both feet and his clogs on, making himself a pain in the mine owners' well padded rumps. He became an organizer for the United Mine Workers at the Trail copper workings up in the Kootenays, and in the coal pits of Cumberland. He was a little carrot-topped firebrand of a Yorkshireman, a self-taught orator with dubious grammar, who practised the art of speech-making by going out into the clearcuts and haranguing the assembled fir and cedar stumps.

He was all right with the men in the pits, and that made him a target for the mine owners. The usual harassments and hindrances failed to deter him, but in the dying months of the Great War, the bosses grabbed for an opportunity to rid themselves of the little red gadfly.

The year before, the Dominion government had

ordered conscription. The army was short of men, and Canada could no longer rely on volunteers to replace the fodder that was being continuously fed into the murder-and-maiming machine of northern France. Even in the remotest Canadian settlements it was understood the life expectancy of a recruit reaching the mud of Flanders could be measured in days. If there was a big push on, the measurement could shrink to minutes.

If Ginger could be pressed into service, he'd no longer be a boil on the mine owners' buttocks. Special handling might even be arranged for him.

There was only one obstacle. When Ginger had duly registered for the draft, the examining doctor had declared him unfit: tuberculosis was the diagnosis, though it may have been the black lung that often choked and killed coal miners who spent too long in the barely ventilated pits.

So Ginger Goodwin should have been safe from the draft. He had no need to run to the woods, as many unwilling conscripts had done — so many that a special paramilitary force known as the Dominion Police had been created to hunt down those whose attachment to King and Country did not overrule their desire to keep hot steel splinters from penetrating their bodies or mustard gas their lungs.

Ginger's lungs were already too scarred from spending half his days in dank, dust-choked tunnels and the other half in crowded slums. But they allowed him enough breath to keep urging his fellow workers to resist the owners and follow him to socialist Zion.

And that was more breath than the owners wanted him to have.

I could imagine how it would have happened; back when I'd been staff speechwriter to a federal cabinet minister, I'd occasionally been a fly on the wall when quiet words were spoken over a glass of Chivas Regal, and someone's fate was decided by a nod and a pass of the hand. Of course, all I was seeing was a patronage plum being plucked and proffered; the quiet word spoken about Ginger Goodwin would have been his death warrant.

Two well fleshed men would have warmed their tweeds before a coal fire at their club, and one would have said, "This bolshie Goodwin, detestable little man. Something ought to be done."

And the other would have harrumphed and said, "Needs five minutes with my old Regimental Sergeant Major."

"Can't be done. Classified not fit for service."

Another harrumph, then, "I'll have word with Algie at the Medical Examiner's Office. Good man, Algie. Knows where his duty lies."

"And, once he's in, send him somewhere not much to his liking, I should think." And then down with their whiskies and in to luncheon.

The quiet word was spoken; an official ear was bent; and the little labour agitator was summarily reclassified into first-class fighting material, and ordered to report to Number Two Depot Battalion in Victoria.

Ginger declined his adopted country's invitation. He reported instead to a little cluster of cabins near a wilderness creek that fed into the far end of Comox Lake, joining a handful of other reluctant heroes who were waiting for the end of the war to end all wars. Sympathetic townsfolk rowed over from time to time, bringing the draft evaders food and other supplies to fill out their diet of trout, berries and the occasional grouse. The authorities grew increasingly unhappy.

Eventually, a local trapper led a posse headed by a Dominion policeman named Dan Campbell to the hideout. The official version of events said that Campbell had surprised Goodwin on a trail leading down to the cabins.

It said that the fugitive had carried a rifle with which he tried to shoot the policeman, but that Campbell fired first in self defence.

The unofficial version — the only version believed in Cumberland — said that Campbell hid behind a fallen log beside the trail, and shot Ginger Goodwin through the throat with a soft-nosed bullet from a .30-calibre Marlin rifle. The slug shattered the little man's spine and blew a gobbet of flesh out the back of his neck, leaving him twitching and dying on the forest floor. It was fired from close enough to leave powder burns.

I'd seen in Mayse's book the picture of the funeral procession, the white, flower-bedecked coffin on the shoulders of men in dark suits. A brass band led the way, and the cortege stretched back up Dunsmuir Avenue as far as the camera lens could reach. The caption below the photo said when the first mourners marched into the cemetery, the tail of the column was still in Cumberland, almost two kilometres behind.

I looked at the scant relics of the man's life collected in the museum case: a hand-crafted, split-cane fishing rod, probably the only thing of value he'd ever owned, ill-matched with a cheap reel; a medal he'd won when he'd played inside forward on a soccer team up in the Kootenays, before his lungs gave out; a little fist-sized model of the odd-shaped tombstone the mine workers union had placed on his grave.

I looked again at the face in the poster-sized photograph. Ginger was looking off to his left, away from the camera. The photographer had caught a thoughtful, almost worried, expression. His hands had come together in front of his chest, the left cradling the fingers of his right. I recognized the stance: catch me thinking about something worrisome, and I might have my hands just like that, the left one spinning the ring I wore on my right.

Ginger already made me uncomfortable. The resemblance made it worse. I had already decided I would not be writing any movies about Ginger Goodwin — even assuming the film rights were available and that I could acquire them. I would not be writing any movies at all, nor the Great Canadian Novel, nor anything else that could lift me out of the trough of hackery-for-hire in which I made my living.

Mo was right: Ginger would make a good movie — not a Hollywood blockbuster, but just the kind of moody, textured piece that Canadian filmmakers excelled at. The man's life had had dignity and pathos. He'd been a fearless little guy who did and said what he thought was right. He'd worked his way into the sensitive creases of some important people and rubbed them raw. So they'd sent a bounty hunter to put a dum-dum bullet through his neck, then whitewashed the murder as self-defence.

Somebody ought to put the Ginger Goodwin story on a screen, ideally on television, to let a few million people know what had happened here. But the somebody was not going to be me.

The night before, I'd lain awake beside Mo's gently snoring warmth, feeling an uncomfortable mixture of satisfaction and guilt. The satisfaction came from knowing that I'd finally faced up to a decision I'd been putting off for a long time. The guilt came because I knew it was not the kind of choice that would have prompted my old man to shake my hand and tell a barman to pull me a pint.

Fish or cut bait, Mo liked to say. Well, I'd decided that I'd take fishing, thank ye kindly, especially the kind of fishing where you put your hat over your eyes, your line in the water and your thoughts about tomorrow on hold.

If I'd ever had an ambitious bone in my body, it had dissolved or atrophied, or whatever bones do when they're no longer holding up anything important. I'd decided that I already had exactly the life that suited me: moderately interesting work that made few demands but yielded a modest income that let me live in a place I loved.

Let others boldly go climbing mountains because they were there. I was here, and here was plenty for me.

Writing movies was not hard. Getting them made was damn near impossible. A movie script, even a good movie script, was in some ways indistinguishable from a lottery ticket. The odds were not good, and the only way to better them was to mount an endless series of suicide charges into the massed ranks of movie makers, who replied with volley upon volley of devastating indifference.

I'd tried the movie biz. I'd let my hopes build on a patch of sand, and after I'd dug myself out of the inevitable wreckage, I'd decided that once was more than enough.

For the foreseeable future, I would just keep doing what I was doing. As a good speechwriter, I could summon up an appropriate Biblical quote: *take therefore no thought for the morrow... Sufficient unto the day is the evil thereof.* Or, to put it in modern English: *Forget tomorrow; today's giving us all the trouble we need* .

I could be proud that at last I'd made a decision, even if I couldn't be particularly proud of the decision itself. But I wasn't looking forward to letting Mo in on the epiphany; she had greater expectations of me than I was prepared to live up to.

I wandered away from the Ginger Goodwin display. He was getting under my carapace, , reminding me that I had become the kind of person my old man wouldn't have be glad to shake hands with or stand a pint – if he'd lived long enough to see me hobnobbing with the denizens of the corporate executive suite. Doing their bidding. Carrying their water.

I drifted toward a series of black and white photographs on the wall. A hand-lettered card said they had been printed from hundreds of glass plate negatives found in the back room of a building that had housed Japtown's photographer at the turn of the century.

The pictures showed serious Japanese miners posing in their excruciatingly clean work clothes, holding their cylindrical lunch pails — *snap tins* said a voice in the back of my head, dredged up from my mother's side of the family: Yorkshiremen, like Ginger Goodwin, mostly steel mill workers, but there was more than a hint of coal dust on my genetic back trail.

I'd had an uncle who'd been lucky enough to apprentice as a plumber at the age of sixteen. By then, he'd already spent two years in a Yorkshire mine.

"Three feet high, the seam was," he'd told me. "You lay on your back, in water, and broke coal off the roof above your head so it fell on you in chunks. Another lad would scrape it back to tunnel. A few shillings a day that was worth, and wages were falling." Uncle Ted had plenty of stories like that one, which all ended with the same moral: "You young'uns today, you don't know you're bloody born."

I walked away from the resigned Japanese, took a look at a display of old telephone equipment and some odds and ends of pottery dug up from the ruins of Chinatown. Someone had taken down the old Campbell's store sign from near the front door, and stood it upright in a corner.

I didn't know why I was hanging around. I had no reason to wait for Sally McMahon, and nothing to say to her. The place was steadily filling my mind with a background hum of guilt. Maybe I was indulging in a little masochism, but enough was enough. I looked at my watch and mimed a mild shock reaction — *goodness me, is that the time?* — as if anyone were watching or would care if they were, and moved toward the exit.

I waved goodbye to the teenage girl in the office and reached to push open the front door. It receded before my hand made contact, pulled open by Sally.

She stopped in the doorway. "Raff," she said. "Mo's not here today."

"I know," I said, and told her about the papers I'd delivered.

She thanked me, and we stood there, each in the other's path, each wondering if the other wanted to carry on a conversation, each waiting for the little body language signals that say, *this one's over, let's move on.*

"Well..." I started, edging aside to let her in.

But I was too late. She'd misread my expectant silence, and now she said, "Have you been looking around?"

"Uh huh," I said. "A little."

She came in and the door swung closed behind her. "I think Mo said something about your being interested in Ginger Goodwin," she said.

"Oh, I guess." Mo talked with his woman several times a week. I wasn't about to confess to Sally the guilty secret I hadn't found the nerve to talk about with Mo. "It's quite a story," I said.

"Mo said maybe a movie?"

I shrugged. "Maybe."

She nodded and looked at her feet. I reached for the door again. "Well..."

She looked up. "Would you need to be doing a lot of research?"

I had the door half open now. "I guess," I said. And then it occurred to me that this might be more than a casual conversation. I didn't know any details, but I assumed that Sally had a stake in whatever happened to Hockney's Woods. Maybe the interruption of her ex-husband's project had put her in financial trouble. Maybe she needed a job.

It was not a subject I wanted to explore. "It's all rather vague," I said. "All up in the air."

She nodded again. "Oh, it's just that Mo seemed pretty strong for it."

"Well," I said again. "You know how these things go."

"I see," she said.

I opened the door all the way. Sunlight came in, and I wanted to be out in it.

"Did you look through the book of transcripts?" Sally asked.

I should have said, "Yes, fascinating," and kept on going. Instead, I said, "No, didn't see it."

Which meant that she had to say, "It's right over here," and lead the way.

And before I knew what I was doing, I was pulling up a stool and sitting down before a display counter, while Sally turned back the cover of the big, leather album Benny Filiatrault had told me about, and I was looking at the testimony of a doctor who had poked his fingers into Ginger Goodwin's wounds after his body was brought out of the woods.

"I've got some things to do in the office," Sally said. "But if you need any help, just call."

"Thanks," I said, and she left me poised over the big book. I would have gently closed its cover and sneaked out, but the office was right beside the front door, with no dead ground to sidle through, unless I wanted to bend my knees until I was below the lip of the front counter, and duck walk through the door.

So I kept reading the transcript of the coroner's inquest. There was something about a gouge on the dead man's left wrist, a mark made by the bullet that had ripped out his throat. The authorities had plainly tried to build a picture of Goodwin aiming a rifle at the Dominion police-man, who had then fired in self-defence.

Despite myself, I was drawn into the testimony. It was

plain that a lot of what was being trotted out for the official record didn't make sense. Goodwin's wounds were not consistent with his having aimed a rifle at Campbell. They were consistent with his having raised his hands as if to surrender, or in a pitiful attempt to protect himself from the high-powered bullet, fired in cold blood, that killed him. There were powder burns on the dead man's wrist and neck, burns that shouldn't have been there if they'd been standing as far apart as the policeman said they were.

I was reminded of the Warren Commission's contorted rationale for the 'single bullet theory,' which described how one slug from Lee Harvey Oswald's rifle had somehow contrived to go through President Kennedy's neck, break Governor John Connolly's wrist, go out and discover the Northwest Passage, and be back in time to be found on a stretcher at that Dallas hospital, looking as fresh and shiny as if it had never even been fired.

Ginger Goodwin's friends and neighbours were right: the inquest had stunk worse than the several-days-old corpse that was its ostensible focus. Clearly, the aim had not been to discover the true circumstances of the little red-haired man's demise, but to wash the blood off Campbell's hands.

The more I read, the louder the background hum of guilt thrummed in my head. I flipped through the pages, came across transcripts of interviews collected in the 1970s and 1980s, the words of people who had known Goodwin. They made me feel worse: if the Cumberlanders had prattled on about the man as if he were some kind of secular saint of socialism, I could have fired up my cynicism generator and put some distance between us.

But the Ginger Goodwin they talked about was all too human. He'd been a hell of a soccer player. A little guy, fast and light on his feet, he'd also been a favourite among the local ladies at social dances, even though his teeth were rotted to the point that they looked like strips of rusty wire.

He liked a good practical joke. Most of all, he loved to be out on the banks of a stream, angling for cutthroat trout with his good rod and cheap reel, his home-tied flies. He had walked the hard cobbled streets between the cold stone houses of northern England, a land where country streams and any life in them were the untouchable preserves of people whose names began with Lord, or Sir or The Honourable — for him, freedom to fish was simply paradise.

I knew Ginger Goodwin. He was the kind my dad would have called "one of us." I felt as if I owed him something, some kind of tribal allegiance. And I didn't want to owe anybody anything.

As I flipped through the pages of collected public record, finding a wealth of material on Goodwin's life and death, a terrible realization crept up and tapped me on the shoulder. I'd fobbed off Mo's urgings that I contact Susan Mayse about the movie rights to her book, telling her that it could cost big money. There would probably be serious competition, if the rights had not already been snapped up by some independent producer with access to government funding.

But it was now clear that I didn't need Mayse's intellectual property at all. It was all here, and it was all in the public domain. Ginger Goodwin had left no heirs. His life story was anybody's to take up and work with. I could start tomorrow.

"Goddamn," I said. I closed the book and slid off the stool. Now I really wanted out of the museum, but I could hear Sally's voice in the office, and the last thing I wanted was to have to give her my impressions of what I'd just been reading.

The museum's main floor had an exit that led to the

adjacent community centre, but to reach it I would have had to pass by another open door, one that connected the office with the display areas. I looked around. A sign pointed to a set of stairs that led to a display of coal mining artifacts in the basement. Perhaps there would be another exit down there.

There was, but affixed to it was a large sign noting that the door was for emergencies only, and that opening it would ring an alarm. On the other hand, basements are often a good place to hide out in, until whomever you're trying to avoid forgets about you and goes away. I decided to poke around the mining exhibits for a while, then come up and see if the coast was clear.

There wasn't that much in the display cases, not when you considered that thousands of men had spent the span of a biblical lifetime mucking through water and black filth far down under my feet. There were lamps and goggles, kneepads and helmets, cylindrical lunch pails of sheet-metal in which the men had carried their lunches.

Some of the equipment was primitive. In the early years of mining in Cumberland, the only source of light underground had been the open flames of lamps fuelled by fish oil, which the miners wore strapped to their caps. Back in Britain by then, the miners' union had long since forced the pit owners to provide safety lamps that insulated the light-giving flame behind wire gauze. The gauze barrier lowered the flame's heat to a point where it would not ignite the firedamp — explosive methane gas — that continually seeped into the mine's tunnels from the surrounding coal.

In Cumberland's early mines, a miner never knew if his next swing of the pick might crack open a pocket of concentrated methane. If it did, the blast would kill him and anyone else within hundreds of metres. Worse than the firedamp, though, was the afterdamp — carbon monoxide — that filled the tunnels as the fiery explosion consumed the oxygen.

Uncle Ted had told tales of the insidious killer, handed down through the generations of my ancestors who had 'gone down t'pit.' Men who had been far enough away to survive an underground explosion could be caught by the afterdamp before they could get to clear air. They'd drop everything and run through the sudden deadly silence, temporarily deafened by the blast, ears bleeding from the pressure wave. But if the following rush of afterdamp caught them in the tunnels, their straining lungs would fill with odourless poison. They'd be unconscious before they hit the railed floor, and dead within seconds.

The dusty display case, with its bits and pieces of the past, was giving me a case of the creeps. I turned away. On a shelf attached to the wall was a model of the headframe over one of the shafts, carefully rendered in hand-shaped miniature lumber and metal parts that would have been machined on some worker's basement lathe. A sign said *PLEASE DON'T TOUCH,* but toys make good antidotes to unpleasant realities, so I gently tugged on a string that made a piston move and a big wheel turn.

Near the model, a large stretch of wall was covered by a mining engineer's map of some of the Union Coal Company's diggings. I went around a corner, and there were more of them. There seemed to have been eight or nine different operations around Cumberland — or in the case of some of them, under it — between the 1880s and the 1950s. I'd written brochures and annual reports for mining companies over the years; they tended to give their diggings evocative names like Greenhills, Polaris or Castle Mountain. But there had clearly been no romantics among the Dunsmuirs or their successors. The Cumberland shafts were all prosaically named Number One Mine, Number Two Mine, and so on.

Some of the tunnels ran out under the glacier-fed

waters of Comox Lake. Others worked their way down toward the sea at Union Bay. It was strange to think just as so much of the Cumberland that stood above ground had remained unchanged by passing decades, under my feet were tunnels, floored in dust and pillared by rough timbers, lightless and soundless except for the occasional creak of wood fibres compressing under constant strain, and filled with the sour reek of methane.

I heard a sound from the stairwell that led down to the basement, then Sally's voice calling my name. I didn't want to talk about Ginger Goodwin or the bad old days any more. I stood still and made no answer. But Sally was the old-fashioned kind of woman who carried things through to a conclusion. She called my name again, and I heard her footsteps descending the stairs.

I cast my eyes around like an actor in a bad farce. There was a rough wooden door with the word *ENTER* on it. I opened it and stepped into dim light glistening off black walls. The museum had built a small L-shaped section of tunnel, complete with narrow gauge rails on the gritty floor and beam-and-post supports every few feet. The rails supported a square-shaped cart of unfinished one-inch planks bolted together with iron fittings, overflowing with chunks of coal the size of my head or larger. Two dummies in checked shirts and filthy jeans, with leather pads strapped over their knees, were frozen in the act of lifting a black lump into the cart.

"Raff?" It was Sally again, on the other side of the door. I moved silently along the short tunnel to the bend of the L, and went around the corner. Picks, shovels and gap-toothed saws leaned against a wall, as if the men who used them had just finished their shift and begun the long walk back to daylight. Another dummy stood here, posed at a hand-cranked drill with an immense bit that looked to be longer than I was tall. The instrument was braced by a vertical jack that ran from ceiling to floor. I touched the wall beside me, and my fingertips came away smudged. I listened for the sound of Sally opening the door I had entered through, but there was only the sough of air being pumped through the little space, giving the walk-in display an extra touch of verisimilitude.

I waited. Suddenly, as Spike Milligan used to say, nothing happened. When nothing had kept happening for two or three minutes, I went quietly to the exit door at the end of the tunnel, where a hand-drawn sign said *PLEASE WIPE YOUR FEET*. I pushed the splintery wood panel open a hands-breadth and peered out. Still nothing. I stepped out, poked my head around the corner of the tunnel display. The basement was empty.

I went back up to the main floor, skirted along the old customs counter until I could see that the office was empty except for the teenage girl who'd taken my three dollars. I waved to her as I went out the front door. She couldn't have known I was also waving bye-bye to the stirrings of half-memories and forgotten allegiances the museum had roiled up from the bottom of my inner sea. Bye-bye to Sally, Ginger, my old man, the whole class war and old Uncle Tom Cobbley and all. Out into the sunshine and Cumby.

Still, despite everything, there was part of me that wanted to make notes, sketch a storyline, envision an opening scene. Even though the prospect of writing anything serious filled my intestines with something cold that turned over and over, as I cranked the Behemoth into life and swung out onto Dunsmuir Avenue, the little man who lives in the back of my mind — the one who handles the actual creativity — was banging on the partition like Wee Willy Winky on amphetamines.

Irony and pity, he was crying through the locks, *They're always suckers for irony and pity. Give them the old I&P and you can't fail.*

I pushed him away, but he came right back — he always

does when he's on a roll. He wanted to show me the key thing in a story like this was point of view, and that there was only one point of view worth looking at in the tale of Ginger Goodwin.

The story shouldn't be told from Ginger's doomed perspective. Nor from Campbell's murderous slant. Nor from the Greek chorus of friends and supporters who helped him and hid him and ultimately buried him.

The most compelling figure was the one about whom the least was recorded, but who played the pivotal role in the tragedy. His name had been Thomas Anderson. He was variously described as a trapper, a miner, a scab.

The government paid him eight dollars to lead Dan Campbell to where Ginger Goodwin was fishing for trout and picking berries. From then on, the trapper was known as 'Scabby' Anderson, and he was nothing but a Judas to the people of Cumberland. He never set foot in the village again.

He was said to have gone to his grave wracked with guilt. For my money, that made him the natural centrepiece to any screen version of the Goodwin story — just the way Scalieri had been the alpha and omega of *Amadeus*.

"Leave me alone," I said to the Behemoth's windshield, but the little guy with the big ideas kept yattering away. I turned on the radio and punched the button for the oldies station. I got Anne Murray doing a Canadian content cover of the Monkees song *Daydream Believer*, with what sounded like the identical arrangement.

But it was better than arguing with Mr. Creativity.

Chapter 4

"Whatever it is you see in that guy," Mo said, "I don't. He's just not funny."

A burst of laughter from the people in David Letterman's studio audience meant they disagreed with the woman I loved, so I didn't have to. The guffaws and whistles were followed by a ripple of titters as the talk-show host opened his mouth and eyes to their widest, and silently mouthed the word, "Wow!"

Mo slapped her pillows into shape and lay down. She pulled the quilt up over her eyes. "He's just making faces at the camera," she said. "Come on, turn him off."

I clicked back to the news. The lead story on the local private broadcaster was the roadblock protest at a bridge on a logging road in Clayoquot Sound. Some of the protesters had brought little kids, stood them out on the dirt road to be arrested with their parents. The kids were scared, some of them crying, as they were led away by the dispassionate RCMP constables.

A group of loggers and their wives who'd come out to protest against the protest were outraged. "This is no place for little kids," said one woman. "Those people ought to be ashamed."

I clicked over to CBC. The public broadcaster was covering the same event. One of the protest organizers was doing her best to put a good spin on the validity of using kids for emotional impact. I doubted they'd do it again.

"Dumb move," I said.

Mo grunted. It sounded like, "Turn it off."

I clicked over to Jay Leno. He was doing a bit on newspaper wedding announcements with odd pairings of names. Somewhere, a Ms. Fuller was marrying a Mr. Bull. I trusted that she would not adopt the modern fashion of keeping both names with a hyphen.

"Off," said a nearby muffled voice.

I went back to Letterman. I wanted to catch the rundown of guests at the end of the monologue. Maybe Teri Garr was on; I hadn't seen her in so long, I was beginning to wonder if she'd retired.

The gap-toothed comic said, "Hey, buddy, fibrillate this." I'd missed the set-up, but it didn't matter — his writers had used a variation of the same punchline a hundred times.

I clicked through half a dozen channels in not that many seconds.

"Hey, buddy," said a throaty voice behind me. "Click on this."

She lifted the covers. A warm scent of bath oil and woman wafted over me. The mingling of musk and flowers opened a passage straight through the cerebellum and down into the limbic system, where it woke up the snuffling old ape and set him to grabbing for the original luxury.

I hit the button on the remote and dropped the clicker beside the bed. The screen glowed pale as a blind cyclops's eye in the sudden darkness. I pulled the covers over both our heads and drew her close.

She slipped her arms around me. I put my lips against her neck and took in the scent of her, ran a hand down past the small of her strong back, curved over the roundness of her wonderful ass, and reached the soft, damp heat at her core.

She made a sound in the back of her throat and let her hand trail down my chest and belly. Now it was my turn to make noises.

This part was good, had always been good right from the start. The fit was perfect. We flowed together as if we were matching components, smoothly oiled, precision-designed.

I moved my hand to her front, cupped her mound and ran my middle finger up the wet divide to the juncture at the top. She pushed my hand away.

"Don't need that," she breathed. "Been thinking about it the whole time I was in the bath. Come on."

She liked it with me on top, said it felt better that way on the hard mattress she'd insisted we buy. It was a good investment.

I went into her. She was like liquid velvet, softly churning around me. She made love as always with silent concentration. Mo gave no *When-Harry-Met-Sally*, mega-decibel performances, but I could tell when she came — she drew in a breath and held it, then she seemed to soften and open like a magnificent flesh-flower, pulling me deeper, squeezing and drawing me deeper, panting softly until the last spasm. Then she would say my name, and other things, whispering fiercely, her breath hot in my ear as I bucked into her.

"Magic," I said, as we lay together, the odour of sweat now added to the mix beneath the covers.

"Mmmm," she agreed and pulled me close.

"Love you," I said.

She didn't answer. She was already gone. She had been stroking my belly but now her hand stopped midway between my sternum and navel. It made a fitful start, as if it might have continued but lacked the commitment, then lay limp. I covered it with mine.

I would have liked to slip down into sleep with her, but somebody had left my brain running. I kept thinking about Ginger Goodwin, about Scabby Anderson.

It wouldn't be so hard to put together a script. I could at least do a treatment, twenty pages of barebones narrative. I could knock off a first draft in a weekend, then fiddle and play with it until it folded itself into the right shape.

But then what? Then came the endless pursuit of the producer: through mail-outs of the treatment, complete with carefully crafted cover letters; through contrived chance encounters at somebody's screening or somebody else's cocktail party; through referrals and introductions cadged from anybody I knew who knew anybody I needed to know; and, if all else failed, by getting on the phone for the hard-assed cold call, where you try everything short of shameless wheedling to keep the reluctant fish on the line long enough to get him to say he'd at least look at the damn outline.

Which he probably wouldn't do anyway. The best you usually got was, "Leave it with us, and we'll get back to you," followed after weeks or even months of waiting by, "It's not what we're looking for." Or nothing at all.

I knew from experience. I'd spent more than two years trying to pry open the legendary treasure chest that screenwriting was supposed to offer. All I'd got was sore fingertips.

I'd begun my screenwriting career with one lucky break — a pay-TV mystery that had almost got produced, until the financing fell apart in the last lap. Since then I'd never even got close enough to smell the dust that the front runners threw back at the rest of us.

I'd heard about writers who had battered away at the business, year after year, wading through waist-high drifts of rejection slips, until they finally got their hands on the hilt of success and yanked that mother screaming out of the stone. They must have had bark on them hard enough to blunt a buck-saw.

All I knew was that, after two years of getting nowhere, my self-esteem was worn right through to the lining. And I didn't figure to let the world scrape any more of it off.

I was a failed screenwriter, but a successful commercial hack. That was good enough for me. My only problem was making it good enough for Mo.

I pushed Ginger and Scabby out of my consciousness and eventually fell asleep, but so late that I couldn't wake up with Mo in the morning. She let me sleep past nine, and even brought me a plate of toast and a steaming mug of black Ceylon before she started her day's work.

The Brentwood didn't have the mordant bite of Uva Highland, but it managed to burrow through the blockages in my synapses. I lumbered out of bed and into the shower, emerging after ten minutes under the hot spray with a reasonable approximation of consciousness. I put on my working uniform of sweat pants and tee-shirt, got another cup of tea, and took it into the office.

"It's alive," Mo said, not looking up from her Power-Book.

I grunted something, sat down at my desk and powered up the 386.

"I guess when I fuck 'em, they stay fucked," she said.

"It's true," I said. "You're way too much woman for a man of my fragile constitution."

I reached for my interview notes on Benny Filiatrault, flipped through them. I told Mo I'd be spending the day putting his campaign material together. "What about you?" I asked.

"I'm wrestling with the pulp mill thing," she said. "The man wants me to figure out a way eight people can do the work of ten."

"Doesn't sound like you're just cutting deadwood."

She made a face. "No, some of this wood is alive and kicking. It's still got to be cut somewhere."

She tapped a few keys and frowned. I watched her spin the track ball to highlight whatever she'd just written, then press a key. The highlighted text disappeared, and she sighed.

I turned back to my own keyboard, created a file called *Hand-01*, and put Filiatrault's name at the top of what would soon be his basic campaign handout. I didn't hear the sound of Mo's fingers clicking on her machine. After a moment, she spoke.

"Sally said you were digging through the Ginger Goodwin book at the museum yesterday."

My fingers hovered over the keys. "When did you talk to her?" I said, without turning around.

"She phoned this morning. You were in the shower."

I said nothing.

"So?" she said.

"Well, there's a story there, all right," I said. I couldn't resist telling her about my feeling that Scabby Anderson was the right path to take into the forest. She agreed.

"Villains are always more interesting than martyrs," she said. "They define the martyrs, don't they? You know what I'm trying to say, light against dark, contrast."

I did. It was almost exciting to think about bringing the players to life in a story. I pushed the thought back down into the pit before it could get all the way out. "It's not Hollywood, though."

"Doesn't have to be."

I couldn't look at her. I hit the enter key on the 386 a couple of times, making some space under Benny's name. "I don't know, Mo."

"Yes, you do."

Now I looked at her, but only for a moment. "Don't know if I could get the rights from Susan Mayse. Might already be taken."

"You could ask. The museum has her phone number."

I shrugged.

"Or I could call her," she said.

"No," I said, "I'll do it. I'll write her a letter."

"Yeah. It'll be good for you."

"I just want to do this job first," I said.

"Sure," she said, and went back to what she'd been doing.

I looked at the shell program display on the monitor and pressed the number key that activated my old Word-Star program. It was the first-word-processing application I'd learned, and the only one I'd ever favoured. I'd started with a really primitive version that had come free with my first computer, and upgraded twice. I wouldn't be up-grading any higher than Version 7, because nobody made WordStar any more. MS Word and WordPerfect ruled the world now. But I was loyal to WordStar; it did everything I needed done, and I'd used the two-letter command codes for so long they were automatic.

I had a recent edition of MS Word on the hard drive, provided free by a Vancouver corporate client after I sent over a 3.5 inch diskette that contained a draft annual report written in WordStar. He faxed back a note telling me to resubmit it after converting the file into basic ASCII, and added, "don't ever send me another goddamn dino-saur's footprint."

After that, I got a conversion program from a client who used his computer and the phone lines to talk to other technofreaks all over the world — he said it was going to be the next big thing. Now I wrote all my stuff in WordStar, then let the conversion program translate it into whatever format the particular client used.

The conversion program was not a commercial product, and its creator had not bothered to make it user-friendly for techno-peasants like me. I couldn't point-and-click with the mouse, and it didn't offer me menus with a choice of individual keys to trigger commands. I had to type in command strings, and if I got one letter wrong, the damn thing wouldn't work.

All of that made converting a time-consuming pain in the ass, but I was not going to knuckle under and be constantly switching word-processing formats every time the market changed. It was like being forced to learn a foreign language. Or maybe it was just a built-in mulishness. Maybe I just liked things the way I liked them.

WordStar loaded itself into the computer's RAM and put the opening menu up on the screen. It was still in black and white, just like the original, although there were a lot more options. Below the menu were the various directories in which I organized my files. There was one marked *MOVIES* and another called *BOOKS* but I didn't go there.

I used the keypad to run the cursor over to the directory headed *WORK* and opened it up. The screen filled with the names of subdirectories, each one representing a corporation or politician for whom I had done work since reinventing myself as a freelance speechwriter. There were a lot of them.

I created a new subdirectory using the first eight letters of Benny Filiatrault's last name, and then sat back and thought about how to fill it. I decided to start with a basic positioning document — a few hundred words of simple, straightforward language that would tell the voters where the candidate was coming from.

If Benny had been a complete unknown, I might have done the kind of *Who I Am, Where I Stand* introductory piece that I had written for Mo's brother Tony when he had taken his half-hearted run at provincial politics. But I gathered that almost everybody in Cumby already knew my client. And, since he'd probably buttonholed each one of them at some time or other, warning them the environmental sky would soon be bashing through their roofs, there was no need to spell out his political philosophy.

I would go straight to the issue on which he was running. When he'd said, "Save Hockney's Woods," my first reaction had been to focus on my possible conflict of interest. But now I thought about it, I could see the issue would have some problems. If Rod Bilder's troubles continued, the old-growth stand wouldn't be threatened – and his issue would evaporate.

So saving the trees wouldn't do. What Filiatrault needed was a classic *trouble in River City* campaign. And that starts with T which rhymes with D and that stands for Development." What Benny really wanted was to warn his fellow citizens not to stand still for any more unchecked development, or their sleepy little village would soon get an abrupt awakening — by the sound of nail guns slapping together a slew of video arcades, fast-food joints and instant-lube drive-ins. There'd be a real-estate office on every corner, staffed by hustlers trying to squeeze another megahome onto a lot originally laid out for a miner's shanty.

Now I knew what I had to write about, so I stared at the monitor, waiting for the guy in the back of my head to come up with something. It took him less than ten seconds to remind me of the obvious: when faced with a creative challenge, the experienced political writer immediately looks for a good idea he can steal, a good idea being defined as one that has already worked.

Stealing is the heart and soul of political writing. I've never met or heard of a political speechwriter who saw anything wrong with lifting other people's words. It was done all the time, and it put me in the same league as presidents and prime ministers.

I'd learned that during my first week as staff speechwriter to the federal Minister of Justice. The guy I had replaced in the job had left behind a well-thumbed copy of *Bartlett's Familiar Quotations.* I later learned he had inherited the book from the long line of word-slingers who had preceded us both — our boss went through speechwriters the way frogs went through flies.

Preparing to put together my minister's first speech, I opened the *Bartlett's* and rooted around for inspiration among the collected *bon mots* of all the really great writers who had come to rest between its covers. I soon learned greatness was no inhibitor of literary larceny. The giants all stole from each other.

It was all in the footnotes. John Kennedy's *Ask not what your country can do,* was adapted from a line in an 1884 speech by Oliver Wendell Holmes. Republican President-to-be Warren G. Harding had woven a variation on the same theme at a party convention in 1916.

Even Winston Churchill hadn't quibbled to lift a line out of a Byron poem to get *blood, toil, tears and sweat.*" Funny thing, Byron had originally coined the phrase as *blood, sweat and tears,* which was exactly what popular memory had credited Churchill with saying.

Benny Filiatrault was at an altogether different layer of the political great chain of being, so I would not be stealing from the likes of Kennedy or Churchill. There was a nearer and more recent store of useful political rhetoric. It had belonged to The Electors Action Movement, a now defunct but briefly successful cadre of centre-left political operatives who had overturned Vancouver civic politics back in the 1970s. TEAM had used modern campaigning methods to unseat the right-wing dinosaurs of the totally partisan Non Partisan Association who had ruled city council since God was still an undergraduate.

The TEAM strategy had been built around one simple question: *whose city was it, anyway?* Was it *ours,* all us ordinary folks who just wanted a decent place to live? Or was it *theirs,* the speculators who wanted to destroy our neighbourhoods so they could retire to Palm Springs?

If it was ours, why were we letting a bunch of money grubbers mess it up?

The *Our City* offensive was precisely the kind of in-your-face, divisive politics that worked well in local elections, so it translated easily into an *Our Village* campaign for Filiatrault. His positioning piece practically wrote itself. The monitor screen filled with short paragraphs, no more than one or two sentences each, that began scrolling out of sight as I ploughed the propaganda furrow deeper.

"How's it coming?" Mo asked.

"Fine," I said. I'd had harder times falling off logs. I wrote another line without taking my eyes off the screen. "How about you?"

She made a noncommittal noise. I turned my head. She was staring at the PowerBook's display screen, tapping a pencil against her teeth. I was looking at her in profile, and I saw the laugh lines at the corner of her eye deepen slightly as she concentrated on her work. The muscle at the hinge of her jaw tightened as she opened her teeth and bit the end of the pencil.

"Anything I can do?" I said.

This time the noise was a definite no. She started typing something on the PowerBook. I went back to Benny Filiatrault and kept at it until I had summed up his *we're gonna lose our village* campaign in less than three hundred words. After I converted it over to MS Word and messed around with different type faces and sizes, it would print out on one sheet of legal sized photocopying paper, with room for a picture of the candidate in one corner and his name across the top in big, bold print. At the bottom, I put *Want to keep Cumby special?* and added the candidate's home phone number. He had no separate campaign office, and even if he had, anyone who wanted to talk to Filiatrault would phone him at home anyway.

I saved the handout file, and WordStar automatically sent me back to the directory. I told the program to create another file, named *Speech01*. The blank electronic page appeared on the screen, and I wrote, *GENERIC CAMPAIGN SPEECH, BENNY FILIATRAULT* at its top. Then I sat back and waited for my internal gnome to feed me the opening line.

Instead, I got a message from another county. The

part of me that liked tea — apparently a very large part — wanted some more. "I'm going to make another pot," I told Mo. "Want some?"

She grunted without looking away from what she was writing. There was an empty cup on her desk, which I collected along with my own and took into the kitchen. I put on the kettle, threw the remains of the first pot into the sink, and washed out the receptacle with hot water.

Some people would have poured the old tea into a cup and nuked it in the microwave. To me, they were no better than the kind of people who bought Da Vinci's *Last Supper* reproduced on black velvet and complained that the picture would be a lot more effective if the painter had given Christ and the apostles really big, sad eyes to match the ocularly enhanced urchins hanging in the guest bathroom.

Put it this way, I could be very flexible on a lot of life's little things — like the choice of people I would writing do jobs for — but when it came to tea, I had *standards*.

Lately, I'd taken to using a tea sock. This was something new to me: a small pouch of unbleached cotton suspended from a wire circle a little larger than the opening at the top of the tea pot. The sock hung down inside the pot; and you spooned the tea leaves into it, poured in the water, then lifted out the sock with its wet clump of leaves once the brew was properly steeped. It made good tea without leaving a mess in the bottom of the cup. Mo said it looked like one of those experimental female condoms she'd seen on the TV news, but she liked the results.

The kettle burbled to let me know the water was boiling. I splashed some into the tea pot to warm it, emptied it out, put in the sock then added three teaspoons of Brentwood Ceylon. I pulled the plug and poured the still bubbling water into the pot, put on the lid and slipped a quilted cozy over the whole thing.

The wall phone rang. I picked it up. "Sid Rafferty."

A very cool, very British voice said, "I see that you are still inflicting your presence upon the world."

It took a long moment for my mental gears to mesh. "Lanc?" I said. "Is that you?"

"It is," he said. "How the hell are you?"

"Mostly astonished," I said. I sat down at the table. "I thought you'd gone over the edge of the world, never to be seen again."

"I was, but now I'm back."

"Back where? Where are you?"

"Back in Port Alberni, god save me."

"What are you doing there again?" I said.

"Something interesting," he replied. "And I'd like you to help."

"You know I'm not a journalist any more," I said.

"Were you ever?"

"More than you on your best day."

"The trouble with you, Rafferty, is that you don't know your place."

"The trouble with you, Sir Lancolm, is that you're an upper class git."

It was as if twenty-odd years had fallen away. And I was glad to be, briefly, back in a time before my life went wrong.

I've had few close friends, and The Honourable Lancolm Bertram Halfnight had not been one of them. Our relationship had been one of those stripped-down associations that you form with people you work with and even booze with, but never invite home. It's a kind of intimacy, but only within a circumscribed range of topics. You might reveal to each other your deepest convictions about politics or philosophy, but you'd never wander over the line into the places where the big stuff was, your real fears and soft spots. If you did, there would be a quick, shuffling retreat under cover of a change of subject.

With Lanc and me, it was politics and class warfare. We met in my last year at university, in what passed for the newsroom of the Simon Fraser University student rag, *The Peak*: Lanc was doing scathing political commentary under a Latin pen name; I was writing movie reviews and satirical features, trying to build up a fistful of clippings with a bold-face *Sid Rafferty* at the top of each, that I could show to a news editor on the *Vancouver Sun* or the *Province*, and maybe get a stringer's job covering city council meetings in suburbs like Coquitlam and Burnaby.

We were a mismatched pair. I was the son of an immigrant labourer, of Liverpool Irish stock. The Honourable Lanc Halfnight was the eldest scion of an Anglo-Irish baronet, and would become Sir Lancolm when he eventually inherited the title. There was no estate or income attached to the rank — there had once been a pension from the Privy Purse, but it had been stopped by Queen Victoria. She hadn't thought highly of the recipient.

The baronetcy had been bestowed on Lanc's great-great-something-grandfather for *services to the Crown*. One late night, over the corpses of a couple of bottles of the raw, red sangria that was all we could afford to drink in those days, he had told me what those services had entailed.

The Crown had been Victoria's uncle, the Prince Regent, later to become George IV, but then widely known as the Georgy Porgy of the nursery rhyme. The 1820's vintage Halfnight had been a roguish County Dublin horse breeder with an unerring eye for high-spirited equine bloodstock and even higher-spirited young ladies of fashion, both of which he procured upon request for His Royal Highness.

"But the thing that clinched it," Lanc told me, "was my ancestor's ability to knock down a house of cards with one fart."

The Prince Regent, who would wager on which way a drunk would fall, bet against Halfnight. The stakes were a baronetcy against Georgy Porgy's pick from the Irishman's stable. The card house was built on a table in the future king's favourite gambling hell. Halfnight unbuttoned his breeches — "Beau Brummel had not by then made trousers fashionable, don't y'know," Lanc said — then bent over, carefully positioning himself at just the right height and angle.

"And then, with a clap like thunder, he blew the Prince's house to smithereens." He raised his glass to his puissant ancestor. "Never was nobility more nobly won."

It was my part in these sessions to play the honest yeoman. "Nobility," I scoffed, working up a poor imitation of my maternal ancestor's family accent. "It were lads like us as went out and won your lot t' world's greatest bloody empire."

He looked over the rim of his glass at me. "You didn't go," he drawled. "You were sent."

"How long you been back in Port?" I asked the phone.

"Just a wee while," Lanc said.

"So what are you doing there?"

"I'm back here in a," — there was a slight hesitation — "in sort of an... advisory capacity. And I have a job for you, if you want it. Good money attached."

"I don't want to work on a newspaper again, Lanc. I'm strictly freelance. My own man."

"Insouciant wretch," he said. "His Majesty should never have signed the damned Magna Carta. Don't worry, your independence will be untrammelled. Actually, a lack of affiliation commends you to the task."

"What task?"

"Not over the phone. Tell you when you get here. Which would be...?"

I thought about it. I could wrap Benny Filiatrault's

speech today, do the phony letters to the editor and any follow-up stuff tomorrow. "I could drive down day after tomorrow," I said. "Be there after lunch."

"Excellent. Do."

"Where do you want to meet? Do you have an office?"

"Not quite the right venue," he drawled. "Remember that squalid little place where we would have a drink?"

I did. It had been the lounge of the old Barclay Hotel, dark and smoky, with a short-skirted waitress who used to make my heart flutter. At his mention of it, I could smell the warm fug that always hung in the air. I'd loved it. "I loved that place," I said.

He laughed. "Well, it's all gone, burned down apparently. But there's a relentlessly bland modern version masquerading under the same name on Redford Street. I'll see you there at two."

I pressed him a little more, but all he would say was it might eat up a week or two of my time, and that I would be paid "a sum sure to exceed your proletarian wants," as he put it.

"You're on," I said.

When I took the tea back into the office, Mo had closed up her PowerBook and was putting the pulp mill papers back into their file. "Who was that?" she said.

"Old newspaper buddy," I said. I handed her her cup and sat down at my desk. "Well, really, older than that." I told her about how Lanc and I had been friends in school, though I didn't mention the Prince Regent's wager. "He has some kind of job he wants me to do. I'm going over to Port Alberni to see him tomorrow. Want to come?"

"I would but I can't, Raff. I'm going back up to Campbell River to present my recommendations."

"You've figured out which chickens get the chop?"

She nodded and sipped her tea. "It's a little ironic — turns out the best thing to do is to eliminate the position of the man who brought me in. He doesn't know it, but he's just a figurehead and a communications bottleneck. If we remove him and let the people under him be a self-directing team, it'll save money and probably increase their productivity by a good chunk."

"Ouch," I said.

She made a wry face. "He'll get a reasonable parachute. Maybe he'll become a consultant and give me competition."

I made one of those sounds men make when they're not being overly compassionate about the misfortunes of others. "Guy can't see a train that's about to hit him, I don't think he's gonna be big competition for a brainy babe like you."

"You think I'm...?" She let it dangle.

"What, brainy?" I said. "You bet."

"No. A babe."

"If I didn't have to write another chunk of deathless political rhetoric, I would take you back to bed and demonstrate the power of your babe-itude in a direct and forthright manner," I said.

"I thought you were all wrung out from last night," she said.

"Somehow, from somewhere, I would summon the resources."

"But you have to work," she said.

"But I have to work."

She shrugged. "I could fit you in tonight." Her eyes told me the pun was deliberate. "I could even buy you dinner at the Old House, make it worth your while."

I said, "You've got a date." Then I smacked my head and said, "No, I just remembered — if I'm going to Port Alberni tomorrow, I should deliver Benny Filiatrault's material tonight. He's going to some kind of public meeting at the village hall, and will probably want to run off a few copies of the handbill and give them out. I'll bet Rod Bilder's going to be there too, so I can give him back his stuff."

"That shouldn't take too long," she said. "I wouldn't mind coming along."

"Sure. But I may have to hang around, see which way the meeting goes, in case Benny wants me to write something about it, maybe a letter to the editor."

We agreed to make it a quick bite at the Black Fin in Comox after the meeting, or a drive-thru burger and chips at MacDonald's if the meeting in Cumberland ran late. I got back to work and she went down to the store to get a few groceries.

Benny Filiatrault's generic speech was still nothing but a heading on my monitor screen. It got no bigger as I finished my tea and stared out the window for a while. I was thinking about Lanc and wondering what kind of job he was offering.

I liked the prospect of seeing Lanc again. And, though I would have denied it under torture, I liked the thought of getting out of town for a while even more. Maybe while I was away, the whole Ginger Goodwin, movie-making idea would somehow fade away.

I wasn't too sure how long I could go on lying to the woman I loved.

Chapter 5

Benny Filiatrault's home suited his principles. He lived in a ninety-year-old, shingle-sided house two blocks off Dunsmuir Street. The place's once-straight lines were now gradually transforming themselves into gentle curves. The ends of the eaves seemed to bend slightly upwards as if the house was thinking about becoming a Chinese pagoda in its retirement years. The walls bulged, but just comfortably. The roofed porch sagged in the middle like a shallow grin, and its boards creaked as I came up the three steps and put my foot on it. I imagined living in the house would be like staying with a slightly dotty old aunt who went around murmuring and muttering to herself, generating a constant, low-level background sound that never rose to the pitch of actual conversation.

Mo stayed in the Behemoth, reading a paperback. The car fitted in well on this narrow Cumberland street, with its cracked sidewalks and creosoted wooden telephone poles. There was nothing younger than the old Ford within a hundred metres.

I was surrounded by the soft, grainy colours of evening: yellow light spilling from Benny's windows and purply black shadows hunkering in the porch corners. If I squinted my eyes and pretended just a little, I could think myself into the skin of a character in some moody story by Ray Bradbury, with time poised to fall out of joint, and a gang of boys in knickerbockers and flat caps about to come racing around the corner, kicking a can.

Benny's door had one of those old-timey bells, stuck in its middle like a protruding navel, underneath the curtained pane that took up most of the door's top half. I spun the black iron key that should have wrung a musical note out of the hemisphere of metal in which it was set, but the bell had been painted over so many times that all it gave was a grating rattle.

It was loud enough, though, and in a few seconds, my client's big shadow moved behind the curtain, and he opened the door. "Come on in," he said. "Sorry there's no light on the porch. The wiring in this place is the shits."

It was a house of small rooms, all with doors. I knew why they used to live like that — it saved on heating costs. Even in a town built on coal, there would have been no money to waste on warming unused space. I remembered living in places like this as a child. On winter mornings, the linoleum floors in the unheated bedrooms would be cold enough to make the balls of my feet ache, even through the socks I'd worn to bed. I'd throw on my clothes in between fits of shivering, then get to the kitchen and its warm stove as fast as I could.

I followed Benny along a claustrophobia-inducing hallway to the kitchen at the back of the house. It was warm and yellow, with appliances and fittings not quite old enough to be antiques. The back door was solid wood with a big old skeleton key lock, but the tongue of the dead bolt stuck out into empty air. Where it should have met a receptacle slot in the jamb there was instead a splinter-edged hole.

Benny followed my gaze. "Somebody broke in the other day," he said. "Kids looking for CDs or something else they can hock fast for beer and cigarette money." He laughed. "Fuck all like that around here."

"They didn't take anything?" I asked.

"Nothing here to take."

We sat at a table with a red plastica top and corrugated zinc trim, perched on matching chairs, and he read what I had written.

There was a time when it made me nervous, waiting while someone went over what I'd been paid to create. Not any more. In this one sphere of my life, my confidence was absolute. Between us, Mr. Creativity and I always got it right.

Of course, when it comes to speechwriting, there's no great trick. People have sometimes asked me how it's possible to write speeches about so many different fields — the forest industry this week, base metal mining last week, and tomorrow it could be telecommunications — when I'm not an expert in any of them. The answer's easy: I'm an expert speechwriter. That means I don't need to know anything but the most elementary basics about the subject, because you need very little information to put together a good speech, and almost none of that information needs to be new.

That's always been the speechwriter's rule of thumb: no more than three pieces of information that the audience doesn't already know. Even then, chances are they'll only recall one or two of them.

So what do I put in a speech instead of new facts? Old facts — especially old facts the audience and the speaker already agree upon. Most speeches — business or political — are exercises in "I'm okay, you're okay." They're part of an occasion where like-minded people get together to reinforce their mutual world view.

That's why Chambers of Commerce don't invite radical environmentalists to harangue the Babbitts at their monthly bunfests. It's why the social democratic party does not ask a spokesperson from the right-wing think tank, the Fraser Institute, to give the key note address to an NDP policy conference.

The purpose of a political speech is not to inform but

to get everybody pulled together and lined up to head out in the same direction. It's the rhetorical equivalent of a fire drill in a kindergarten. Benny Filiatrault's generic stump speech was designed to make his fellow towns-folk feel good about what they shared and worried about losing it — worried enough to turn up at the polls and put an X next to his familiar name.

He read the eight pages of text carefully, line by line, then laid them flat on the red plastic, put his extra-wide hand flat on top of them. "I like it," he said. "It's so simple, heartfelt."

"Well, that's the trick," I said.

He went through the draft hand-out just as carefully, then started on the half dozen letters-to-the-editor I had crafted. One was for him to send in under his own name; the rest would be copied out by willing supporters in their own handwriting, then signed and delivered to the *Free Press* and its tabloid competitor, the *Record*.

While he was reading, I heard water running some-where else in the house, then Davey Clemmer came into the kitchen. If he wasn't wearing the same clothes, he had duplicates.

"We're almost out of soap," he said. He ignored me.

"Just fine," I said. "How's your own self?"

He grunted to let me know my sophisticated brand of humour was wasted on him. He picked up the speech text from the table and glanced through the pages, letting each one fall as he finished with it. Halfway through, he sniffed, let the remaining sheets drop and wandered out of the room.

"I'll get some tomorrow," Benny said, his nose still in the letters to the editor. Clemmer wandered out of the kitchen into the hallway that led to the front door. Benny called after him, "We need to go over to Christopher's and make some copies of this handbill before the meeting starts." There may have been a grunt in reply.

I gathered Christopher was that extremely useful element in a political campaign: a supporter who owned a photocopier. "Will you need anything more from me?" I asked.

"You're going to come to the meeting?"

I nodded. "Sure."

"I might ask you to write something after."

"Okay."

He led me back down the hall. A door that had been closed before was open now on a tiny living room — when the ancient house was built it would have been called a parlour —containing a couple of overstuffed armchairs and a ratty old couch, the kind you buy for ten or twenty bucks apiece at the Salvation Army thrift shop. Benny was apparently telling the truth when he said the house contained nothing worth stealing. Perhaps he was able to stuff hundreds and fifties into envelopes and give them to deserving freelance writers because he was a whiz at economizing on overhead.

But it wasn't the poverty of the room that drew my attention, nor the sight of Clemmer reclining on the sofa, reading one of those modern magazines, the kind where the editors put all their effort into visual design, producing page after page of garish, almost unreadable graphics.

What got my attention was the neat, round bullet hole in the room's small window, with the web of cracks running to the edges of the frame. I stopped in the doorway, then leaned in to take a closer look.

"That's a bullet hole," I said.

"Yeah," Benny agreed. "Couple of days ago. It's no big deal. I figure it was a spent bullet, somebody shooting in the woods or up at the lake. I dug it out of the wall, there." He showed me a hole in the plaster and lathe — no drywall in those days — a few inches below the ceiling. "Only went in half an inch. Just a fluke."

Clemmer flicked a page of his magazine, saying

nothing but saying it loudly. Benny noticed. "Davey thinks somebody's warning me to back off, not run for council." He blew out his cheeks and let the air rasp over his lips in a succinct expression of opinion. Clemmer rattled the pages again.

I looked at the hole in the wall and at the one in the window. A spent bullet would have come in on a descending trajectory. Which meant it had to have bounced off the roof of the neighbour's house, which wasn't much further than I could have thrown Davey Clemmer.

"Where's the slug?" I said.

It was on the mantelpiece over the Lilliputian fireplace. To me, it just looked like a slightly blunted cylinder of soft metal. I assumed it had to have come from some kind of rifle because it seemed to me that pistol rounds were shorter than this. I was no ballistics expert, but I thought Benny must be right: the bullet couldn't have had much force behind it, if it had made such a shallow impression in the room's flimsy inner wall. Maybe it had come over the neighbour's roof, through the window, then bounced off the carpet and hit the upper wall. Stranger things have happened.

"What did the cops say?" I asked Benny.

His eyebrows went up. "Nothing," he said. I didn't call in any cops."

I didn't say anything, but my face must have, because now Benny showed a little exasperation. "You're as bad as he is," he said, twitching a thumb in the direction of the junior nihilist. "I mean, what's with you guys? It's no big deal."

I hated to share an opinion with Clemmer, but I was being paid to think about this kind of stuff, so I said, "Could be useful in a campaign. It's an attention-getter, good media stuff, potentially draws sympathy."

"Bullshit," said Benny.

"It's part of my job to make these suggestions."

"Sure, but that one is bush league. It would make me look like a hysterical asshole." He spread his hands, palms down. "No, we don't use it. It's bad enough Davey goes around telling some of my supporters about it, and I have to say, 'Don't do that any more,' but we're not going to the media. Is that understood?"

"You're the boss," I said.

"Good."

He showed me out.

Mo tucked a bookmark into her book as I got into the car. It was Michael Ondaatje's *The English Patient* which had already won half the Booker Prize and the whole Governor General's Award. It was the kind of book she loved, but for me it was all pearls and no string. I could appreciate fine prose, but I needed a strong storyline to carry me along.

"Are we finished?" she asked. "I'm starting to get hungry."

"There isn't really time to get something to eat," I said. "I've got to meet Benny at the community centre in less than an hour. Unless you just want to get a burger or something." Cumberland was not known for its cuisine; the good restaurants were in Courtenay and Comox.

She made her life-is-generally-yucky face. The expression was a fleeting survival of her childhood, from all the years when there had been a Maureen Migliorini I had never known, and never would. She didn't like me to probe her about what it was like being the lawyer's daughter, being big sister to her brother Tony and the other sister I had still not met. About her marriage, she had told me almost nothing; he was a jerk, it was a mistake, and that was that.

"We could go up to the lake," I said. "Get some fries, sit on a log. I hear it's a summer tradition in Cumby."

That got me a smile. "We haven't done that yet," she said. "Okay."

I wheeled the Behemoth up past the museum and the community centre, swung onto the lake road, and followed the narrow two-lane blacktop.

Less than kilometre out of the village we passed a tiny wooden cabin, windowless, with its door boarded up. Next to it was a big display board under a peaked roof. It was the kind of touristy thing I routinely left out of my day.

Mo was different. "Have you seen that?" she said.

"Uh uh."

"Pull over."

I put my face into my own version of the expression she'd shown me outside Filiatrault's.

"Humour me," she said. "It won't hurt a bit."

I pulled over onto the gravel patch between the cabin and the road and we got out. I followed Mo over to the cabin, but there was not much to see.

"Not much to see," I said. It stood at the top of a wooded slope. It was hard to believe anyone could have lived in such a small space — at the most three metres by two — made of rough logs, the gaps between them unchinked. I tried to peer through a thumb's-width space at about eye level, but the sealed structure was as black inside as a mine-owner's heart.

"I've known chickens that wouldn't live in a place this bad," I said.

"Look here," Mo said. I dutifully trudged on to where she was now standing and reading the notice board. The local Visigoths had spray-painted unintelligible markings here and there, but I could read most of what the museum wanted me to know. I learned the cabin had been the home of the last resident of Cumberland's Chinatown, who had moved out in 1968. The old man's name had been Mar Ho Shui, but he was known locally as Jumbo.

Mo added to the sparse information on the board. She said the village council had rescued the tiny building from what would have eventually been its certain fate: to be the centrepiece in a Cumberland Halloween bacchanal. Cumby's wilder teens — joined by like-minded hoodlums from all over the valley — liked to celebrate Samhain by igniting anything left lying around.

I knew that much. It was not unheard of for the mayor to read the Riot Act and call out the volunteer fire brigade to hose down the celebrants as well as their bonfires. One memorable year, someone had attached stolen blasting caps to a propane tank outside the elementary school. It was only the punk's ineptitude that had prevented him from properly wiring the caps to blow. Otherwise, said the explosives experts from CFB Comox who disarmed them, the resulting blast would not only have converted the hopeful firebug into pieces too small to tempt a dust mite — it would have demolished more of central Cumberland than the great fire that took out three blocks of Dunsmuir Avenue in the 1930s.

"So they moved the cabin up here," Mo said. "It was the last vestige of Chinatown." She looked around. "Amazing."

"What's amazing about it?" I said. "I could move this little building myself in an afternoon."

"Did you ever see the pictures of Chinatown in the museum?"

I shrugged. I might have, but they had left no impression.

Mo said, "There were several streets, dozens of houses, stores and a theatre with two-storey false fronts, a whole little town just up the road from Cumberland."

I looked around. "It must have been near here."

"Very near," she said.

"So, where? On the other side of those trees?" I pointed downslope.

"No. Under them."

That was enough to tap my curiosity on its usually heedless shoulder. I went down the slope a ways. It was thick with undergrowth and fast-growing deciduous trees, the kind I'd heard foresters call weed species — aspen and alder, I thought — that spring up on any clear-cut where there was open sky and no one to bother them.

I pushed branches aside and followed a faint trail that could have been made by deer or kids. In the back of my mind was a hopeful expectation that, a step or two farther into the summery green, I'd come upon a clearing, and there would be a vista of dilapidated bricks and boards, a Chinese ghost town, with creepers twining up the porch posts and birds perched on sagging roofs.

But there was nothing but the trees and the bushes. "There's nothing here," I called back to Mo. She hadn't come down after me.

"I know," she said. "That's what's amazing. It's all gone, like it was never here. That's why they saved the little cabin."

I climbed back up the bank, and we got the Behemoth out on the narrow road again. Mo was being quietly thoughtful. I would have broken in and offered a penny for whatever she was mulling, but I suddenly didn't have the leisure.

As soon as we pulled away from the cabin, an old beater full of teenage boys roared up behind us and surgically attached itself to the Ford's bumper. I could hear the beat from their stereo — I'd bet it was worth more than the car — even with the windows rolled up.

"Couple more years of that," I told Mo, "and their eardrums will have the elasticity of sun-baked rawhide. The Archangel Gabriel can blow like Dizzy Gillespie, and these guys'll still sleep through Judgement Day."

Mo sad nothing, just made one of those faces that say, *I heard what you said and I'm happy to agree so long as I don't have to actually discuss it.*

There wasn't room on the twisty little road to pull over and let the bass-thumping testosterone-mobile pass.

I sped up and paid close attention to the driving for the next few kilometres, especially after we swept around a curve and almost mated with a Winnebago with Alberta plates that was slow-hauling a power boat up to the lake.

I swore. "Whatever happened to the good old days, grandpa and grandma are sitting on porches, complaining about them dagnabbit young folks?" I said. "Who the hell thought old fuds ought to be crawling along public highways in studio apartments on wheels?"

The kids pulled out and baboomed on by, passing us and the wanderlust-filled retirees. I glanced sideways as they paralleled the Ford, and thought I recognized a face, but it went by too quickly to be sure.

We stayed behind Mom and Dad Tourist the rest of the way to the gates of the lakeside park, where the mobile turned right toward the boat-launch ramp. We went straight ahead to the parking lot above the swimming area, and I put the Behemoth next to the old heap that had passed us. It was a rust-eaten Nova, but it was actually two years younger than what I was driving.

The boom-box kids had disappeared somewhere around the curve of the densely wooded shoreline. They'd taken their suitcase-sized ghetto blaster with them, far enough away that it almost blended with the natural sounds of ripples on the little man-made beach and the wind in the trees behind us .

Comox Lake has the casual beauty that many British Columbians take for granted: clear glacial water, tree-lined shores and genuine hold-up-the-sky mountains. Cumberlanders had trucked in sand to make the beach, then they added washrooms and a few picnic tables, strung a floating boom of chain-linked logs to separate swimmers from boaters, and a put up concession stand that dispensed hot dogs, fries, cokes and other traditional beach-goer fare.

The parking lot was separated from the beach by a line of logs. We sat on them, eating pretty good French fries out of cardboard dishes, and waving away the yellow-jackets that hovered around us like mosquitoes on steroids. I pulled the plastic lid off a discarded paper cup, laid it upside down a couple of metres down the log we were sitting on, and poured some pop into it; the wasps eventually drifted over there and tanked up on sugar and caffeine.

"No wonder they're so aggressive," I said.

Mo said nothing. Something was cooking in there, and I thought I knew what it was. I got my lines ready, then I asked her, "What are you chewing on?"

She sighed and shrugged. She generally had a so-so sigh, but her shrugs almost always made me want to put an arm around her shoulders and draw her to me. This one worked its magic, and then she was warm against my side, the top of her head against my jaw. Her hair always smelled like love.

But still she said nothing.

"Come on," I tried. "What?"

"I don't know," she said. "It's just..."

While I waited, I ran my hand up and down her outer arm.

"I'm just wondering where we're going," she said.

"Where no man has gone before." Sometimes, when I'm caught by surprise, I say the first dumb thing that stumbles across my tongue. And Mo had taken me completely unawares. Instead of a duck-and-dodge over Ginger Goodwin's cinematic potential, we had wandered into the discussion all couples must eventually visit. A little chill scaled my back, and it had nothing to do with the gentle breeze from the lake.

"Can we be serious?" she said.

At least I know not to keep on saying dumb things. "Yeah, okay."

She squinted at the speckles of light bouncing on the water. I saw the laugh lines beside her eye deepen again.

"I don't know," she said again. "Maybe it's from hanging out with the women at the museum. You know, they've all got lives and families, and, I don't know..." She moved her hands, "...connection, continuity."

"You mean kids." Might as well get it out in the open. I can be brave when there's no choice.

"No," — she shook her head, then nodded — "well okay, maybe I do mean kids. Maybe not. I mean, it's not that clear to me that I can say, 'I want a baby, that's what I want.' I don't *know* what I want, but I want *something*, something more solid."

I didn't say anything for a long beat. I didn't know what was the right thing to say. I knew what a lot of the wrong things would be.

"I don't know what to say," I said.

She shrugged again, then put her hand over mine where it rested on her shoulder. "I don't know what I want you to say."

"I like what we've got," I said.

"I know you do. So do I, but..."

"But...?"

"But is it enough?" She looked at me. "So far it's been enough, it's been great. But is it going to be enough a year from now, or ten years, when we're like those old dears in the Winnebago? Are we ever going to be like them? Are we going to be together when we're old like that?"

From somewhere inside, a voice was muttering to me, *Don't have this conversation, now. Let it slide. Whatever you do, don't tell her what you really think.* But I ignored the inner voice, as I dependably do when it's talking about anything important.

"Who knows?" I said. "We might be dead tomorrow. Can't we just take it one day at a time?"

Even before it was completely out of my mouth, I knew I had just produced the all-time, number-one platinum winner on the hit parade of wrong things to say at that precise moment. She'd walked me up to the big door, because she wanted us to take a peek through it together, maybe think about some day stepping across the threshold. And I'd just reached past her, grabbed the handle and slammed it shut.

Mo moved a little away from me — a few centimetres that could have been measured in parsecs. "Sure," she said.

"I shouldn't have said that."

"Sure you should've. That's how you feel. I don't want a man who just tells me what I want to hear. I can't stand being lied to."

"Mo," I started.

"Now you think you're in trouble, don't you?"

"Aren't I?"

She sighed. "Let's drop it, Raff. It's okay. At least, it's more me than you."

Time to be brave again. "We should talk about it."

"Some other time."

I knew her well enough to disbelieve that one. Mo Migliorini was not a dropper or a putter-offer. In her private dictionary, procrastination was a synonym for ducking your responsibilities; see cowardly, spineless, and other things your mother didn't raise you to be.

"I want us to talk about it," I lied.

"Nice try," she said. "But don't patronize me."

And from there it could have become the kind of genuine eye-opening, muck-dragging, here's-what-we're-all-about conversation recommended in all the best psychobabble books — the kind that kills way more relationships than it saves.

But, fortunately, as we'd been tugging each other toward the precipice, the background noise had been climbing steadily. The kids with the boom box were coming back along the shoreline, probably having finished a doobie out of sight of the parking lot where the Mounties occasionally appeared. The *whump-bump! whump-bump! a-whump-bump!* of their portable thought-suppressor made dignified conversation increasingly difficult.

They passed behind us, uniformed in hightops, saggy jeans and hooded sweatshirts, the peaks of baseball caps sticking fore or aft of heads that were as shorn of hair as a clearcut was of trees. I caught a whiff of weed from them. I turned to watch as they headed back to their car, and now I could put a name to the face I'd almost recognized when they'd roared past us on the road. It was Titch Haglund, whom I'd last seen kneeling in the bloody grass, yelling at me to get some help when there could never be enough help to undo what had happened to his father.

His gaze slid over me as the group went by, but if my face meant anything to him, he gave no sign. I thought he didn't look good: there were hollows in his cheeks and darkness under his eyes, and a tightness to his shoulders that smoking a joint ought to have eased. He got into the beater with his buds, and they laid a linear cloud of dust and grit across the gravelled parking lot.

"We'd better go," Mo said. She stood up. "That meeting starts soon."

"Oh, love," I said. Something was turning over in me. I hadn't known I was big enough inside to hold so much sadness.

She gave me a smile I hadn't seen before. "It's all right, Raff. Come on."

We walked back to the Behemoth, she leading the way. I unlocked the door and opened it for her, and she got in. Her strong, lithe body suddenly seemed much more self-contained, as if she had been redrawn with a darker outline. I closed her door softly, but it still made that solid, chunky sound of big-car finality.

We didn't talk on the way back to Cumberland. As we came down the top end of Dunsmuir Avenue, I could see a line of cars on either side of the street near the village hall, and people walking in twos and threes toward the big community centre beside the municipal office. There was a small crowd outside, waiting for the doors to open.

I put the Behemoth in a spot around the corner on the street beside the museum. Mo and I walked the few metres back to Dunsmuir, stopping at the curb to let a couple of cars go by. I could hear the thumping of the teenager's blaster again, not too far off. It was rap music — one of my favourite oxymorons — and coming from not too far away.

"There's your client," Mo said.

Benny Filiatrault was coming up the gentle hill that lifted Dunsmuir Avenue between the village hall and Cumberland's little downtown. A sheaf of paper was under one arm while the other sawed the air in front of him as he made some point to the black-clad stick figure who matched his pace.

Mo and I stepped off the curb, angling across the street to intercept them. I turned to her to say something uncomplimentary about Davey Clemmer, and saw her eyes widen involuntarily. I snapped my head around to follow her gaze, and there was Titch Haglund and his crew boiling across the blacktop, shouting something over the noise of the boom box they'd left in the car.

The rap chorus dropped in intensity for a few beats, and I heard the kid's thin voice clearly say, "...killed my dad, you fuck..." before the chanting voices came back and drowned him out again.

Mo's hand involuntarily tightened its grip on my arm. But she didn't need to hold me back. I had no inclination to keep Davey Clemmer from a kicking — for all I knew, he'd set the trap that had killed Titch's father, and so deserved much worse. I wasn't worried about Benny either. My client didn't look to be a skilled street-fighter, but I figured he was big enough to pick up any one of the five teenagers, if necessary, and use him to club the rest.

I patted Mo's hand, said, "Don't worry, I'm not getting into this. Benny looks to be able to take care of himself."

I stepped forward, meaning to get close enough to watch, without being drawn into whatever was about to happen. But Mo set her heels and pulled me half around. "He's not going to fight them," she said. "Everybody knows he's a pacifist."

"Oh," I managed.

Her eyes were the colour of the sea in winter and just as uncompromising. "He needs your help," she said.

Oh, shit, I thought, but what I said was, "Okay," and turned toward the little knot of trouble and strife.

So far, it was mostly yelling, the kind that young bulls do when they're pawing the ground, working themselves up to the pitch of making that first lunge, but still not sure they want to come out of the chute. Young Haglund was generating most of the noise. He did not command a rich vocabulary of epithets, and he seemed to consider *cocksucker* the deadliest insult in his arsenal.

Filiatrault stood between the teens and his companion, like a Disney cartoon bear facing down a pack of hyperactive coyotes. I looked behind him to see how Clemmer liked being the centre of attention.

I'd expected him to be scared. Hell, I was and I hadn't even stuck my head in the hornets' nest yet. But I knew it was never an even match: one middle-aged writer against a half-dozen teenage punks. After all, one of the prime reasons armies draft adolescents is because they don't need much encouragement to get excessively violent. Guys my age would be hunkered down in the bottom of the trench, waiting for a lull in the machine-gun serenade, but kids like Titch Haglund would be out in no-man's-land, ignoring the bullets busy all around them, vaulting over the shell holes and casting about for a belly they could stick a bayonet in.

But Davey showed no sign of fear. He was alert, feet

spread and knees bent for balance, his hands about waist high, shoulders loose and easy. He looked *ready*. His eyes flicked from one to another of the five boys, calmly and calculatingly. I suddenly knew that though Benny might think he was protecting his disciple from the kids, the reality was the other way around.

A few more Cumberlanders had congregated around the disturbance by now, although nobody looked ready to interfere. The yelling intensified, and now came the first actual contact.

Titch moved to step past Benny. I saw Davey's knees bend a little more and his right fist came up and back, chest high now, while his eyes locked on the Haglund boy.

But it was Filiatrault who reached out an arm and gently but firmly swept the teenager back toward his friends. I couldn't hear what he said, but Titch's *Fuck you!* came through loud and clear.

It wasn't over. The kid was plainly going to come on again, and this time the others would be part of it. I looked over to the storefront cop shop. It was lit, but there was no cruiser out in front tonight. Inside, there would be a civilian volunteer, who was probably already on the phone to the main RCMP station in Courtenay. But the nearest cop could easily be ten minutes away, in which case the volunteer should also be calling for an ambulance.

I looked back to the stand-off. The kids were leaning forward on the balls of their feet. Benny's hands were spread wide. Clemmer was still as a coiled spring. *Here it comes*, I thought.

And here I go. I could feel Mo's eyes on my back. It was time to earn some of the regard in which she held me. I stepped forward, and took hold of Titch's collar and pulled. "That's enough," I said. "Back off."

Old Jim Anderson from *Father Knows Best* could have aced it. Ward Cleaver wouldn't even have had to loosen his tie. Any of the black-and-white role models from my childhood could have chilled out a teenage rumble without breaking a sweat, just by flexing their natural authority.

In real life, my own old man could have done it, too, although he would have terrified the little bastards. Titch and his buds would have taken one look at my dad's bulging eyes and flared nostrils, and they'd have known right away, down in the oldest circuits of the brain where sheer savagery still hummed as the constant carrier wave, that here was a man who spent his days hoping, praying, that someone would come along and pull his cork, so he could go absolutely, terminally, retributively ape-shit all over them. And they'd be lucky to leave the scene with any one part of them still connected to another.

But, as somebody must have said, our generation is the diminutive progeny of giants. Titch Haglund was not cowed by my intervention. He spun around, his feet skittering as he regained his balance, and shook himself out of my grip.

The surprise in his eyes gave way to recognition. I stepped back and opened my mouth to say something generically pacifying, but before I could launch the first syllable, the kid threw the word "Cocksucker!" into my face and followed it with his right fist.

I dodged most of it, so that the blow glanced off a cheekbone, and put my hands up to ward off the next one. But that next one turned out to be about twenty, as the boy windmilled his arms and came at me like a demented threshing machine.

I stepped backwards. None of the blows was actually causing me much pain. I felt more ridiculous than threatened. But then the rest of Titch's crew must have reached the conclusion that I was an even better target than Clemmer, because they all joined in.

I backed again, and tripped on something — maybe a teenager's outstretched leg — and I went down. I managed to twist as I fell so that I landed on my hands, but now it was time to start worrying. The kids crowded in, a dark mass above and around me. They wore work boots — probably steel toed — and I knew what those could do the delicate grey jelly inside my skull if anyone landed a good one.

I felt the first kick in my belly. It was not high enough or hard enough to knock the wind out of me, but there was no doubt it hurt. I curled up and put my arms over my head, like Muhammad Ali playing rope-a-dope. I could hear Mo yelling something, and Benny's voice too, but mostly my ears were full of the excited yelps and bleats of the kid pack.

Fortunately, these guys had gained only scant experience in the art of organized head kicking. Only a few boots were getting through — mainly they were just getting in each other's way. But then I felt a toe connect squarely with my left shoulder, the same one that I'd dislocated three and a half years earlier in an explosion. Jagged pain shot through my arm and back like ice and lighting. I screamed.

The sound left my mouth and then somehow it was picked up and amplified. It went on and on, drowning the voices of the teenagers and Benny and Mo and the rapper on the boom box and every other noise in the universe. It seemed to be coming from everywhere at once, including the inside of my own head. *Christ,* I thought, *what have they done to my ears?*

But then I noticed that the kicks had stopped. I uncovered my face and looked up. There was more light above me, and I saw Mo's face, full of fear and concern. Then Benny Filiatrault hove into view. He got his hands under my armpits and hauled me to my feet, setting off the pain in my shoulder again — but only second degree, which was bearable.

Mo put her arms around me, and Benny said something I couldn't hear, because the noise still hammered at us. I looked around. Most of the people who had gathered to watch the fight had their hands over their ears, and everybody, participants and spectators alike, were turned toward the source of the sound.

It was a chrome plated air horn — actually, it was three of them — mounted on the cab of one of those goofy monster four-by-fours, the kind that crawl over school buses and clapped out wrecks at truck-and-tractor shows. This was one was standing still in the middle of Dunsmuir Avenue. Its wheels were easily four feet in diameter, with treads that could have crunched across Antarctica, and the suspension put the driver high enough up in the world that he could peek through second-storey windows.

But this driver was looking down, at us. His head and left arm leaned out of the open window, while his right hand held steady pressure on the roof cord that connected to the air horn. He had black hair, long and slicked back, a heavy-featured face and two days' stubble that made him look like a cheap knock-off of Stephen Seagal. By the black-leather car coat and thick gold neck-chain, I guessed that Seagal was indeed the look he was going for.

He eased off on the air horn, and it was as if silence rushed back to comfort us, although I could still hear the rap number on the kids' boom box across the street, and the thrumming rumble of the monster truck's oversized engine.

The driver opened his door and stepped down, leaving the motor running. He moved slowly. We were all watching him, and I could see he found the pressure of everyone's attention to be no burden. He was loving it. When his feet were on the ground, he took time to shift his shoulders under the jacket, like Joe Pesci in a mob flick. Then he moved close to Titch Haglund and did a little chin lift that went with the shoulder thing.

"The fuck you doin'?" he said. The voice was a tone or two higher than he probably wanted it to sound, but he was doing the best he could with it. He leaned in closer, making Titch pull back and duck his head. "You ain't got enough trouble, you doin' this shit in the street?"

The kid mumbled something I couldn't hear.

"Get your ass home, alla yez," he said, and did the chin move again.

The kids made no further argument. They split up to go around the big truck, heading back across the street to the boom box. They got their old beater going, and trundled up Dunsmuir toward the lake road turn-off, like a slow-moving genie who travelled in his own cloud of blue smoke.

The little crowd watched them go, then the people remembered what they were doing there and began moving toward the community centre again. In a moment, there were only Filiatrault, Clemmer, Mo and me standing with the man from the truck.

His gaze passed over us, came to rest on my client. "Benny," he said, and did a kind of ripple trick with his eyebrows.

"Trick," Filiatrault said. It took me a long beat to realize that was the guy's nickname.

"How's it goin'?"

"Well, you know," Benny shrugged.

"Yeah." He gave Davey, Mo and me another round-up look. "These people with you?"

Benny pointed us out. "Sid Rafferty and Davey Clemmer," he said. "They're helping with the campaign. Mo's with Raff." To us, he said, "This is Trick Ketterich."

Ketterich moved his tongue around his side teeth, like Letterman doing his dumb guy shtick, but without the irony. He looked at Filiatrault sideways, and I started wondering how many mannerisms this guy could have, and how he managed to remember them all.

"You've been talking about Hockney's Woods," he said at last. "You should maybe find another place to worry about."

"We've moved on since then, Trick," Benny said. "It's the whole village were thinking about now."

Ketterich sniffed, then ducked his head and looked up at my client, squinting from under his brows. *James Dean,* I thought. I was starting to keep count of his moves on my fingers now. "You know," he said, "if it's a money thing..."

Davey spoke up. "It's not a money thing."

Ketterich looked at the green activist as if he were a precocious kid who'd just butted into the grown-ups' conversation. "I seen you in those woods," he said.

Davey said nothing.

"You should stay out of places you got no business," Trick said. "People gettin' hurt."

It could have gone somewhere from there; Davey Clemmer was no more scared of Trick Ketterich than he had been intimidated by Titch and the boys. But I caught a flash of blue lights from the corner of my eye. An RCMP cruiser was coming up the street, siren off. It stopped beside the monster truck, and the young constable who'd been in the storefront when Haglund died got out and came around to the sidewalk. He looked us over. "What's going on?" he said.

They all looked at me. My shoulder hurt like hell. "Nothing," I said. "Just talking politics."

The cop turned to Ketterich, touched the monster truck. "How about you move this?"

"Was just gonna," Trick said. He gave me a nod and a wink — I couldn't quite place from whom he'd copied it— got back into the truck and went the same way as the kids' old beater. The cop followed in the cruiser.

Mo put an arm around me. "You okay, Raff?" she asked.

I rubbed my shoulder. "No," I said. "My old shoulder injury is not benefitting from the traditional clog dancing."

"I'm glad you didn't say anything to the cop," Benny said. "I'll talk to Titch's mom, straighten things out."

We followed the flow of Cumby folk toward the community centre. "So that was one of the Ketterich boys," I said.

Davey snorted. "Asshole."

"Actually," Benny said. "Trick's the nice one. If Butch had seen a bunch of the locals kicking a stranger, he'd've probably joined in."

"Lot of town spirit, Cumberland," I said.

We had reached the door of the community centre. A hum and buzz of conversation was bouncing off the quonset style roof. "Yeah," Benny said, reaching for the door handle, "so if you feel like getting up and saying anything during the meeting, it's probably better you don't."

He was looking at me as he said it, but then his eyes flicked to Davey's face and stayed there. The kid deepened his built-in sneer a notch, but he didn't argue.

Chapter 6

The Cultural Centre was bestowed upon Cumberland-ers by a grateful New Democratic Party government for having put their Xs against social democratic candidates' names in every election since the party had been hatched. In most of those campaigns, the NDP's chances of taking power were somewhere between "like Hell" and "I don't think so," but the Cumberland electors consistently voted their convictions over their expectations. When the NDP at last made it back into power, the faithful were rewarded for keeping the flame hot.

It was a two-storey building set against the museum — Mo said there was a connecting door somewhere — and somebody had talked the designers into giving its exterior an old-timey feel. Along the side facing Dunsmuir, across from the village hall, the cultural centre wore a two-storey facade of clapboard false fronts, like a row of nineteenth-century wood-framed shops and offices, each one labelled with the name of an authentic business from a hundred years before.

"Wow, major cute," I'd told Mo, the first time I saw the place. "Looks like a location shoot for Hopalong Cassidy."

"It's nice," she said. "It'll look better when the wood's aged a little."

Inside, it was a generic community centre, with a seniors' lounge down below and a large public room at the top of a double flight of steps. Mo and I mixed our-selves into the moving crowd and let it carry us upstairs into the big room, with its neutral coloured walls and flu-orescent fixtures. A string of Christmas lights straggled all the way around the room, just below the ceiling, either left over from the holidays, or to provide low-cost mood lighting for community dances.

The place was filling fast. I looked around for Rod Bilder, to relieve myself of the thick envelope of his bumpf that was tucked under my arm, but couldn't see him. Mo and I sat in the last of a dozen wide rows of tube-and-plywood stacking chairs, divided by a centre aislefacing a low wooden dais at the far end. There was a single microphone holding a floor stand at the end of the aisle.

Most of the seats in front of us were full. I automatically did a reporter's rough head count, multiplying rank by file, and calculating that there were at least three hundred people already in the room, with more still coming in behind us.

"Big turn-out," I said. I had to raise my voice a little to be heard over the rumble of conversation.

"Lot of town spirit," Mo quoted.

Benny had rendezvoused with some of his friends, and they had fanned out to distribute copies of his broadside. A few of the people glanced at the text and laid the sheet down or rolled it up into a tube, but most read carefully through it, and more than a few looked up to give Benny a voiceless attaboy with a thumb or nod of the head.

"Is that Sally?" Mo asked me, indicating a blonde head near the front.

I peered forward, then said, "Not sure." The hair looked right but not the set of the shoulders. Sally had the kind of perfect posture people tend to expect of a physiotherapist; the woman in front of us was slumped in her seat like a sack of potatoes suffering from low self-esteem.

"It's her," Mo said. "Come on."

Mo was right, as usual. We made our way down the centre aisle to the row where Sally sat. There were no empty seats to either side of her, but there were two vacant ones in front, and we sidled our way to them.

Sally didn't notice us when we sat down. She was examining the pads of her fingers as if she had never seen them before. Again, I noticed that ferocity of concentration that seemed to be at the core of her personality. She was not an off-hand kind of woman. She locked onto whatever she was looking at and held steady.

Mo spoke her name, and Sally's head came up as if a spring had popped open. She blinked, like someone coming back fro m somewhere far away. "I'm sorry," she said. "How long have you been sitting there?"

"Just got here," I said. I looked around the room. "I was looking for Rod. Have you seen him?"

"No, not for a couple of days, I guess."

"I've got the background stuff he gave me for the brochure. I want to get it back to him."

She just nodded.

"Everything okay?" Mo asked.

Under the skin, the human face is intricately muscled, those muscles being connected to a tracework of major nerves that lead back to large portions of the brain. Together, all of those components can rearrange the features into hundreds of different expressions, only a few of which — like grin, frown or pout — have ever been named. Sally McMahon's face now shifted rapidly through two or three unlabelled dispositions, before settling on one that most of us would have identified as indecision.

"I don't know," she said, confirming what her face had already said. "I don't want all this fuss about the woods."

"It must be hard," Mo said.

Sally nodded. "It is."

The mayor and council entered now from a side door at the back of the room. *Had themselves a little pre-meeting meeting, to make sure everybody's singing the same song,* I thought, having covered enough get-togethers of this sort way back when I'd been a reporter. *Whatever comes from the floor, the councillors will present a united front.*

But then I changed my mind. At least two of the seven people who took seats on the dais looked unhappy about whatever had just been decided in the back room. One was a balding man in an old tweedy sports jacket he was paunching out of. The other looked like a farmer, with a wind-roughened face and big, knobby hands. They took the last two seats on the dais. As they sat down, the farmer said something that made the bald one look down the line of chairs at the mayor and shake his head.

A smooth young man wearing a smooth grey suit and a silk tie came out of the back room, carrying a lightweight metal easel and a large white display board. He set the easel up to one side of the dais, put the card on it and nodded to the mayor.

The mayor wore a well used checked suit, and a striped tie. He was surprisingly small, as so many politicians are off camera, but he had the compensating attribute of nervous speed. He looked as if he could go to his left or his right, or straight down the middle, whichever way the ball bounced.

He lifted an FM cordless mic to his lips, flicked the on switch and called the meeting to order. He read carefully from a piece of paper. This was to be strictly an information meeting, he said, with no decisions "to be taken at this point in time." A few months ago, the village had "engaged a town-planning professional" — we all looked at Mr. Smooth — who had gone out to "gather input from various stakeholders" on the "elements of an official community plan." Now, the gathering of elements having "approached a level of critical mass," it was time to "seek initial feedback from the community as a whole."

He came to the end of the written text, which I would have bet the most precious parts of my body had been scripted for him by that same town-planning professional, then said, in his normal diction, "So no decisions are gonna get made tonight. Council's here, but we just want to hear what you've got to say. So don't none of you get all worked up about any of this, 'cause it's early days yet."

He reached down and handed the mic to the planner, and I settled in with professional interest to watch the young man try to weave a spell. Within a minute, I knew he wasn't bad, but I also knew he wasn't going to be good enough to win this crowd if they took against him. On the other hand, unless they got riled enough to scare the complacent majority on council, it wouldn't matter. I'd covered enough city councils back when I'd been a young reporter; I knew how these things worked.

Canadian municipal politics is almost always about land use. Federal and provincial governments long ago grabbed off all the big portfolios, from social welfare to air quality. So land is about the only jurisdiction left in municipal control, except for the challenges of garbage removal and pothole repair.

Town councillors get to decide if and how private and public property will be developed. The craft the zoning and building bylaws that decree what can be put on the little segment of the earth's surface that a property owner calls his own: it could be a complex of luxury condos surrounding an up-market shopping centre; it could be a row of modest single-family homes; it could be a park. Depending on which use the town council designates for the land, the owners could make a flat-out fortune, a sweet little profit, or a cup of coffee.

Most town councils favour growth the way hogs favour twice-daily deliveries of swill. Growth translates into real-estate commissions, which is why most town councils are nesting grounds for realtors. Federal and provincial governments deal with bigger problems — justice, health care, international trade — so it's no coincidence that very few realtors turn up in provincial legislatures or the federal parliament. But it's a rare town council that lacks representation from the local real estate board.

In British Columbia's small towns, councillors are paid about one-tenth what the unionized cleaning staff get for polishing the mayor's gavel and sweeping out the council chamber. So only the most selfless and community minded citizens run for office, and it's a curious coincidence that the most altruistic people in many towns and villages turn out to be licensed real-estate agents, or to have a relative in the business, or to be the recipients of campaign donations from people whose names are linked on lawn signs with the words "For Sale" and "New Listing."

Mr. Smooth introduced himself to the people of Cumberland. He said his name and I instantly forgot it — that's why I always took copious notes as a reporter. He told us he had been engaged by the village to help prepare a comprehensive plan for land use in Cumberland.

"Now you might be asking," he said, "'Why do we need an Official Community Plan'" — the way he said it I could hear the capitals he placed on the words — "when we've got along all these years without one?"

As a good speechwriter, I knew if I ever set up a speaker to ask a rhetorical question, I'd better supply the answer to it in the very next line, before some rude and negative voice from the audience did so for us. Mr. Smooth didn't know that rule, or maybe he was just too confident in his professional stature. He allowed the question to hang in the air, and I heard the inevitable scrape of a chair somewhere behind me as someone rose to the temptation.

The planner was suddenly fluttering his hands in front of him, patting the air as if it were a big, overly friendly dog that had risen up unexpectedly to lick his face. I looked around and saw that his gesture had dissuaded the old man in a worn but carefully mended Canadian Legion blazer who had been getting to his feet, under the impression that he'd just been invited to a debate.

"Please," Mr. Smooth said, "there'll be lots of time for

questions later."

I heard the chair scrape again as the disappointed Legionnaire sat back down.

"Now, where was I?" said Smooth. *Asking stupid rhetorical questions*, I said to myself, and then thought about getting up and saying it out loud. But I let it pass. I was supposed to be wallpaper tonight.

The young man in the soft suit started over again. I soon tuned him out. It was generic blah-blah. Growth was inevitable, he told the Cumby folk: people wanted to move to Cumberland, and couldn't be stopped. Growth was good: the newcomers would make jobs for the community's young people, and generate more taxes for public services.

As a reporter, I'd heard the same spiel in a dozen community halls, the old siren refrain of, "Give me your town for just a little while and I'll give it back to you bigger and better than ever."

But it was always hooey. You never got your town back, and if you did, you wouldn't recognize it or want it any more. Not after you let the place where you made your life and your living be used by somebody who was just out to make a killing.

I was feeling an unaccountable urge to get up and argue with this soft young man and his smooth sell. I wanted to say that growth was never inevitable. People wouldn't come unless developers built houses for them, and the developers wouldn't come unless there was cheap land. No cheap land, no growth.

If Cumberland took the developer's bait, hoping they'd be doing the right thing by their kids and grandkids, they'd soon see those hopes melting away like an ice cream cone dropped on a sidewalk. There would be no flood of entrepreneurial newcomers to start up high-tech companies that would pull young Cumberlanders off the streets and turn them into systems analysts. Most of the inflow would be retirees or people like me, ex-urban downshifters who got their incomes from the world outside.

Even the construction boom wouldn't touch many of the local unemployed, unless they already had a trade qualification. The out-of-town contractors would bring in out-of-town workers: most of them would be non-union, mixed in with a few jobless dues-payers who left their union cards at home and signed on for half the union scale. The best the home-town kids would get would be a chance to pour the newcomers' coffee or sell them burgers. And those jobs would be part-time at minimum wage with no benefits.

And, yeah, the tax base would grow, but the demand for services would swell even faster. More and bigger roads, more and wider sewers, more and brighter street lights, more water lines and pumping stations — all of that would drive up the taxes faster than any corresponding expansion of the tax base. After all, if a broader tax base meant lower taxes, then the owner of a split-level in Vancouver ought to pay less than the owner of an equivalent home in upcountry hamlets like Horsefly or Yahk.

Hokey little stores would close as the Dunsmuir Avenue rents went up, and the up-market boutiques would move in. The old Cumberlanders would see the cost of living going up while their incomes stayed level. Give them ten years and many of them would find themselves surrounded by a gentrified town in which they could no longer afford to live. They'd have to sell the house grampa bought from the mining company — a helpful realtor would be standing by — and move someplace the downshifters hadn't yet got .

The suit from the planning department droned on, and I listened with half an ear as I looked around to see whether Rod Bilder had come in yet. I was surprised he hadn't been here from the opening: if the official community plan decreed Hockney's Woods would be preserved as park land, his whole development plan would come apart like smoke in a sea breeze.

"...augmented physical infrastructure...," Mr. Smooth went on, "...broadened tax base leading to enhanced quality of community life..." He actually used the word "multi-factorial," which I wouldn't have doubted he made up on the spot.

I tuned him out again. He was nowhere near as good at working a crowd as he thought he was. But I guessed he had a solid majority of the council backing his plans, so he probably figured he only had to spread a thick layer of verbal schmaltz over the people at the meeting — "stun them into blinking, stumbling submission under a creeping barrage of polysyllabic verbiage" was how the Hon. L.B. Halfnight used to put it, describing the technique he used on fellow undergraduates in university seminars — then send them home so he could get on with redesigning their village.

I had my own grab bag of tricks for manipulating crowds, if I chose to use them. Back when I'd been an aide to the Minister of Justice I'd learned a lot from watching my boss handle constituents at the "accountability sessions" that became obligatory during the Trudeau years. Nowadays they were called "town-hall meetings," but it was the same old same-old: sometimes you steered a crowd this way, sometimes that way, and occasionally you just let them blow off a head of steam. The main thing was to get them to leave feeling good about the people who were running things for them — or at least not feeling mad enough to cause a change of management.

It would have been fun to mix it up with the planner a little, use a few of those old politician tricks. But I was supposed to be invisible, so I kept my mouth shut. Besides, this was Filiatrault's show. I doubted my client's pacifism would prevent him from rhetorically biting off pieces of Mr. Smooth until there was nothing left but the tip of his condescending nose.

I looked around for Benny, and saw him sitting quietly in an aisle seat, four rows back from the front. It was a good placement, I thought: when he got up to speak, he would rise from within the crowd, but also from its fore-front. A spin doctor would call it "good optics." More and more, I was coming to see the big, shambly Cumberland-er as a political natural.

I found Davey Clemmer's sneer further back in the crowd, seated just behind a knot of seven or eight envi-ronmental activists of both sexes and a variety of ages. The greenies were identifiable by their natural fibre shirts and dresses, mostly topped off by Cowichan sweaters of unbleached grey and white wool, with native Indian designs knitted in black on the back and front panels. Compared to the organically correct greenies, the rest of the small-town Cumberlanders were big-city sophisticates, and Clemmer was a crow with attitude hovering over a flock of pigeons.

The planner was winding down. I swung my eyes over the room again. It was so crowded now they had run out of chairs, and more than a dozen people were standing at the back of the hall. I saw Trick Ketterich leaning against the wall near the double doors. But there was still no sign of Rod Bilder.

I turned in my seat to look over my left shoulder and felt a stab of pain like white hot lava rush through my shoulder. I gasped and reached around with my right hand to press the epicentre of the pain, about three inches below the top of the shoulder.

"Are you okay?" Mo said.

"No," I said. "Suddenly it hurts like hell where that kid kicked me."

Sally leaned forward. "Who kicked you?"

Mo quickly told her about Titch and the fight.

"I'm sorry," Sally said.

"It wasn't your fault," I said. "It's an old injury."

Mo gave me a look that let me know I was being dense again. Women say they're sorry to express sympathy; men only say it to acknowledge when they've done something wrong.

"I'm sorry," I said to Sally.

"Come to my place after the meeting. It's only a block. I'll give it a little ultrasound."

"Thanks," Mo said, which meant that was settled.

The man with the plan had finished talking. He sat on the edge of the low dais and called for questions. I turned — carefully this time — to watch Benny, but he was biding his time, letting some of the other Cumberlanders troop up to the microphone and address the suit.

The old man in the Legion blazer was first at the microphone. The placement of the sound equipment meant that he had to stand with his back to the room, addressing the planner and the council. Smart optics there, too, I thought — the crowd's focus will remain on the planner and the council, not on any opposition.

The Legionnaires' shoulders looked narrow and frail under the worn blue cloth, but he held them squarely back. He did what all amateur speakers do when confronted by a microphone — he tapped it. *Bop, bop,* said the speakers.

Mr. Suit waited blandly, swinging one foot so that the heel thumped softly against the wood of the dais. The old man leaned into the microphone, too close, so that we could hear his breathing. Then he said his say, going all the way back to the planner's original rhetorical question.

"This town," he said, the voice thin as gruel, "has been here since 1871. I was born here. So were my mom and dad. We never needed this kind of foofaraw, and I don't think we need it now."

There was a mumble of agreement from scattered parts of the hall. The planner began speaking even as the old man marched slowly back to his seat. He used one of the standard techniques for dissipating opposition to change: he minimized both the extent of the change and its effects. Thus, the Official Community Plan became just a reference document, a "set of broad guidelines that assists the community in determining general directions for land utilization. Nothing about it is carved in stone," he finished.

The next questioner was even less trouble than the old man. He was an athletic man in his thirties, wearing a dark wool jacket with white leather sleeves. It had a team crest of some kind sewn onto the breast, and the name MIKE on the right sleeve. Mike wanted to know when the village was going to build some more ball fields so that local softball teams wouldn't have to go down to Courtenay to play. The planner didn't bother even to stand up to bat that one away.

Now Benny Filiatrault got up. He walked sedately to the front of the room and put his hand on the microphone stand. But instead of turning his back on the crowd and hunching over the mike to address the planner and council on the dais, he deftly pulled the instrument out of its stainless steel holder, flicked its wire free of the stand like Tony Bennett preparing to wow a room full of Vegas punters, and spun smoothly around to face his neighbours.

"Well," he said, "I just want to say I think this meeting is a fine idea. It gets all of us together to talk about what kind of town we want to live in, what kind of town we want to hand on to our kids."

And it was *take it awaaaay, Benny.* Thirty seconds into it,

I had no doubts at all; this guy was a genuine natural. He worked the room like a complete pro, doing everything right: the way he made eye contact with people here and there in the crowd, keeping his tone gentle and folksy, looking down at his feet as if stuck for the right phrase, then bringing his head up exactly on the beat to deliver one of the homespun lines I'd crafted for him.

"He's good," Mo whispered to me.

"He makes good look bad," I answered. "Check out the planner droid."

So smooth was Filiatrault's style, the man in the soft suit still hadn't realized he had lost the meeting. Even he had fallen under the spell, just like the villagers — who were all Benny's now, and the big blond man was reeling them in. The phrases wove their way effortlessly among the collective memories of the Cumberlanders: "our little old village, ...these familiar streets and corners, ...our home town, ...this place where we belong, and that belongs to us."

And on he went, as close to perfect a performance as I'd ever seen. The bland room somehow grew warmer, the fluorescent lights glowed more softly. Every eye was on Benny's round, homely face, but I knew the people were looking straight through him into their own deepest sentiments.

Now, way too late, Mr. Smooth woke up, but he was not looking so smooth any more. One of the councillors — a comfortable real-estate man who wasn't looking at all comfortable — had leaned forward in his chair, almost hunched over in a crouch, to direct a forceful whisper at the young planner. I couldn't hear the words, but I thought I saw the realtor-politician's lips form the words, *Shut that fucker up.*

The technocrat brought the cordless mic to his lips, swallowed, and said, "Uh, sir, this is not a proper occasion for speechmaking. Did you have an actual question?"

"Oooh," I told Mo, "wrong tone."

Benny's segue was as smooth as Elvis Stoyko on ice. "I think we've all got the same question on our minds tonight. And that's," — he paused for a beat — "whose village is this? And whose village is it going to be five years, ten years from now?"

He looked around the room, doing the eye-contact thing again.

"Uh, sir..." the planner began.

Benny turned and faced the young man, then rode right over him. "This is our home town! But who are you planning it for? For us and our kids? Or for a bunch of outsiders who'll come in here and change it all? People who don't know — and don't give a damn — who we are and what we've done in Cumberland."

The voice was not so soft now. He turned back to the crowd. "Do we want a town full of strangers, just come here for cheap land?"

There were several "No's" from the Cumberlanders.

Benny moved the power up another notch. "This is our home. Our folks paid for it with sweat and pain, down in those goddamn mines. Some of them never came up, and their mangled flesh and crushed bones are down there still. This place is in our blood, because our blood is in the ground."

He paused and looked down at his feet again.

"Man," I said, under my breath. I watched the planner bring his mic to his lips, take a breath and open his mouth. He never had a chance.

"Are we going to hold what we've got?" He looked to every corner of the room, his eyes stabbing into them now. "Are we going to preserve this special place of ours?"

The crowd rumbled, and individual voices broke out like foam bursting from a cresting wave. "Damn right!"

I heard the man in the Legion blazer say. The softball player was nodding furiously; his eyes looked wet to me.

Benny turned to the dais. He ignored Technoboy completely. The functionary no longer existed for him. He looked straight at the mayor and council as he said into the mic, "Well then, let's take a vote right here and now. No community plan without a referendum. It's not official until we say it is."

More voices came out of the crowd, not a murmur of dissent among them. Benny swung back to them. "All in favour? Opposed?"

Surely there ought to have been some people in the rows of seats who wouldn't have minded selling their land to developers and moving on down to Arizona. At least there must have been a few real-estate agents who'd come to the meeting with visions of fat commissions dancing in their heads.

But if they were there, they were either swept up in Benny's oratory or understandably reluctant to breast the emotional tide that was surging through the room. I turned gingerly, the pain nagging my shoulder again, and saw a forest of hands raised above the crowd. When Benny asked for dissenters, there were none.

After the vote was taken, Filiatrault looked down at the floor for a beat, then brought his head back up, slowly and swept his gaze over the meeting.

"Thank you," he said. Then he let the mic's cord trail through his grasp, so that it descended like a slow-motion yo-yo. It touched the floor, and the speakers said, *Ack*. Benny let go of the wire and walked slowly up the aisle: but not to his seat — instead he went all the way to the double doors.

He hadn't gone two metres before the first few scattered claps began. Then there came a thickening of the sound, until it was like fire catching in dry tinder, and now the applause rattled and roared through the low-ceilinged room, the Cumberlanders getting to their feet, knocking back the lightweight chairs against the knees of the people behind them, who didn't care, because they were all watching Benny Filiatrault walk slowly to the exit, where he turned, half raised his hand, bowed his head once, and was gone.

I looked back toward the dais. Some sculptor — I think it was Auguste Rodin, the one who did *The Thinker* — once created a group of statues that represented the leading citizens of a French medieval town, being led out with ropes already round their necks, to be hanged by an irate invader. The pro-development majority on Cumberland council could have posed as models for a modern recreation.

Beside them, the hold-out councillors, the farmer and the too-tight tweed jacket, were pounding their palms together so hard they wouldn't have noticed if their fingers flew off. And the mayor was clapping politely along with the crowd, a thoughtful look on his well practised face.

The planner still had his FM mic halfway to his lips; his mouth was open, but nothing was coming out. He seemed to have shrunk maybe ten per cent inside his custom-made suit, making him look like a teenager wearing a big brother's hand-me-down.

I'd been to a lot of political meetings, either as a reporter or as a coat-holder for my boss the minister. Occasionally, I'd seen conflicts come to a head and be resolved, with metaphorical blood on the floor, and careers made or broken. But I'd never seen anyone's ass so thoroughly kicked through the goal posts as the planner's had been kicked by Benny Filiatrault.

I said as much to Mo and Sally.

"That's the kind of people we grow here," Sally said.

"I wish I belonged here," Mo said. "I wish I had your kind of roots."

Sally gave her a sad smile. "No, you don't," she said.

"He's right about the blood and bones."

It was a long time before the applause finally died. The Cumberlanders may have been hoping their new star would come back and do an encore. But Elvis had left the building.

Gradually, then suddenly, in that odd way of crowds, the clapping diminished and died. The people of the village took their seats, those who had them, and they all looked at the kid in the suit. He looked back at them.

"Well," he said. Then nothing. There were titters in the crowd.

"Well," he tried again. This time, it was a ripple of laughter.

The mayor reached down and tapped him on the shoulder, gesturing for the mic. The young man passed it gratefully.

The mayor waited until there was silence. "Yeah, well," he said, and let the laugh come and go. "I think we've had a pretty convincing expression of what people want. Now, a vote here tonight has no legal standing," — there were rumbles from the crowd — "but I will personally put Benny's motion for a referendum on the agenda at the next council meeting. And that vote will count."

The mayor's applause was second-best to what the Cumby folk had given Filiatrault's performance, but it was a good save.

"Now let's hear what people have to say about the planner's proposals," he said.

"I'm going to duck out and see if Benny's out there. He said he might want me to write something. I won't be long."

"Sure," said Mo.

There was nobody outside the double doors. I checked the washroom, found it empty, then went down the stairs. I pushed through the main doors and looked up and down the street. There was still no sign of Benny.

That struck me as a tactical mistake. I knew political enthusiasm is like a spark in tinder: if you don't keep blowing on it, it goes out. Benny should have hung around. He could have used his successful intervention in this evening's event to pull people to him, get them committed beyond a round of applause at a community meeting and give them something to do in his campaign. It's an old rule of politics — when someone offers to help, immediately give the volunteer a job.

Maybe Benny wasn't as much of a natural as I thought. I re-entered the community centre and made to reclimb the stairs, only to find my way blocked by a small man in jeans and a checked shirt. He was standing in the middle of the staircase, a couple of steps up, but he was short enough that he was looking down on me from not very much of a difference in height.

I said, "Excuse me," and went to go around him, but he moved sideways, so that again the way was barred. I moved to the other side. So did he.

"Thanks for the dance," I said, "but..."

"His name's Rafferty," said a voice above me. I looked up. Trick Ketterich was leaning over the bannister enclosing the stairwell. He wiggled his shoulders. I knew I'd seen some actor do the move, but I couldn't place it.

"I'm supposed to give a fuck?" said the miniature man. His gaze never left mine.

"Something I can do for you?" I said, in my most neutral tone. I had spoken to the one in front of me, but it was Trick who answered.

"Maybe," he said, levering himself up off the railing and coming down the stairs. He stopped when he got down as far as the little man. "This is my brother, Butch," he said.

I didn't say, *Pleased to meet you.* I only tell lies for money, and even then I can be choosy. "Does everybody in this town have a nickname?" I asked.

Trick flicked his eyebrows up twice, and opened his mouth in a lazy grin. I almost got that one. Kirk Douglas, maybe. No, somebody else — if I stopped trying to place it, it would come to me. Trick would have made a good impressionist — maybe not a great one like Frank Gorshin, but easily as good as a David Fry or a Rich Little.

But I didn't have the leisure to study Trick's act. I was keeping my attention on Butch. The larger man had some good heft on him, and looked as if he'd know his way around a street-fight. But the little one was by far the more dangerous.

He didn't move. I couldn't even see his chest lifting, though he had to be breathing. His arms hung loose like a puppet's with its strings cut. He had sharp little features, a ungiving mouth that turned down at the corners, and eyes as dark and dead as a dogfish's. If those eyes had lids, he didn't use them much.

"What's happening here?" I said.

"Wanna talk to you, is all," said Trick. He held his head up and back, half closed his eyes and looked down his nose at me. This time I got it: *Jack Nicholson*, I thought. The voice was not too close, but the face was spot on.

"So talk," I said.

"You hanging out with Benny." Trick apparently did all the talking in the Ketterich family. I didn't really want to know what purposes Butch fulfilled.

"I'm working for him," I said.

"He pay you well?"

"I don't work cheap."

"We want to hire you too."

I said nothing.

"We want you to keep an eye on Benny and that kid, wears the black clothes."

"What do you mean, keep an eye on them?"

"Just see where they go, what they do. Specially the kid."

"Why?"

Butch didn't like me asking questions. The skin around the lines at the corner of his mouth turned a little yellow. Trick still kept up the Nicholson impression, but now he was starting to sound like Jack Torrance up in that isolated hotel once the snow closed in and the ghosts came out. He tilted his head a little sideways, tucked his pupils down in the corners of his eyes, and squinted at me. I began to wonder if maybe these two were equally dangerous; it could be that one of them just had a longer fuse.

"Because that's what we'd be paying you to do," Trick said.

"I don't spy on people I work for," I said.

"That like a rule with you?"

"Kinda."

Butch leaned forward, craning his neck and shoulders to shorten the distance between us. When he spoke, his breath was a whisper of stale air against my forehead. Maybe my first impression was right: he didn't breathe as much as normal human beings, so the contents of his lungs lost their freshness waiting for a chance to get out.

"Make an exception," he said.

The fact was, I intended to do just that. I had this one figured out. The Ketteriches had money — probably a lot of money — tied up in Rod Bilder's housing development. Benny was a potential blockage in the pipeline of profits the brothers were expecting. He made them nervous, and they wanted to buy themselves some insurance.

Fair enough, I thought. Whatever they wanted to offer, I would take. I didn't figure Benny was up to anything in private that he wasn't also doing in public. Any reports I made would be innocuous.

Clemmer was another matter. Somebody had laid those traps around Hockney's Woods, and if it hadn't been him it was only because he hadn't thought of it yet. I wouldn't be surprised at anything he might do. I also didn't expect him to do any of it when I was around.

If Cumberland's marijuana cultivation kings wanted to waste their money, they might as well waste it on me. I wondered how high they would go.

"Okay," I said. "I just might make an exception. If you make the right offer."

"A thousand," Trick said.

"Two," I said, automatically. Butch's upper lip twitched. If he leaned any farther forward, I'd have to catch him when he inevitably toppled toward me.

"A thousand is just for looking," Trick said. "You find something, it'll be a lot more."

"What am I looking for?"

"You'll know it when you see it."

Usually, my face doesn't show much of what's going on behind it. This time, the facade must have slipped an inch or two, giving Trick and Butch a hint as to how little I was enjoying their act.

"We need to show him," said Butch.

"Okay," said his brother. "We'll show him."

It didn't occur to them to ask whether or not I wanted to be shown. They moved me out of the community centre with an economy of force — more an implication that force was available in overwhelming quantities if I encouraged them to bring it into the open. I didn't think much encouragement would be necessary.

A minute later, we were in Butch's maroon four-by-four, watching through tinted glass as the last lights of Cumberland dropped past us into the darkling forest. I knew the road, though I'd only been on it once. We soon reached the clearing where Stu Haglund had died, but we kept going another couple of hundred metres, while the road became a two-rut track, and then the track became a trail that disappeared into a thicket of salal and salmonberry bushes.

Butch stopped the vehicle and we got out. He went

straight through the gap in the undergrowth. Trick nudged me to follow, and I did. Under the trees the air was grey and purple. The sky above the woods might still be full of late summer light, but down here among the big sticks, night was already making itself comfortable. The ground was thick with ferns big enough to have been cast as extras in *Jurassic Park*.

Butch set a fairly rapid pace, considering the shortness of his legs. We marched a couple of minutes into the gloom, then he stopped and gently pushed aside a big fern. He held back the fronds for his brother and me to get off the trail, pointing to a log he wanted me to step on, and a bare rock after it, so we would leave no trail for others to follow.

Beyond was a downslope. We descended to where a fallen log crossed a small stream, no more than a trickle over a mat of wet leaves and needles at this time of year. Then we climbed to a low ridge and made our way along its crest a ways, slipping between the trees until we were standing above a place where a big one had gone over, its roots apparently loosened in the shallow soil by a sudden rush of melt water in the little stream a year or two back.

"This is it," said Trick.

"This is what?" I said. There was nothing to see but another anonymous patch of ferns and berry bushes, with the big log cutting across it, its black roots reaching up into the air like the freeze-frame negative image of exploding fireworks.

Butch moved down the slope a little, got a stick and moved aside a thorny blackberry creeper. "There," he said.

I stooped and looked. It was hard to see in the gloom, but there was a green stalk sticking out of the ground. It was a little thicker than my thumb, and would have come up to my knee. Butch moved more blackberry runners out of the way, and I saw more of the truncated stalks.

Ding, went the small chimes in the back of my head.

"You were growing dope here," I said.

"Two hundred and fifty-plus plants," Trick said. "A hybrid Kush strain, we bred it ourselves, flowers three weeks before your normal outdoor grow. Thirty per cent THC. Best in the world. You know how much money that is?"

I didn't.

He was doing Jack Nicholson again. "Retail, it would make around a thousand a plant. Wholesaling it to our regular customers, more like three-fifty. Altogether, call it ninety grand. That's a lot of money."

There was a silence. I realized I was supposed to say something. "Somebody ripped you off, took your crop," I said.

"Uh huh," said Trick.

"It wasn't me," I said.

"Well, we know that." In the dusk, it could have been Nicholson himself.

"So, why am I here?"

"Because there's only so many people we figure it coulda been. Most of them are too dumb to shit and blink at the same time. We been checkin' around, lookin' in their places."

"Eliminating the suspects," Butch put in. I wondered if he meant that literally.

"But there's three people been coming into these woods that might be smart enough to rip us off and get away with it. And you know what the funny thing is?"

"What?" I said, not expecting any humour.

"You're hangin' with all three of them."

"You mean Benny?" I said.

"And that freak, Clemmer," Trick said. "We seen him goin in and out." He'd switched to another voice, but he wasn't giving me enough to recognize the new impression.

"Who's the third?" I said. Suddenly, I got a chill. "Not Haglund?"

Butch snorted. "No," he said. "Bilder."

"But I thought he was partners with you guys."

"You're pretty well informed for a guy don't even live here," said Trick. It definitely wasn't Nicholson now — more like the actor who played Andy Sipowitz on *NYPD Blue.* "Whatta you think, cause people are partners, they're not gonna screw each other?"

"Sheesh," said Butch, shaking his head.

"So now I know what I'm looking for," I said. "About a half a tonne of marijuana. What makes you think it's still around?"

"Cause if it weren't," said the New York cop voice, "we woulda heard about it. There's only so many people could move that weight, and they woulda told us."

"Nobody likes a thief," said Butch. "Bad for business, people start raidin' the crops."

"You got that right," said his brother. "This ain't Chicago in the Prohibition times. We got established lines of distribution, people been growin' and shippin', ten twenty years."

"Maybe the cops took it," I said.

"Nah," said Trick, the Sipowitz character voice getting even better with practice. "Cops pull 'em out, roots an' all. Whoever did this, he just took the leaves and buds."

He reached down and pulled a stalk out of the ground, held it up to my nose. "Smell that?"

It was sharp and resiny, the same smell I remembered from university days, but much more pungent. "Wow," I said.

"Wherever they're hidin' the stuff, in the garage, down in the basement, the whole house is gonna smell like that," he said. "You happen to be in somebody's place, you smell that smell, you let us know."

"We'll take it from there," said Butch.

They turned to leave, and I followed. Then something caught my eye. "What's that?" I said.

It was where the big tree had fallen, tearing a wound in the slope above the little watercourse. The spring runoff would have swept through the little gully, filling it with brown swirling water and eroding the edges of the hole. Each rainfall since would have continued the work.

Something pale gleamed in the darkness. I stepped over the stream and poked around. "Bones," I said. They looked like ribs.

Butch joined me. "Probably a deer," he said. "Maybe a dog. Pretty old, anyway."

He was right. The bones were greyish green and crumbly to the touch. There looked to be more of them under the leaf mold, but I didn't feel like digging further. I had a sudden image of worms or maggots, teeming clumps of them, pullulating just under the surface, ready to cling slimily to my hand if I broke through the damp black soil. "Best leave it alone," I said.

But Butch and Trick were already climbing back to the top of the ridge. I went after them. They gave me a lift back to the community hall, then sped off in a cloud of hydrocarbons. I went upstairs to see how the meeting was going. Of course, it was all anticlimax after Benny — predictable questions and bland responses. Mr. Smooth had got some colour back in his cheeks and seemed to feel at least adequate again.

The greenies in the Cowichan sweaters trooped back and forth to the microphone. They didn't ask questions, but made heartfelt little speeches about preserving wilderness, encouraging more recycling. Most of it went down well with the Cumby folk, because the environmental enthusiasts were their own kids or cousins or nieces and nephews. I took notes, listening for common themes, local trigger words that could be worked into future speeches and hand-outs. But I didn't imagine Benny Filiatrault would need a whole lot of help from a hired gun like me.

Davey Clemmer stayed for the whole thing. Toward the end, he slouched down the aisle to the mic, tossed a few apocalyptic predictions into the crowd, which generated some head scratching and a couple of rebuttals in the form of anatomical noises. When he went back, he sat in the same row as the local greenies — and I noticed that he left with them when the meeting was over.

Rod Bilder never showed. As the proceedings wound down, I stood up and scanned the now half empty room, but the big red head was not to be seen.

I was not sure of the protocol involved in asking Sally about her ex-husband's whereabouts, so I asked Mo instead. "Do you think Sally would know where Rod is?" I whispered.

"Ask her," she said. So I did.

"Probably at his office," Sally said.

"I thought he would have been here for the meeting," I said. "Rezoning those woods for mixed development is part of the community plan."

Sally had nothing to say about that. "Try his office," she said. "But first come to my place, and let me check out your shoulder."

Chapter 7

"Hoo!" I said, with lots of breath and a slight shiver. "Cold."

Sally pulled her hands away from my bare shoulder and rubbed them briskly together. "Sorry," she said.

I shivered again. The big front room that she had fitted out as her home-based physiotherapy clinic had been shaded all day by a large cedar on the front lawn, and by evening it was definitely chilly for a man who was stripped to the waist, even in summer.

"Sorry," she said again. Today was my day off, so I didn't have the heat on in here at all. We'll go to the parlor, and get warm."

I didn't really want to be in either room, for two reasons. In the first place, I had this peculiar attitude toward pain: I thought it was something I was just supposed to endure. As long as it didn't actually prevent me from standing up or remaining conscious, my sentiment was: forget it, it will go away.

It was a holdover from my upbringing, back in the days before Canada adopted a national medicare program. The Raffertys were working poor; when my dad was working, it was almost always at low-end jobs that offered no medical benefits. There was no money for running to the doctor just because some part of me hurt or had turned a funny colour. If it got so bad I fainted or ran a fever that made me babble, then it was time for a professional to take an expensive look.

The other reason I didn't want to be under Sally's ministrations was it meant being in the same room as her and Mo. Talk might easily turn to a certain movie project that I wanted the woman I loved to believe was cooking right along, at least until I could find some plausible excuse for ditching it.

I trailed after Mo, who followed Sally's sturdy figure down a dark hallway to a closed door. I was thinking I would try to steer the conversation into other topics. Benny Filiatrault was probably a safe bet. If we could just chat about that while Sally did to my shoulder whatever she and Mo thought was necessary, I might get away without further injury.

That hope hit the ground with a morbid thump the moment Sally pushed opened the door and led us into a parlour that might have been lifted whole and intact from a 1930s movie. It was a small room and crowded with overstuffed furniture, beaded lamp shades, a dark and massive sideboard with scrolls and curlicues carved into its doors and drawers. Most of one wall belonged to a deep fireplace framing a small electric heater. Above was a wooden mantelpiece across which sailed a flotilla of black and white photographs, of people and places untroubled by the decades stretching between us and them.

There was a mirror behind the pictures. I looked odd standing there half undressed, my shirt bunched in my hand.

Sally flicked a wall switch that activated the heater. The elements soon glowed with warmth, but not a lot of it was reaching me yet.

"This is so nice," Mo said.

"Like time travel," I said.

"It was all up in the attic. When I moved back here after Rod and I ... you know, well, I just brought it down."

Mo went to take a look at the photos. "That's the sign," she said. "Look, Raff."

I peered at the framed snap. It showed half a dozen people, four men and two women in what I took to be

1930s dress, on the sidewalk outside a small store. A big sheet-metal sign stood straight out from the building above their heads, with the name CAMPBELL'S not only painted on it, but outlined in light bulbs. I'd seen the same sign on a wall in the museum, its paint long gone, its electrical sockets blind and empty.

"All the stores on Dunsmuir Avenue burned in a big fire, didn't they?" Mo asked Sally.

"Most of them," was the answer. "During the Depression. Somebody found that old sign in the village dump a few years ago, and hauled it down to the museum."

"Are these your people?" Mo asked, indicating the men and women in the photograph.

"That's my mother on the right," Sally said. "She worked for the Campbells from when she was a young girl until the store burned. My grandfather worked there too, as a clerk."

Mo peered at the four men in the photo. "Which one is he?"

"He's not there." She indicated another picture. "Here he is."

It was a family portrait, a couple with their young daughter, dressed in their formal best. The woman was somewhere in her twenties, but the lines in the corners of her mouth and the dull stare she turned on the camera said youth was already forever gone. The man was a few years her senior, and though he showed all the stiff dignity with which pre-Jazz Age Canadians posed for posterity, the photographer had nonetheless caught an air of puzzled apprehension in the arrangement of his features. *Something happened to this feller,* I thought. *Luck turned against him and left him asking himself, 'why me?' all the way to the end.* I knew how he felt.

"He died in the war," Sally said. "1918. This was taken just before he went away. The house was his." She looked around the room. "Then it was my mother's. Now it's mine. That's mom, on Grannie's lap. She'd be about five there. We were both born in the same bed."

We looked at the little girl in her little dress and pinafore. Her head was canted to one side as if she were too tired to hold it erect, and there were dark smudges under her eyes.

"Poor thing," Mo said. "She looks worn out, like she'd been sitting there all day."

"It was TB," Sally said. "She and Grannie both had it. It was common enough in those days."

"My god," said Mo.

Sally shrugged. "It's how it was. Now let's fix your man here."

She ushered me toward a wooden chair with a brocaded cushion and back. "Would you sit here? And, Mo, would you mind bringing me the white machine that's on the trolley-table-thing in the clinic? Oh, and the tube of gel that's on top of it."

Mo left, and Sally positioned me on the chair. She stood beside me, took my left arm in her still cold hands, and slowly rotated the shoulder, gently pulling and pushing, while asking me, "Does this hurt?" and "How does that feel?" which I answered with "A little," or "No," or "No big deal."

Mo came back in with a machine about the same size and shape as the Nintendo deck my twin boys got from their fat-cat stepfather. She put it on an end table next to where I was sitting, then stood over me and watched as Sally had me extend my left arm straight out from the shoulder, telling me to resist as she pushed down on it. I tried, but the limb went down like a well oiled pump handle. Then she switched to my right arm, which stayed stubbornly up even when she put on some real pressure.

"Hmm," she said, and frowned in that worrying, annoying way that practitioners of the healing arts almost inevitably acquire.

"What is it?" Mo asked.

Sally didn't answer. "You said there was an old injury?"

I told her about dislocating my shoulder in an explosion at an industrial park three years ago. Emergency room doctors had put everything all back together. Since then I'd had the odd twinge, but it hadn't bothered me. Not until Titch Haglund put the toe of his Doc Martens into it.

"Shoulders are complicated things," Sally said. "There's a lot of little micro-muscles that connect this way and that. You damaged some of them three years ago, and they haven't recovered."

"It hasn't hurt or anything," I said.

"You're sure you're not just being all male about it?" Mo put in. "Don't want to admit a weakness?"

I assured her I was not being all male. Until I'd been kicked in it, my shoulder had gone about its business without bothering me, and I'd returned the favour.

"Well, there's bruising and inflammation where you got kicked," Sally said, "which is what you'd expect. But there's also weakness from the old injury, and we need to fix that."

"How fix?" I said.

"This," she said, indicating the device Mo had put on the end table. It had buttons and knobs on the top, with a springy telephone-type cord coming out the side, which connected to what looked like a microphone with a solid steel disc at its end.

Before she did anything with the machine, she picked up a tube that might have contained toothpaste, but which turned out to be full of some kind of clear gel. Sally squeezed a glob of it onto her fingertips and spread it on my shoulder. I shivered again.

"Ultrasound doesn't conduct very well through air," she said. She pushed a button and turned a dial, causing the machine to emit a tiny polite hum. She freed the hand-piece from a clip that attached it to the side of the box, applied its steel disc to my skin — another source of cold, but by now I already had all of my goosebumps deployed — and moved it in slow, small circles.

"You sure it's working," I said after a few seconds. "I don't feel anything."

"If I hold it still, you'll feel the warmth," she said. "Like this."

She stopped the circling, and I felt an odd prickling inside my shoulder. Then she moved it again, and all I felt was the steel gliding through the gel on my skin.

We sat there, not saying anything for several seconds, Sally concentrating on the treatment. "You have to be careful not to put it on bone. That can hurt," she said.

"Isn't this what they use on pregnant women?" Mo said.

I carefully didn't look at her.

"Similar," Sally said. "Different frequency. This vibrates in the tissue, deep down. That generates heat, which stimulates circulation and relaxes muscles when they're in spasm. They've also recently found that it makes cell membranes more permeable, so that the tissue reabsorbs fluids. That combats inflammation — like what you've got here."

She'd been concentrating the hand-piece on the spot where Titch had kicked me. It seemed to me I did feel a subtle, spreading warmth deep in my shoulder. My goosebumps had gone to half mast. I turned my head to the left, felt only a faint ache where before there had been jagged pain. "I think it's working," I said.

I found myself looking at Sally's face. I noticed she quite resembled her grandfather in the photo on the mantelpiece. But the animating expression behind the features was different. There was no puzzled wonderment to the set of Sally McMahon's countenance; her face again showed such an intensity of concentration that it was almost uncomfortable to be so close to her, like sitting too near a bright light.

I turned to see what Mo was doing. She was looking though the other photographs on the mantelpiece. "Raff's going to see if he can do a movie about Ginger Goodwin, at least write the script," she said to Sally's reflection in the mirror.

"Oh, yes?" said Sally, her eyes never leaving my shoulder.

"If I can get the rights," I said.

"It was a terrible thing," Sally said. She lifted the ultrasound applicator clear of my skin and stared into the fireplace. "He was in this house, once. Toward the end, when he was on the run."

"Really," I said.

"The people at the store asked my grandfather to keep him a day or two, till they could row him over to the other end of the lake. They didn't think the Dominion Police would look here, because our family had nothing to do with mines or unions." Her eyes remained fixed on the glow of the electric fire. "A terrible thing," she said again.

"It's a hell of a story, though," Mo said. "Tell Sally what you were thinking about."

"What?" I said.

"About the trapper."

"She doesn't want to hear."

"Sure she does."

Sally had gone back to work with the ultrasound. She didn't look up.

I told her about my idea to build the script around the Judas who had turned Ginger in for money.

She nodded. "Everybody hated Scabby Anderson. He couldn't show his face in town ever again. He died all alone at St. Joe's over in Comox."

"Perfect," Mo said. "Like Salieri in Amadeus."

"That's a little ambitious," I said.

"You ain't heard nothin' yet," she answered.

I looked at her. There was a way she could make her eyes seem to dance when she had something she was dying to tell me. Normally, I loved it.

"What?" I said.

"I had an idea," she said.

"Uh huh."

"On the way back from the lake."

"Uh huh."

"Aren't you going to ask me what it is?"

As if I had a choice. "Okay," I said, "what's your idea?"

"Well, I was thinking, I'm good at organizing things and dealing with people."

"Yes."

"And I've been thinking it's time I did something a little more, I don't know, *rewarding* than the stuff I've been doing. And I could afford to take some time off to work on a project."

It was like standing in front of the firing squad without a blindfold, while the officer in command kept padding out the interval between *ready, aim* and *fire*. So I pulled the trigger myself, just to get to the pain and suffering without further delay.

"You want to produce the movie," I said.

"Ding," she said.

Oh, god, I thought. "Oh, good," I said.

She was smiling at me with two hundred watts worth of teeth. A literary thought crossed my mind: there was no incompatibility between love and despair. Both could inhabit the space between a man and a woman.

"It's an interesting idea," I said.

The smile dimmed just a little, and the tiniest of lines appeared between her eyes. "I think we should produce something together," she said. "Don't you?"

"Sure," I said. I'd already made my big mistake up at the lake. "I think it's a great idea."

"I'm glad."

"Be a big learning curve, though. Lot of ins and outs, the movie biz." You don't survive in PR or politics without learning the basics of stalling and playing for time.

"But you know people who know the biz, right?"

"Right."

"Like that man who was going to produce your pay-TV movie. Isn't he still in Vancouver?"

I could have lied and said I'd lost touch with Roger Gambowsky, but his name and numbers were in the address directory of my computer. "Uh huh," I said.

"And your old office neighbour who used to run the Telefilm office? Didn't you tell me she was an agent now on West Fourth?"

I couldn't deny that either.

"Well," Mo said. "There it is."

Sally's ultrasound machine said, *Meep.* "You're done," said Sally. "Right," I said. I noticed the goosebumps were back.

❧

We walked back to the Behemoth, my left shoulder feeling looser, while the rest of me seemed to be tightening up. It was full dark now, with just a touch of a moon. It lit up the few puffs of cloud that clustered over the Beaufort Range like empty dialogue balloons for cartoon characters who had nothing to say.

I tossed Rod Bilder's package of background bumpf onto the back seat; I didn't know where he lived, and I doubted he'd be in the office this late. But when we drove down Dunsmuir Avenue, the window of the space he rented above Tarbell's glowed with quiet yellow light.

I pulled over. "I'll just be a minute," I told Mo.

"I'll come with you," she said. "He sounds like a real character. Maybe I'll cast him for a part in our movie."

"Oh," I said. "Sure."

We went up the outside steps, the old wood creaking and commenting on our combined weight. I tapped on the door at the top, but got no answer. I could hear nothing from inside. I knocked, louder, then tried the doorknob. It turned and the door opened.

There was a small unlit vestibule, then Bilder's office beyond, the yellow light from the partly open door arranging itself into a bent parallelogram on the linoleum floor and the opposite wall.

I stood on the landing at the top of the outside stairs and called, "Mr. Bilder? It's Sid Rafferty."

There was no answer. There would never be any more answers from Rod Bilder, unless the question was phrased as something like, *Don't blink, don't breathe and don't move at all if you happen to be severely life-impaired.*

He was sitting behind his desk, one arm resting on his thigh, the other dangling loose. His chin was on his chest and his eyes were open. I thought that he looked like a man who had just had depressing news and was sitting there, slumped, thinking about it — in a sense, I guess he had received bad tidings, the worst tidings of all: *excuse me, Rod, it's your life calling — just want you to know I'm over.*

Mo came into the room after me. I heard her gasp. "I don't think he's going to be available for the movie," I said.

She went past me, and felt his throat for a pulse. I'd seen it done on TV, but had no idea where you actually found the beat of life. I don't think Mo did either, because the moment she touched him, she pulled her hand away as if he were a hot stove.

She looked at me and a little shiver rattled her shoulders. "He's stone cold. He must have died hours ago."

"Yeah," I said. "Otherwise he would have come to the

big meeting."

"We'd better call somebody — ambulance, or maybe the police."

"The cops," I told her. I crossed to the window that looked out on Dunsmuir to see if there was anybody in the storefront police unit across the street. The lights were out.

Mo had moved away from Bilder's body, went all the way to the door to the vestibule, where she stood, not looking at the corpse, holding her elbows.

I reached for the phone.

"Maybe we shouldn't touch anything," she said.

I looked around the office. There was no sign of a struggle, no holes in the corpse. No bruises or blood. "Why? This is natural causes. Probably a stroke. He was taking medication."

She shrugged. I found a phone book and looked up the number of the RCMP detachment in Courtenay. The Comox Valley didn't have a 911 system yet, although the local politicians were talking about making the multi-thousand dollar investment.

The cops were there in five minutes. Mo and I waited outside in the Ford until a cruiser came up Dunsmuir, with its lights flashing but no siren. There were two Mounties, both of them familiar faces: Corporal Mikhailovsky, who had come to our house a few days before, and the young constable who had gone to see about Stu Haglund.

"It's Mr. Rafferty, isn't it?" said the corporal.

"It is."

"And another body?"

"I'm afraid so."

I told them where Bilder was and the noncom went upstairs, leaving the constable to take our statements. The younger man just stood there and stared into my eyes, a technique he'd probably learned in Cop 101 at the RCMP

Academy in Regina, some slick behavioural science expert telling the rookies that people would blurt out the most surprising things, if you just skewered them on the old steady eyeball.

After ten seconds, I gave him what he wanted. I said, "We must stop meeting like this."

I can usually trust my instincts — trust them to be wrong, that is. Sitting at a keyboard, with Mr. Creativity on line, I can generally hit the board somewhere between pretty good and brilliant. On my feet, with only my vocal apparatus to work with, I am a danger to myself.

The young constable gave me another ten seconds of his Buster Keaton impression, then took out his regulation issue notebook. It didn't take long to answer his questions, first me, then Mo to confirm what I said. Before we finished, Mikhailovsky came down the stairs, radioed for an ambulance, then stood listening to what we were telling the young cop.

The constable closed his notebook and tucked it away in his breast pocket. The four of us stood in the middle of one of those brief silences that seem to go on forever.

"I guess it was a stroke," I said.

The corporal turned a bland gaze toward me. "Why do you say that?"

"He was on high blood-pressure medication," I said. "When I came to see him the other day, he was taking them. He tended to get worked up about things, shout at people on the phone, punch holes in the wall."

The constable took out his notebook again, and made some additions to my statement. "You knew him pretty well, then?"

"We were practically strangers. I spent less than an hour with him, and that was spread over two separate meetings.

And that reminded me of the other thing that had

been on Bilder's desk. I asked the corporal, "Did you find a sheet of paper with letters cut from newspaper headlines?"

Now the noncom's gaze was not bland at all. "Why do you ask?"

I told him what I had seen peeking out from under the architect's drawings. He wanted to know more. I told him I had only had a glimpse, that it had been something about staying away from Hockney's Woods or there would be trouble, and the name Earthstrike!, complete with dramatic punctuation, at the end.

The corporal thought this was worth writing down in his own notebook. "You didn't report it," he said when he was finished. It was not a question.

I shrugged. "It was just a piece of paper sticking out from under something on his desk, not anything he discussed with me. I thought it was none of my business."

Mikhailovsky said, "Still, after what happened to Mr. Haglund," and left it there while he gave me his variation on the Cop 101 stare. It was a lot better than the constable's. I hadn't done anything, and I was nervous.

"It was a busy day," I said. "I had to go see a new client, then run some errands. It just slipped my mind."

He made another note. "I see."

Ever the big sister, Mo Migliorini stepped in. "Corporal, can we go? It's been a long day. You know where to find us."

The Mountie weighed it up. "Okay," he said, after a moment. "Would you come and see me tomorrow morning, Mr. Rafferty?"

"I have a meeting with a client in Port Alberni in the afternoon," I said.

"I won't need you for long."

How could I refuse?

The old Ford was pulling itself effortlessly up the long curving hill that led into Comox. We passed the place at the top where the big forest company Crown Zellerbach used to have a fancy lodge for visiting executives. Now CZ was almost a forgotten name, its operations long since absorbed by Fletcher Challenge, an international conglomerate out of New Zealand. Around the lodge had been the last tiny stand of old growth on the Comox peninsula. The first British farmers who had come up by coastal steamer had begun to clear the ancient Douglas firs in the 1860s, and by the 1950s, they were pretty much all gone, except for a few dozen that shaded Crown Zellerbach's elite and incidentally formed as hilltop gateway to the town of Comox.

The New Zealanders who ran Fletcher Challenge were of that lean, mean, and bottom-line worshipping breed that kicked ass in every quarter of the new world economic order. They quickly sold the lodge and grounds to a developer, who deconstructed the old building, then made room for all the up-market condos that the site could hold by chopping down many of the giant trees.

Horrified local folks had begged Comox council to try to save the old growth, or at least to throw roadblocks in the developer's way, to give the aroused citizenry time to try to raise funds and buy the site for a public park. But the elected reps had dawdled and dithered and done nothing. The chainsaws had ripped, and the firs had come crashing down. Then winter brought gale-force winds off Georgia Strait, stronger than the thinned out stand could bear, and more of the remaining trees were blown over.

"Ticky-tacky boxes," I said to myself.

"What?" Mo said.

"Never mind. Do you want to go straight home, or should we go somewhere and eat?"

She looked at her watch. It was after ten. "By some- where, you mean the Black Fin?"

I nodded. The Fin wasn't the only place open — the Leeward and the Lorne would still be going strong, along with the Griffin out by the airbase — but it was the one I liked best.

"I guess," she said.

Five minutes later we were at a window-side table over- looking the harbour and the marina. The eastern side of the basin was crowded with grey-hulled fishing boats waiting for another brief seasonal shot at the salmon runs. The western side, enclosed by a riprap mole topped by a wooden boardwalk, was choked with colourful sailing craft — everything from twenty-five foot day-trippers to sleek, ocean-going live-aboards. The water beyond, dead calm, was a sheet of oiled steel in the twilight, broken by a forest of masts and rigging.

It was less tranquil on our side of the window. A dozen or so boat people — the kind that can afford to take the whole summer off to cruise between Puget Sound and Alaska — had pushed three or four tables together and were rounding out dinner by telling each other their best stories. But by the time our drinks had arrived — Shafte- bury cream ale for me, red wine for Mo — they'd moved up to the upper part of the Fin's split-level layout to throw darts at the tournament boards.

I watched them for a moment, then said, "Remember in the old war movies where the Americans would ask sus- pected spies baseball questions?"

Mo sipped her wine and gave me the face that says, *and so?*

"I was thinking how we could spot Americans if they were pretending to be anything else, just by the way they throw darts." I indicated one of the boaters, who was winding up to hurl his little missile. I watched as he let it fly with almost enough force to put it through the wall and into the living room of the old lady in the apartment across Port Augusta Street.

I looked out at the harbour again. "Hell of a day," I said.

Mo didn't answer. She had her chin in her hands and was looking up at the boat that was suspended upside down from the middle of the Black Fin's vaulted ceiling. There was a write-up about it on the back of the pub's menu.

The long, sleek rowing vessel was a replica of a Boston Whitehall, a design that dated from the 1820s. The Fin's specimen was no older than the pub, however, having been specially made by a craftsman from down near the southern tip of Vancouver Island to be chained among the wisps of cigarette smoke the floated above the dining area.

The Whitehall, the menu said, was not a ship's boat but a vessel intended for harbour and coastal use. In the age of sail, the type had been common on every North American waterfront, ferrying passengers and provisions to and from the square-rigged ships at anchor. The narrow, deep bow cut through harbour chop, while its wide flaring sides kept sea spray from coming inboard, allowing land-lubbers to reach ship or shore with their clothes dry and their stomach contents unheaved.

The menu waxed lyrical about the boat's wineglass stem and its deep skeg — apparently the afterpart of the vessel's keel — which made it fast and reliable. The White-hall's racing design was perhaps the reason rowing had become the most popular sport on the American eastern seaboard in the mid-nineteenth century.

I knew very little about boats. To me, a boat was a wooden lining for an extremely expensive hole in the water. But even I could see the Whitehall was a work of art. If it had been down where the drinkers and diners could get at it, it would have drawn hands to stroke its white curve of hull and slide along the dark amber of its varnished tiller.

"I said, *hell of a day,*" I reminded Mo.

She made a sound somewhere between the back of her throat and her closed lips. I had no idea what it meant.

"You always stare at that boat," I said.

She made a similar sound. "Poor Sally," she said.

"You mean, poor Rod, don't you? All of his prospects just became severely limited."

She shrugged.

"Besides, now Sally can sell those woods to the village for a park, and all the craziness will be over."

The waitress came and we ordered. Then we sat and looked at this and that, and said nothing for quite a while.

Finally, I said, "I'm sorry about up at the lake. I said the wrong thing."

She smiled. "I'm always jumping you when you least expect it," she said.

"If you really wanted a kid...," I began.

"The pin is back in the grenade," she said. "No need to throw yourself on it. We'll make a movie instead."

"Yeah," I said. "A movie."

The food came and we ate. We talked about my kids and the air show and how beautiful it was on the other side of the window. I told her there were some beautiful sights on this side, too. Then we went home and made love, which we were still pretty good at.

Chapter 8

There were two words on the screen, the same two words that all movie scripts begin with: *FADE IN*, followed by a colon. I looked at them, then at the flashing line of the cursor under the blank space immediately after the colon.

I moved my eyes down to the keyboard, to where my fingers rested on the frame just below the space bar, then came back to the screen. I depressed the control key and used the old WordStar keystroke command to put the cursor beneath the *F* in *FADE*, then entered the command code that enclosed the two words and their attendant punctuation mark in bold face.

Then I stared at the screen and waited. I was opening the inner door, as I always do, so that Mr. Creativity could feed me the opening concept, first line. Usually, he wouldn't take more than a few minutes, but today something wasn't working right. Nothing was coming through.

I shifted in my chair. I didn't seem to fit into it right today. My shoulder ached where Titch had put the boot in. I stretched it carefully, and thought about going back to Sally for another ultrasound. But that made me think about Ginger Goodwin, and that brought me back to the two words on the screen.

The room wasn't particularly warm — it hardly ever gets uncomfortably hot in Comox — but there was sweat under my lower lip. Something was crawling lazily around the walls of my stomach. I belched, and it left a taste of sulphur in my mouth.

Come on, I said to the guy in the back of my head, *we can do this.* I could almost feel him, as if he were a real presence somewhere in the unvisited rooms of my mind. He wasn't happy either. I imagined him kicking at a locked door, beating on it with his little fists, like a hyperactive kid who'd been sent to his room.

It was a strange feeling, and far from a pleasant one. It wasn't writer's block, whatever that is, if it even exists. The part of me that did the writing was on deck and ready for action. But there was another part of me that was saying *No* with an exclamation point. I recognized the sensations that flowed from the fragment of my psyche that was vetoing the work — they were the symptoms of fear.

I was having a phobic reaction. I remembered the prof's lecture way back in Psychology 101 at SFU. It was one of the courses Halfnight and I took together, an introductory survey of the main schools of thought concerning the science of the mind. "An unusually intense fear of an animal, object or situation," the lecturer had said. "Some people are terrified by houseflies, some can't bear the thought of dust settling on them, and some are horrified at the prospect of leaving their own homes. The cause is usually some traumatic event or unresolved conflict, the emotional load of which has been transferred to the apparently unrelated object of the phobia. Identify that cause, and the fear is soon dispelled."

To which Lanc Halfnight had said, "Bullshit. I bet I could cure most phobias in a weekend."

Halfnight had sampled the various schools of psychological thought presented in the first few lectures, and decided that B.F. Skinner and the behaviourists had it right. "It's all conditioning and reaction to stimuli," he would say. "You're afraid of spiders? I'll start by showing you still pictures of them, then movies, then rubber models, then the real thing in a cage. Give me a few days, I'll have you handling tarantulas."

To Halfnight, all the world was a Skinner box, albeit a big, complicated one, and all the people in it were no more than dressed-up pigeons pushing buttons to get a food pellet or sidestep an electric shock.

"You'd give half your victims — sorry, I meant *patients* — heart attacks," I would reply. I'd become a convinced Jungian, on just as little evidence as had driven Halfnight into the behaviourist camp. But Jung's concept of the divided psyche, of different elements combining to make up what we called the Self, made instant, intuitive sense to me. I'd always known there were diverse parts to the inside of my head, that different aspects of my personality would take over the controls, depending on the situation I was in.

Besides, Jung's anatomy of the psyche justified my life-long habit of talking to myself. "If I give up Jungian thought," I'd told Halfnight. "I'll have to admit that I'm just nuts."

"There's no such thing as nuts," he'd said. "There's only appropriate or inappropriate behaviour. Context is all."

"You keep believing that," I'd said. "It looks good on you."

Right now, though, I wouldn't have minded being a behaviourist for an hour or two. Then I could have worked my way through my inappropriate responses to what should have been inoffensive stimuli, and *written the damn movie for Mo.*

I tried it. I said to myself, *This is bullshit! Write something!* It was what I would have said just about any other day of my professional life. Working writers don't have the luxury of being blocked; we leave that to the more delicate blooms in the literary garden, those who pen moody poems and exquisite pensées and who are published in academic journals read almost exclusively by those who contribute to them. Pros produce prose the way pea plants produce pods, and any accompanying flowers are merely by-products of getting the job done.

But nothing was ripening on the vine today. The more I tried to force it, the sicker I felt.

I checked my watch. It was 10:30 — I'd been at this for an hour. Mo was out: some kind of follow-up meeting in Elk Falls, to go over her report on the mill's reorganization. I stared at the two words on the screen, sighed, and moved the cursor to the next line. And waited.

I got up and went to the kitchen, took the cozy off the big teapot and poured myself another cup — the strong stuff, with Mo away, Murchie's Uva Highland. It smelled sweet and heavy, like a hay barn at a dairy farm. I stirred in a little milk and went back to the keyboard.

Part of me was saying, *Come on, let's do it for Mo,* while another piece replied, *Don't touch that — it burns, it bites.* It was like pushing your hands together, the way Charles Atlas used to recommend in the back of comic books. Isometric Dynamic Tension was supposed to build the kinds of biceps and pecs that turned ninety-eight-pound weaklings into bully-thumping, babe magnets. But all that was coming out of this test of strength was futility. The two words sat there on the screen.

The psych prof had been wrong. I knew what was causing the problem. In the early 1980s, I'd lost my wife, my job and custody of my kids over the course of one lousy year. It wasn't that I'd been made to feel a failure — I had failed, and I'd spent ten years flagellating myself for not measuring up.

And then, in a matter of a few weeks, everything had changed. My old friend who was now an agent had talked me into writing a movie script for a pay-TV service. The project had taken off and soared. Suddenly, I was back up in the clear air where you can see forever. I came back to life, moved to Comox, started making plans.

And then it all crashed. No movie, no money, no hope.

Back to scrabbling for assignments, doing the one thing I was reliably good at — turning Mr. Creativity loose, and writing corporate crap for cashable cheques.

When it came to writing anything else, I had lost my nerve. Part of me might want to get back on the horse, even if it was only to please Mo. But that part was outvoted by the rest of my inner crowd, who didn't want any more punishment.

My tea had gone cold. I closed the script file, and created one called *Notes*. If jumping in headfirst wasn't an option, maybe I could grow the story organically. Maybe if I could get something down, some seed planted, the thing would send out roots and shoots and crack the barrier of fear. I typed the name *Ginger Goodwin* from the first column of the first line, then centred it. And waited. And then waited some more.

I tried forcing it. Who killed Ginger Goodwin? I typed. That could be a working title. But it wasn't right. I erased it and tried again: *Who sold Ginger?* Then I hunted around for additions to the thought: *Thirty pieces of silver.* I snorted to myself. Melodrama.

Who wasn't the story, I realized. The story was *why*. Why did the trapper do it, becoming the hated Scabby Anderson, never allowed to show his face around his old haunts again? For a few bucks?

Maybe. I tried it. *He would have sold his mother for a bottle of homemade whisky*, I typed. But the words looked ridiculous on the screen. Sure, there were people who would sell their children for a bottle or a fix. But they didn't make a good story. They were pathetic, not heroic — all pity, but no redeeming irony. What was needed was the old inner conflict, with the good man forced to do wrong to prevent some greater evil.

Something was coming. Mr. Creativity was breaking through. I urged him on, *Come on, we can write this sucker. All we have to do is do it.*

I flicked the cursor down to the next line, and poised my fingers over the keyboard. I could feel the stirrings, like the rumble beneath a drill rig before the oil comes gushing into the light. *Here we go*, I said to myself.

The phone rang. B.F. Skinner would have loved the Pavlovian response that made me automatically answer it. "It's Corporal Mikhailovsky," said the little speaker in my ear. "Could you come down to the police station, please?"

"When?"

"Now would be helpful."

"Is it important?" I said. "I'm just in the middle of something here."

"It's important," he said. "I have the results of the Bilder autopsy."

"I see," I said, although I didn't.

"It won't take long," he promised.

I looked at the few words on the screen. Whatever had been about to bubble up had cooled. I pressed the function key that saved the file, and said, "Okay. I'll be right there."

The RCMP station in Courtenay has one of those blue metal roofs that are supposed to outlast the pyramids. The brightness of the colour gives the building a cheerful, almost whimsical air, as if it were a kid's playhouse that had grown up to be a cop shop.

Corporal Leon Mikhailovsky's little office off the main squad room set the record straight. It was all business, a study in straight lines and right angles. The in- and out-baskets were each one inch from their respective corners of the regulation steel and particleboard desk. The promotion and proficiency certificates on the wall were aligned and spaced at precise intervals. The corporal himself was so perfectly positioned behind his green blotter that he could have been put there by an RCMP Academy drill master with a measuring tape and set square.

There might be a worse place to make a few derisory observations concerning the Mounties' recent decision to license their image to the Disney Corporation, but offhand I couldn't think where it would be. I sat on the edge of the interviewee's seat — I doubted that Mikhailovsky ever had folks who just came to visit — folded my hands and answered the cop's questions.

When he'd come to the house after Haglund was killed, his questions had been direct and to the point; he'd been building himself a word picture of what had happened and in what sequence. This morning, he was using a different approach, wandering all over the map, poking in and out of different subjects, it seemed at random. It was hard to figure out just what he was after, and I guessed that was his intent. On the phone, he'd said he had the results of the Bilder autopsy; but now he'd been questioning me for five minutes, and the subject hadn't come up.

He asked about my working background, and I told him: freelance commercial writer specializing in speeches for corporate execs and politicians; ex-reporter for the *Vancouver Sun* and the Ottawa bureau of the long defunct *FP* chain; former speechwriter to the federal Minister of Justice; and a short stint as a public relations staffer at a middling-sized forest company. I laid it on a little heavy about the involvement with the justice minister, but not with much conviction. Mikhailovsky was the kind of cop who would have written up Jean Chrétien for a loose tail-light on the prime ministerial limo.

He was also the kind of cop who would have already found out everything officially recorded about me — and probably a few things that were jotted down unofficially in the margins. I felt like a Pekingese being sniffed by a pit bull, even though I hadn't done anything.

He asked about Stu Haglund — did I know him? What

about the kid, Titch? I shook my head.

"But last night you and the boy were involved in an altercation in the middle of Dunsmuir Avenue."

I explained about going to Benny Filiatrault's aid, about his being a pacifist.

"Mr. Filiatrault, is he a close friend?"

"He's just a client."

"Do you normally get into street brawls on your clients' behalf?"

It was Lenin who said, *everything is connected to everything else.* I didn't mention old Vladimir Ilyich to Mikhailovsky — Mounties with eastern European names tend to have decided opinions on Bolsheviks and anyone who quotes them without spitting. But over the next couple of minutes, I proved the old revolutionary right as I sought to explain to the cop why I had so uncharacteristically jumped into a fistfight that was none of my business. I told him the gist of Mo's and my disagreement at the lake, then a little bit about the Ginger Goodwin thing, and then I wrapped all of that into an explanation of my not wanting to disappoint the woman I loved by standing there while a guy I didn't care for at all — Davey Clemmer — got knocked around, and another guy I liked but hardly knew — Benny, that is — got hurt trying to stop it.

Mikhailovsky made only a couple of notes throughout the entire saga. When I'd finished, he said, "This Clemmer, what do you know about him?"

I didn't have enough information to give a useful answer, but I had enough impressions and opinions to give a long one. At some point, Mikhailovsky put up his hands to stem the flow of words, and said, "Do you know where we can find him?"

"He's staying at Benny's."

"Not any more. He left late last night. No forwarding address."

There was nothing I could say.

"If you run into him again, you might let us know."

"I will."

Then we were off on another tangent. The Mountie looked at another piece of paper on his desk. "What is the nature of your relationship with Dodd and Colin Ketterich, also known as Trick and Butch?"

I thought about the thousand dollars the dope growers had put in my hand. It was sitting in an envelope in my desk drawer together with Rod Bilder's so-sorry money and Benny Filiatrault's advance payment. Together it totalled thirty-two hundred dollars.

It had occurred to me that none of them was ever likely to declare me as an expense on a tax form. If I didn't put it into a bank account, it would be untraceable. It was my first participation in the grey economy, the world of cash under the table that is not usually available to people like me, who got most of their income in the form of cheques signed by some corporate bean counter.

Mikhailovsky was patiently waiting for an answer to his question about the Ketteriches. I wondered if he was drawing as much information from my delay in responding as he would from what I was about to say. Which was, "I don't think I have a relationship with them. I hardly know them."

The Mountie glanced at a piece of paper on his desk. I knew he was just doing it for effect. He would no more require written notes in an interrogation than Horace Rumpole would need *Bartlett's Familiar Quotations* to toss out a line from Wordsworth. "Constable Tonn reports seeing you and Trick Ketterich engaged in a conversation right after the altercation on Dunsmuir Avenue."

"Ketterich broke up the fight. I didn't know who he was, just some guy in a funny truck who thought he was Rocky Balboa."

"He intervened in the same spirit of altruism that prompted you to protect Mr. Filiatrault?"

Objection, calls for speculation, my counsel would have said, if I'd had one and if this had been a court of law, instead of a friendly chat with the local heat. I fell back on the standard reply I'd learned as a working-class teenager faced with police queries. "I don't know," I said.

"Somebody also thought you might have taken a ride with the two of them, out into the woods," he said.

"People think the strangest things," I said.

That got me thirty seconds of the inquisitive eyeball, then without any segue we jumped over to the note with the cut-out letters I'd seen on Rod Bilder's desk. I repeated what I'd told the corporal the night before. He probed for more details, but there were none.

We jumped again. "Why did you assume Rod Bilder had had a stroke?"

"He was taking Enalapril. That's a medicine for high blood pressure. And he acted like a guy who would have a cranial geyser ready to pop."

"How do you know what Enalapril is prescribed for?"

"My old man took it."

Only ten seconds of eyeball this time, then we were heading down yet another passage in the labyrinth. "You left last night's meeting with Sally McMahon, the dead man's estranged wife."

I told him about the old shoulder injury, and Sally's offer to treat it with ultrasound. Then I had to explain about Sally and Mo and the museum exhibit on women's work. He listened patiently and made a couple of more notes, then asked me what I knew of the business arrangements between Sally and Bilder.

"Nothing," I said, then thought about it. Mo had mentioned something when she'd promoted me to Rod through Sally. The cop watched me thinking, then said, "Well?"

It was a vague. I hadn't paid much attention when Mo had talked about it. "My girlfriend told me something a few weeks ago. Before he died, Sally's husband and Bilder had a company, and they were going to develop that land, the woods where the logger got killed."

Mikhailovsky made a note. "Yes?"

"Even after the man died, the deal was still going ahead. Something about there being two kinds of shares in the company — A and B shares, where only A shares could vote. They had equal shares, but Bilder had more of the A's and Sally had mainly B's, so she got half the profits, but no say in what the company did. Mo said they had lawyers talking about it, then Sally dropped it."

The Mountie made another note. "What about other investors in Mr. Bilder's company? Know anything about that?"

"I heard gossip that those Ketterich guys were backing him."

"Heard it where?"

"I don't know. Just around Cumberland."

"Do you use marijuana?"

That came out of the blue. "Not since I was in school," I said. "It used to fuzz me up too much. I like to know what I'm thinking."

"Uh huh," he said, and closed the file on his desk. "Thank you for coming in, Mr. Rafferty."

I wanted to be out of there, but I didn't move. "Wait a sec," I said. "Is there something going on that I should know about?"

"I don't know," he said, his eyes on the closed file. "What kind of thing might that be?"

"I'm starting to wonder," I said, because I was. "I mean, I happened to be there when Haglund was killed, okay, but it was just a coincidence. And then Bilder has a stroke, and I find him. But that was just a coincidence, too."

He said nothing, didn't look at me. *Dammit*, I thought, *he's playing me and I'm flopping around like a fish on a line.* But I couldn't be coy and cagey; you do that when you've got something to hide — but I had nothing to cover up, just a growing creepy-crawly sense that I was in the middle of some kind of trouble, but I couldn't see just what kind of trouble it was.

"Am I suspected of something?"

He looked at me now. "And what might you be suspected of?"

"I don't know. Nothing," I said. "But you're filing reports on who I talk to and who I leave meetings with."

"Whom," he corrected.

"I know the difference," I said.

"Good," he said.

I waited. "So?"

He didn't answer. Instead, in that annoying cop way, he asked another question.

"When Mr. Haglund was killed, you were waiting for Mr. Bilder?"

"Yes."

"He didn't show up?"

"That's right."

"Why not?"

"I don't know. I just assumed he was late. People get behind schedule sometimes."

"Still, he wasted a portion of your day. Did he apologize afterwards, offer any explanation?"

"No, he just gave me money."

"And you didn't ask?"

"He looked to have enough troubles, the next time I saw him."

"Thank you for coming in," he said again.

I didn't like being in the room with him. But I couldn't leave yet. "I asked you if I was suspected of something."

"I know you did."

"Well?"

He said nothing.

"Look," I said. "I want to know what's going on. If you

don't want to answer me, I'll see about getting somebody to ask the questions for me, somebody you'll have to give an answer to."

He smiled at me. It was the first time I'd seen anything on him but the Great Stone Face of Mountiehood. It was an oddly pleasant smile. "That's a bluff," he said. Then he went back to the granite jaw. "Nobody can make an RCMP officer divulge information about an ongoing murder investigation."

Ding! went the bell in the back of my head. "You said Haglund's death was probable manslaughter," I said.

"Did I?"

"Yes."

He smiled a second time. "People underestimate you a lot, don't they?"

"Never mind that," I said. "Does this mean Bilder didn't die of a stroke?"

He opened the file again and looked at a piece of paper. "The autopsy was this morning. The coroner's report will be filed this afternoon, and it will be in the papers tomorrow."

"So tell me now."

He shrugged, the first human gesture I'd seen him make. "Mr. Bilder did not have a stroke. He died of prolonged anoxia. Do you know what that is?"

"Lack of oxygen to the brain."

"Right."

"He wasn't strangled," I said. "There was no bruising, no marks at all."

"Still," said the corporal, "he died from lack of oxygen, which meant something stopped his breathing. *Somebody* stopped his breathing. Somehow."

"You don't think it was me?"

He gave me a few more seconds of the cop stare. "No, I don't," he said, and closed the file again. "Now, thank you for coming in."

Mo got back sometime after three in the afternoon. I had spent the time since lunch staring at the monitor screen, my Ginger Goodwin *Notes* file no fatter than it had been when Mikhailovsky had interrupted me. Whatever might have been about to erupt past the doom-criers that populated my inner spaces had sunk back down into the depths, and all my hopeful fishing for it had brought up nothing.

I'd sat, I'd stretched, I'd gotten up and walked around. I'd tried forcing a few words out. I'd tried random typing, filling the screen with letters and punctuation marks — I'd read somewhere that blocked writers could lubricate the literary pump just by moving their fingers in the familiar motions. I might as well have sacrificed a goat and danced around widdershins. Nothing was coming.

"Working on the script?" Mo asked when she saw me hunched over the keyboard. "How's it coming?"

"Fine," I said.

"Can I see?" I heard her footsteps coming up behind me.

"Not yet." I saved the file and switched off the computer.

"Are you concentrating on the Judas angle?"

"Yes," I said. "Very promising. Irony and pity, you know."

"Great," she said. "Well, I'm finally finished with Elk Falls, so I'm going to get into this full time for a while. When do you think you'll have something we could show around?"

"I don't know. I've got to go down to Alberni about that job, and there's still some stuff to do for Benny Filiatrault."

She shrugged and tossed her head just slightly. For the umpteenth time, I wished I could have known her through all those years when we had been strangers who didn't know that we were swimming inexorably toward each other. I would have liked to have had the full experience of her: to have sat behind her in school, too shy to do more than pull a pigtail; to have danced with her at sock hops; to have fumbled under her blouse in the darkness of the movie theatre while James Bond suavely lit a cigarette; to have been her first lover; to have married her when we were both little more than kids and then to have grown into middle age together, our lives twining into one inextricable twinning.

Instead, she had burst into my life like sunlight flooding a sombre room, late but not too late. She had lifted me out of the ruins of my hopes and become the new focus of my life. I'd seen TV commercials that were shot in washed-out black and white, but with the product — fruit juice or something — colourized to stand out, golden against the shades of grey. That was Mo to me. She was an ember glowing in a bed of ashes, warmth and light amid the flyaway flakes.

Her smile still lit up the room. She opened her PowerBook and brought it to life. "Okay," she said. "Give me Roger Gambowsky's number and that agent. I'll call them while you're away, get things rolling."

I dug them out for her, and she entered them in her address file. "This is going to be so great," she said. "You and me."

"Oh, yeah," I said. "So great."

Chapter 9

I tuned in the last hour of Peter Gzowski's *Morningside* show on CBC radio as I rattled down the old coast-hugging Island Highway. He had on some cultural maven from central Canada, and they were asking listeners to write or phone in with their suggestions for the quintessentially Canadian song of all time.

"*Summer Wages,*" I told the slotted grill in the Behemoth's dashboard from which Gzowski's quintessentially Canadian voice spilled. "By Ian Tyson."

The maven talked about *Un Canadien Errant,* as I might have expected, and *Rise Again,* a nice little song about a sunken Maritime fishing boat. Typically, there was no mention of anything originating west of the southern Ontario heartland, that small enclave that had welcomed the original United Empire Loyalists. By the CBC's unofficial definition, only that narrow realm was authentically Canada, and every other part of the country was attached to it as merely a "region."

But for my money, Canada was a lot bigger than any latte-sipping Yonge Street-wandering Hogtowner could get his head around. And nobody could beat Tyson the cowboy poet for capturing the soul of a run-of-the-mill, salt-of-the-earth, Western Canadian working man. *Summer Wages* was his best. It was the lament of a sadder but wiser guy, after he's gambled away his money and his woman, and faces going back to crewing a coastal tow-boat wearing his slick-soled city shoes. The words, simple and almost monosyllabic, laid bare all the melancholy fatalism that is so often to be found in a lunch-bucket or an hourly pay-packet.

"In a decent country," I told Gzowski, "they'd name large buildings and significant geographical features after the likes of Ian Tyson, while the Rita McNeills would be lying on their living room couches, reading chunky novels with Fabio on the cover." Instead, McNeill inexplicably had her own weekly hour of television, and it was a rare day I heard an Ian Tyson song on the radio — unless it was Neil Young and Emmy Lou Harris doing that interesting old version of *Four Strong Winds* .

But Gzowski wasn't listening to me, so I punched the button for a Vancouver oldies station, and got the Four Seasons singing *Walk Like a Man* — the latest stone-age rock and roll single whose title had been grabbed for a totally forgettable Howie Mandel movie.

"I should start a betting pool," I said to the tailgate of the pick-up truck I was following through the seaside village of Union Bay, where the ancient hulks of captured warships and square-rigged sailing barks made a breakwater for the long-demolished coaling pier. "Everybody puts in a dollar and picks a Top 40 single from between 1955 and 1970. The one who holds the name of the very last baby-boomer hit that's used in a movie or TV commercial wins the pot."

I would have put my money on Crazy Arthur Brown bellowing *I am the God of Hell Fire* in his echo chamber, but it was probably already slotted for an antacid spot.

A few hundred metres offshore, a Vancouver Island legend floated above Mac's oyster beds. Fore and aft anchors kept the pale blue *Samarkanda* from joining the outflowing tide. The long, low ship with its knife-sharp bow had begun life in Portland, Oregon, in 1945, built to lay anti-submarine nets for the U.S. Navy. By the 1960s, retired from military service, it was a Panamanian registered coastal freighter. And it was flying that flag in 1979, when it entered local history.

The *Samarkanda* was at the forested head of Sydney Inlet in Clayoquot Sound, where the long rollers come in off the Pacific Ocean. The crew was unloading hundreds of bales of cargo when an RCMP task force swooped in to seize the ship, its crew and 33.5 tonnes of prime Colombian marijuana neatly stacked on the beach.

The dope went up in smoke in North Cowichan's municipal incinerator, while shotgun-toting members of the Mounties' SWAT team stood guard. The ship was sold at a Customs and Excise auction. And, ironically, the weed smugglers went on to make legal history.

At the trial in Victoria, their lawyers argued that they had never meant to land their marijuana in Canada. The cargo had been intended to meet the needs of Alaska's many pot puffers. But rough seas had forced the pharmaceutical entrepreneurs to seek shelter in Sydney Inlet, where they ran aground and had to offload cargo to lighten the ship. It was not known whether it was the lawyers' skilful arguments or the sheer chutzpah of the defence that led the judge to accept that the accused had landed $56 million worth of wacky tobacky out of sheer necessity, and — necessity being a cogent legal defence — to acquit them all.

The crew's lawyers could have tried another defence: that bringing marijuana to Vancouver Island made as much economic sense as bringing coal to Cumberland during the heyday of the Dunsmuir mines. The Island was not an import market for dope; it was where some of the highest-grade, most sought after cannabis was grown, and from where it was shipped to the rest of Canada and down into the States. Weed Connoisseurs all over the world praised its potency .

I'd read about it not too long ago in a three-part series that ran in the Victoria *Times Colonist*. It said the weed I remembered using back in the Sixties, supposedly dynamite strains like Acapulco Gold, Panama Red and Maui Wowee, contained anywhere from one to three per cent of the psychoactive chemical THC. The stuff growing in the perfect climate of Vancouver Island topped the potency charts with a THC load of thirty per cent.

Based on a retail value of a grand per mature plant, the cops estimated the total value of British Columbia's annual marijuana crop at a cool billion dollars. That was half again the combined worth of all the tree fruits, berries and vegetables grown between the Rocky Mountains and the Pacific Ocean.

For the folk who cheerfully planted and reaped this bonanza, the proceeds were not only tax-free but almost completely without risk. Growers picked remote patches of Crown land, places that got enough sun and had reliable water supplies. They'd go in in April, plant the seeds, and then not come back until the plants were ready to harvest in the summer.

The police flew around in helicopters, from time to time, looking for the tell-tale bright green of ripening marijuana, and occasionally they found a few score plants. But, unless they happened upon them just as the harvesters were at work — and somehow too occupied to notice a police copter — all they could do was pull the crop up by the roots and fly it off to the incinerator.

And even if the growers were dumb enough to get caught, the worst that would happen would be a little fine and a stern wrinkling of the brow from a provincial court judge. To my knowledge, there hadn't been a cultivation bust in the four years I'd lived in the Comox Valley, and the only case I'd heard of — a guy with a few dozen plants on his own land somewhere down Island — had earned the grower a five hundred dollar slap on the wrist.

No wonder the Ketteriches were pissed off. Growing dope on Vancouver Island was about as profitable as owning a chartered bank. I knew how bankers felt about people who made unauthorized withdrawals. I was willing to bet that Butch and Trick could be just as indignant.

The *Samarkanda* dropped out of sight as the road moved inland. I rolled on past the Fanny Bay Inn, which I'd heard had just been named number one in some poll of the best pubs on the Island, and once again made myself an instantly forgotten promise to stop in some day for a pint. I did the same thing as I passed the *Brico*, the old telephone cable-laying ship that had been converted into a roadside seafood restaurant.

Then it was down the twisty, dangerous two-lane black-top, lined with nodes of tourist motels and retirement cottages, and suffering the usual summer constipation caused by motorhomes towing little cars at ten klicks below the posted speed limit, which alternated between sixty and eighty every few minutes. I passed through Bowser then came down into Qualicum Beach, beloved haunt of sand-castle builders and topless sunbathers. Nestled in an un-ending line of tourists, I chugged along the beachfront at under fifty — which the Behemoth's American speedom-eter translated into the grand speed of twenty-eight miles per hour.

As Qualicum's long, smooth beach petered out beside me, I swung west at the junction with Highway 4 and began the steady climb inland. The farms and woodlots around the little village of Coombs soon gave way to more serious second-growth stands. Fifteen minutes later, I was easing the big old Ford around the edge of ice-cold Cameron Lake, the road looping in and out, as if it were tracing the edges of pieces from a giant jigsaw puzzle. Overhangs of rock bulged above me on the left and deep green water lay patiently to my right. Local legend said the lake was bottomless, which meant it was deep enough that nobody would dive down to recover the drowned contents of any large automobile that took a curve too fast and briefly broke the smooth, mountain-reflecting surface.

Past the lake, I encountered the usual clutch of tour buses and recreation vehicles jamming the narrow road that passed though MacMillan Provincial Park. I'd never heard anybody refer to the park by that official name, which commemorated the old lumber baron who had dedicated a small patch of old growth in perpetuity. Instead, it was always known as Cathedral Grove, for the immense, ancient Douglas firs and spruces that loomed over the groups of pastel-clad Japanese tourists huddling together on the carefully manicured trails. They pointed their Nikons skyward, as if at any moment they expected to snap a candid of Godzilla pushing aside the needled canopy, doing his extenuated elephant call, way up there.

Greenies worshipped Cathedral Grove — sometimes literally. It was everything they wanted in an old-growth temperate rain forest: big trees with thick coats of moss, a springy carpet of mulch underfoot, and — once you tuned out the tourists — lots of solemn quiet. It was the romantic city-dweller's image of nature at its most sublime.

But any forester could have told them the main reason it was so still among the towering stalks was that there was precious little for animals to eat in a decadent, over mature stand of timber. Most of the living greenery was fifty metres above the ground, where it would stay until a once-in-fifty-years hurricane finally barreled in from the Pacific and slapped the big old trees down flat. Until then, not enough sunlight would reach the surface to grow the forage that deer need, or the berries that draw bears.*

A forester had made it clear to me one day, during my short stint as a public relations staffer for WestCan Forest Products in the early eighties. My first week, the old newspaper buddy who headed up the department, and who had given me the staff writer's job, sent me out to all of the company's mills and operation zones, to get a look at how trees were turned into useful products like newsprint, two-by-fours and shareholder dividends.

"Catch a ride on the Goose," he said, "and spend a morning with Tony Elberson at Sproat Lake. He doesn't bite people who ask him dumb questions."

The Goose was the company's almost antique Grumman flying boat, which could deploy wheels to land on a runway. That day, we didn't need the wheels: we dropped down over the pass that newcomers to Port Alberni soon learn to call The Hump, dodged the plume of smoke from the pulp mill, then slid past the town and on to the shore of Sproat Lake, a long, crooked finger of water that starts just above Alberni and stretches west for fifty kilometres. WestCan had cutting rights to a lot of Crown-owned timber adjacent to the MacMillan Bloedel tenure at the southwest end of the lake.

I'd lived on the B.C. coast most of my life, but like most British Columbians, I'd done that living in modern cities or well set up small towns. I had never been out in the really wild lands, the places that supported the resource industries that in turn carried the provincial economy. I'd seen what I took to be the original forests, like those on the steep mountains across Burrard Inlet from the steel and glass boxes in downtown Vancouver. But those thick, green slopes that Vancouverites are so proud of are nothing but second-growth, though they're wild enough to swallow and digest a few naive hikers every year. The real old stuff was cut down before the twentieth century dawned and carried away, to make masts for sailing ships and roof beams for houses from San Francisco to Peking.

It wasn't until I flew out to Sproat Lake that I learned what a real old-growth forest looks like, and what logging does to it. The Goose came in from the northeast, over the Martin Mars water bomber base, two of the big planes riding at anchor, the third up on shore for the mechanics to get at, then banked a little to the left before the long pull across the tranquil water and a shuddering glide that ended in a gentle touchdown.

We taxied to the WestCan wharf. The grey-haired pilot cut the engines and gestured to the door with his thumb. I got out, legs a little shaky after bouncing around in the air pockets between here and Vancouver International Airport, and looked around.

The western horizon was about forty degrees up and maybe fifteen kilometres away, a saddleback ridge thickly packed with big timber. But between the edge of the sky and the shore of the lake, there was scarcely a vertical line to be seen. All the trees that had once stood on the slopes running up to that ridge were down.

Some of them were in the water, chained into long, skinny booms that would be towed to the mills in Port Alberni, where the best timber would be cut into lumber and the worst processed into pulp, with both products being shipped from the town's deep sea docks. Some were stacked on shore, waiting to be sorted and graded, or to be trucked to other WestCan mills.

But a lot of what had been standing timber was now lying down in the most godawful vista of mass destruction I'd ever seen. The clearcut stretched almost as far as I could see in every direction except the lake behind me. It looked like there'd been a battle, and the trees had lost.

"Man," I said, "that is one hell of a fucking mess."

"Oh, Christ," said a voice beside me, "why do they always send them to me?"

He was tall, blond and blue-eyed, loose-limbed and gangly, and his jeans, boots and checked shirt make him look like some kind of Swedish cowboy. "Are you Rafferty?" he said.

I admitted I was, and he told me he was Tony Elberson, WestCan's chief forester. "First time seeing a clearcut up close, huh?" he said, looking at me, not at the debris field I was gawking at.

"Uh huh."

"Big mess, right?"

"Right."

He rocked on his heels and looked out over the lake. "Ever seen a baby get born?"

I nodded. I had been there for the twins' debut.

"That's pretty messy, too, wouldn't you say?"

I would. I did.

He continued to watch the water ripple its way to the dock. "But you don't expect it to stay that way, do you? All bloody and covered in...yick?"

He was talking to a speechwriter. I knew arguments that relied on analogies were inherently weak: sure, A may be like B, but A also has to be *unlike* B, otherwise it would *be* B. I pushed him back to the here and now. "But this is pretty radical deforestation," I said. "I mean, every damn tree has been cut down, and it looks like half of them are smashed up and just left there to rot on the ground."

He came around real fast. I had obviously trod on a toe that had been stepped on before. "This is not *de*forestation. The street you live on is deforestation. The fields that grow your corn flakes, *that's* deforestation. That's land that used to be forest, but it's never going to grow trees again, because you'll mow down any seedling that pops up among the special hybrid grass you call a lawn, and Old MacDonald's going to plough and harrow the soil once he gets his crop in."

He waved his arm to take in the scene of destruction that ran down to the shore. "You see the little green things sticking out of the ground all over the place?"

I saw them, a lot of them once I started to look. "Baby trees?" I said.

"Since you're now in the business, you should call them seedlings. We plant two of them for every one we cut down."

In those days, I liked to argue. "Okay, but are they natural? I mean, the original forest, nobody planted that. How is this the same thing?"

It turned out Elberson liked to argue just as much as I did. And why wouldn't he? He had all the facts, while I had only impressions and city-boy notions.

"At least now you've got a half-assed point," he said. "That is to say, you're half-right. This place wouldn't green up so fast with original species if we just left it to nature. You'd get a lot of alder and maple — weed trees, we call them — and they'd dominate for years, until the spruce and fir got tall enough to regain control. But eventually, the land would grow the same species we cut down."

"How do you know?"

"Cause that's what it's been growing since the glaciers melted. Listen, you want to see unnatural forests, go to Sweden, where they grow imported Scotch pine. Go to New Zealand — it's all radiata pine from California, totally unnatural. Here, we only plant what would grow naturally if we kept to nature's timetable. We just hurry it up a little."

He told me the mess I was looking at was a forest; I couldn't see it as a forest because I was looking at the earliest phase. "Come back in a few years," he said, "it will be greened up with waist-high saplings. Send your grandkids here in fifty years, there'll be big trees all over the place. They'd have to look pretty damned hard to find any evidence this land was ever cut over.

"You could no more deforest British Columbia than you could make it stop raining," he said. "The trees will always grow back. Fire won't stop them. Volcanoes and hurricanes won't stop them. A billion weevils and borers and bark beetles won't stop them. A hundred-thousand-year ice age won't stop them. They *own* this place. They are the dominant life form. All we do is give fireweed and blackberries and salmonberries an interregnum for a few years, to feed the bears and the deer. But then the trees come up and take it back again."

I thought about Elberson as I came down Johnston Street into Port Alberni, the precipitous grades and tight turns of The Hump safely behind me, and passed the company's boarded-up plywood mill down by the Somass River at the east end of town. I turned onto Third Avenue at the lights and headed out toward the big MacMillan Bloedel pulp mill, which roofed half the town with its smoke plume and — back in the bad old days — used to coat every outdoor surface with tiny flakes of white ash .

The site of the old ivy-clad Barclay Hotel on Stamp Avenue was now a Mohawk station and a rent-a-car booth. The new one was at Third and Redford. Its facade was mostly unpainted grey concrete, a continuation of that stark neo-fascist vogue that Arthur Erickson had started with his design for Simon Fraser University in the mid 1960s. I had once spent an afternoon, on behalf of the student paper, punningly named The Peak, in a search of the entire mountain-top campus. I'd been looking for a curved line. When I finally found one — the only one — I didn't write about it; I figured it had to be an oversight, and if I told the world about its existence, someone would come and get rid of it.

SFU had come to mind because that's where the Hon. Lanc Halfnight and I had begun our desultory friend-ship, back in 1969. He didn't look much different when I found him in the sports-oriented lounge of the new Barclay Hotel. A little jowlier, perhaps, and the sandy hair thinning, but he's always been one of those red-faced, pop-eyed British types who look much the same at fifty as at twenty, and I had no trouble spotting him when I came in the door from the lobby.

He put down an almost empty pint glass of something dark. "Good god," he said. "It lives."

"If you want to call this living," I said. And we shook hands in his reserved Anglo way, then summoned the waitress to bring us pints, Guinness for him and Shaftebury cream ale for me. When they were in our hands, we toasted each other.

I wiped the foam from my upper lip, and said, "Well."

He said, "Well, indeed. No beating around the herbal configuration, my old proletarian consort. I am prepared to offer you employment."

"Are you just?" I said. "Swinking in t'pit for tuppence-ha'penny and all the forelock-tugging I can take?"

He looked at me over the rim of his glass, supped a good measure of the inky liquid, then said. "We'll pay you five hundred a day."

The offer meant that fun time was abruptly over. He was ringing two kinds of bells inside my head. One was my come-and-get-it signal — five hundred a day was good money, especially when the number of days was left indefinite. But the offer also set off my watch-it alarm: when they hold out the money before they tell you what you have to do for it, you'd better be prepared for a serious good news, bad news conundrum. Especially, when Half-night hadn't even told me who exactly were the we who wanted to buy my services.

"It sounds interesting, which I always like," I said, stepping carefully. "Also mysterious, which always worries me. And, judging from your reluctance to talk on the phone or to meet in your office — wherever that is — it also comes across as possibly dangerous or illegal, or both."

He moved his mouth in a way that was equivalent to a shrug. I noticed that he had grown a couple of lines that sloped down from the corners of his lips. Somehow it made his mouth look both soft and hard at once.

"So what do you want me to do?" I said.

He smiled. It was not the old smile I remembered. "A bit of spying," he said. "Watch the little green folk for us."

"Little green folk?"

"Those people who are making all the fuss about Clayoquot Sound ."

Chapter 10

The anti-logging campaign at Clayoquot Sound in the summer of 1993 was the largest incidence of mass disobedience in Canadian history, according to the protesters. I was willing to bet the Winnipeg General Strike of 1919 might have outclassed it for the numbers of people involved — not to mention the fact a few of the strikers were shot dead by troops, while the worst the Clayoquot road-blockers faced was a video camera on the shoulders of a guy from the MacMillan Bloedel PR department and a special detachment of polite Mounties who carried them off to the community recreational hall in the coastal village of Ucluelet.

There, their particulars were taken down and they were released. The RCMP advised the arrestees in due time they would be summoned before a judge in Victoria who would be less than pleased they had chosen to ignore his injunction not to block the logging road at Kennedy Lake. The flouting of the judge's order being "open, continuous and flagrant," the protesters would have to answer for criminal, not civil, contempt of court.

The road blocks had been going on since early July, and by time they were finished three months later, more than 850 people — hippies and housewives, grannies and mystics, artists and academics — had been hauled off to Ucluelet to have their names put on the honour roll.

Celebrities of various kinds came and went: Bobby Kennedy Jr. flew in with his media hype machine at full roar; an Australian rock group threw a free rock concert in the woods; old-timey California activist Tom Hayden married a British Columbia-born movie star on the beach near Tofino, promising to love, honour and preserve each other and Clayoquot Sound. The federal NDP's loosest cannon, Svend Robinson, MP, stood with the blockaders on the opening day of the campaign, but was not charged until someone figured out that there was no reason why he shouldn't get the same treatment as the rank and file.

But all the other celebs — including the core of organizers who spoke to the media before and after each day's mass arrests — made sure they were never at risk of getting to see the inside of the Ucluelet rec centre. They made their practised noises at the cameras, but when the little people were being hauled off the road and into the system, the international green lobby's elite members were already setting up their next photo op. At least I could content myself with knowing I wouldn't be the only cynic to have dropped into Clayoquot Sound in the summer of 1993.

Of course I was going in, though I didn't jump at the bait quite as quickly as Lanc and his friends thought I might. For a start, I wanted to know just who those friends might be and why they were waving lots of money at me.

"Who are you fronting for?" I asked. "The Forest Alliance? The SHARE groups?" The Alliance was supposed to be a broad-spectrum lobby of industry reps, scientific types and community activists from towns that depended on the forest resource, but it had been put together by one of the world's most high-powered public-relations firms, Burston Marsteller, and its entire budget arrived in the form of cheques that bore the names of major forest companies.

The SHARE groups were a chain of grassroots citizens' organizations from small forest-dependent communities out in the boonies. Their members were mostly laid-off loggers and the small-business people who sold them groceries and four-by-fours. They had looked down the road past a shrinking Annual Allowable Cut, past more and more forest land being turned into parks and preserves, past tighter restrictions on the forest industry mostly, past more anti-logging protests and boycotts,and they had seem themselves standing in modern ghost towns.

The Alliance tended toward professionally written brochures and newspaper ads to counter those of the protesters. The SHARE folks wanted to show up wherever the protesters were and take them on, one way or the other.

"Whom," Halfnight said.

"Yeah, and ee-by-gum to you an' all," I said. "Now, for whom are you fronting?"

"Not the Alliance. Not SHARE," he said.

"Half an answer is not better than none," I said. "It is the same as none."

He looked around the mostly empty pub. It had been designed as a place where mill workers would feel comfortable arguing about disputed hockey goals and the merits of various front lines. This time of day, there was nobody there who looked as if he might be doing counter-espionage for Greenpeace.

Still, Halfnight lowered his voice. "I represent a corporate interest."

"A forest company?"

He shook his head. "A business that is somewhat forestry dependent," he said. "And which is well able to afford substantial consulting fees."

He probably expected me to be content with that non-answer and its accompanying wave of the money wand. I said nothing, letting him think I was considering the offer. Instead, I was backtracking over what I knew of The Honourable Lanc Halfnight's career, looking for pieces I could fit together.

He had stayed on to complete his degree at Simon Fraser University while I dropped out to work at a succession of low-paying weekly newspaper jobs. After two years of working my way up from part-timer to full-time reporter to news editor, I was offered a chance to edit a newly founded weekly in Port Alberni.

In those days, I hadn't yet learned to ask key questions of prospective employers: questions such as, how the hell do you expect me to write all the editorial copy and take all the pictures required to fill twenty-eight to thirty-six tabloid pages, every week? The owners, a pair of local businessmen who were not widely experienced in the news business, thought that one guy ought to be able to handle it all. I'd been so in love with the idea of being an honest-to-god newspaper editor — with the business cards to prove it — that I'd actually stuck it out for three horrendous weeks before reality struck, in the form of complete exhaustion.

So, as the third edition went to press — printed on contract by the Green Sheet, up in Courtenay — I informed my employers that they could either get me a reporter and a photographer or they could roll their paper into a tight tube and file it where their grannies would never find it. Surprisingly, they didn't quibble.

Their lack of resistance should have been a clue: getting more money out of weekly newspaper publishers is usually only slightly less difficult than extracting a grizzly bear's teeth without anaesthetic. But I put my success down to the overwhelming force of my personality.

I called up a local camera enthusiast who had dropped by to show me his portfolio and negotiated a retainer and per-shot agreement. Then I phoned Lanc Halfnight in Vancouver and asked him if he wanted a job. He came over on the early ferry the next morning, the ink on his degree still damp, and we started putting out what, we thought, was a pretty good community weekly.

The paper stayed in business almost an entire year, then the whole jury-rigged, jerry-built facade came tumbling down. When I thought about it later, I was surprised my so-called publishers had been able to keep all the balls in the air for so long. There must have been times when they were running on nothing but financial fumes.

I didn't know it when I signed on, but the tabloid was only meant to last three or four months, six at the most. It had been nothing but a scam from its conception. The two entrepreneurs who signed my paycheques — they bounced a couple of times, which should have been a clue — launched the paper with the expectation that they would soon sell out at a good profit. Their plan depended on their becoming a bit of grit in the far-seeing eye of the most powerful new figure to burst into the Canadian news biz since Roy Thomson.

Their target was Conrad Black, who at the time was adding small-town newspapers to his growing Stirling Ventures chain almost as fast as Imelda Marcos was filling her closets with shoes. Canada's budding newspaper tycoon was said to be using the appendix to Senator Keith Davie's report on Canadian media ownership as a shopping list, running his manicured finger down the roster of independently owned dailies, and putting check marks beside those that were good candidates for *the treatment.*

The treatment consisted of phoning the owner of a targeted paper and offering a good price for the operation, cash on the barrel head. If the owner said no, a few weeks would go by, then the phone would ring again, and one of Conrad Black's acquisitors would be back with an even better price. The treatment would be repeated as often as necessary, the offer rising higher and higher, until the answer was finally yes.

Like many small towns, Port Alberni had its own independent. The *Alberni Valley Times,* a metro-sized paper that printed five days a week, had been a fixture in the area for decades, dominating its small market and chugging along nicely under the ownership of a competent publisher. Then one day, the phone rang, and the owner received an offer to sell to the Sterling syndicate. He'd said "no thanks," and the treatment began.

Very often, events that transpire inside a newspaper owner's private office — though it be only scant metres from a newsroom full of reporters — never seem to make it into public print. I've known politicians who would sell whatever was left of their souls for the kind of immunity from media scrutiny that publishers accept as their birthright. So Conrad Black's wooing of the *AV Times's* owner should have been a strictly private seduction. But trying to keep a secret in a small town can be like trying to keep water in a sieve.

It might have been a secretary who liked to gossip about what she overheard at the office. Or maybe it was a waitress at the Beaufort Hotel who tuned in on diners' conversations. One way or the other, the news that *the treatment* was being applied to the owner of the local daily stole into the receptive ears of two men who digested its meaning, and came to the conclusion here was a way to make some money.

They set about giving the impression they were starting up a newspaper. It wasn't hard: they just rented a cramped and uncomfortable office, bought a few used typewriters and desks, leased some computerized typesetting equipment and made a deal with the owner of the nearest printing press. Then they hired somebody who knew enough about reporting and editing to produce those twenty-eight to thirty-six pages.

It was particularly easy because the pseudo-publishers never intended the paper to come even close to breaking even. Circulation wasn't an issue: the paper was distributed free to every household and business in town. That would have automatically made the tabloid attractive to advertisers, but the two hustlers deepened the attraction considerably by setting their advertising rates at bargain basement levels. They quickly creamed off the ad budgets of the local retailers, and pumped out a fat little weekly — chock full of high school sports pix, gardening tips and coverage of the municipal council meeting — that was bound to cause genuine problems for an established daily that had to make a profit in the same market.

Of course, it meant the hustlers had to reach into their own pockets every month for the couple of thousand dollars their imitation paper was losing. But that didn't matter, because the whole intent of the venture was just to put a wrinkle in the on-going seduction of the *AV Times*. When the owner of the daily finally said yes, Conrad Black would just have to reach a little deeper into his suitcase full of money and buy up the annoying weekly too — debts and all, with any luck — and shut it down.

Nothing about the deal ever appeared in print, of course, but eventually the *AV Times* changed hands. And, at the same time, the plucky little tabloid was also acquired by new owners, and summarily ceased to publish.

I wasn't there to see it happen. After six months, I had moved on to a job on a real paper, the *Vancouver Sun*. Lanc had taken over my corner desk at the tabloid — I'd never had an actual office — and the title of editor. When the tab died, Halfnight had not suffered, however; a reporter's job came open at the daily. He signed on, and eventually rose to be its managing editor.

By then, I was in Ottawa, newly assigned to the Parliamentary bureau of the *FP* chain. Lanc and I had lost touch. At some point I heard, the way you always hear things in the small professional community that is B.C. journalism, that he had gone to Australia.

Now he was obviously back, and I thought I could trace where his movements had led him. "Conrad Black owns some newspapers in Australia, doesn't he?" I said.

Halfnight did a good dead pan. Too good. "I believe he does," he said, and sipped his Guinness.

"Which is where you've been lately."

"You always had that remarkable ear for accents. True, my once beautifully former plummy vowels were somewhat flattened during my extended stay in the Antipodes. Better that than to have my nose given the same treatment. Australians do not care for English mannerisms, especially from those blessed with inherited rank."

"Back to the point," I said. "Are you working for Hollinger?" Hollinger Inc. was the corporate vehicle in which all of Conrad Black's assets rode .

Halfnight gave me his blandest look. "I am not at liberty to say." He drained another inch of stout from his glass. "Does it matter?"

Ultimately, it didn't. I had written for every sort of client, from the presidents of ultra-respectable public utilities to the scam artists of the Vancouver Stock Exchange. What counted most was whether the cheque cleared.

"What exactly do you want me to do?"

Over the next five minutes, he told me. Then he gave me a cell phone; "Strictly for emergencies," he said. He also gave me a cheque for thirty-five hundred dollars. "Your first week's fee," he said.

I looked at it. It was a standard business account cheque, with my name and his signature on it, drawn on a Vancouver bank. But where the name of the company to which the account belonged should have been, there was only the initials *BC*, followed by a string of numbers, and the word *Limited.*

"I'm working for a numbered company?" I said. Normally, numbered corporations were shell companies, temporarily incorporated to hold assets — like stocks or real estate — whose ownership was changing hands.

"It seemed best," he said. "That way, if you're asked, you can't tell. No names, no blames."

Something about it made me uncomfortable. "For all I know, I could be working for the Iranian secret police."

He finished his pint, and said, "I'm sure you would

exercise the same professionalism for them as you will for us."

There were still a few things I wanted to know. "How did you decide to offer me this job? How did you find me?"

He signalled the waitress for another Guinness. My glass of Shaftebury was only half gone, so I declined her offer to bring me another. "A mutual acquaintance told me where you were and what you were doing. I naturally thought you would be perfect for the role."

"Who? Who told you?"

"Doesn't matter. As I said, no names, no blames."

I prodded him further, but it did no good. If I wanted the job, I'd take it under the terms he offered. I put the cheque in my pocket, and said, "Okay."

He gave me details on where and when the protest organizers rendezvoused with new recruits in the mornings, and suggested I find something different to wear. I was in my standard freelance writer outfit — slacks, shirt and sports jacket, no tie, nondescript shoes — which I agreed would not be appropriate for an indefinite camp-out in the Black Hole. Besides, I wouldn't be much of a spy if I stood out like a Sikh at a Mennonite prayer meeting. I told him I would pick up something that would help me blend in with the green crowd.

By then I had finished my pint and would have liked to have reminisced a little about old times. But Halfnight drained his glass and rose. "Not good to be seen together," he said. "Compromise the mission, and all that. Good to have seen you."

He offered his hand. I shook it, rising at the same time. "Maybe sometime we can get together, like when the job's done."

His voice gave assent, while something about the look in his eyes said the opposite. He turned to go, then stopped. "Watch yourself, Raff," he said. "It's not like when we used to lark about on peace marches. Some of those people are bloody serious about trees."

"I'll be careful," I said.

When he was gone, I went out into the lobby and rented myself a room for the night. Then I drove around until I found the local Goodwill store. Twenty minutes and forty dollars later, I had outfitted myself with two pairs of jeans, three wool shirts and a knitted sweater, and a well worn pair of work boots that looked sturdy enough for clambering around a clearcut. I spotted a fuzzy wool cap that resembled the kind I'd seen local greenies wearing around Comox, and added it to the pile. A well used knapsack cost me another two bucks.

I went up Third Avenue to the Saan's store for underwear and socks, then bought a khaki jacket and a rainproof poncho at a military surplus store — the Goodwill had had nothing useful in my size. West of the mountains on Vancouver Island, even in summer, and at any time of the day, you can suddenly find yourself in a downpour that would make Noah say, "Hey now!" If I was going to play environmental warrior, I didn't want to pick up pneumonia along the way.

When I was fully kitted out, took all my new gear back to the Barclay and put it in my room. Then I drove over to the *AV Times* offices. A pleasant receptionist showed me to a small, empty office near the front desk. One wall was an immense open cupboard, the shelves of which supported fat stacks of newspapers, bound month-by-month. The binding wasn't fancy: the papers were sandwiched between two slats of wood held together by stainless steel bolts along the fold side. I lifted out the papers from the same month last year, took them to a table and chairs set aside for browsers, and sat down to bone up on Clayoquot Sound.

Like any British Columbian who had read the papers and watched the TV news over the past few years, I was generally aware there had been trouble between loggers and environmental activists on the west coast of Vancouver Island, occasionally involving the interests of the six Indian bands that made up the Nuu-cha-nulth Tribal Council. But, because most of my information had come from the big city media in Vancouver and Victoria, I had only a sketchy notion of what was going on. The dailies and TV news rooms covered the issue only sporadically, and usually built their stories around attention-getting stunts by one side or the other.

Reading the detailed local coverage, I came across several events I hadn't heard about before. I also got a good grasp of how complex the long-running, multisided dispute truly was. The standard media treatment of the issue was David meets Goliath, with MacMillan Bloedel as the big bone-crusher and the greens as the plucky little partisans. The TV news did the worst job, as always, employing the usual let's-tell-it-in-pictures-and-a-couple-of-quotes approach that was really only useful for covering car crashes.

The big city dailies were not much better. Their downsized news staffs — constantly shrinking as the economics of print continually faltered — weren't equipped to deal with any issue that couldn't be explained in under a few hundred words. But the Clayoquot story had been growing and evolving for almost ten years. To cover it properly would have meant backing up each new development with masses of background information.

They'd have to explain the findings of a decade of consultations, task forces and steering committees. They'd have to at least outline the basic — and frequently changing — positions of communities, native bands, unions, a range of often conflicting industrial interests from tourism and fish-farming to mining and forestry, government agencies and protest groups. And they'd have to define abstruse scientific concepts like monocultures and biodiversity, about which not even the professors at the world's forestry schools were in agreement.

Any newspaper that actually tried to cover Clayoquot in all its diversity would have ended up with what one of my old editors used to call "vast, grey prairies of print, across which the readers wander until, one by one, they perish from exhaustion." It was much easier to snap a picture of a goateed teenager with his head bicycle-locked to a logging truck, then mix and match some standard quotes from Greenpeace, the forest company public relations spokesperson, and — if he didn't see the reporter coming — the Minister of Forests. *Rounding up the usual suspects*, it was called.

I had winnowed through three months worth of coverage and was carrying the fourth volume back to the table when a voice said, "Rafferty?"

I turned to see a small, completely bald man holding a manila file folder and peering at me over the tops of his eyeglasses. "It is Sid Rafferty, right?" he said.

There was something vaguely familiar about him, mostly the eyes and the shape of the mouth. But I couldn't place him. "Sorry," I said. "Do I know you?"

"I'm Ted Fletski," he said.

"No, you're not," was my automatic response. Ted Fletski was a little butterball of a man, all winks and quips, who had been a general assignment reporter on the *AV Times*, way back when. He'd come the closest I'd ever seen to being an actually spherical human being, almost as thick in the diameter of his waist as he was tall, and he'd had a thick halo of black curls that made his head look like a small moon that had been captured by the gravitational pull of his body.

"I'm what's left of him," said the man, in a voice as thin and dry as a styptic pencil. He came forward and offered a small, cold hand. It felt like a bundle of sticks wrapped in soft leather.

"What the hell happened to you?" I said, as he sat down across the table from me.

"Cancer," he said. "I beat it, but it whittled me down to the core."

"It did that," I agreed. "If there was any less of you, you'd be a deficit."

He laughed, and it was a ghost of the sound I remembered pouring out of him twenty years ago. "Yeah," he said, "I have to be careful stepping on sewer grates, case I fall in." He and I had always competed at topping each other's lines.

"So you're still working for the *Times*," I said.

"Desk man," he confirmed. "They stopped sending me out when I started scaring women and children. What about you?"

I told him what I'd been doing since leaving Port Alberni, at least the minimalist version.

"I remember hearing you were working for WestCan, got married, kids," he said.

"Yeah," I said, "the full catastrophe."

"And now?"

"Freelancing."

His almost nonexistent eyebrows went up. "Here?"

"Up in Comox. I came down here to meet an old friend."

"Anybody I would know?"

"You ought to. Lanc Halfnight."

"Here?" he said again. "Halfnight, here?"

"He's not working with you? On the paper?"

Fletski's head moved from side to side. "Haven't seen him in years. Went to Australia or New Zealand, far as I know, never came back."

I said nothing, which is usually the best thing to do when you've already said too much.

The little man had always had a good nose for a story. Cancer hadn't diminished that organ's effectiveness. He leaned forward and rippled his fingertips in a tattoo on the table top. "So you're telling me Halfnight's in town and he's hiring freelance. What's the story? Where's it gonna run?"

I tried out a few nameless facial expressions involving rolling the eyes up and twisting the lips into various odd shapes. And said nothing.

Fletski read the upside down type on the page I'd been scanning when he saw me. "Clayoquot," he said, and nodded knowingly. "He's got you doing research and legwork. He'll write the piece? Or are we talking video? I always figured Halfnight was slick enough, he'd end up in front of a camera." He waited for me to respond, and when I didn't he said, "Well?"

"Can't tell you," I said. "Wouldn't have mentioned it if I hadn't assumed he was still connected to this place."

Fletski smiled, and I almost saw the old cheek stretching grin make a comeback. "Which means he hasn't told you who you're working for. Interesting."

"Whom," I said. "I know *whom* I'm working for. I just don't know for whom *he's* working. But, as long as the cheque doesn't bounce, I don't much care."

He shrugged his bony shoulders. "Fair enough. But now I know Lanc's in town, I'm going to send some eager beaver reporter around to see what we can find out. With *whom* he meets, and so on."

"Can't prevent you doing it," I said.

"Maybe we'll pick up something you don't know. Something you'd like to know."

"It could happen."

"Then we could talk again. Trade a little information."

"Could be," I said. I'd never put much stock in the old saying what you don't know can't hurt you. Some of the worst hits life had landed on me had come as complete surprises.

"Tell you what," I continued. "How about you fill me in on Clayoquot Sound? All I know is what I read in the dailies and see on the TV news."

"Then you don't know squat," he said.

"So tell me squat," I said.

He moved a chair over so he could sit across from me. For a moment, he rested his sharp elbows on the table and tented his fingers, organizing the information that filled his head. "What you need to know," he began, "is there are not going to be any happy endings in Clayoquot Sound, not this summer or any time as far down the road as I can see."

"Both sides dug in too deep?" I prompted.

He shook his head. "Too many sides," he said. "Too many agendas. You've got the companies, you've got the protesters, sure. But you've also got the government in Victoria, which doesn't know whether to shit or go blind, because they've got the forest unions on one side and the greenies on the other, and those are two of the key groups that got them elected.

"But the key to the whole thing is the First Nations ," he went on. "Ask the industry, the government or the protesters, they'll all tell you they've got the tacit support of the Nuu-chah-nulth Tribal Council. Meanwhile, the natives just give everybody the same thousand-yard stare and stay neutral. As far as they're concerned the only issue is this is *their* land, and they want it back."

But it didn't matter which way the natives finally came down, if they ever did. There would not be any compromise. "At least nothing that will last. The green position is no more cutting old growth, that's all she wrote. But it'll be thirty years before there's enough second growth to keep the local economy going even at half speed."

"So it's win or lose for somebody," I said.

"Yep."

"So who's gonna win?"

He shrugged his bony shoulders. "Can't tell yet, but I'd bet on the greens. They got a lot of money behind them, a lot of volunteers willing to go to jail. Besides, this is not a part-time thing with them. This is what they *do*, full time, year round, and they're good at it."

He figured the forest companies would fight as long as the economics made sense. "But once the game is no longer worth the candle, they'll write off the losses and go cut trees somewhere else."

One of the losses the suits would write off would be the loggers living in places like Port Alberni and Ucluelet. They'd be looking at permanent unemployment. The banks would take their houses and four-by-fours, and they'd end up living in trailers and working at tourist traps for maybe a quarter of what they used to get for risking their lives in the woods.

"That's if they're lucky enough to find work. We're talking about forty- and fifty-year-old guys with grade-school educations. Most of them will just get sucked into the welfare whirlpool."

I could see where this was leading. Things could get rough enough during strikes, when all that was at stake was wages and benefits. When people were seeing their lives destroyed, there was every possibility somebody would get seriously hurt, maybe even killed.

"There have been some incidents," Fletski went on, and ticked them off on his meagre fingers. A couple of hundred loggers had surrounded a busload of white-collar protesters who had chartered a bus to bring them up from Victoria. It had taken a squad of RCMP to rescue them. In Ucluelet, pushing and shoving between a logger and a protester outside a bar ended in the logger being charged with assault — the victim was a television news cameraman who moved in to shoot the fracas, and got pushed over a wall.

"And it's not all on one side," he said. "Most of the greens — almost all of them — are into non-violence. But some of them aren't. Some of them are frigging nuts. Last year, they burned down a logging road bridge and torched a MacMillan Bloedel boat. Couple of months back, they tried to burn another bridge, and a security guard came this close to getting crisped."

The incidents kept building: a Port Alberni millworker's tires slashed after he decorated his car antenna with a pro-logging yellow ribbon; two hundred liters of human excrement dumped at an information tent run by an anti-logging organization near Tofino; MacBlo's forestry information centre in Ucluelet trashed by a mob of eco-warriors who cut phone lines and threatened staff.

"I hadn't realized it was that bad," I said.

"The city media play it down. They've made this into a good-guys/bad-guys scenario, and they've elected the greens to be the good guys. So they concentrate on what's happening at the Kennedy Lakes bridge — all those noble, hymn-singing youth being loaded into paddy wagons — and barely mention the firebugs and the tree spikers.

"But somebody's going to get hurt."

It was the kind of situation in which I preferred to maintain strict neutrality. Instead, I was hiring myself out to one side, playing secret agent for half a grand a day. Or at least that's the motivation I had let Lanc Halfnight think was sending me into the war zone. To myself, and nobody else, I would admit that I liked the idea of spending a week or so away from home; maybe, when I got back, Mo would have lost the movie bug and moved on to something that didn't make the bottom drop out of my belly, every time I thought of it.

Back to the Barclay again, to change into my undercover clothes. I looked at the result in the full-length mirror on the bathroom door. I was too old for the counterculture look, but I wouldn't stand out. The desk clerk gave me a funny look when I came downstairs carrying on a hanger the guise of respectability I had worn to meet Lanc.

I asked her if she knew someplace I could park my car indefinitely. She directed me to a gas station on Third Avenue. I put my slacks and sports jacket in the Behemoth's trunk, then drove over to the garage. For twenty bucks, the owner let me put the Ford in a locked shed out back. I walked the couple of blocks back to the hotel. It was getting on to supper time, but I thought I'd better check in with Mo.

She answered on the first ring. "The police just left," she said.

"I talked to Mikhailovsky this morning," I said. "What's the trouble now?"

"Somebody tried to break in. They got in the back door to the garage somehow and were trying to get into the house."

"Were you home?" I remembered the pair of hired thugs who had held us at gunpoint in my own living room, the first time she'd come to visit. I remembered, too, how brave Mo had been.

"No," she said. "Don across the street noticed them hanging around and called the police."

"Good old Don," I said. My neighbour was a retired army major who kept an eye on our end of the street, and would call the cops if he saw anything hinky. His loud announcement that he was doing just that was what had scared away the two gunmen four years before. Sometimes a nosy neighbour is a godsend.

Mo told me the rest, how the constable figured the burglars must have had a lookout, because when his cruiser came up Back Road they were already gone into the woods; how he'd need a dog and handler to track them, but the nearest canine team was sniffing for dope out in the Merville farm district, and couldn't be at our house for an hour or more.

"Did they take anything?"

"Doesn't look like it." That figured. I wasn't the kind of guy to have a garage full of pawnable power tools. About the most valuable thing there was a rake with a split handle I'd bound up with black tape.

"But all that money in the envelope in your desk drawer?" she went on. "I took it to the bank and told them to put it in your account."

Oh well, I thought, *so much for the grey economy.* "Thanks," I said.

"When are you coming home?" she said, and I could hear a little note of worry behind her usual confidence.

I'd felt shabby before, knowing I was ducking being with her when she wanted me to do something I didn't want to. Now I was leaving her to fend for herself when criminals were lurking in the shadows. Sure, chances were they were just fourteen-year-olds looking to grab a quick handful of CDs to pawn for beer and smokes money — the most common crime in peaceful Comox — but I still felt the way a salmon smells three days after it spawns and dies.

"I've got this job on," I said. "Money's good, but it's going to be a few days."

"What job? What did your old friend want?"

"It's kind of a research thing, check things out, make a few notes, assess the situation first-hand."

"Raff," she said, "why do I get this feeling you're trying not to tell me something?"

Because you're smart and you know me, I thought. But what I said was, "I'm not too sure, myself. I'll explain when I get back. Maybe a week."

"Well, where are you going to be?"

I told her I would be off the side of a road, in a camp.

"What camp? A logging camp?"

"No, actually the opposite."

Mo read the papers and watched the news. "You're going to cover the protesters at that camp," she said, "what do they call it, the Black Hole?"

It was close enough. "Yeah, I'm going to spend a few days there."

"And you're going to write an article or something."

"That's kind of up in the air," I said. You can't write political speeches and not learn how to dissemble.

Her tone changed. "You're not going to get arrested? This is not one of those *twenty-four hours in the life of a pro-tester* thing? Listen, Raff, they're charging those people with criminal contempt, not civil. I heard on the radio one of them's just been sentenced to six months in prison and a fifteen hundred dollar fine, criminal record, the whole megillah."

"I won't be getting arrested."

"Well, be careful," she said. "You know I worry about you sometimes." Now the salmon was five days dead, and the days had all been warm and sunny.

"I know."

"Oh," she said. The way she said told me she'd remembered something. "I called your friend, the movie maker. I'm going to go over and see him, day after tomorrow. He says he knows some people I could talk to about development money."

"Great."

"Find a phone and call me that night. I'll be back on the six o'clock flight. I'll tell you how it went."

"Sure."

"Okay, don't do anything silly."

"I won't."

"Love you."

"Love you," I said.

At five a.m., I paid my bill at the Barclay, bought a couple of chocolate bars from a machine for breakfast, and asked the night clerk, a thin woman in her thirties, what was the best way to get to the Black Hole.

She set her mouth in a way that accentuated the smoker's lines furrowing her upper lip, and said, "I don't know."

"I'm not one of the protesters," I said.

She looked at how I was dressed, the knitted wool hat on the back of my head and the knapsack over my shoulder.

"You're not one of us," she said.

I knew how most people in Port Alberni felt about the thousands of strangers who'd come from all over Canada and even from far-off parts of the world to stop them from making a living out of the woods. I'd read letters to the editor in the *AV Times*, full of outrage, bewilderment and bitter sarcasm. Chances were almost certain this woman was the wife, daughter, sister, girlfriend, or neighbour of someone who had been put out of a mill or forest job in the past few years. The greens said it was automation and downsizing that was causing growing unemployment in forest communities; the people in those communities tended to put the blame on the folks who stopped them from going to work.

"I'm a writer," I said.

The information didn't seem to raise my status in her eyes. But after a long beat, she sighed and said, "You know Johnston Street?" I nodded. "Go down to Johnston and Somass, by the river. When you see a van full of hippies, stick out your thumb. They'll be going where you want to get to."

"Thanks," I said. Then, maybe because my conversation with Mo already had my guilt lapping at the high water mark, I added, "I'm not on their side."

The information was not going to change her life. I went out of the grey hotel into the pre-dawn chill, and walked the kilometre or so to the place she'd recommended. I knew, somewhere over on the far side of the Hump, the sun would be thinking about getting up, but right now the morning belonged to the fog that had drifted in from the Alberni Inlet.

I stood at the designated intersection. There was almost no traffic this early, and the drivers of the few vehicles that came by in the first few minutes had enough to do to steer through the mist. I couldn't be more than a dark spot in the opaque air. I groped my way back from the sidewalk, until I came up against the stuccoed side wall of a store. I set my backpack on the grass and sat on it, leaning against the rough plaster.

I thought about what I ought to do. It was not the kind of thinking I was accustomed to, but I gave it a try. Mostly, I was used to thinking about what I had to do just to keep on going — find some work, do the work, chase the client for the money, pay the mortgage and bills, then find some more work so I could pass go and collect another two hundred dollars.

But that wasn't the problem right now. I had Halfnight's money in my jeans, not to mention Benny Filiatrault's retainer. Besides that, I had another breadwinner in the household — some months, Mo made more than I did. We'd actually got to the point where we ate out just because neither of us felt like cooking, which is as precise a definition of being middle class as anything Statistics Canada ever came up with.

For the first time in as long as I could remember, it was a question of choice instead of necessity. And the choice was pretty simple: would I join the woman I loved in a project that, however irrationally, gave me the collywobbles? Or would I stall and tap dance and prevaricate and generally treat her as if she were no more to me than a bank manager until she gave up and moved on?

It wasn't so bad, thinking about these things in the chill, wet hush of the morning fog. As long as I sat here in the pearly indefiniteness, at an intersection I couldn't even see, the questions were as abstract as the world that might or might not exist beyond the mist.

But then a breeze came sneaking in from somewhere and herded the fog back out onto the water. Once again the world was black asphalt and the green poles of streetlamps, then suddenly it was also a beat-up old Westfalia camper van that could have driven straight out of a time warp — it actually had flowers painted on the side.

I stood up and stuck out my thumb. The van stopped, and I climbed in.

If you'd asked me, I would have told you that I had made no decision about what I ought to do. But if you pressed me hard enough, I might concede that avoiding a decision was in itself a choice. And I had just made it.

Chapter 11

The kid driving the van had long dreadlocks the colour of sandstone and an opinion about the tax system.

"There was a time," he said, "letting businesses deduct expenses from income tax made sense. Now it's mostly bullshit."

"Uh huh," I said. Back when hitchhiking was how I got to places that were too far to walk, I'd learned not to contest the opinions of the people who gave me rides. With some of them, the only reason they picked up hitchers was to have a captive audience for their particular idiosyncratic views on how the world ought to be organized.

"Used to be," the driver went on, "a simple connection between business spending and the general good. A company put up the money for a factory. The factory created jobs. People worked at the jobs and paid taxes."

"That's for sure," I agreed. We had climbed a little since crossing the Somass River and heading west down the two lane blacktop that was the sole entry and exit for the communities on Vancouver Island's Pacific coast. We passed the turn off to Sproat Lake Park, where I used to go and throw stones in the water twenty years ago, while I thought about giving up weekly newspapers and becoming a novelist.

The park was a little postage stamp of grass and sandy shoreline, with a sheltered swimming area. It was a quiet place, except when the giant Martin Mars water bombers based just up the shoreline cranked up their four massive piston engines and flew off over the mountains to knock down some forest fire. A couple of times, I'd seen them doing practice runs over the long, skinny lake, coming in low and slow, engines booming like a giant humming to himself. Then the bomb bay doors would open and, in three seconds, enough water to overfill a swimming pool would race the plane's shadow down to the surface of the lake.

Because the plane was travelling at better than two hundred kilometres an hour, the airstream would blow the edges of the payload into a halo of spray. From the shoreline, it looked as if a gentle cloud of mist was descending to the water. But I remembered going out to the bomber base one spring day to interview the manager for a feature. The gentleness was an illusion, he told me.

"Inside all that spray is a thirty-tonne glob of water, and it's arriving at high speed. If you're ever in a situation where you see one of our planes coming toward you with its belly open, what you better do is hit the ground, face down with your head in the direction of travel, and put your hands over your neck. Cause anyone standing up when that water hits is going to be lying down afterwards, and he won't be getting up again."

One of those same bombers would be thrumming over the Beaufort Range to give my kids a thrill at the air show in a few days. It was like a part of my own past rising up out of Sproat Lake and dropping in on the contemporary me. The big red and white plane would be just the way it had been when I'd been a twenty-something wondering where my talent would take me. Everything else would be different.

We passed the sign that said *Bomber Base*, with an arrow showing which way to turn. It occurred to me my life could have been a whole lot better if there had been arrows pointing me in the right direction at some crucial intersections. Assuming I would have followed them, that is.

Dreadlocks spun us past the base and accelerated along the long straight stretches paralleling the lake. He was warming to his theme of revolutionizing the tax system. "So the factories made more jobs. With more jobs you had more taxpayers, so you could spread the load of public spending. It was in everybody's best interest to let business deduct its costs."

I played along, prompting him with, "But then..."

He picked up the ball and ran with it. "But then, along came high-tech and the information economy. Nowadays, you open a new plant, it employs only half as many people as the one it replaced.

"Now you got fewer people working, so the lucky ones who still have jobs pay more taxes so they can support the unlucky ones who've been downsized out of the labour force."

He shrugged, but kept both hands on the wheel. The road had begun to wind. "And we're supposed to subsidize a business that's throwing people out of work? Give 'em a deduction like they deserve a reward for dumping a bigger share of the overall tax burden onto us?"

"You're right," I said, dutifully. "It's bullshit. But whatta ya gonna do?"

As I expected, he had an answer. "What we gotta do, we gotta make the tax system reward businesses that serve the general good. We need, like, an Index of Social Usefulness" — I could hear the initial capital letters in the way he said it — "and then we rank each kind of business according to how much it adds to the common good."

"Or takes away from it," I said, just to keep the ball in play. The sun was up behind us now. We were following the road along a narrow valley bottom. This was MacMillan Bloedel territory, part of the company's Sproat Lake logging division. I remembered how it had been twenty years back, the overlooking hills clearcut to the ridge tops, the grey mess of stumps and slash, with the roads crisscrossing the slopes like thin pale scars on a well whipped back.

But it was all greened up now, thick and bushy young spruce and fir. *It bounces back and keeps on going,* I thought. Was there a message for me in that observation, some Pollyanna part of my psyche telling me to buck up, take heart, get back on the horse?

If there was, I was tuning it out to listen to the tax visionary.

"Say a company's in the business of cleaning up pollution, or curing diseases. Maybe it's doing something that helps people with disabilities be more self-sufficient."

"Okay," I said.

"Well, that company's making things better in general, not to mention it's saving us money in the long run. So we let it deduct all of its capital and operating costs. In fact, if it's doing something really positive, we give it a bonus — maybe let it deduct a hundred and fifty per cent of its spending."

"Cool," I said.

"Yeah, but if it's some bullshit business, you know, like poking holes in teenagers' eyebrows or flipping commercial real estate, then we only let 'em deduct fifty per cent or forty or whatever. And if they're totally bogus, like..."

He was stuck for an example of a completely useless enterprise. "Psychic hotline," I said.

"You got it," he said. "If that's your line of business, you don't get to deduct zip."

"Yeah, fuck 'em," I said, entering into the spirit of the thing. I wondered where a freelance corporate speechwriter would stand on this guy's Index of Social Usefulness. Probably not too far above Princess "E" and her 1-900 number.

There was more. Dreadlocks wanted to extend the principle of social usefulness to the manner in which businesses were run. Any business that created jobs could still deduct wages and benefits; but a business that hired people off welfare or long-term pogey would get a bonus, because it would be taking some of the load off you and me.

A company that restructured its work week to share existing jobs and prevent layoffs would get a tax break. But a company that downsized to increase shareholder value — that is, profits — would slide down the social usefulness index. It would still make a profit out of throwing its employees into the dumpster, but it wouldn't get to write off the cost of making life more difficult for the rest of us.

I nodded and voiced the right noises on cue — it's another of my talents. Privately, I thought it was a brilliant idea. It was also completely unworkable. Not because the Index of Social Usefulness would be a devastatingly complex and arbitrary system of deciding who pays what — the tax code we already had was only slightly less complex than the total genetic blueprint for making a human being .

I threw in an observation. "I knew a guy used to be an assistant to the Minister of National Revenue in Ottawa," I said. "He told me they had all these experts that were always writing new rules and regulations. And as soon as they were written, that was it, they were the law, the tax law. Then they'd send them out to all the private sector tax lawyers and chartered accountants, and those guys would immediately start figuring out ways to reinterpret the rules so they could get around them.

"He said it was like that old cartoon — you remember *Pogo*?"

Dreadlocks nodded. "No, I don't think so."

"Before your time," I said. "Anyway, there was this character called Albert, he was an alligator, and he had a friend who was a turtle called Churchy."

"Churchy?"

"Yeah, it was short for Churchy LaFemme."

"Jesus," said the tax visionary. I could have told him that humour evolves with the passage of generations. These days, hardly anybody throws bricks at village idiots for a laugh.

"The thing was," I said, "Albert could write, but he couldn't read. And Churchy, he could read but he couldn't write."

"How could that be?"

"It was a comic strip, you play along."

"I guess," he said.

"So Albert would be writing these long compositions, and then he would have to get Churchy to read them to him, so he'd know what he'd written."

"And this was a comic strip?"

I told him it had been in lots of papers. "Point I'm making," I went on, now wishing I had never started on the subject, "actually, the point my friend who worked for the tax minister was making, was that the experts at Revenue Canada and the tax practitioners out in the real world were like Albert and Churchy."

"Oh, I get it," said Dreadlocks. "You got one guy writing rules, doesn't know what they mean until another guy twists them around."

"That's it," I said.

"Okay," he said. "Funny, I guess."

And that was the end of the conversation for a while. We watched the road flow towards us, and I took in some of the scenery.

"But that's an interesting idea, about the taxes," I said.

"You mean interesting from a hippie in dreadlocks driving a VW van?"

I shrugged.

"I run a retreat just this side of Tofino," he said. "A little meditation, a little group stuff. But five years ago, I was an investment advisor with Midland Walwyn in Toronto."

"You can't always judge people by the way they look," I said.

"You got that right."

The road twisted and dropped for a few kilometres. A fast-moving stream appeared along the right shoulder, then built itself into a small river of mostly white water broken by polished black stone outcrops. A few more kilometres and we left the water behind, to climb through hairpin curves and switchbacks, with lichen-stained grey rock to our left and empty air to the right, then curving down to the inland edge of the narrow coastal plain. I looked up at the scalped hills falling behind us, the angled white scars of logging roads running up to the ridge tops. It looked a real mess.

"That's it up ahead," Dreadlocks said. "The Black Hole."

The road was straighter here. I could see cars and vans on the gravel shoulders, and a couple of big flatbeds pulled way off to the side. They were loaded with what looked like pipes and plywood. I wondered if the protesters were laying in a water system, building themselves a squatters camp. It wouldn't have been the first one in the area.

The ex-investment adviser stopped in the middle of the highway and let me out. I thanked him, slung my pack over one shoulder and stepped off the blacktop into the Black Hole.

The name was part of the PR battle the protesters were waging through the media, a couple of memorable syllables to conjure up connotations of lifeless desolation and permanent ruin. In reality, the Black Hole was a nameless stretch of flat land between the highway and the hills close behind. It had been logged and the slash had been burned to speed up the reabsorption of nutrients into the soil. Then it had been replanted. A lot of the seedlings had been trampled down by the herd of city kids who had come west to save the forests.

The campsite was not well organized. Tents of all sizes and shapes were dotted around the roughed-up ground, some of them cobbled together from plastic sheeting and scraps of wood. There were cooking fires and what looked like a communal kitchen. But most of the activity seemed to be happening around the big trucks. I went over to take a look.

"What's happening?" I asked a skinny kid in a plaid jacket.

"Midnight Oil," he said. "They're settin' up here, 'stead of the bridge."

Which might as well have been Swahili. I didn't ask any more questions, because while the kid was being incomprehensible, it had suddenly dawned on me that I had no idea how to be a spy. I didn't know what I was looking for, or how to recognize it if I found it. And I sure as hell didn't know how to blend unobtrusively into the scenery .

Halfnight had said there were environmental monkey-wrenchers in the camp at the Black Hole — bridge burners and tree spikers. He wanted me to get next to them and, supposedly, win their confidence so I — or he — could turn them in to the cops.

It was the kind of idea that sounds simple and straightforward over pints of ale in a pub, especially when someone is offering large amounts of money. Now that I was standing amid scorched logging debris and the mess made by hundreds of inexperienced campers, some of the unforeseen complications were making themselves known.

I moved away from the Swahili speaker and found a tall stump I could lean against. I figured my wisest course was to learn as much as possible from passive observation before I tried quizzing anybody else. Nearby a knot of people had gathered around a sharp-featured woman with long brown hair. She was telling them something, and from the look on the listeners' faces, it wasn't good news. I drifted closer, hoping to learn a thing or two.

I learned Midnight Oil was an Australian rock group that had volunteered to take a break from a North American tour to play for the protesters and anyone else who wanted to come. They had planned to set up an outdoor stage and sound system on scaffolding at the Kennedy Lake bridge, where the sit-down arrests usually happened. The greens must have seen it as a golden opportunity to draw international media attention to their protest.

But as they were preparing to set up, some elders of the Nuu-Chah-Nulth peoples had arrived to tell them the concert could not take place on their land. In the game of political correctness, Canadian-style, first nations are trumps, so the disappointed greens had to turn the trucks around and haul their stage and sound system away.

The sharp-faced woman didn't say why the Nuu-Chah-Nulth had nixed the concert. Maybe the natives had decided blasting the wilderness with rock music from speakers the size of compact cars wasn't the best way to protect it. Whatever the reasons for the turndown, the protest organizers had fallen back on the Black Hole as their back-up site.

I watched for a while as what looked like a few professional roadies, assisted by a horde of volunteers, began to put the stage together and erect towers for the speakers. They wheeled up a thumping big diesel generator to provide the power. I didn't see anybody who looked like a rock star, but the band might have been staying away until it was time to make a big entrance.

I did see media: TV crews with betacams, radio reporters with their tidy little black cassette recorders, print types with the same kind of spiral-bound steno notebooks I'd used twenty years ago. They formed a knot at one end of the camp, smoking and drinking coffee and — if nothing had changed since I was a reporter — swapping personal and professional gossip, intermixed with did-I-ever-tell-you tall tales that grew taller and funnier with each retelling. They ignored the activity, except for one cameraman who was shooting footage of the stage-building, just in case his reporter needed to pad the day's item.

The media lethargy was typical. At any well organized media event, reporters spend most of their time waiting until the prepared stunt is ready to roll. When the actors are ready for their cues, the cameras, recorders and pens busily go to their brief work. The carefully scripted words and precisely symbolic deeds are duly captured, and then it's back to the coffee and gossip.

The media herd brought in for today's event knew the story would be handed to them, predigested and packaged, and well before they needed to file tape or copy for deadline. They trusted the Greenpeacers to be professionals. The environmental protest group might have been launched twenty-odd years ago by a gaggle of rag-tag counter-culture Galahads out to save whales and ban bombs, but it had since grown into multi-million dollar, transnational enterprise. The spin doctors running the outfit in 1993 were every bit as savvy as my ex-wife Karen and her second husband Lyle Pastorel, who were about as slick as oiled ice. I'd spent some time as a minor back-room operative in political high places, but compared to the Greenpeacers with their satellite up-links and on-call helicopter, I was a bumpkin.

Any wrinkles the Nuu-Chah-Nulth's refusal might have put in the day's plan looked to be smoothed out by now, and the preparations for the concert rolled serenely on. As the sun climbed above the bare ridges to the south, the trickle of arriving Midnight Oil fans and protest recruits swelled into a steady stream. The Black Hole began to fill up, with at least five thousand true believers standing and sitting amid the burned out logging debris by the time the band came onto the makeshift stage.

There were some speeches to start with, but they got plenty of support from the crowd. I moved back and up a slight rise to get a better look at what was going on. When the music started, the crowd started bopping along, more than a few dreadlocks bouncing up and down on denim-clad shoulders. I sat on my sleeping bag and watched the action, idly wondering what Halfnight thought I could accomplish for him here.

At one point, I thought I saw Davey Clemmer's black-clad form working his way along the edge of the crowd. It looked as if he was scanning faces, searching for someone. Then he disappeared into the glare of one of the klieg lights blasting mega-candlepower across the clearcut.

Eventually, the band played its last number, someone gave the last rah-rah speech, and the crowd began to break up. Those who had come just for the concert were flooding onto the road, piling into cars, vans and pickups. I moved against the flow, going deeper into the Black Hole, looking for a place to spread my sleeping bag for the night. Tomorrow, I would tag along with the crowd heading for the protest site at the Kennedy Lakes bridge, and try to figure out what practical use I could be to Halfnight and whoever was the ultimate source of my five hundred a day.

Since I'd arrived I hadn't heard one word about tree-spikers or monkey-wrenchers. There might be some among the crowd — I'd be surprised if there weren't — but they weren't wearing identifying T-shirts. All my eavesdropping on the campaign organizers or anybody else who appeared to be more than just a protest grunt had got me nowhere. As far as I could tell, this was a civil disobedience operation, pure and simple. People went out onto the road to get themselves arrested in front of the whole world, and the RCMP and news media cooperated fully.

I wondered what I was supposed to do next — try to stir something up, play *agent provocateur*? Could I see myself sidling up top some wispy-goateed eighteen-year-old and saying, "Hey, dude, wanna spike some trees?" I remembered the painfully obvious undercover cops who used to prowl through the crowds at the Stanley Park be-ins in the sixties, in their leftover beatnik attire, buttonholing stoned-out hippies and loudly asking them, "Got any pot, man?"

I found a relatively flat space with a slight slope toward the road, arranged my bag so that my head would be higher than my feet, took off my boots and climbed in. I used my knapsack for a pillow. The noise from the road gradually dropped as the crowd melted east toward Alberni or west to the ocean.

I looked up at the stars, spread across the sky like a slash from an abstract artist's dripping brush. In Comox, I could look up from my deck and see ten stars for every one that was visible in Vancouver. Here, away from even the lights of a small town, they were multiplied a hundredfold.

I found I could let it all fall away — this ludicrous spy caper, the Ketteriches, my disgraceful tap dancing around Mo's movie dreams. I could just be a pair of eyes staring up at immensity. And then, the perspective unobtrusively switched, and I was hovering over a vast empty space dotted with flecks of light. Suddenly, the sky was no longer presenting its fictional self, the apparently solid dome we unconsciously raise above our heads; instead, I was looking out and down into true nothingness, cold vacancy and aching vacuum stretched all the way to infinity, and I was a very small flicker of consciousness whose eventual snuffing out would not trouble the universe by a fraction of a whit.

I closed my eyes and got a more comforting darkness. I rearranged my shoulders to smooth out a lump in the ground, pulled the bag up to my chin and drifted away.

I awoke to a bright light only inches from my eyes. I tried to sit up, but there were weights on the edges of my sleeping bag. I moved my arms within the confinement but couldn't get them free. *Feet*, I realized. *Somebody's standing on the bag.*

"Is it him?" said a voice from behind the light. I didn't recognize it.

"Yeah, that's him all right." The second voice was one I'd heard before, but not often enough to place it immediately.

"Let's get him up," said the first speaker.

"What's going on?" I said.

The light went away as the flashlight reversed. All I saw was orange and yellow circles. Then the butt end of a long battery case rapped against my forehead, not too hard, but hard enough. "Shut up," said the first voice.

It sounded like good advice. The light came back into my eyes, blinding me again but I knew there were more than just the two who had spoken. I heard boots scraping on the scraps of scorched bark and charcoal that littered the ground, and breathing sounds.

"Okay," said the one with the light, "lift him."

Hands grabbed the edges of the sleeping bag on both sides, and I was hauled upright. With the edges of the bag gripped tightly by at least four hands, I still couldn't free my arms. "Go through his pack," said the one giving orders.

There were rustlings in the darkness. "I found the cell phone," said a third voice.

"Let's see," said the light bearer. He shone the beam on the instrument Halfnight had given me, then thumbed down the first speed dial button. The phone absentmindedly chirped a string of tones to itself, there followed a buzzing of a faraway ringer wherever the other end of the connection was, then a faint recorded voice said, *This is the Share BC Hotline. Please leave a message after the beep.*

"Well," said the man with the flashlight, shining it back in my face. "I guess that settles it."

"Told you," said the almost familiar voice. Then the tones fell into place. It was Davey Clemmer.

"Let's go," said the man behind the light. The hands holding the bag pulled and I tipped backwards. Now the bag was an inclined stretcher, and they were hauling me downslope, my heels dragging on the ground through the padded fabric.

It occurred to me the last time I had been in a sleeping bag, I'd been stuffed into it by a mobster who then shoved me into the trunk of his car. Now, as I was carried through the night in another one, I decided I would never insert so much as a toe into one of the damn things again.

The lightman put the beam on the ground so the others could see their way. My vision cleared as my eyes adjusted to the darkness. The Black Hole was dimly lit by a few smouldering campfires and a couple of low-power electric lights. Now I could see shadowy shapes on either side and others following along. There must have been seven or eight of them.

"Where are you taking me?" I said. "You know, this is kidnapping." Even as I said it, I knew it sounded lame. If these were the kind of people I thought they were, true believers who laid man-traps in forests, sank boats and burned bridges, a little bit of involuntary confinement wasn't beyond their scope.

"It's not a kidnapping, asshole," said the one who'd done most of the talking. "It's an eviction. Now shut the fuck up. There's people here gonna put it on the line tomorrow. They need their sleep."

We reached the road. They stood me upright again, but then the hands that had been holding the sleeping bag let go and the sack drooped and slid down to below my knees. I probably looked like a soft sculpture of a potted plant, and felt just about as effectual.

The flashlight beam slid along the road toward Uclue-let. "Uke's that way," said the man holding it. "You'll be there by dawn. Watch out for bear and cougar."

They all laughed. While they were doing it, and with the light still in my eyes, somebody planted a hard one in my middle. All the air in me decided it was time to go on vacation. I bent over, presenting a target for the boot of one of the ones behind me. I pitched forward onto all fours. Sharp gravel dug into the heel of my right hand and I felt a stab through the old injury in my left shoulder. I heard my knapsack hit the ground beside me, then they all turned and followed the beam back into the Black Hole, weaving among the sleepers and debris. I could hear their voices and chuckles fading.

When I could breathe again, I kicked free of the sleeping bag and got up. My belly hurt and my hand stung. I thought very briefly about rolling the bag up, but it felt better to give it several good kicks, until it flew off the road into the darkness, and out of my life forever. I sucked a couple of shards of stone from my hand and spat them out, then scooped up the knapsack and opened its flap. My boots were in it. So was the cell phone, and under it was its battery hatch, but the battery was gone.

I said a short word, and repeated it several times. Then I put on the boots, slung the backpack over one shoulder and set one foot in front of the other on the road to the sea. It wasn't long before the dim glow of the Black Hole was behind me, and the real dark closed in. The stars gave just enough illumination to tell me where the road was.

The clumping of my boot heels on the asphalt sounded like *Dumb, dumb, dumb*. I couldn't argue with their opinion of me or my situation. And it was becoming clear to me, as I thought about it, just how much of a patsy I'd been.

And if patsy wasn't the right word for it, there were others — decoy, maybe, or pawn, or that old favourite: the sacrificial lamb.

Being spotted by Clemmer could have been a coincidence, a little bad luck. A nihilistic kid who fancied a career as an environmental terrorist would obviously be attracted to Clayoquot Sound in the summer of 1993. It was the biggest and longest running environmental hotspot of the year — Greenpeace was spending a lot of money and effort to keep jabbing it into the public eye. So he might happen to spot me and, knowing my background, put two and two together.

But the cell phone's speed dial connection to the Share organization was too much. It was like being caught wandering around the Pentagon in the mid 1950s with the phone number of KGB Central inked on the back of my hand. Halfnight might as well have tattooed *SPY* in block capitals on my forehead, with a subhead reading *incredibly inept,* for those who wanted the full story.

The only logical conclusion, now that I'd had my face rubbed into it, was that Clemmer and Halfnight were connected. Clemmer was the real undercover operative, and I was the throw-away piece whose unmasking by the intrepid Junior G-Man would establish his bona fides with the Black Hole's inner circle. If there were any clandestine monkey-wrenchers, Clemmer would now be a long step closer to finding them.

Hindsight brought it all into focus. Clemmer had attached himself to Benny Filiatrault because Benny was an outer islet of the archipelago of activists and organizations connected with environmental issues on Vancouver Island. Benny would have provided an introduction to the Cumberland members of the Friends of Clayoquot Sound, a loosey-goosey group that had chapters all up and down the Island. Clemmer would have come down to Clayoquot with a contingent of the Friends, and with their credibility to recommend him, then he would have proved himself the right kind of guy by unmasking a SHARE spy posing as a freelance writer.

When he'd come across me at the Bar None, I must have looked like a ripe contender for the stooge's prize. And when he'd suggested my name to his boss, my old buddy the Hon. Lancolm Bertram, the synergies would have been obvious. I was only surprised that Halfnight hadn't advised me to wear baggy pants, size forty-eight shoes and a red rubber nose.

The road lit up in front of my feet. A vehicle had come around a curve somewhere behind me. I got over on the gravel, where my boot heels switched their monologue to, *schmuck, schmuck, schmuck* Then it occurred to me the smart thing to do was to turn around and stick out my thumb, see if I could hitch a ride into Ucluelet or Tofino, where I could probably catch a bus back to Alberni in the morning.

The vehicle was too big to be a car, too small to be a semi. Full-size pickup, I figured. All four headlights were on high-beam, and a brace of low-mounted yellow fog lights were adding to the blinding glare. The road was straight here and it was coming on fast.

I squinted and tried to shade my eyes with my free hand. The truck wasn't slowing down. It reached that point all hitchhikers recognize, where if it's still moving that fast, it isn't going to stop. I dropped my thumb and turned to walk on.

I was already seeing after-images from the truck's brights, but the sudden eruption of flashes and sparks in my field of vision took me by surprise. There was a funny sensation on the back of my head, a coldness as if someone had doused me with a bucket of water. And for some un-fathomable reason, I was toppling slowly forward. I put out my hands to break my fall, and for the second time in less than an hour, the gravelled surface ripped into my palms and the impact sent a spike of pain through my left shoulder. I saw the tail lights of the truck shrinking into the distance, then everything switched off.

The next thing I knew, I was lying face down on the edge of a dark road, wondering where the hell I was and how it seemed such an odd place to be waking up. A couple of seconds later, I remembered the truck with the high beams, then the rest of the day's events snapped back into focus. I would have preferred the respite of amnesia.

I had no idea how long I'd be lying there, the gravel scrunching its little points into my cheek. I pushed myself up to my knees, my cut palms registering a protest. The back of my head was wet, and there was something sharp under the hair, something I could pull out. I brought it around to my nose and sniffed. It was beer.

That puzzled me. I couldn't remember drinking. Then the gears in my consciousness made another half turn and produced an explanation. As the pickup had gone by, somebody with a good aim had thrown a bottle of lager. The combination of the truck's speed and the added momentum of the throw had smashed the bottle into my head with enough force to shatter the glass and knock me down and out.

I felt around some more. Not all of the wetness was beer. There was at least one fair-sized cut under the hair, and a long, skinny shard of glass was dug into the flesh of my upper neck. I pulled it out, then felt a fresh trickle run down and under my collar.

I was still seeing plenty of colours and shapes. The back of my head still felt numb, but now a throbbing ache was rising up behind my eyes. I wondered if I had a concussion. If I did have one, I told myself, the best thing was to take it somewhere that had people in white coats who would do something about it. I stood up, and that seemed to go all right. I bent down to pick up my pack, and almost rejoined it back on the gravel shoulder.

I straightened back up and waited for the world to stop dancing in the dark, then tried slowly squatting down until I could reach the pack without moving my head. I straightened up, while somebody in another part of my disordered psyche commented, *Always lift with your legs.* That made me laugh, which made my head move, which was not a laughing matter.

I kept the dizziness at bay by staring straight ahead at the grey strip of road between the dark masses of trees to either side. I heard water moving over rocks somewhere nearby, and suddenly my throat felt half stuck together by thirst. But the sensible part of my scrambled consciousness showed me a little private movie in which I stumbled across uneven ground in the pitch blackness under the trees, ending up in a deep river, running cold and fast at the bottom of a steep gorge.

I kept walking toward Ucluelet, wondering if bears were attracted to the combined odour of beer and blood. The experts all recommended playing dead until a curious bruin got bored and wandered off. At least I wouldn't have any trouble doing that. I'd only be half faking.

My boot heels weren't saying much now, mainly because I was doing more shuffling than marching. After a few minutes, my head cleared and I picked up the pace. I still saw occasional sparks and flashes of light in the corners of my vision. I remembered from Psychology 101 that the occipital lobe at the back of the head was the brain's vision centre, and that a blow there could make you see stars. I wondered how long they took to go away.

The road lit up in front of me again. I turned and looked. From the size and height of the headlights, this one was a car. I shaded my eyes with my left hand and stuck out my right thumb.

The car slowed as it approached me. When there were only a few metres left between us, its headlights began to flash and a flicker of red and blue lights erupted from a rack on the roof. It stopped beside me and the passenger window rolled down. A flashlight lit up my face from inside the car.

"Can you give me a ride to town?" I said. "I'm kind of hurt."

"Mr. Rafferty," said a voice that sounded familiar. "I thought it was you."

The flashlight clicked off and the overhead dome light came on as an arm in a khaki sleeve reached over to open the passenger door. Between the paisley shapes dancing before my eyes, I recognized the man in the car.

"Corporal Mikhailovsky," I said. "This is a coincidence."

"Not really," he answered, putting the car in gear and moving us from one stretch of dark road to another. "I was heading for Ucluelet to spend the night, so I could come and look for you in the morning."

"Why?" I said, then a terrible cold fear rushed up out of my belly and froze my throat. "Has anything happened to Mo?"

"She's fine," he said. "She told me where you were."

"Then what did you want me for?"

"Well," he said, "I might have to place you under arrest."

Chapter 12

"I think I'm going to throw up," I said.

"Roll down the window," said the Mountie. He sniffed the air between us. "Too much to drink?"

I shook my head, which turned out to be not an activity I would recommend. The police car seemed to move in more directions than my inner ear could handle, but by rolling down the window and putting my head into the slipstream of cool air, I managed to avoid the almost inevitable consequences.

"Nothing to drink," I said, when my internal settings came back down from the red zone. I told him about the bottle of beer thrown from the pick-up. "I'm worried about concussion," I said.

"I'll take you to a doctor in Ucluelet," he said.

The doctor was a large man with surprisingly small hands that appeared to be well versed in tweezing small pieces of glass out of people's heads. I wondered aloud if a tossed bottle was a common local greeting.

The doctor grunted. "You should get this x-rayed," he said, threading a curved needle with silk and preparing to stitch me up.

"Will I be able to play the violin?" I said.

He almost walked into it, but was quick enough even after midnight to check his automatic response and ask me in return, "Could you play it before?"

"All the best jokes have been taken," I said.

He pulled the second stitch through, knotted it and cut the line. "Okay," he said, "the doctor comes into the examining room and says to the patient, 'Mrs. Jones, it looks as if we'll have to operate.'

"The patient says, 'But I'm not Mrs. Jones.'

"The doctor says, 'Well, you know, medicine's not an exact science.'"

I laughed. It made my head hurt.

"You shouldn't laugh," the doctor said.

"I thought laughter was the best medicine."

"You also shouldn't read *Reader's Digest.*"

"Are you finished?" Mikhailovsky said.

It looked that way. We thanked the doctor and went back into the night. The pubs were closed, and the working-class town of Ucluelet was mostly asleep. Mikhailovsky drove us through the little grid of civilization, only a few blocks deep, at the southern end of a narrow peninsula that parallels the coastline of Vancouver Island, past steel-hulled fishing boats and white frame houses, marine-supply and grocery stores.

I'd never spent any time in Ucluelet. I'd only come this way before as a tourist, and like most tourists, I'd gravitated to the bigger, classier town at the other end of the long spit of land, past the glistening flats of Long Beach: Tofino of the curio shops and vegan eateries and charter boats that would take you out to annoy a passing whale.

Ucluelet has a small RCMP station. We parked behind it, and got out. Mikhailovsky opened the trunk of the cop car and took out a small suitcase. He gestured toward the back door of the cop shop, and said, "Inside."

"Wait a minute," I said. "Am I under arrest?"

"I don't think so," he said.

"You don't think so," I repeated.

"It's kind of a grey area," he said. "Come inside and we'll talk about it."

I hesitated. Who wouldn't?

"Have you got anywhere else to go?" he said.

I didn't.

"Then come inside. You can sleep in one of the cells."

"Will the door be locked?"

"That depends on how you answer a few questions."

In the main room of the station, a couple of uniformed RCMP were filling in forms at a table. A radio crackled with semi-decipherable code words from Mounties driving around in the darkness.

Mikhailovsky waved to the two uniforms and led me to an interview room in the back of the cop shop. There was a table and two chairs. I sat at one and he said, "You want coffee?"

I checked with my stomach, then said, "Sure. Cream, no sugar."

He brought two styrofoam cups and took the seat across from me. We sipped, then he took a leather-bound notebook from his hip pocket, flipped it open and read whatever he found there.

"Ms Migliorini deposited more than three thousand dollars in hundreds and fifties into your chequing account yesterday," he said.

"Yeah, so?"

His gaze came up off the page and flung at me . "Do you mind telling me where that money came from?"

"Why?"

A movie cop might have said, *Why don't you just let me ask the questions, buddy?* Mikhailovsky just kept boring into my abused head with his bright blues. I should have been intimidated, but maybe the knock on the head was affecting my judgement. I felt like getting mad at somebody, and he was the only one around.

"Fuck this," I said. "My head hurts, somebody just stepped all over my ego, and I'm too tired for games. Stop farting around. Treat me like I've got a working brain, or charge me with something so I can go and lie down."

He kept the cop stare going for a few more seconds, then switched it off.

"I don't think there's any reason to charge you," he said. "I just need to know where the money came from."

I sighed and sipped the coffee. It wasn't bad, for coffee, especially for cop coffee. "You tell me why, I'll tell you what you need to know. I'm just tired of being messed around."

He thought about it for a few beats. "Okay," he said. "Two of the bills Ms Migliorini deposited in your name bore traces of a fluorescent marker, a dye that we use to trace money as part of a drug investigation. I am fairly confident you're not dealing drugs..."

"High praise indeed," I said.

"...but it would be useful to an on-going investigation if you would tell me who gave you that money." He sipped his coffee, and waited for my answer.

My anger was fading as quickly as it had come up. My head throbbed now. "I don't know," I said.

He put the cup down. "You don't know if you're going to tell me, or you don't know who gave it to you?"

"I don't know who gave it to me. Although I can give you a short list." I explained that, contrary to my usual way of doing business, I'd had a brief influx of cash in envelopes over the past week: from Rod Bilder, Benny Filiatrault and the Ketterich brothers.

"You told me you had no relationship with the Ketteriches," Mikhailovsky said.

"I don't. They said, 'Here, take this thousand dollars.' I got a sense that they'd be disappointed if I didn't, and it seemed to me they might react in a forceful manner. I'd already had one kicking that night, and I didn't want another."

He made a note in his book, then closed the cover. "You can sleep in a cell," — he met my question before I asked it — "the door will be open. I'll ask the duty constable to keep an eye on you overnight. Concussion can rebound on you."

"Are you heading back to Courtenay in the morning?" I asked.

"Yes."

"I left my car in Alberni. Could you give me a ride?"

"Might as well," he said.

The cell was reasonably comfortable, if you happened to be exhausted and further debilitated by bodily injuries. I soon got used to the faint background odour of vomit and disinfectant, and dropped off to the sound of the pain throbbing behind my eyes. I was awakened twice during the night by a serious young woman in a khaki shirt who wanted me to count her fingers, then by Corporal Mikhailovsky just after seven.

"How are you feeling?" he said.

I shook my head gently. Nothing seemed to be broken inside. "Not too bad."

We went to a little restaurant up the street from the police station. I munched toast and made it through half a cup of coffee-flavoured acid while the Mountie inhaled a breakfast that would have weighed down King Kong. I offered to pay, in exchange for the free bed, but Mikhailovsky insisted on separate cheques. "Policy," he said.

We drove out of town. As we reached the turnoff to Highway 4, a paddy wagon was coming from the direction of the Kennedy Lakes logging road. The vehicle sat low on its springs, so I guessed it was carrying the morning load of protesters.

"What do you think of civil disobedience?" I asked.

"No comment."

"I'm not a reporter," I said. "I'm just making conversation."

He gave no answer, and I figured the discussion was

over. But after a moment, he said, "If people want to break the law, they should be prepared to take the consequences."

"Well that's the idea," I said.

"But they don't," he said. "They get themselves lawyers and they go into court, try and tie up the docket, prevent the system from dealing with them, so then they have to be let off."

"They want to use their day in court to preach the message. They're talking past the judge and to the people through the media," I said.

"But the value of civil disobedience is that you're willing to suffer for what you believe in," the Mountie said. "If you'll go to jail to make a point, then people will say, 'Hey, maybe there's something to what he's saying, if he's that's serious about it.' And if a whole lot of people are willing to go to jail, then the society and the lawmakers have to take notice.

"That's what Gandhi and Martin Luther King did, and they were right. They prevailed, not because they were willing to break the law, but because they were willing to suffer."

We were passing the Kennedy Lakes logging road turn-off. He gestured toward a second paddy wagon that was approaching the highway. "These people try to talk their way out of what they've done. That's no way to do it. If you're going to be a martyr, then be a martyr. Don't be a weasel."

I heard an echo of Mo Migliorini: *make your choice and stick to it.* I decided to change the subject. "Speaking of weasels," I said, "you were asking the other day about Davey Clemmer."

He turned his head part way toward me, his eyes staying on the road. I took it as a signal to go on.

We were just coming up on the Black Hole. The bandstand was gone and the flatbeds. People were moving around the campfires. "He's in there, somewhere," I said. "He was the one sicced the heavies on me last night. I didn't see him, but I recognized his voice."

Mikhailovsky shrugged.

"You're not interested?" I asked.

"No."

"I think you should be."

"Why's that?"

I told him, in detail, my opinion of Davey Clemmer, and what I thought he'd been up to since he came out from Ontario. I'd pieced it all together the night before, walking down the dark road before the hurtling bottle of beer gave me other things to think about. I told the Mountie about Halfnight and how he'd hired me to be a decoy so that Clemmer could expose me and cement himself with the folks who were running the Black Hole. I described Clemmer as an *agent provocateur*, a spy who wouldn't scruple at nailing spikes into trees or rigging trip wires. I said I suspected that he was responsible for Stu Haglund's death, and that he may have hassled Rod Bilder into some kind of fatal seizure.

"I figure he sent that threat with the cut-out letters, and he fired the rifle shot through Benny Filiatrault's window," I said.

Mikhailovsky's head came around sharply. "What rifle shot?"

I told him about the slug in the wall. "He would've done it to impress the Cumberland greens. He wanted to look like some kind of desperate radical monkey-wrencher, so he could work his way into the leadership of the Clayoquot Sound and spy for Halfnight. The little shit."

When I finished, there was only the sound of the police cruiser's tires humming on the asphalt and the wind flying past the windows. Mikhailovsky put a portion of his lower lip between his teeth and said nothing.

"We should go back there and get him," I said.

He looked at me, with an expression that translated as *What do you mean, 'We?'*

"He's a bad guy," I insisted.

The Mountie thought about it for a while, working the same spot on his lip again. "Maybe," he said after a while. "But I've got nothing to justify a charge, or even bringing him in for a talk."

"What about ratting on me last night, getting me thrown out and smacked around?"

"Being a Judas is not an indictable offence. Fact is, police work depends on a continuing supply of Judases to tell us who did what. We cherish them."

We were leaving the coastal flat land now. The road snaked up into the hills, with one S-curve following on another, lichen-streaked grey rock on our right, empty air to the left. Mikhailovsky swung the car around the bends with easy assurance.

"Funny thing is, he came to us and offered to spy on you," he said when the road briefly straightened out.

"On *me?*"

The road curved again, and a pick up swept around a shoulder of rock toward us. It might have been the one from last night, but it was gone and I wanted to hear more about Clemmer. "What do you mean, spy on me?" I repeated.

"Well, really on the Ketteriches. He was the one who told us about you talking to them and driving off together. Which, as I recall," he added, "you lied to me about."

"As I recall, I gave you a noncommittal answer," I said.

"I'd have to check my notes on that. Anyway, he was looking to sell somebody — anybody — to anybody who was buying. He first came to us wanting to know if there was a reward for turning in marijuana growers. We said there might be a few bucks if he could zero us in on a growing site when the cultivators are on the scene to take out the harvest. He looked disappointed when we told him there was no big money."

"Did he try you on the idea of catching tree-spikers?" I asked.

"Yeah, pretty soon after Mr. Haglund was killed. But we told him, there's no reward budget for that kind of thing. The RCMP certainly isn't in the business of hiring civilians to spy on the public. If he had information about a crime, we hoped he would recognize that it was his duty to come forward and inform the authorities."

"I guess he tried the SHARE people next," I said, "and got a bite."

"Maybe," said the Mountie, "if that's who your friend Halfnight is working for."

"Whom," I corrected him. He didn't thank me.

"Anyway, we checked Clemmer out, just to be sure," he said.

I wanted to know what he meant by *checked him out*.

He told me the Courtenay RCMP had queried the local force in Clemmer's home town of Dundas, as well as the Ontario Provincial Police. Nobody had an official file on Clemmer, but he was known. "He did the same kind of thing when he was a kid, offered to give information on the local young offenders, if someone would pay him. Apparently, he always wanted to be a spy. Somebody thought he'd heard that he'd applied to CSIS," — I recognized the acronym of the Canadian Security and Intelligence Service, the national spy agency — "but they turned him down."

"So he came out here and went freelance," I said.

"I suppose," the Mountie agreed, "but he won't get anywhere. We have our own people in the protest camp, and it's strictly civil disobedience this time. The organizers know any monkey-wrenching will cost them the public relations battle. There are no tree spikers in the Black Hole."

"There's at least one," I said.

"You think he set the trap that killed the faller and sent a warning note to Mr Bilder. But Clemmer didn't arrive in Cumberland until two days after Mr Haglund's death."

"How do you know when he arrived?"

"We asked around. Strangers in Cumberland get noticed. Especially if they stand out from the crowd."

"I still think he's a bad guy," I said.

He gave me a considering look, then turned back to the road. "It's a mistake in police work to pick a suspect and then look for evidence that inculpates him. Better to gather the evidence first, then see which way it leads you. An open mind solves cases, a fixed idea leads you in the wrong direction."

"Then who do you think set that trap?"

"At this point in the investigation, we have no suspects," he said.

"I'll bet you it was Clemmer," I said. "And I'll bet he's preparing to set some more in Clayoquot. Then he'll *discover* them and collect the reward."

"No," Mikhailovsky said. "There are...informal channels of contact between us and the protesters. We'll arrange to let them know. And they'll remove him the same way they removed you."

We drove the rest of the way in silence. When we crossed the Somass River and entered Port Alberni, I directed the corporal to the garage where I'd parked the Behemoth. "Are you all right to drive?" he asked me as I opened the police car's passenger door.

I said I thought so, thanked him for the ride and closed the door. Three minutes later, I was warming up the Ford's four hundred cubic-inch V8 engine and wondering what to do next.

Finally, I put the car in gear and tooled over to the *AV Times*. Ted Fletski was in the newsroom, editing somebody's copy on a widescreen monitor that also let him fit it into the eventual layout of the local news page. He looked up as I came in and said, "Short trip. Have fun at the big concert?"

"They had me in stitches," I said. Then I sat down and told him the whole story: Halfnight, Clemmer, the abortive spy caper and the bottle of beer. I took him through Haglund's death and Bilder's, what the Mountie had told me. From time to time, Fletski smiled. It must have sounded funny the way I was telling it. Maybe in a few years it might even sound that way to me.

When I was finished, he laughed and said, "Well, you had fun at the fair."

"So glad I brightened your day," I said. "So what did you find out about Halfnight?"

"Nothing," he said. "He was never here."

"He was here. I saw him."

"Then you were the only one. Old Lancolm has become a man of mystery. I phoned around, asked a few people who ought to know. They didn't know any more than I did. So I got interested and dug a little harder. Still nothing hard and fast. All I can tell you is he's not in the news business at all anymore. He's just maybe connected to a couple of security firms, the kind that perform unspecified functions for corporate clients in return for big bucks, and nothing gets mentioned in the report to shareholders."

"Industrial espionage?" I said.

"That's how it looks," he said. "Not the kind of thing I'd want to do, but I can see it suiting Halfnight."

I had to admit it, so could I.

"Well," I said, "you're welcome to the story. You want to run it, go ahead. Just call me Mr X or something."

"What run it?" he laughed. "There's nothing to run. But I'm sure as hell gonna tell it a few times."

"There's a story here," I argued. "You got a guy turned down by CSIS, hooks up with a shadowy operative from an industrial espionage firm back east. He comes out here, worms his way into the Black Hole. You got booby traps and dead bodies in Cumberland. It's a hell of a story."

"Yeah, and what am I going to hang it on?" He started counting my troubles on his sticklike fingers. "The only piece of evidence you've got is a cheque from a numbered company, and it's even money neither the company nor the bank account even exist, so we can't follow that trail. You've got a cellular phone that used to speed-dial SHARE BC. Now, with the batteries out, it won't remember how to do that, and even if it did, so what? The cops are not treating either Halfnight or Clemmer as suspects."

He rubbed his thumbs and index fingers together, like a man getting rid of crumbs. "All you can give me is the unsupported word of an ex-reporter who tried to play spy games at the Black Hole and got hit on the head by some passing loggers." His stripped down face showed sympathy behind the amusement. "To the guy with the stitches in his head, this can sound like desperate drama. To the rest of us it's mostly farce. Sorry, Raff."

"There's a story here," I repeated.

"Sure," he said. "Somewhere. But you don't have enough hard facts to write it. And anyway, this is not about the story. You're not a newsman any more. It's a bitch," he finished, looking at me dead on. "You've been screwed, blued and tattooed. All of which might make a good movie, but it ain't gonna see print in this newspaper."

He was right, and I hated it. I'd been suckered, hosed, hornswoggled, gulled, played for a noddy, and every other phrase in the thesaurus. I wanted to get my own back, but I probably never would. I'd never see Halfnight again, nor Clemmer.

I might as well go home, with tail well tucked.

"Roger Gambowsky loves the story," Mo said. "He says we don't even have to worry about getting the rights to Susan Mayse's book. It's all in the public domain, he says."

"Great," I said. "Let me put down my suitcase."

I squeezed past her. She followed me from the front door to the bedroom. "He says he knows some people who are looking for, what did he call them, *docudrama features* based on BC history, and this could fit right in. He wants a treatment right away, and if they like it he thinks he can get us some money for a full script."

She paused to take a breath, then said, "What happened to your head? Are those stitches? My god, let me see."

I'd never thought I'd be grateful for my souvenir of Clayoquot Sound, but I was glad to get Mo off the subject of movie making. I let her fuss over my gallant wounds, demanding to know what foolishness I'd been up to, while I wondered if I could call Roger and explain that I didn't want to play this game again, get him to back off. He'd probably understand.

But I put the idea away. I was guilty enough without asking a decent guy like Roger to do my lying for me.

I told Mo a short version of how I had been tossed out of the Black Hole, making it sound like just bad luck. I dwelt a little more on the whack on the head, shamelessly playing for sympathy, and even more shamelessly accepting it when it was offered.

Then I segued into Corporal Mikhailovsky and the marked money. By the time we'd talked that over, I could honestly say I was bushed. I took a shower and headed for bed.

Mo was waiting for me under the covers. "Poor baby," she said, sliding one arm under me, while her other hand stroked my belly.

I nuzzled my nose into the warm, soft spot where her neck met her shoulder. She smelled like musty honey.

"Mo," I said. "About the movie. I don't know if I can do it."

"Course you can," she said. "Roger says it'll be so great. Besides, you've already done half of it, haven't you?" She stroked lower. "So all you have to do is finish."

I wanted to say, *I've lost my nerve, I'm afraid to get back on the horse.* But her fingers were cupping and encircling, while her nails traced slow patterns that sent lines of white fire racing along my most privileged nerves.

I let my hand descend the long flat length of her abdomen, over her mound and into the liquid velvet below. I did the things she liked, and now her breath whispered across my ear, gently panting.

She freed her arm and levered herself up, then got onto her knees and straddled me. Part of me jumped up to greet her, and she got hold of it, first with her strong, warm hand, then with a softer, hotter grip. She gradually let herself sink all the way down, and rested there for a moment, palms flat against the tops of her thighs, while she looked at me. Her eyes were as wide and green as the sea, and just as knowing.

She rotated her hips. "How's your head?" she said.

"What head?" I said, and thrust up and into her.

In the morning, Mo wanted to talk about the movie but Benny Filiatrault called while we were having breakfast. He needed an op-ed piece for the local papers. I told him I'd be over in a little while, finished my tea and gathered up my note-taking gear.

Outside, the Comox Valley was posing for a postcard again, which it does very well. At the bottom of Comox Hill, the Behemoth became the rattle in a thick-bodied snake of metal and glass, its belly filled with tourists, which was turgidly crawling along the Dyke Road and over the elevator bridge that crosses the Puntledge at 17th Street.

But instead of heading up 17th to Cumberland Road, I swung right onto Cliffe and drove a few blocks to a phone store I'd seen in the mini-mall that housed the government liquor outlet. I came out ten minutes later with a Motorola cell phone, a black oblong whose bottom flipped open when you wanted to talk. It was almost like the little props James Tiberius Kirk used to flip open when he needed beaming up, although without the cool sound effect .

Five minutes later, I was climbing Cumberland Road. I averted my eyes as I passed the cemetery and the stand of old growth above it where Stu Haglund had died. Instead I fiddled with the radio but found nothing good to listen to,

Filiatrault's front door was open, so I knocked and went in. I looked in the living room and didn't find him, then went down the hall to the kitchen. He was sitting at the table, a notepad before him. He'd been making notes. "I've been thinking," he said as I sat down across from him, "that we should be zeroing in on the Hockney's Woods issue."

"No," I said, "I've been thinking about it, and we definitely shouldn't."

"But it's tangible," he said. "The our-village, their-village thing isn't."

"All the better. People can put their own meanings into it. Whereas Hockney's is where Haglund died. He's got a lot of friends and relatives who are upset over his death. They're going to blame the greenies, but if you stick your foot in there, some of that blame will rub off on you."

He looked doubtful. "Listen," I said, "the basic rule is to have a simple message and keep repeating it. You scored at the meeting. Now you follow up with an op-ed piece that says the same thing, then put your hand-out through every mail slot in town. Any reporter asks you about anything, you tell him the election's all about whose village this is."

"What if I'm asked about Hockney's Woods?"

"You say, 'That's a difficult issue, and we need to take a long, hard look at all the ramifications. But this election is about whether Cumby is our village or the developers'.'"

He looked at me as if I'd just invited him to bet on which card the queen of spades was under. "And I'll get away with that?"

"It's done all the time. If the media don't ask the question you want to answer, you slide past whatever they ask you and answer the question you wanted to hear."

"Huh," he said.

"So," I said, "I didn't really need to come up here. I'll write the op-ed so that it's the same as the hand-out and your speech to the meeting."

He shrugged. "If you're sure."

"I'm sure."

"It just sounds so cynical when you say it that way."

"You're the client," I said. "To you I speak candidly."

He put up both hands. "Okay. I've put in a fax machine. Send me the draft." He gave me the number.

I got up. I'd come up to see him because it got me clear of Mo and the movie for a while. But as I'd driven past the cemetery I'd had an idea. "Before I go," I said, "I'd like to take a look at Clemmer's room."

"Why?"

"Young Davey was not all he seemed," I said. I told him about what had happened at the Black Hole and a digested version of what Corporal Mikhailovsky had told me.

"Huh," he said again. "I thought I was a better judge of people than that."

"You were dealing with a guy who'd been playing at being an undercover agent since childhood."

He took me up the narrow staircase to a small space that would once have been a child's bedroom — probably several children at once back in the days before contraception. It was empty except for a narrow bed covered by a bare mattress and a beat-up chest of drawers.

I opened the drawers, found nothing. I lifted the mattress, saw only a half dozen wooden slats.

"He had a sleeping bag," Filiatrault said. "Took it with him."

But when I let the mattress drop, I heard a soft sound. Something had been pinned between the bed and the wall and it had fallen. I pulled the bed away from the wall and saw a rough-textured glove, the kind you'd wear to clear out nettles from a garden. Even as I bent to pick it up, I was getting a whiff of a pungent odour, and when I brought it up for a closer look and saw the dark green stains on the palm and the fingers' inner surfaces, the rank smell rushed up my nose.

"Oh, ho," I said, holding the glove for Filiatrault to sniff. "I think we know who harvested the Ketteriches' crop."

"Jeez," he said. "He didn't strike me as that stupid. Who could he sell it to?"

"He never meant to sell it," I said. "The Mounties told him they needed to catch the grower with the crop — that's what they'd pay for. So Clemmer comes up with a plan. He must've stashed the dope somewhere, hidden it. Then he contacts Butch and Trick, arranges a meet to let them recover it. But he also tells the time and place to the Mounties. They catch the brothers with the dope, they've got a case for the Crown prosecutor."

"What does Davey get?"

"Money, for sure, but that's not what he's really after. The arrest makes him a successful undercover agent. Maybe he thinks he can get some kind of reference from the local detachment, so he can go around to other towns doing the same kind of thing."

Filiatrault threw the glove into a corner. "Except now

he's working for that old friend of yours, so he's a real spy at last."

"*Friend* is not the word I would use," I said. "But, yeah, he thinks he's got bigger fish to fry. About which he is wrong, because the Mounties are going to burn him with the Black Hole crowd, so his career as an industrial spook is about to come to an abrupt end. Ten to one, he comes back here and restarts Plan A."

Filiatrault shrugged. "I don't care. Why should you?"

Good question, I thought. Because the kid was a lying, scheming little schnook? Or because he and Lancolm Halfnight had made a fool out of me? Or because focusing on Clemmer's sins took my mind off the lying and scheming I'd been doing, that was making a fool of the woman I told myself meant the world to me?

The answer I gave was none of the above. "Because the Ketteriches would pay good money to know who ripped them off."

"Actually," he said, "Ketterich money is bad money. You might want to think about that."

As I came down Filiatrault's walk and out onto the street where I'd parked the Behemoth, I ran into someone I didn't want to see.

"Raff," she said, "how's the shoulder?"

"Sally," I said. She hadn't asked about the movie, so I could tell her the truth. "Not so good. I took a fall, caught myself on my hands. I don't think the impact helped."

"Come to my place," she said. "Another dose of ultra-sound will probably help."

"I can afford to pay you," I said.

"Nah," she said. "Come on."

Her place was only a couple of blocks up Dunsmuir Avenue from Filiatrault's. I left the Ford and walked with her. We went in silence. It seemed to me there was something on her mind, something that made her keep her eyes on the sidewalk in front of us while she chewed on the inside of her lip. I'd worn a worried look through enough of my life to recognize it in others.

"Everything all right?" I said.

"Sure," she said. She straightened and took her hands out of her pockets. "Just life," she said. She gestured to the old buildings that lined the street. "As it is lived in Cumby."

The room with the ultrasound machine was warmer this time. She had me move my left arm around and pushed and pulled on it from different directions, then put the gel on my flesh and began circling with the applicator.

"How's Benny's campaign coming?" she asked.

"Fine. He's got all the instincts."

"Comes by it naturally. His grandad was a big man in the union, back when the mines were going great guns."

Another silence. The applicator circled over my flesh and bone. I was thinking of Davey. After a moment, I said, "You know that kid who was hanging around with Benny for a while?"

"Clement? Was that his name?"

"Clemmer."

"What about him?"

I indicated my shoulder. "He's responsible for the latest damage."

"How so?"

I told her a truncated version of the Black Hole saga, leaving out the bit about how I'd been sold out by my former friend, the Honourable Lancolm Halfnight. "He wants to be a spy," I said. "But he's been having trouble finding someone to spy for."

When I told her about my suspicions about the Ketterich crop, she said, "That's stupid. You don't mess with those guys."

"I don't think Clemmer's gears fully mesh," I said. "He does dumb stuff, like shooting a rifle through Benny's window."

The applicator stopped for a second, then began to circle again. "A rifle?" she said. "Where'd he get that?"

"I dunno. Probably he got rid of it. Maybe stashed it where he hid the dope, figured he'd also get Butch and Trick on a weapons charge."

She made a little sound in her throat. "Why can't people leave well enough alone?"

I shrugged and noticed that it didn't hurt so much as it had lately. "This ultrasound really works," I said. "How much do I owe you?"

"Nothing," she said. "You're trying to do something for the memory of Ginger Goodwin. In Cumberland, that gets you everything on the house."

"After all these years? How big a deal can it be?"

She stopped working my shoulder. I turned and looked up at her. Her face had taken on the stark planes of those women in the old black-and-white photos of generations gone by. "It's a big deal," she said.

She went back to work. "Almost done," she said. "What happened to the bullet at Benny's?"

"It's on his mantelpiece. I just saw it."

"He didn't take it to the cops?"

I shook my head. "He thought it was just a spent round that ricocheted off the neighbour's roof."

"Oh," she said. "But you think it was the Clemmer kid."

I didn't see why I should be fair to the little rat, but I said, "Benny could be right. If it had been an aimed shot through the window, it would have had more force to it. But it was half-sticking out of the wall."

"Huh," she said. The machine's timer beeped and she did something with its controls, then wiped the excess gel from my shoulder with a paper towel. "You're all done."

"Thank you," I said. Slipping back into my shirt, I felt less pain. "I appreciate it."

"It's nothing."

"Listen," I said. "Do you want to do me another favour?"

She was putting away the machine. "What?"

"If you see Clemmer around town, would you give me a call?"

"Maybe you should leave him alone."

"Maybe. But I owe him one."

"People like that," she said, "they usually get what's coming to them."

"That hasn't been my experience," I said. "A lot of people get away with murder."

"No," she said, "they don't. They get punished."

"I still think Clemmer's responsible for Stu Haglund's death. If that wasn't murder, it was pretty close."

She had that stark look again. "You really think that?"

"I do. The cops don't. But I do."

She sighed. "Even so," she said, "you should leave it alone."

"Maybe I'll change my mind," I said. "But, still, if you see him, will you call me? On my cell." I fished out a card and a Pentel rolling writer , jotted the new phone's number on it, and offered it to her.

She looked at me in silence for a moment, and I had no idea what she was thinking. Then she took the little oblong of pasteboard and glanced at it. "Sure."

I could have driven back home, but Mo might be there, wanting to see my draft treatment. Then I remembered something Benny Filiatrault had told me about the Ketteriches and drove around the small grid of streets that was the heart of Cumberland until I saw a two-storey house that was having its roof relaid. A monster four-by-four with blacked-out windows was in the driveway. I parked, went up to the front door, and knocked.

Butch answered. He didn't say anything, just leaned against the jamb, his tongue making a bulge in one cheek, his eyes widening and his eyebrows scaling the slope toward his hairline — all adding up to a look of bemused expectation.

"Jack Nicholson," I said.

He smiled, a wide one. "Pretty good," he said. Then his face went into repose. "What are you looking for?"

"No, it's what you're looking for. I think I might have a line on who stole your dope."

His gaze went past me, looked up and down the street. I said, "You want to pat me down, see if I'm wearing a wire?"

That made him laugh, though there wasn't a lot amusement in it. "No," he said. "Who was it?"

"I don't want to say until I've got it confirmed."

"We can do the confirming."

"That's what I'm worried about. Maybe I get somebody a beating and he doesn't deserve it."

"Friend of yours?"

"No."

"Then what are you worried for?"

Having this conversation didn't seem as good an idea as it had when I'd come looking for it. "General principles," I said. "The thing I want to know is what's it worth to you if I find the guy?"

He looked at me flat-eyed for a long pause. He might have been working out whether it was worth it to beat the information out of me right then and there, so he and Trick could get onto the next step. Finally he shrugged and said, "We gave you a grand up front. We'll give you another for the name."

"And if I give you not only the guy but the location of

the dope?"

"If it's still good, another five."

"Thousand."

Nicholson was back. "Those are the units we deal in."

"I'll be in touch," I said, then turned and started down the stairs.

"That," he said to my departing back, "would be a smart move. You wouldn't want us to think you'd found the stuff and decided to sell it yourself."

I looked up at him from the walkway. "I've been called a lot of things," I said, "but stupid isn't one of them."

He nodded, considering, then said, "Good exit line."

"You're welcome to it," I said.

Chapter 13

Mo wasn't there when I got home. There was a post-it note on my monitor telling me she'd gone up to Elk Falls for a meeting with the mill manager who was doomed but didn't know it. She might not make it back for supper.

It was lunch time. I heated up a can of soup and ate it with bread and cheese. Then I sat down at the computer and let the guy in the back of my head take a run at Benny Filiatrault's op-ed. The sentences and paragraphs rolled out with their usual fluency and at one point I asked the empty air around me, "If you can do this, why can't you write Mo's movie?"

No answer came, just the next thread in the *our village versus their village* narrative. I finished the draft — it was only eight hundred words — made myself a cup of tea, then sat down to polish the text. Twenty minutes later, it was on the fax and winging electronically to the sagging old house in Cumberland. I poured myself another cup of now-strong Ceylon and went out onto the deck to see what the birds were doing down on Farquharson's Farm.

Not much, was the impression. The fields were deserted. I went back inside, dumped the half a mug of tea into the sink and rinsed the cup and my soup bowl. *Now what?* I asked myself. I had no work to do, except for the work I wasn't able to do, but should have been doing.

I could go into the office and sit at the keyboard, the Ginger Goodwin file open, but nothing on the screen except *FADE IN:* and a blinking cursor. Perhaps something would turn over, down in the well of my psyche, and the words would start to flow.

More likely, I would just sit there and keep on sitting there while I got more and more miserable. I looked out the window over the sink. The Comox Glacier, slung between its grey peaks, ignored my gaze. But my mind was wandering from one loose thought to another and now it settled on Hockney's Woods and the patch that the Ketteriches had used to grow their hybrid Kush strain.

If someone had stolen the weed to sell it, they would have hauled it out in plastic garbage bags and stowed it in a garage or basement, preparatory to disposing of it out of town. But if Davey Clemmer had clipped the crop with the intention of ratting out Trick and Butch and winning his spurs as a confidential informant, he needn't have taken it far. The dope could be in the woods. It might be only a couple of hundred yards away from where it had grown, down a hole or even hauled up on a rope into the trees.

It was worth a look. If I found it, even if Clemmer didn't return to Cumby, the Ketteriches would pay me a five thousand-dollar recovery fee — more than enough to take Mo on a vacation for a couple of weeks, to someplace where I might find a way to broach the subject of how, and why, I'd been lying to her these past couple of weeks.

It was not the best idea I'd ever had. But right now it was the only one I could come up with. I changed my city shoes for the pair of boots I'd bought for my short-lived spy assignment in the Black Hole, and headed back over the river and up Cumberland Road.

I retraced the route the Ketteriches had taken, past the site of Haglund's last stand, but didn't push the old Ford as deep into the bush as the brothers' jacked-up four-by-four had gone. I got out and walked the rutted track until it became a trail, then pushed through the gap in the salal and salmonberry thicket.

I hadn't been paying close attention to the route the first time, but I remembered that we'd followed the trail to a particularly large fern, behind which was a big fallen log that we'd walked along until we'd come to a boulder. I tried a few ferns until I found the right one, walked the log and stepped onto the rock. Then it was down, across another log that bridged a small stream, then up to a ridge and along its crest to the big fallen tree. A few pokes around the undergrowth, and I found the severed stalk of a marijuana plant.

Okay, I told myself, *now we spiral out.* I'd read that that was the way to look for a trail if you were tracking someone and lost the scent. I found the far edge of the dope patch and started with a fifty-foot circle, eyes on the ground and, more important, nose sniffing the air for the skunky odour of a mass of marijuana. I figured that, even if it was tied up in garbage bags, the smell would be noticeable once I got close enough.

The trees here were huge, the trunks maybe twelve feet in diameter. Although the individual cedars and firs were widely spaced, the canopy of branches high overhead was so interlaced that no direct sunlight reached down to the thick carpet of needles on the forest floor. It was like walking through some dimly lit, pillared ancient temple. And it was solemnly quiet, no rustles in the undergrowth because there wasn't much to eat — plant life was thin on the ground except for the ubiquitous ferns. There were birds up in the heights — I could hear them calling to each other — and from somewhere in the gloomy distance came the sudden *rat-a-tat-tat* of a woodpecker.

As I traced my widening spiral, I saw that a little distance off to one side there was more light. A great tree must have come down some time in the past, opening enough room above for sunlight to penetrate and for faster-growing trees to take advantage of the opportunity for growth. *Like bacteria getting into a break in the skin,* I thought, *until the forest grows up another giant to overshadow and starve them out.* It would take centuries for the hole to be repaired, but old growth forests are living lessons in the power of vegetative persistence.

Gradually, I worked my way over to the better-lit part of the woods. I'd expected to find a fallen trunk, mouldering into the detritus of the forest floor. Instead I found, rising from a thicket of salal and salmonberry, a ten-foot-high trunk, its sides pocked with the man-made slots into which the long-ago fallers had put planks to stand on, while they worked the great saw back and forth through centuries of growth-rings. A huge cedar had been taken down here — apparently in pieces, from the top down; if it had been toppled, it would have made a far greater gap in the canopy, and might well have taken one or two of its neighbours down with it as it crashed to the floor.

I wondered why someone had surgically removed one tree, all those years ago — at least a century, judging by the size of one of the broad-leafed trees that had grown up in the gap. Then my mind switched gears as I caught the first rank whiff of high-grade marijuana. I took in a good noseful of the laden air and let the odour lead me around the huge stump. The smell got stronger as I pushed through the salal and I followed it across the light-well, the mid-afternoon sun streaming down through the thinner canopy in this half-healed wound in the forest.

I didn't see any bags of bud, although the strength of the odour told me I couldn't be more than a few feet from them. But I did see the remains of a camp: a place where someone had cut down the undergrowth to make a ten-foot wide clearing. On one side, bracken and ferns had been piled up to make a rough bed. Beside it was an oil lantern, the kind they always lit up the bad guys' hide-outs in old westerns. A blackened fire-pit dug through the compacted leaf-and-needle floor, some firewood stacked nearby, and a plastic grocery-store bag half-filled with wrappers from ramen noodle packages and empty sardine and beans cans, completed the tableau.

And that, I thought, *is how Davey Clemmer was around long enough to rig the trap that killed Haglund, without Cumberlanders noticing the stranger in their midst.* He must have camped out here while he scouted Trick and Butch's grow-site. Then when the Mounties turned down his offer to burn the Ketteriches, he'd moved over to his secondary target, working his way into the local greenies, with an eye on the Back Hole.

I squatted on my heels, poking through the grocery store bag in case there was something incriminating there — like a spool of fishing line — and finding only garbage. But I was thinking that what I'd said to Benny Filiatrault was not a bad guess: now that the Mounties were going to blow Clemmer's cover in the Clayoquot Sound protest, there really was a strong chance that he might fall back on Plan A. The dope was still here, somewhere — my nose was telling me in no uncertain terms — so the circumstances could still be manufactured to connect the Ketteriches to it and bring the cops down on them.

Which meant the would-be snitch would be back. I was glad I'd asked Sally McMahon to tell me if she spotted him. Maybe I should broaden my surveillance by asking Benny to do the same. The more I thought about that idea, the better it seemed. I would drop in on my client on the way out of Cumby.

But I still hadn't done what I'd come into the woods to do. I stood up and sniffed again, trying to gauge where the reek of marijuana was coming from. It was so strong, I couldn't see how it wasn't right under my nose. I picked up a stick of Clemmer's unused firewood and poked at the ground, thinking he might have dug and disguised a pit, but wherever I tapped I found only solid earth.

Behind the sleeping place some salal had grown up. It was dry and parched; there had been no substantial rainfall for several weeks. I pushed aside the branches with my piece of firewood and it seemed to me that the smell grew stronger. I pushed through the thicket, following my nose, the dry salal scratching against my sleeves, giving me its usual resistance. Then suddenly I was pitching forward, my foot snagging on a low-level creeper at the same time as the thicket in front of me abruptly thinned then disappeared.

I had sense enough not to throw out my hands to break my fall, which would have once again undone all of Sally's ministrations. Instead I turned so that I fell on my uninjured side. It gave me a jolt but I got no more than a sympathetic twinge from the old war-wound. I raised myself up on one elbow, the stench of prime bud overwhelming now, and looked around.

In the midst of the salal thicket was an open space, roughly square and six feet on a side. It was floored in something dark, and when I got to my knees I saw that heavy, squared timbers — railroad ties, I thought — had been laid side-to-side. The end of one of the ties, on the far side of the space, was higher than the others. I circled around the square, my feet pressing down the salal. I didn't want to step on the timbers because my last visit to the Cumberland Museum had given me an idea of what I had stumbled upon.

When I got to the up-lifted chunk of creosoted wood, I was not surprised to see that a pale, nylon rope passed underneath it. The other end of the rope went into the salal. I tugged on it, but it held firm, anchored no doubt to a broad-leafed tree that I could see standing on the other side of the thicket. I turned back to where the cord went under the up-lifted tie. I still had the length of firewood and I used it to lever up the squared timber. It came easily, and from the darkness below came an even stronger gust of marijuana.

I pushed the tie right up and threw it over to crash into the salal on the other side of the square. In front of me now was a tie-sized slot in the ground, and although the sunlight was slanting down onto it, the gap looked pitch-black except for where the pale rope disappeared down into the darkness.

I kneeled, took a one-handed grip on the cord, and pulled. The weight was too much for me to raise. Two-handed, I probably still couldn't manage it. If I was serious about it, I'd want to bring a tripod and a block and tackle. But I had no need to do so. The Ketteriches' marijuana could stay right where Clemmer had left it: suspended over the deep and narrow emptiness of an closed-off ventilation shaft that went and down until it met a tunnel in one of Cumberland's many decommissioned coal mines.

That's why the big cedar had been taken down, all those years ago: to make a clearing for the men who had brought in the equipment to dig the shaft. I worked my way around the square again, levered up the tie I'd removed, and let it fall back into place. Then I pushed my way back through the salal, trying to be careful not to trample the branches too much. Back in the camp, I tried to see if I'd left any evidence of my poking about. I positioned the grocery-store bag about where I thought I had found it.

I took one last look around and my gaze fell on something I'd missed before: a scrap of yellowy fabric under the salal and salmonberry near where I'd come in to the open space. I went to it, knelt, and tugged. Something slid out from under the thicket, a long bundle of old-fashioned oilcloth wrapped in twine. I slid the string off one end and unfolded the flap that sealed it. When I pushed the wrapping down, from the package emerged the rusty muzzle and front sight of a rifle.

Ho, ho, ho, I said to myself, *Davey boy, I've got you now.*

Benny Filiatrault called later in the day. He wanted a couple of minor changes in the op-ed text and I saw no reason not to accommodate him. I told them I'd run them through the word-processor immediately and fax them back to him.

"Fine," he said.

"Okay, talk to you later."

"Wait a minute."

"What?"

"When you were here before, did you take that bullet that was on the mantelpiece?"

"No," I said. "But when I looked into the living room I saw it on the mantelpiece. Now it's gone?"

"Yeah." He sounded puzzled.

"Maybe Davey's been by."

"You think?"

"You leave your front door open," I said, "anybody could zip in and out." I decided to tell him about the camp in the woods and the rifle wrapped in oilcloth. "Let's say the bullet came from that gun. And let's say I'm right that he wants to use the rifle to frame the Ketteriches. He wouldn't want the cops wondering what Trick and Butch had against you, and why they'd be so dumb as to shoot at your house."

"Cause they wouldn't," he said.

"The shot through your window was part of a different scam. That didn't work. The bullet only complicates the con he's working now."

He was silent for a moment, then he said, "I really misjudged that kid."

"He was telling you what you wanted to hear."

"Maybe I shouldn't be in politics if I'm that easily fooled."

"Nah," I said, "there's already too many of the other kind. You'll learn the tricks of the trade."

He grunted. "Some tricks," he said.

I completed the thought. "Some trade."

"Huh?"

"Never mind. Will you let me know if you see him around town."

There was silence for a moment, then he said, "Yeah, I will."

⌇

Mo called to say she'd be late for dinner. The manager her review had doomed had apparently got an inkling of the fate he had unknowingly designed for himself and was now fiddling with her consulting assignment's terms of reference in an attempt to save his job.

"It isn't going to work," she said over the phone. "The numbers don't lie." She sighed and I could hear the fatigue in her voice.

"Look on the bright side," I said. "You charge by the hour."

"Money's just money," she said. "At some point, the dance has to stop. You can't just keep on spinning around to the same tune."

"Are we talking musical chairs?" I said.

"I don't know what we're talking. I'll see you later."

She came in around ten, her face drawn, and said she was going straight to bed.

"Want company?" I said.

"Just sleep. I'm bagged."

I watched *NYPD Blue* then the news. The Clayoquot protests were still topping the bill on the local CBC newscast. There'd been some more road blockades, some more arrests. Crown prosecutors were asking for the greenies to be tried en masse to prevent them clogging the courts. Defence lawyers were protesting.

I switched channels and found a *Barney Miller* rerun, the one where Yemana and Harris get stoned on hashish-laced brownies. After that, it was Letterman, and I hung on till my eyes were swimming from the effects of yawning, even though I found Brother Theodore's presence on the show to be incomprehensible. But at least I didn't have to defend the show to Mo. With this episode, I wouldn't have had a leg to stand on.

I crawled into bed beside her. She was warm and smelled of lotion, and her breath was soft against my cheek. When I stroked her arm, she made an indistinct sound and turned over. I ran my hand down her back and patted her hip, and for a moment I had an impulse to wake her up and tell her how stupid I'd been. But I let it pass, turned my back to hers, and lay there thinking until I faded away.

The phone rang while I was making the morning tea. It was Karen.

"Can you take the boys earlier than we discussed?" she said. "The project I was going to start next week has been moved up."

"When?"

"Today would be best. I can put them on the ferry if you can pick them up in Nanaimo. They like the ferry. It has video games."

"I can do that," I said. "Which sailing?"

We made the arrangements. I would pick them up just before one p.m. As I hung up, Mo came into the kitchen, eyes still heavy with sleep.

"I've made tea," I said.

"Coffee," she said, and started doing things with the grinder and some beans. When the noise subsided, I told her about my sons' coming over early.

"Is that all right?" I said.

She sat at the table while she waited for the kettle to boil again. Her eyes were focused on a point in the air maybe ten inches in front of her. "Why not?" she said.

"I'm happy about it. They can be here for Nautical Days as well as for the air show."

"You think they'll like Nautical Days?" she said, then yawned.

"What's not to like?"

"It's kind of corny for the Nintendo generation."

She was right about that. Nautical Days was an annual celebration of the historical relationship between the town of Comox and the sea. It took place on the early August long weekend and began with a parade along Comox Avenue; the floats were homemade and amateurish, although the military bands from the airbase and the Sea Cadets station down on the Goose Spit were well rehearsed.

Then the action moved to the harbourside park, which filled up with booths and tents where you could buy anything from perogies and sausage to hand-made wind chimes or tie-dyed tee-shirts. A service club would put up a big tent and sell beer, and there'd be some small-time rock and country music acts.

"They've got to like the canoe jousting," I said. "It's slapstick. And the build-bail-and-sail is always funny." In the latter event, teams of two had four hours to slap together some kind of vessel from plywood and other materials donated by the local builders supply store. Then they had to carry them down the boat-launch ramp into the salt-chuck and paddle out to a buoy and back. Most contenders never made it.

The weekend after Nautical Days, we'd have the air show out at CFB Comox. "That they'll love," said Mo.

"They always do."

I sat down across from her with my tea. She extended the ten-inch stare to me, looking at me across the rim of her cup as she sipped.

"What?" I said.

She lowered the mug halfway to the table, took a breath. I suddenly went cold inside. She looked at me for several heartbeats — I could hear them in my ears — then she let the breath go. "Nothing," she said.

I drank half my tea, threw a look at my watch. "I'd better go. I got to gas up the car and it's tourist season on the highway."

"Yeah," she said.

I leaned over and kissed her on the cheek she lifted to meet me. "You going to be here when I get back?"

"No, you should have some dad-and-sons time."

"You'll be here for supper, though?"

She nodded, sipping her coffee. "You making?"

"Macaroni and cheese," I said. I made it working-class British style, lots of grated cheddar and baked in the oven, sliced tomatoes on top. Bill and Dick liked it.

"Okay."

"See you."

And I was out the door, still feeling that chill inside me. I climbed into the Behemoth with a silence singing in my ears and the certainty that something bad, very bad, had just passed me by.

You're going to have to tell her, I told myself as I fitted myself into the stream of Winnebagos and towed power boats rolling south down the highway. It wasn't going to be easy while the next few days were filled with the twins, but it wouldn't be much easier if they weren't there either.

I hadn't been raised to admit weakness, nor to turn away from trouble. *Get stuck in* could have been the family motto. It wasn't expected that I should win every battle, but the minimum requirement was to square up and do your best. So I wasn't just letting Mo down, but my mom and dad and all that long line of ancestors fading back into the shadows. Hell, I was even letting Ginger Goodwin down, and I'd never even known him.

"I'll do it," I told the Ford's windscreen. "I'll find the words. I'll make it up to her. It'll work out."

A semi-trailer blew by me heading north. The sound of its passage could have been saying, *Suuuuure.* I didn't like its tone.

I got to Departure Bay well before the ferry came in and was waiting at the arrivals door when the twins came rampaging up the passageway along with a hundred or so passengers. I had them throw their carryalls into the Ford's trunk, while they made derisive comments about the vehicle's age and size. But once they were settled in the back seat, with the plush upholstery and the fold-down middle armrest, they decided that the old piece of iron was actually pretty cool.

"I thank you," I said, "and Detroit thanks you." The big car still had four hundred cubic inches of power under the gigantic hood, so when we got the first passing lane on the road north, I put my foot down and we burned up the asphalt.

Mo was gone when we got home, so we dropped off the bags, after first getting out their swimming trunks and towels. I took them to White Spot for lunch and then out to Kye Bay, where you could walk half a mile out into the sea and have the water come no higher than your chest. The sandy bottom was littered with starfish and sea urchins, crabs scuttling away from our feet, and darting fish no bigger than my little finger.

Then it was over to the Filberg Festival, an annual crafts fair held in a park that used to be an old-time timber baron's summer retreat. The fair was invitation-only and drew some of the best handicrafts from a part of the world in which first-class artisans had proliferated since the sixties. I wasn't entirely sure that it would appeal to a couple of coltish fourteen-year-old city boys, but Bill pronounced the kaleidoscopes made from some dark satin-surfaced wood, "Awesome!" while Dick bought a fist-sized burl of polished yellow cedar that contained a secret drawer so carefully cut into the wood that I couldn't see it until he showed me how to tease it open.

"Excellent stash box!" he said, to which his brother answered, "Totally!" And then they both looked at me in a way that prompted me to say, "I didn't hear that, and I'd better not hear it again."

We stayed to listen to some of the bands that played on a stage off to one side of the fair, but they were a little too folky even for me. I took them back to the house on Back Road and left them to their own devices while I assembled the macaroni and cheese.

Mo arrived while I was slicing the tomatoes, said hi, and went out into the back yard where the kids were hanging out. I heard laughter and the kind of braying sounds that only a teenage boy can emit. When I stepped over to the window and glanced out, Dick was hanging by his knees from a low branch of the pear tree the original builder of the house had planted forty years ago. Bill was walking on his hands.

I took it for a good sign. They hadn't spent much time with Mo, and none at all since she'd moved in. If they were competing to show off for her, any ice that might have formed had been broken.

I put the macaroni and cheese in the oven, positioned a baking tray on the shelf below to catch the inevitable drips, and set the timer. Then I went out onto the little roofless porch that overlooked the back yard.

"Dinner in about an hour," I said.

The boys did most of the talking around the table, in between inhaling huge quantities of pasta and melted cheddar. Mo ate half of what I put on her plate, but downed more than half of a bottle of a Chilean red wine she'd brought home a couple of weeks back and that had got lost in the cupboard under the counter. I had a glass, but it was a bit raw for my taste.

When the plates were cleaned away, I told everybody to get back in their seats then went to my office and brought back a set of the board game *Risk* that I'd picked up in Vancouver a while back.

"I used to play this when I was a kid—" I began.

"So why should we be any different?" said Dick.

"It's a good game," I said. "Clean, family fun. Plus you get to conquer the world."

Bill had opened the box and was lifting up the folded board. "Where do you put the batteries in?"

"Ha, ha," I said. "Unfold the board and pick a colour while I shuffle the cards."

It turned out they'd both played the game at friends' houses, and Mo had played with her brother when they were teenagers. It also turned out that the rules had changed since the original version, so the boys had the unequalled pleasure of setting their father straight. After that, it seemed that they also ignored strategy and position and spent most of their time attacking me, until I was soon driven out of the game and had to turn over my cards to Mo, who swept in and finished me off after Bill and Dick had reduced me to a pitiful remnant.

"See?" I told the two of them while they grinned and smirked as only fourteen-year-olds can do. "Now she's going to clean your clocks."

But she didn't. She played without the ruthlessness that the game requires, while finishing the bottle of wine. Eventually, she was forced out, and the twins settled in for a war of mutual attrition that Lord Kitchener would have recognized. As the dice rolled and the little plastic men were carried off the battlefield, Mo yawned and said she was going to bed.

I joined her an hour or so later. She was a still lump under the covers. If she wasn't asleep, she was doing a good impression. I slid in beside her in the darkness and ran my hand once up the middle of the back that was turned to me. She didn't respond.

I rolled over and lay there, staring into the dark. I could hear the twins talking and giggling from the spare room. After a while, they settled down. I continued to look at nothing, the same pointless thoughts running through my mind. At some point, I fell asleep.

The build-bail-and-sail was a hit. We left the park after the last flimsy craft had sunk and went to White Spot again for burgers. Mo said she had to do some work on the Elk Falls reorganization, so we dropped her off at the house and I took the twins up the old logging road — now paved, I was glad to discover — that led up to the ski country on Mount. Washington and we walked through meadows that would be cross-country ski fields come winter. From up there you could see the whole of the Comox Valley, with the sea beyond and then the mountains of the coastal range on the far horizon.

"Look at that one," Dick said, pointing out a classically conical peak. "It looks like a volcano."

"It probably is," I said. "We're part of the Ring of Fire. There are volcanoes all up and down the coast." I told them I'd seen a *Nova* documentary about it a while back.

"Active?" Bill said.

"Or extinct?" Dick finished for him.

"Dormant," I said. I explained about the big Pacific tectonic plate that was pushing itself under the one beneath Vancouver Island, lifting mountains and causing hot spots. "One of these days...kablooie! Major earthquake, nine or ten on the Richter scale."

"And volcanoes going off?" Dick said.

"We've already had Mount. St. Helen's. So why not?"

The twins fell to discussing what it would be like if a major quake brought civilization to a halt and they had to survive in the ruins. They agreed it would be totally radical. In the midst of it, my cell phone buzzed in my pocket.

I flipped it open and heard Benny Filiatrault's voice. "Benny," I said, "I can't do much for you this week. I've got my sons over from the mainland."

"I'm not calling about work," he said. "You wanted to know if I'd seen Davey?"

"Have you?"

"No. But a guy I know said he picked him up hitchhiking a couple of days back, dropped him off in Cumby."

"So he's back."

"Yep. I asked around, but nobody else has seen him."

That figured. He'd be keeping out of sight, and I knew where he'd be doing that.

I was tempted to go right now and check out the camp in the woods. But I had the kids with me, and Davey Clemmer had a rifle. He'd killed Sid Haglund and hadn't shown any upset about it, and he'd had no qualms about delivering me into a beating. I called Mo at the house, but she said she needed uninterrupted time to work. In fact, she was thinking of catching the ferry over to Powell River and driving down to her brother's place in Sechelt for a few days to get the damn thing done.

"I'm sorry," I said. "I didn't think the kids would be so loud and busy."

"They're fine," she said. "I just need some thinking space."

Part of me wanted to ask her what kind of thinking she needed to do. But a bigger part of me was afraid to ask. "Okay," I said. "The air show is Friday and Saturday. Sunday they'll go back to Karen's."

"I'll come back then," she said.

I told her that would be okay. I told her I would miss her. I told her I loved her, after walking a few feet away from two pairs of fourteen-year-old ears.

"Yes," she said, and hung up.

I closed the phone, then a moment later I opened it again. Then I had to get my wallet out of my back pocket and fish around in its folds until I found Sally McMahon's card. I punched in the number and she answered after a few rings.

I identified myself then told her what Filiatrault had told me. "So he's around. Will you keep an eye out for him and let me know if you see him?"

"Oh, yes," she said. "Count on it."

"But be careful. He has a rifle."

"Has he?"

"I think it's something he found in the woods. The ammunition's probably out of date, but it could still be dangerous. Especially if he's bought a fresh box of shells."

"I'll be careful, then," she said.

Nautical Days always concluded with a military tattoo at sunset, put on by the Sea Cadets who had spent the summer at HMCS Quadra, a training camp on the Goose Spit that jutted out into Comox Harbour. The boys and girls marched in columns into the harbour park, dragging a pair of field guns with them. They executed various drills and manoeuvres culminating in firing the guns. The cadet band played stirring old sea songs and the cadets sang about conquering and fighting again. I was surprised to find myself tapping my foot to the band's rendition of *The Maple Leaf Forever*, which I realized I hadn't heard played on anything but a World War II documentary since my childhood.

"That's a good old song," I said to the twins, "though the lyrics are crap." But they were more interested in the cannons.

By the time the cadets marched off the field, still singing, the sky was darkening. The crowd moved down toward the water's edge. Out in the harbour, a barge floated, loaded with fireworks. The people waited patiently for full dark to come on, except for the usual clutch of hyperactive kids who ran around and had to be pulled back from possible fatal injury when they tried to climb over the boardwalk railings above the rip-rap mole of boulders enclosing the boat basin. A gaggle of teenagers on the edge of the crowd drank beer from paper bags and goofed around like teenagers always do.

Then we heard a dull *thump* from out in the water and a few seconds later a great fiery blossom appeared over our heads. *Oooh,* said the crowd, then *Aaah,* when another burst just behind the fading remnants of the first. And so it went for twenty minutes. No accompanying music like they did in the big-city events. No astounding pyrotechnics. Just a small-town event for small-town people, who, when it was over, filed out of the park talking quietly, parents herding their over-tired kids and carrying toddlers on shoulders, couples holding hands, old folks and teenagers, all mixed together as they rarely ever were.

The twins and I walked up several blocks, the curbs lined with parked cars, to where I'd found a spot for the Behemoth. I was missing Mo. We hadn't done a Nautical Days fireworks display yet, and I would have liked to have held her hand and been part of that summer-night crowd that might have stepped out of a Ray Bradbury story.

We drove home and the house was empty. The boys would have stayed up, but I half-threatened, half-cajoled them into turning in. Twenty minutes later, they were sound asleep.

I went into the office and turned on the computer. I opened the file that was supposed to contain the Ginger Goodwin treatment. The Bradbury mood that had hung over the park was still with me, but when I put my fingers to the keyboard, nothing came. I stared at the monitor and waited to see a picture in my head, something that I could turn into words. But all I saw was my own reflection in the dark glass.

I struggled with it, the way I'd never had to struggle before. The words had always come, whenever I needed them. This should have been one of the easiest writing jobs I'd ever tackled; I already knew the story, the whole middle, beginning, and end of it. I had decided on the point of view from which to tell it. The rest should have been mostly typing.

But it wouldn't come. Whatever the part of me was that did the writing was just refusing to work. It was like the time I'd had minor surgery on my knee. I was in my mid-twenties, before I found out the chronic pain in the leg was the result of a fragment of cracked-off bone that had lodged in the joint years before, after I'd been kicked in an elementary school soccer game. When I was back home recovering, lying in bed, I steeled myself to endure the pain then tried to move the injured leg so I could get up and go to the bathroom. But it just wouldn't move. No signal was being transmitted from the brain to the muscles. The lines were down.

I tried typing random words, then the one about the quick brown fox and the lazy dog. I'd heard that that was one method of overcoming writer's block. But nothing happened. The words remained random, the fox jumped but the dog wouldn't hunt.

"Crap!" I said, aloud. "What's the matter with you? Write the goddamn thing!"

I tried to use the anger to push through the inertia. Nothing. I suddenly found myself thinking about Davey Clemmer, and then about Lancolm Halfnight, and the way they'd set me up. I knew they had nothing to do with what I was really angry about, but what the hell? Getting mad at myself wasn't accomplishing anything. At least I could look forward to rubbing Clemmer's nose in his own mess. And maybe, somewhere down the road, I could find a way to pay Lanc back for the way he'd messed me around.

I let myself daydream about that for a while. *Nothing wrong with my imagination*, I concluded. *I bet I could write that scenario in no time flat.*

But that didn't solve the problem staring at me from the darkness of the monitor. After a while, I shut off the system and went to bed. I could smell Mo's shampoo on her pillow, but when I ran my hand over the place where she would have lain, the sheet was cold.

Chapter 14

The boys and I continued to do the sights and attractions of the Comox Valley for the next couple of days. Then came the air show. The day began with the Snowbirds, all nine of the red and white jets, flying arabesques over the town, making windows rattle and dogs duck for cover.

"Cool!" said the twins in unison, as we went out onto lawn to watch the display. The sky cleared, the contrails beginning to spread, and we waited to see if they'd come back for more. But the come-on was over, so we turned back toward the house where we'd left our breakfast of toaster-heated waffles on the table.

But Bill said, "What's that?"

I looked to where he was looking, saw a small dark shape just above the southern horizon. It rapidly grew larger as we watched, a dull black object flying toward us in perfect silence. It was roughly triangular in shape, and for a moment I had the absurd thought that it was a giant-sized version of one of the old cast-iron, wood-stove-heated irons that housewives in Ginger Goodwin's day would have applied to the household sheets and shirts.

Then it passed almost right over our heads, all three of us with our necks tilted back as far as they would go. It must have been going at least two hundred miles an hour because it was over our heads for no more than a few seconds.

"F-117!" said Dick. "Radical!"

"Totally!" said Bill.

"We gotta go there," they both said to me in unison.

I looked at my watch. The air show wouldn't open its gates until 10 a.m. "Eat first," I said.

When the gates opened, we had already been waiting forty-five minutes. The boys were among the first half-dozen through the barrier, and they ran past the hangars and airbase buildings to the wide concrete apron where the planes were parked. I caught up to them where they were leaning over the rope-on-posts barrier that surrounded the American stealth fighter, studying its oddly angled fuselage and cockpit.

"Listen," I said, "I'm not going to be able to keep up with you so we need a time and place to rendezvous." I looked around, spotted a hot-dog stand with a big sign that said it was being operated by the local Lions Club.

"There," I said, "at three o'clock."

"Got it," they said. But I made sure they had my cell phone number as well. If anything happened, and I told them sunstroke was not out of the question on an open airfield in August, they could find a phone and call me.

"Yeah, sure," they said. There was a CF-18 fighter parked maybe fifty yards away, its flight-suited pilot standing within its roped circle and talking to the crowd that had gathered around.

"Hot dog stand, three o'clock!" I called after them as they ran. Bill raised a hand in dismissive acknowledgement.

I wandered around, said hello to a few faces I recognized, watched as a smoke-trailing biplane performed an aerobatic routine over the airfield, the daredevil letting the antique craft fall out of the air only to recover control just a hundred feet above the tarmac. I walked through a giant C-130 Hercules transport, the kind that could deliver any military cargo, from a whole company of infantry to the tanks that would support them on a battlefield. I climbed into the gondola of a tethered Goodyear blimp and found it surprisingly roomy.

By then, my interest level had pretty well been reached. I wandered past a display of radio-controlled miniature planes and helicopters flown by local hobbyists, then headed for an open-sided marquee tent where the Elks were selling cold beer to a thirsty and grateful crowd. I got a plastic cup of lager and found an empty folding chair in the shade. I sipped and watched what I could see of the air show, which from that vantage was mostly people passing between me and the airfield.

Way out on the grass beyond the apron and runway, I could see some kind of activity going on: uniformed figures moving objects they were unloading from a couple of trucks. Seated a few feet from me, an older man with a military mustache was watching the activity through a pair of binoculars.

"Excuse me," I said. "Can you see what they're doing out there."

He lowered the glasses and turned to me. "Building a forest," he said. I would swear his eyes actually twinkled. "For the Martin Mars," he continued.

"The water bomber?"

He explained the air force was putting up some cardboard and plywood trees soaked in aviation fuel that they would set alight as soon as they got a signal from the plane that it had filled its hold from Comox Lake and was back in the air. The bomber would come in low over the airfield and let go six thousand imperial gallons of water onto the blaze.

"Now that would be worth seeing," I said.

"From a distance," he agreed.

I thanked him and watched the world go by, sipping beer. When my cup was half empty, my cell phone rang.

"Is that you, Sid?" said a voice I didn't recognize.

"Who is this?"

I heard a throat being cleared. "Sally McMahon. You asked me to call if I saw that guy."

I sat up straight. "Did you?"

"I'm looking at him right now," she said.

"Where are you?"

"On Dunsmuir. He's in the grocery store. I'm parked across the street."

"Don't let him spot you," I said.

"He doesn't know me. I almost didn't recognize him." She told me Clemmer had a beard now and that he'd ditched the granny glasses. The all-black clothing was also gone, replaced with a jeans and checked-shirt ensemble that would let him blend right in with Cumby's street scene. "I'm going to follow him," she finished.

"Be careful." I was already up and moving, the phone to my ear as I made my way out of the beer tent and wove through the crowd toward the parking area. "I'm on my way. Call me back in ten minutes."

I closed the phone and looked at my watch. It was just gone 11:30, plenty of time to do what I needed to do and get back in time to rendezvous with the boys. But as I got into the Ford and started it up, the question raised itself: just what exactly was I going to do?

The general answer was easy enough: I was going to settle the score with Davey Clemmer. I owed him for some aches and pains, including a near-concussion that wouldn't have happened if he hadn't set me up to be booted out of the Black Hole. I also wanted to clue him in on the reality that he wasn't the slick operator he thought he was. And I would enjoy letting him in on the fact that I had only to call Trick and Butch Ketterich and he'd be in for a world of hurt.

As I headed down Ryan Road toward the Fifth Street Bridge, I spoke those words aloud. "A world of hurt, Davey boy." But by the time I was over the bridge and working my way over to the Cumberland Road, the more rational part of my psyche was stepping forward, raising a finger, and saying, "Hey, wait a minute."

The quickest, easiest way to deal with Davey Clemmer was to make sure he was holed up where I thought he'd be, then make a quick phone call to the number in my wallet, and drop the Ketteriches on him. It would also be a profitable move, because Trick and Butch would be moved to reward me for not only ratting out the guy who had stolen their dope, but for telling them where the marijuana was stashed.

But should I also tell them Clemmer had a rifle? I didn't think that would deter the brothers. It would just make them show up at the hidden campsite with whatever arsenal the modern Cumby dope grower considered to be appropriate to the nature of the business. Probably AK-47s and nine-millimetre pistols, according to what I'd read in the papers.

Did I really want to precipitate a gunfight? Maybe a murder? And if the confrontation ended with the Ketteriches gunning down Clemmer and dropping his body down the same ventilation shaft in which he'd hidden their purloined pot, what would happen next?

I could imagine Trick saying to Butch, "That Rafferty guy knows something that could hurt us."

And I could see Butch doing a thoughtful impression of Jack Nicholson saying, "You got that right."

Or I could call Corporal Mikhailovsky and tell him Davey was holed up in possession of the dope and a weapon. That would bring armed Mounties in bulletproof vests down on Clemmer's head. But then I'd have the problem of explaining how I happened to know about the dope and the gun. Worse, I'd have to explain to Butch and Trick why I called the cops instead of them, after they'd so kindly given me a thousand bucks.

I was passing the Cumberland cemetery with a mile or so to go when the phone on the seat beside me rang. It was Sally again.

"He's left the store and is heading toward the lake

road," she said.

"On foot?"

"Yeah. I'm following in the car."

"Stay way back," I said. "I know where he's going."

"Where?"

"He's been hiding out in Hockney's Woods. I've seen the place."

"Uh huh," she said.

I asked her where she was, and she told me she was just at the turn-off to the lake road. I was only a few minutes away. "Wait there for me. Let him get into the woods, then I'll go in after him."

But when I pulled up beside where her car was parked at the turn-off to the lake road, she was standing beside it, dressed in jeans and a wool shirt, wearing boots. I made the passenger side window go down and said, "I'll take it from here."

"No, you won't," she said. Her face was drawn and pale. She looked like one of those women in the old photographs at the museum, the ones who spent every day with the knowledge that at any moment word might come death had once again stalked through the underground galleries and it had claimed their men.

She pulled open the Ford's passenger door and got in, sat there with arms folded, staring straight ahead. "Go," she said.

"Sally, this could be—"

"They're my woods," she said. "You can't tell him to bugger off, but I can."

"He might be armed."

She didn't look at me. "And you're bulletproof?"

I put the Behemoth in gear and turned onto the lake road. I couldn't see Davey Clemmer, but after I had eased along for a while at thirty kilometres an hour, I spotted him walking along the side of the road, half a klick ahead, plastic grocery bags dangling from both hands. I stopped the car and watched until he went out of sight around a curve. Then I drove slowly forward until I was close to the curve. I parked and got out, easing the door closed so it wouldn't make its big-car *thunk*. Sally did the same on her side.

We walked around the inside of the curve, shaded by trees growing close to the road. When I could see down the next straightaway, I saw Clemmer still hiking along. He was passing the spot where Haglund had died. Soon he would come to the old growth stand, and the place where the track led to the hidden trail that led to the Ketteriches' marijuana grow. I watched until I saw him leave the road and plunge into the bushes.

"Okay," I said, and went back to the Ford. Sally came with me. I drove slowly down to where the track started. "This'll do," I said.

I got out of the car and stood, listening. I could hear nothing but the sounds of a chainsaw stopping and starting somewhere back toward town, and a couple of ravens conversing up in the canopy. Then I heard the thrum of heavy plane engines, distant but coming closer. I turned to Sally.

"I really don't think you should come."

"What are you planning to do?" she said.

"Tell him off," I said. I realized I had made the decision. "Put a scare into him, tell him I'll sic the Ketteriches on him." Her eyebrows went up and I explained. "He stole their dope."

Her jaw was set. She looked off into the trees. "I'm not scared of him," she said. "Besides, he's got a lot of damn nerve living on my land, poking around where he's not wanted."

"Well, stay behind me," I said. There was no hurry. I got my boots out of the trunk of the car and changed my footwear. Then I set off down the track. Once again,

I found the big fern and the fallen log and the boulder. Before too long, I was at the site of the harvested marijuana crop. I looked toward the place where the big cedar stump marked a break in the canopy. I saw grey tendrils of smoke rising through the sunlit air. A moment later, the faint breeze shifted and I caught the odour of burning wood.

"He's there," I whispered to Sally. The forest floor was a thick mat of dried needles and cedar that silenced our footsteps. I used the widely separated big trees for cover, and went forward in a crouch. When I came to the thicket of water-starved salal and salmonberry that surrounded Clemmer's camp, I paused. I supposed that some commando could wriggle forward, belly to the ground, and pass through the barrier silently. But I couldn't, so with a glance back at Sally, close behind me, her eyes wide in a face that had gone pale, I breasted my way through the scratchy branches.

The noise warned Clemmer someone was coming, so that by the time I could see him he had risen from where he'd been sitting on his rolled-up sleeping bag on top of the pile of ferns and bracken he's made for a bed. He'd rigged an arrangement of sticks that supported a cooking pot over a bed of embers that lay in the pit. The wrappers of a couple of noodle packets lay on the ground, their contents swirling in boiling water. I thought he'd been dumb to leave the fire to burn down to coals while he went to town for supplies. The woods were dry as tinder.

He was standing on the other side of the firepit. In his hand was a hatchet, the kind with a rubber grip over a steel handle, and on his face was an aspect of fear that quickly faded away when he recognized me. If I'd had to put a label on the expression that took its place, I would have called it puzzled amusement. It didn't change when he saw Sally come out of the thicket behind me.

But he kept hold of the hatchet as he said, "You two weren't looking for a secluded spot for — what would people your age call it? — a little nookie?"

"We were looking for you," I said. "And we knew just where to look."

Now he was wearing a knowing look. "I thought someone had been by during my absence," he said. I could see the gears turning in his all-too-clever mind as he thought it through. "But you didn't take the dope." He was waiting for me to say something, but I stayed quiet. "The guys who grew it would pay a pretty good reward for its return," he said.

"Five grand," I said, "If I throw in the guy who stole it."

That clashed with his take on me. I could see him processing the information. "You?" he said. "A snitch for a couple of dopers?"

"They paid me a grand just to look around," I said. I paused, savouring the effect of what I was going to say next. I took out my cell phone and opened the cover. "I've got their number on speed dial. Can you appreciate the irony?"

He made a sound like a half-swallowed snort. "Give me a—" He broke off, his eyes going past me to Sally. "Hey, leave that alone!"

I turned my head enough to see, from the corner of my eye, Sally had gone to where the oilcloth still lay under the edge of the salal. She ignored him and, stopping, yanked the bundle out. Clemmer stepped around the fire pit towards her, the hatchet raised threateningly. But before he could reach her, she had the rifle out of its covering. She worked the bolt and a piece of dull brass arced off into the thicket. Then she raised the weapon and aimed it at him.

He stopped a few feet from her, and now he looked genuinely worried. "That's a really old gun," he said. "It might blow up in your hands."

"No," she said, her voice tight. "If it was going to do that, it would have happened when you took the shot through Benny's window."

He was looking at her differently now, and again I could see the gears turn. "What do you want?" he said.

"Drop the hatchet," Sally said. When he let it fall to the ground, she followed with, "Over here," and stepped back, gesturing with the rifle for him to move toward me.

"Okay," I said to Clemmer, closing the cell phone, "here's what you're going to do."

"Sid?" Sally said, her eyes still on Clemmer.

"What?"

"Shut up now."

I looked at her, my face saying, "Huh?"

He was watching her, his face uncertain, as he came around the fire pit toward me.

"Stop," she said.

He looked at me, then back to her. Now I could practically hear his mental gears whirring. "What's going on?" he said.

"Just do as I say and everything will be all right."

"Sally," I began, but she pointed the rifle at me. In books, people who have guns pointed at them always focus on the muzzle. But that's just an artistic conceit. In real life, you watch the face of the person holding the weapon, because that's where your fate lies. In Sally's face I saw cold, hard determination. Whatever was going on here, she had already thought it through and come to terms with it. Nothing I said was going to make it better, and could only make it worse.

She held the rifle one-handed, the butt under her arm. I saw that it didn't waver much. With her free hand she reached into a pocket and brought out a handful of cords, the kind of line people in Cumby still strung across their back yards to dry their washing on. She threw them at Clemmer's feet.

"Tie his hands," she told him.

This time I had to speak. As he bent to pick up the cords, I said, "Sally, what's this all about?"

Her face didn't alter. "Just do as I say and everything will be all right." It sounded like something she'd rehearsed for the occasion. That, and the fact that she'd brought the restraints with her, cut to a useable size, worried me.

She told me to turn around, and I did. "Take the phone and put it on the ground," she said, and Clemmer did as he was bidden. Then she had him wrap the clothesline several times around my wrists and knot the ends. I could feel the flesh swelling as the blood pooled in my hands.

"Sid, you lie face down," Sally said, then to Clemmer, "and you lie beside him. I'm going to tie your hands, but if you try anything the rifle will be handy and I'll shoot you in the head. Even if the ammunition's deteriorated, it will still probably kill you."

"All right," Clemmer said. "Be cool."

I was lying on my belly, face turned to the side and I saw him lie down beside me. The look on his face was cool calculation, but behind it was fear. Then he looked the obvious question at me, and I gave him the only visual answer I could: that I had no more idea than he what this was all about.

He grunted as Sally knelt on his back, the rifle's muzzle touching the back of his head but angled in at forty-five degrees from the right side. Quickly, she pulled his wrists together and tied them. Then she was up and standing over us, tucking my cell phone into a pocket of her jeans.

"Now are you going to tell us?" I said.

She was silent. I raised one shoulder and turned my head to look up at her. She had given off an aura of studied determination while she'd been getting us under control. Now I saw a face filled with misery.

"Come on, Sally," I said. "How bad can it be?"

It was the wrong question. The hardness came back.

"Bad, Sid," she said. "As bad as it gets in Cumberland."

"I don't understand."

"I know."

"Then make me understand."

My position was giving me a crick in my neck. I lowered my head until I was looking at Davey Clemmer again. He was thinking hard. I heard her sigh, and when she spoke her only emotion was weary resignation. "What good does understanding do? It doesn't change anything."

Of course it didn't. But an explanation took time, and in that time something might happen, someone might come along to alter the direction of the events I was increasingly sure were about to lead to me dying, right here beside a pot of noodles. So I said, "You've got to tell me. What did I do?" I clutched at a straw. "Do you think he and I were responsible for Stu Haglund's death?"

There was no humour in the short half-moan of laughter that came from above me. "God, no," she said, "that was me."

"What?"

"I spiked some trees and strung some traps," she said. "They were damned obvious. And I sent Rod a warning with cut-out letters." I heard her swallow, and her voice thickened. "I just wanted them to back off. I thought Stu would see the fishing line or maybe trip over it. I didn't think he'd miss it, at least until it was too late."

"But why?"

"Because these woods can't come down," she said. "There's a secret buried here, and it has to stay buried."

"What secret?"

She said nothing.

Davey spoke up. "The bones. Where I found the rifle."

"Aren't you the smart one?" she said, but there was no humour in it.

"Look," I said, "whatever it is, I promise I won't tell anybody." I looked at Clemmer. "We both do, right?"

"Sure," he said.

I heard that painful laugh again. Then I heard her letting out a long breath. "It will be a relief to be able to tell somebody," she said, more to herself than to me, "after all these years."

She paused — I supposed she was gathering her thoughts — then she began to speak.

Thomas "Scabby" Anderson hadn't known where Ginger Goodwin and the other conscientious objectors were hiding out at a place called Alone Mountain above the west end of Comox Lake. The fugitives, knowing that someone would come looking for them, had been too careful. But there were people in Cumberland who knew the general location, the select few at Campbell's store who packed supplies up to the southeastern shore of the lake and rowed them down the long stretch of water to a spot on shore where a trail came down out of the woods.

"My grandfather was one of those few," Sally said. "Philip Hockney, his name was. His dad was a miner, but Philip didn't have the stamina for it. Bad chest, probably TB. There was a lot of that around in those days.

"So he got a job in the store. And when Ginger and the boys went into the woods, he drove the truck that took their supplies up to the lake and he helped row the boat. So he knew where the trail met the water.

"The word was out, the Dominion Police were paying for information that would lead them to the objectors. My grandfather knew he wouldn't live a long life, and he had a wife and child to provide for. You have to remember that, in those days, there were no widows' pensions or welfare. Christ, that was what Ginger and the unions were fighting for."

She told me her grandfather had been gradually buying the stretch of woods that still bore his name. Woodland was cheap in those days — it was everywhere — but on a store clerk's salary it would have taken years for him to save it all up. But the man who owned the timber knew what the consumptive Philip Hockney was trying to do for his family, and was willing to let him pay a dollar a week on an agreement of sale.

"He'd been paying that for almost two years," Sally said, "and it would have taken him another two years to pay off the rest. But he didn't have the time. The TB was getting worse, and he knew he might not live to complete the deal.

"Meanwhile, the Dominion Police were offering a hundred-dollar reward for Ginger Goodwin's whereabouts." She paused and sighed. "He never thought they meant to kill him. Just bring him in, put him jail for the duration. And it looked as if the war wouldn't last too much longer, now that the Americans were in it."

So her grandfather met with Constable Dan Campbell and his superior officer, Inspector William Devitt, out in the woods. He told them where the trail came to the water near a couple of distinctive boulders, drew them a map. The policeman took that information to Scabby Anderson, who went out and scouted the area, and came back to say he'd seen footprints and knew where the fugitives were coming down to the water to fish and bathe.

"That was all Dan Campbell needed. He took his rifle and went to wait behind a log at a bend in that trail. And when Ginger came down, carrying his fishing rod, Campbell shot him through the throat.

"And that was that."

The Dominion Police paid Philip Hockney his reward. The clerk had come home with an envelope full of five- and ten-dollar bills bearing the images of Kings Edward VII and George V, the men who ruled the Empire for which Ginger Goodwin was expected to be happy to give his life. The store clerk sat in his shabby little parlour, pale and trembling, until he was seized by a fit of coughing that left his handkerchief spotted with red.

He had attended the coroner's inquest — at which not a single miner was empanelled for the jury — and heard it deliver its neutral, no-blame verdict. He saw the photographs of Goodwin's body, heard Dan Campbell's self-serving testimony, saw the .30-calibre Marlin rifle that had fired the fatal shot.

He did not go out with the rest of the town for the funeral, telling his wife and friends the walk was too far for a man in his condition. But with Cumberland virtually empty, he had gone to the hall where the inquest had been conducted, pried open the back door and the coroner's evidence locker, and stolen Campbell's rifle.

When Beatrice Hockney came home with her young daughter from the graveside, she found a note on the kitchen table. Beneath it was the envelope containing the hundred dollars. The note instructed her to tell anyone who asked that Philip had gone off to volunteer for the army. It told her to use the money to pay off the rest of the sum owing on the timber land. And it told her where in those woods she would find her husband's body, after he put the Marlin's muzzle in his mouth and pushed down with his thumb on the trigger.

Beatrice followed his directions. Out in the woods, she found her husband had brought a shovel with which he had considerately dug his own grave and laid himself in it before shooting himself. He'd even brought an oilcloth to lay over himself before firing the shot, so that she wouldn't have to see the mess the .30-calibre made of his skull. But Beatrice Hockney was as practical as a woman of her time and circumstances needed to be. The rifle was valuable. So she wrapped it in the oilcloth and tied it tightly with some string she had in her pocket and laid it beside her dead husband. In time she might come back for it.

Then she said a Hail Mary, picked up the shovel, and put back the earth Philip had piled to one side. She rolled a length of fallen log over the grave to keep scavengers away, and went home.

I interrupted Sally McMahon. "Over near the Ketteriches' grow, there were some bones that had been washed out of the ground by a stream."

"Huh," was all she said. She paused for a moment, then continued the tale.

Her grandmother had told anyone who asked that her husband had gone for a soldier and she began taking in washing. She moved into the smaller bedroom with her little daughter, and rented out the larger room to the first of a succession of boarders. She lived on what she made from these endeavours and gradually used the money her husband left her to buy the woods in which he lay. Once she owned them outright, she hired men to cut the timber, a few trees at a time, and sold them wherever she could.

But the stretch of old growth surrounding her husband's grave remained untouched.

"And so it would have," Sally said, "if my damned husband hadn't got greedy."

When they cut the trees and bulldozed the land, they would have found the body. And the rifle. The make and calibre would have guaranteed every eye in Cumberland would have turned toward Hockney's Woods, and every tongue would have begun to wag.

"Sally," I said, "it was a long time ago. Nothing to do with you. You hadn't even been born."

She said nothing. I turned my head to look up at her again. She was looking down at me with the same face she probably would have shown me if I'd told her Tinkerbell would flutter down from Never Never Land and make everything tickety-boo.

"There is no long time ago in Cumberland," she said. "It's always right now, all the time. And it doesn't matter when I was born. They'll know I've always known. Nobody will ever speak to me again. They wouldn't spit on me if

I was on fire. My life, everything and everybody I've ever known, all over, finished."

"No," I said.

"Yes!" Her face was full of agony for a moment, then the grim curtain came down again. She kneeled on Davey Clemmer's lower back again. He'd heard out her confession in silence, though I'd seen his brow knitted up in thought. Now he squirmed fruitlessly beneath her and said, "It's nothing to do with me! I won't tell anybody! I promise!"

Again she sighed. "Sure you will. My grandfather hated being an informer. He did it to save his family, then killed himself for it. But you, you never wanted to be anything else!"

"No!"

But she wasn't listening. I saw her reach forward and place her index and middle fingers of each hand carefully on either side of his throat toward the front. Then she pressed inward. I was looking at his panicky face and in a moment I saw the light leave his eyes and the tension go out of his straining neck. His eyes closed and his head hit the pad of dried needles.

"It's painless," she said. "I press on the carotid synapses. The pressure sends an impulse along the vagus nerve that fools the brain into thinking there's a sudden dangerous spike in blood pressure. The system responds by drastically lowering blood pressure. After a while, the brain begins to be starved of oxygen so it triggers the breathing reflex and the person wakes up."

While she was saying this, her hands were moving off Clemmer's neck. One hand went over his mouth, the thumb and fingers of the other pinched his nostrils shut. "But when the reflex is triggered, if no air comes into the lungs..."

I saw it happen. A spasm shook the young man's body. It lasted only a second. His eyelids flickered but did not open. All the rigidity seeped out of his muscles. He lay flat and inert beneath her. She kept her hands in place for several more seconds, then she released their grip. Davey Clemmer was gone.

"You did that to Rod Bilder," I said. I was horrified, not just by the enormity of what she'd done before me, but by the ease with which a life could be snuffed out — an act no more difficult than pinching a candle flame.

She was getting to her feet. "He wouldn't listen. It was a dirty trick, that business with the A and B shares."

"You killed him!"

"He was going to send in men with metal detectors to look for the spikes in the trees. They'd have found the rifle."

"Except Clemmer already found it," I said. "He didn't know what it was. He was going to use it to frame the Ketteriches, get them nailed on dope and a weapons charge."

She shrugged. "I didn't know that then. By the time I did, it was too late."

She reached down and grabbed hold of the dead youth's collar, lifting the upper part of the body, then she looked to where the rope led from a tree to the old ventilation shaft. Somehow, the matter-of-fact way in which she proposed to dispose of Clemmer's body galvanized me as not even his murder before my eyes had done. I rolled on my side, drew up my knees, and began to struggle to get upright.

Sally let go of the collar and the corpse's face dropped onto the ground. She picked up the rifle and pointed it at me. "This," she said, "will hurt a lot more. The ammunition's seventy-five years old, and I might have to shoot you several times to get the job done."

I'd gotten my knees under me. Now I froze. "Sally, you don't need to do this."

"Yes, Sid, I do. Mo told me how you were digging into the whole Ginger Goodwin business. 'Coming at it from the villain's point of view,' she said. You would have turned up something."

"No," I said, "it wasn't like that. I..." But then I couldn't tell her I'd been lying to Mo all along. Besides, we were past that now. After what Sally had told me, what she'd let me see, she couldn't let me live.

"Sorry," she said, but her face was full of hard purpose. She resumed her grip on Clemmer's collar and laboriously dragged him, one-handed, over to the far side of the fire pit, to the spot where the railroad ties covered the shaft opening. She leaned the rifle against a tree, and without taking her eyes off me, levered up one of the squared timbers, then another.

Then she heaved the body forward until it was bent at the waist, head and shoulders aimed downward into the long, dark drop. Without a pause, she stooped and lifted Clemmer's ankles. The body disappeared into the shaft. If it made any sound when it struck the probably water-filled gallery far below, I couldn't hear it.

Now Sally picked up the rifle again. She looked at me.

"Sally, no," I said. "You know I don't deserve this. I've got kids."

"I'm sorry, Sid," she said. "But I don't deserve to lose everything. Ginger didn't deserve to get shot. My grandfather didn't deserve to get TB. Deserve doesn't come into it."

She hefted the rifle and came around the fire towards me. Clemmer's pot was bubbling, the noodles swirling in the boiling water like a frenzy of pale eels. Above us I could hear the cyclical thrum of heavy airplane engines.

I got to my feet. She stopped a few feet away and raised the weapon. "Don't make this worse than it has to be," she said.

"You mean worse for you? It doesn't get much worse for me!" There was no point running. First I would have to breast my way through the salal, and that would give her time to come up right behind me and shoot. I had no doubt she would do it, and I'd seen how far a bullet from that rifle had gone into the wooden wall of Benny Filiatrault's house. A hole driven that deep in my skull would mean that the bullet would be bouncing around in my brain.

But there were other things I could do with feet besides running. I started around the firepit to meet her.

She backed up. "Don't, Sid." She backed away, but there was no fear on her face, only that look of studied concentration. She raised the rifle, put the butt to her shoulder.

A fresh shot of adrenaline flashed through me. *This must be what it's like in a war,* I thought. I wasn't afraid anymore. I was just as determined as she was. My thoughts were hard and clear as crystal: I would kick the rifle out of her hands, then I would kick *her,* and if necessary I would jump up and down on her until she was no longer a danger. Part of me was shocked at the violence I was intending to do, but it was a part of me that was standing off to the sides, watching while the dirty work was done.

She backed up against the mass of bracken that had been Davey Clemmer's bed. The uneven footing unbalanced her for a moment, and I saw my chance. I rushed forward, my mind so sharply focused I saw I had to go right foot first, then left, and that would leave my right free to swing the kick.

It all happened slowly. My right foot came down, my left was in the air and about to land. It was then I saw the flash of fire from the muzzle. I even saw the shape of the transient flame, like a long, thin spear-point. At the same moment, the .30-calibre slug hit me square in the middle of my chest.

It was like a punch from a giant's fist. I felt my breastbone crack, or maybe that was the sound of the shot. I was still moving in slow motion, but not forwards anymore.

The force of the blow spun me a little and my left foot came down in the firepit.

My leg knocked the pot flying, boiling water and noodles spilling out over the ground on the far side of the pit. My boot landed in the coals and immediately I felt the heat. I wanted more than anything to get my foot out of the fire, but I was still falling sideways, following the pot. My left elbow struck the ground less than a second after the pot's boiling contents, and my shoulder plunged into the scalding mess.

Instinct told me to yank my left foot out of the fire and get my shoulder off the noodles. I told instinct to shut up. Two hundred million years of distilled experience left my reptile and mammal brains in no doubt as to the right course of action when an appendage encounters live coals. But my human brain had its own agenda. Even as my shoulder was being scalded, even as my boot felt as if it had been replaced by one of the Inquisition's red hot shoes, even as the cuff of my jeans caught fire, I dug my foot deeper into the fire and kicked out, sending a shower of burning coals toward Sally.

Because she was methodically working the Marlin's rusty breech action, jacking the empty brass cartridge out to disappear into the salal. She was just about to slam the bolt forward to put another round in the barrel when the chunks of burning charcoal landed on her lips, chin and upper torso.

I knew it must have hurt, because by now I was actually on fire. But I felt no sympathy. Scalded and burning, with every neuron of my reptile and mammal brain circuits telling me I needed to jerk my foot out of the coals, I did just the opposite.

Because my human brain had noted that Sally had dropped the rifle and put her hands to her blistering lips. I pushed myself upright, left foot still in the coals, and stepped out of the firepit to plant a kick on the Marlin.

My right foot connected and sent it flying into the salal.

I spun around, intending to continue with my earlier, interrupted plan to kick Sally into submission. But it seemed that all the components of her brain were also turning over at full revolutions. She ignored the pain in her mouth and even the wide, smoldering spot on the front of her shirt, to put her hands on my arms in a firm grip. Instantly, she pushed me to one side then, as I automatically resisted the pressure, the side of her foot hit my right ankle and I toppled over.

I landed on Clemmer's bed, and Sally landed on top of me, which was apparently her plan. Sometime in the past, she must have studied one of the martial arts, because the push-kick-and-topple maneuver was straight out of a ju-jitsu book I'd studied as a kid.

I wished I'd recognized it earlier, because I might have pulled free and got in a kick. Now I was lying on my back, my hands tied and pinned beneath me, and Sally was manoeuvring herself to kneel with her legs on either side of me and her hard buttocks resting on my belly. The weight made it hard to breathe.

She touched a finger to her blistered lips and I saw a flash of irritation. Then it was replaced by that familiar look of grim intent. She didn't offer me any more expressions of regret. She simply reached for the spots on the front of my neck where oblivion waited to greet her educated touch.

I bucked, I thrashed, I tried to kick the back of her head. My knee connected with her spine and she grunted. But all she had to do was lean forward, and she was out of reach.

I didn't yell for help. I didn't plead. But sounds came out of my throat. Not words, but animal snarls. I was not going gently into the dark.

I felt her fingertips touch my flesh. They were cold. I jerked my head to the side, tried to push her fingers aside with my chin. No good. She carefully, knowledgeably, explored the structures of my throat, seeking the flaw in the anatomy that would kill me.

Still I bucked and thrashed. My left foot connected with something hard, something that went *crack!* I tried once more to knee her in the back. But her fingers had stopped moving now. She had found the spots. Her burned mouth set itself.

I had time to think, *Here it comes,* then a sheet of flame erupted behind her, followed by black smoke and a stench of burning kerosene. The pain I had been ignoring in my left ankle suddenly increased tenfold and engulfed the whole leg. I'd been on fire before. Now I was seriously ablaze.

But so was Sally McMahon. The back of her shirt had caught fire and the flames had reached her hair. She wasn't overruling her primitive neural circuits. She jumped up, her hands slapping at the back of her head, making wordless sounds. I wriggled backwards then rolled off Clemmer's bed of dried vegetation and kept rolling until the flames that were consuming the lower left leg of my jeans were smothered. The cloth still smoldered and the flesh hurt like hell. But I knew that was a good sign: the burn hadn't gone deep enough to kill the nerves.

I got to my knees. I felt the post-adrenaline shakes, wondered if I was at risk of shock. Then I saw Sally, after putting out the fire in her hair and having flung herself down on the ground to kill the flames on her back, was sitting up. No shock there. I would have admired the woman's determination if it hadn't been so focused on killing me.

She was getting to her feet. Now would have been the perfect opportunity to kick her senseless, but other priorities were rapidly emerging. In my struggles to avoid her quick-and-easy method of instant death delivery, my left leg, complete with burning cuff, had kicked over Clemmer's old-time kerosene lantern. It must have had a well-filled reservoir, because it had ignited and spread.

His bed was on fire. The salal behind the bed was on fire. And the flames were spreading through the bone-dry thicket and reaching for the trees around it with a speed and appetite . I'd seen this happen once, back in my forest fire-fighting days, when the crew were back-burning a stretch of semi-open woodland and the fire got away from us.

It had raced across the ground, igniting the dry grass, spreading like a shockwave. When the line of the flame reached a thirty-year-old spruce tree, the flames licked into the dead, dry branches that are always to be found near the bottoms of evergreen trunks. The Métis had shown me they made great kindling, and the wildfire showed me that in spades. With a *whoosh* and a roar, the spruce went up like a match.

The difference between then and now was that, all those years ago, I'd been with a crew of experienced fire-fighters, who were equipped with the right tools. Plus the wind had shifted. But today I was half tied-up, with no one to help and a fire that didn't need any wind to spread itself. The initial blaze had already expanded more than halfway around the ring of dried-out salal, and soon it would complete the circle, after which I'd be surrounded by enough ferocious heat to cook me where I stood.

I turned and threw myself into the bracken, the stuff scratching my face, my feet being snagged in branches. I didn't care. I could hear the fire roaring louder beside me, could feel its heat, already bad and building, and I kept going until I broke free into the little clearing of fast-growing broadleafed trees.

Now it was time to run. The little patch of second growth in which I stood was catching fire almost as fast as the salal thicket. The ancient woods surrounding the little clearing had no undergrowth to ignite and spread the fire. But the canopy above was as dry as the salal and it was all linked together — plus there would be desiccated, dead timber up there, the naked white spars that you would see always sticking up above the still-living timber. And between the ground and the upper world were plenty of those excellent-tinder dead branches.

And now the still-growing blaze the spilled kerosene started was throwing a tornado of sparks and flaming flakes up into all that excitable, ignitable fuel. I had seen what happened when flame reached a dense, dry canopy, back in my youth: it was a phenomenon called *crowning*, and it would spread a fire through a canopy faster than a man could run. A lot faster, if that man's hands were tied behind his back.

I didn't look behind me. Sally was a problem for later. If I was lucky she'd catch on fire before she got out of the burning ring of bracken. It was not a kind thought, but I discovered my love of humankind did not extend to fellow members of my species who tried to murder me.

I got my bearings by sighting on the big cedar stump they cut down to make some room to work in when they'd dug the ventilation shaft, and I started running. It wasn't easy to cover rough, uneven ground with my hands tied behind my back. But I had determination going for me.

What I had working against me, beside the fire, was the hard-faced determination of Sally McMahon. I hadn't covered fifty feet before she caught up to me and gave me a hard shove from behind that sent me staggering off balance. My foot caught on a root and I went down, twisting as I fell to land, with painful irony, on the bad shoulder she had helped heal with ultrasound.

I rolled over onto my back, fast as I could, knowing what was to come. She was looking around, and I realized she was searching for something with which to batter me into helplessness before she applied her carotid death-pressure. She moved a few feet to one side and picked up a fallen branch.

But it was ancient and rotten. It snapped of its own weight when she gave it a tentative trial swing. She looked around again, and found nothing. So many centuries of needles and other detritus had fallen to the floor of this cathedral-like grove that any handy rocks had long since been buried.

That had taken her only seconds, and I'd been using the time to try to get to my feet. I made it to my knees before she came quickly and kicked me in the solar plexus. All the air went out of me and a great stab of pain flooded in to take its place. The blow reminded my sternum it had been cracked by the impact of the .30-calibre bullet, and it added its own sharp complaint.

I went down again, gasping and wheezing, landing on my back. She looked down at me, studying my condition, and I saw the decision form in her countenance. I tried to kick at her, but I was still too short of oxygen for my legs to be of much use. She sidestepped, then dropped to her knees beside me, her face showing that look of deliberate purpose. Her hands came toward me and I realized her face and hands were was the last sight I would ever see.

Except for what I saw above and behind her: the great sea of flame that was spreading high overhead, as fast as a floodtide racing over shallows. Burning twigs and flakes of carbonized wood and bark were beginning to rain down, and the sound of the fire had become a steady roar.

"Sally!" I said. "For Christ's sake, you'll burn!"

But nothing would divert her from her intent, not even the bit of burning debris that landed on her shoulder and made the wool fabric smolder. Her fingers touched my throat. I felt no pressure, only the coolness of her touch. Then I felt nothing at all.

Chapter 15

It was like breaking through the surface of a pond after swimming up from the dark depths below. As I came back to consciousness, I was sucking in a great draft of air, my brain having decided enough was enough, the tissues needed fresh oxygen.

At first I did not know where I was or what had happened. I was lying on my back, looking up into darkness. I tried to rise and found I couldn't move my arms. I was cold and shivering, and a moment later I realized I was soaking wet.

And then it all came flooding back. I rolled over on my side, bent my legs, and struggled to get them under me. After a few moments I managed to get to a kneeling position. I looked around.

The ancient woods were a sodden mess, every branch dripping with water. A few dozen yards away was the big cedar stump, and beyond it a tangled mass of charred black sticks that had been the thicket and the second-growth trees surrounding Clemmer's camp. The fire was out though its remains were smoking a little. Then I realized what I was seeing was mostly steam. I could hear a hiss from the still hot wood.

Around me, the ancient forest floor that had been so clear of undergrowth was buried beneath a field of half-burned debris: leafless limbs of deadwood as thick as my thigh, charred and scorched branches and twigs of all sizes, and flakes of ash filtering down like a black and grey rain. And with them came an actual sprinkling rain of dirty water, dripping everywhere — including on the face of Sally McMahon, who lay beside me, her body half curled as if she had gone to sleep.

But that wasn't sleep. Her eyes were open, and as I looked down at her, a piece of grey ash floated down to touch one cornea. The eye did not reflexively blink.

She was dead and after a moment, I saw why. Lying on the ground behind her was a thick length of barkless deadwood, its grey, weathered surface streaked with char — and halfway along its length was a splash of red that was being slowly made pink by the drips from above.

High up there, I could see a hole in the canopy, blue sky and some moving cloud, then a shaft of sunlight reached down through the steam-filled air. As I looked, a broad white wing passed over the gap, and I realized I was still hearing a roar — but it was the sound of heavy airplane engines, as the great Martin Mars water bomber made another pass over the site of the fire, to make sure the blast of its cargo of Comox Lake glacial runoff had done the job.

It had certainly done all that was needed, as far as I was concerned.

It took me a while to get my hands untied. Clemmer's hatchet helped, once my head cleared enough to remember it. The rubber had burned off the steel handle, but the blade was sharp. I wasn't squeamish about digging my cell phone out of Sally's pocket. It still worked, and I called the Courtenay RCMP office and asked to speak to Corporal Mikhailovsky. I asked him to send someone to the air show to rendezvous with my twins at the Lions Club hot-dog stand. I wouldn't be able to meet them because I'd be waiting for the corporal to meet me under the hole in the roof over Hockney's Woods. And afterwards I expected I'd have to spend a fair amount of time at the cop shop giving a statement.

And probably trying to talk my way out of a different kind of hole: the one I'd dug for myself by withholding evidence in a number of now-related cases.

Mikhailovsky told me to stay right where I was. A fire crew was already on its way, and I was to tell them to stay away from the crime scene.

I closed the phone then opened it again and called Karen. I got her assistant, who wanted to know if it was urgent. Delayed shock was catching up with me by then. The hand holding the phone to my ear was shaking and I guess there was an edge to my voice when I told the young woman to get my ex-wife on the line, right-fucking-now.

"Are the boys all right?" were Karen's first words.

"They're fine. It's me. I've... ." I couldn't begin to explain it all, so I just said, "I've been in a fire."

"Are you burned?"

"No, just a little shaken up. But I'm going to have to spend some time with the police."

All concern for me fled her tone. "You mean spend some time under arrest?"

"Maybe."

She wanted to know what the hell I'd been up to. "Practicing history," I said. I didn't suppose the short, involuntary laugh that erupted out of me helped the situation.

"Are you drunk?"

"No." I didn't tell her it sounded like a good idea.

"Where are the boys?" she said.

"I've asked the RCMP to look after them."

"And whatsername, where's she in all of this?"

"Mo?" The mention of her name called up another shiver. I'd have to call her, too. "At her brother's place in

Sechelt."

There was silence on the line, except for a clicking sound. That would be Karen tapping a pen on something while she thought. Then she said, "I'm going to see if I can get them on a flight this afternoon."

I might have said that I could drive them down to the ferry, but the truth was I didn't know if I'd be spending the night in a police cell. And maybe an indefinite time after that. "Okay," I said. "Let me know."

She didn't say goodbye. I closed the phone, thought again about calling Mo, then was relieved not to have to make the attempt. I heard voices and turned around to see figures in heavy boots and firefighters' coveralls coming toward me.

I met them halfway.

I arrived home late that night. I'd been questioned for hours by two plainclothes Mounties. During the ride in the back of a cruiser from Cumberland down to the station, I'd decided I wouldn't mention the marijuana at all. I stuck to the most basic parts of the story: that I knew Davey Clemmer had got me in trouble at the Black Hole — Corporal Mikhailovsky could confirm that — and that I wanted to have it out with him. When Sally McMahon called me to say she'd seen him, I went to have the confrontation. Everything else that happened was a surprise, I said. That part of the story had the advantage of being completely true.

They'd taken my sodden clothes when I arrived at the station. I was wearing jeans and a sweatshirt from somebody's locker, plus a pair of sneakers that didn't quite fit. At some point, they brought in a doctor to have a look at me. He said I had some bad bruising and probably a cracked sternum. My leg burns were only first-degree. Let the air get at them, he said, and for God's sake don't put butter on them. He gave me some painkillers, then handed me back to the interrogators.

The hardest part was making them understand the role Cumberland's history had played in all of this. The Mounties have always tended to move their personnel around the country; that meant I wasn't dealing with a couple of locals. When I started to explain the background to Sally McMahon's murder spree, I found myself being looked at in that way cops will look at you when they think they're being bullshitted.

Finally, I told them to go and phone the mayor of Cumberland — or anybody else they trusted up in the village — and ask him what would be the probable fate of anyone who was discovered to be descended from the person who ratted out Ginger Goodwin. They went out, came back ten minutes later, and one of them said, "Okay, tell us that part again."

By then the painkillers were kicking in. Coupled with the exhaustion that went with being shot, almost killed, and then grilled for hours, the drugs were enough to have me nodding off in the interview room. They decided to call it a night.

Corporal Mikhailovsky came in, looked me over, and added one last surprise to the day when he said, "You can go."

The cops had had the Behemoth towed to the impound yard, and I was in no shape to go recover it and drive home. I called a cab and went outside to wait for it.

That was a mistake. Two reporters — one print, one radio — were waiting outside the cop shop. The moment I appeared, a young woman accompanied by a cameraman got out of a van and hurried over. I waved them off with a, "No comment. Call me in the morning." I figured they'd have plenty to run with as it was.

The house was dark. The twins' bags and their stuff were still there. I'd have to put them in the freight compartment of the highway bus in a day or so. I fell across the bed, still wearing the borrowed clothes. I was asleep in seconds. But I came awake before dawn, clawing my way out of a nightmare. The deepest levels of my psyche knew that we'd been killed back in Hockney's Woods and were not ready to calm down about it. I rolled over on my back and looked up at the dark ceiling. For the first time, I thought about what had happened.

To fight for your life, to come within a hair of dying, and to win that desperate battle can leave even combat-experienced soldiers with post-traumatic stress. But I hadn't won the battle. I'd been licked and I'd known it. As Sally's cold fingertips had found my throat, I'd had no doubt it was all over. I hadn't accepted it, hadn't gone quietly. I'd still been bucking and thrashing, but I'd known it was all over for Sid Rafferty.

It had been pure chance the Martin Mars bomber, having tanked up on glacial meltwater for the stunt at the air show, had been wheeling majestically back from the end of Comox Lake when the pilot had seen the flames leaping into the canopy from the hole in the old growth.

The first officer had switched the radio from the air base's frequency to the forest service's emergency channel, reported the fire, and asked permission to squelch it. Somebody had already spotted the smoke — the rangers keep a close watch when the woods are dry — because the bomber got an immediate you-betcha.

The huge airplane adjusted its course, lined up, came down to near-treetop level, and let fly. The weight of the thousands of gallons of water, arriving with an airspeed of almost two hundred and fifty miles per hour, had smashed the hell out of the canopy. Big chunks of wood, dead and living, had come crashing down to the forest floor.

And one of them had cracked Sally McMahon's skull,

just as she was reaching to pinch my nose and seal my lips, to deny my aggregated brains the oxygen that would keep us all alive. The fact I was now lying on my bed, looking up at my bedroom ceiling and still breathing, was nothing but pure luck. Or, depending on your point of view, it could be seen as an offer of a second chance.

Or even a message from the deity of my choice — or from the great karmic wheel of the cosmos — that I had something to do before I went down into the big dark.

Lying there, in a lesser darkness that was yielding to the pre-dawn grey, it was definitely worth thinking about.

I must have slept some more, this time dreamlessly, because suddenly I realized I was looking at a ceiling lit by the full glow of the morning sun. I got up, went to the bathroom then to the kitchen to make a pot of tea. I saw the message light blinking on my combination telephone and answering machine. The red digits of the readout said I had ten messages. But I wasn't going to hear any of them until I'd had at least half a cup of strong black Ceylon leaf.

While I was rinsing out the pot I saw motion through the window. I eased over and peeked around the edge of the frame. There was a full gaggle of reporters on the lawn, their cars and vans parked on both sides of the street. A TV crew was interviewing the retired army major who lived across from me. I hoped he was feeling charitable towards his poor suffering neighbour.

I made the tea and set the pot on the table to give it time to brew. I put a china mug beside it and got a jug of milk from the fridge, then sat down. I kept watching my hands as they performed these mundane actions. I was thinking it was a wonderful thing to have hands and to be able to use them. I kept taking deep breaths and letting them out slowly, my chest feeling as if I was filling up with helium.

I poured myself a cup and took a good, hot mouthful. And that was wonderful, too. I was beginning to think almost getting killed and being miraculously saved at the very last moment was the kind of thing I ought to do more often. I finished the tea, poured another mugful, then went to stand over the phone. I punched the playback button and heard a CBC radio reporter's voice asking me to call him back as soon as possible at the number I didn't bother to record.

The next message was from another radio reporter, then one from the *Vancouver Sun,* and another from the Victoria *Times Colonist.* The other seven messages were from other media, including the *Globe and Mail.* I didn't figure there was any need to return the calls; by now, every news organization that wanted to hear from me had a reporter on my lawn.

I erased them all, then finished my tea. I got changed into something more respectable than my borrowed cop clothes, and went out onto my front step. The crew across the road immediately abandoned my neighbour and hurried over to join the rest of the scrum, who flocked toward me bristling with lenses, microphones and tape recorders, shouting questions, the most common of which was "How do you feel?"

I'd noticed it back when I was a reporter. In the days of Edward R. Murrow and his Canadian equivalent, Matthew Halton, reporters used to ask interviewees "What do you think...?" about whatever the issue was. Somewhere back in the 1980s, when news was being rebranded as entertainment and we were all giving up being citizens of a society to become consumers in an economy, the big switch had been made. Consumers don't think about things, they feel their way into a relationship with the brands that give them their sense of identity.

"I feel fine," I told the scrum. "Now I'm going to make a statement. I won't answer any questions. There is a police investigation going on and you can get everything else from here on in from the RCMP."

I told them the basic truth: I had been the victim of an attempted murder. In the struggle, a forest fire had been accidentally started. I was immensely grateful to the crew of the Martin Mars water bomber who had saved my life. And now I was going to step back and let the police and the courts do their jobs.

"And that's all I have to say. You can camp out on my lawn for as long as your assignment editors want to keep you here, but you won't get another word out of me."

Of course, they tried. But I smiled and waved and went back inside. The phone rang. I let the machine answer it and heard a reporter's voice asking me to name the person who attempted to murder me. I looked through my front window and saw a man with a cell phone to his ear, waving at me. I shook my head and turned down the volume on the answering machine. For good measure, I also switched off the ringer.

I made myself breakfast on a tray and ate it sitting on the couch, with the TV tuned to CBC *Newsworld*. The murder-cum-forest fire story was getting covered as breaking news. I saw video of a body on a stretcher being loaded into an ambulance on the lake road, firefighters coming out of the woods, Corporal Mikhailovsky on the cop shop steps saying that a second body was being recovered, that the suspect had been found dead at the scene, and that suicide was not involved.

Then the anchor was cutting to a new report, coming in live. I saw one of the scrum reporters looking out of the screen at me, with my house in the background, setting up the clip to come. A moment later, there I was, saying my say, then disappearing back through my front door.

The anchor and the reporter agreed there was more

to come on the story and that CBC would keep the viewers up to date as it unfolded. That was followed by some stock footage of the Martin Mars dropping a load of water on a fire somewhere. I turned the set off and took my tray back into the kitchen.

The answering machine's read-out said it had silently accumulated ten more messages. That seemed to be its limit. I erased them all without listening to them. The crowd outside had thinned, but three reporters had been left on picket duty, in case I changed my mind and decided to become talkative.

I picked up the phone, heard a dial tone, and called Karen. She told me Bill and Dick had got home safely, that they'd been worried about me, but they'd just seen me on TV. Their reaction had been to declare that I was pretty cool for a father.

"I'm sorry about the trouble," I said.

"Who tried to kill you?" she said. "And why?"

"That's a long story."

"I've got time. Tell me."

So I did. When I was finished, she said, "Jesus. What are they, hillbillies?"

"They're good people, up in Cumby," I said. "Salt of the earth. But that earth is full of the bones of their dead, and they don't forget."

She made a dismissive noise. I decided not to argue with her. It had never done much good. I told her I'd ship the boys' bags over on the bus and call her when they were on the way. She told me to be careful.

"Too late," I said.

I went and watched the TV news some more, in case there was some new development from the police side of things. But after I'd seen myself twice more, I switched off.

The media pickets outside were gone. I saw my neighbour picking up some of the trash the scrum had left. I thought about going out to help, but he'd probably get more indignation — and thus more enjoyment — out of doing the chore all by himself.

There were only three messages on the machine now. I turned up the sound and played them. The first two were reporters and I erased them. The third was from Mo.

"Are you screening?" she said. "If so, please pick up. There was silence for a long moment, then her voice continued. "Maybe it's better this way. I saw you on the news. I'm glad you're all right." Another pause, then, "But.. ." The silence this time went on even longer before she said, "Before I left, I looked on your computer. I just wanted to see how the treatment was coming along, before I talked to Roger again."

More silence.

Her voice, when it came again, wasn't angry, but bewildered. "Raff, why would you lie to me? Why would you make me look like a fool?"

If she'd been angry, I could have stood it better. But she sounded so sad. "I trusted you. Why couldn't you trust me?"

There was a click as she hung up the phone. In the movies, you would always hear a dial tone. But in real life, all you hear is an empty silence.

I dialled her brother Miggs' number. A machine answered. When I heard the beep, I said, "I'm sorry. I was afraid to tell you that I was...afraid. Please call me back."

But she didn't. Instead I got a call from Miggs. "She wants to know a time when you're not going to be there. She'll come and get her stuff, but she doesn't want to see you."

"Miggs—"

"Don't bother. I never thought you were right for her."

Miggs was a paraplegic who climbed the outside of skyscrapers with equipment he'd designed and made himself. His motto was *Never give up*. I'd never be able to explain myself to him. He wouldn't know a phobia if it came up and bit him on his rear end, which he couldn't feel anyway.

"Okay," I said. "I'll let you know."

"Jesus," he said, "I never knew anybody who quit so easily." He hung up and I was listening to nothing again.

I packed Mo's clothes and make-up and the knick-knacks she'd acquired while we were together. It didn't take long. I went down into the office and boxed up her files and the other materials from her consultancy business. I piled them near the door.

I looked around the work space we had shared. Then I sat down in my chair, closed my eyes, and thought about how it had been to have her just behind me when I was working, so I could turn my head and see her there, staring at something she'd written on her PowerBook , tapping her teeth with the eraser end of a pencil.

I opened my eyes and saw my own face in the darkness of the monitor's screen. After a moment, I reached out and booted up the 386. When the DOS prompt appeared, I typed in WS and few seconds later I was looking at the opening menu of WordStar.

I found the movies directory then clicked on the word *GINGER*. One of the files listed was *TREATMENT*. I clicked to open it and saw the two words followed by a colon and the flashing cursor.

I closed my eyes and tried to call up Mo's face. Instead, I got Sally McMahon's, looking down at me with that look of determination. It should have horrified me, should have set the reptile and mammal brains thrashing about within our shared cerebrum.

But it didn't. I opened my eyes and looked at the empty space in front of the cursor. The words came out of me, without thought. "I'm still here. I won."

I put my fingers on the keyboard. For a moment I sat there, waiting. Then the image came, and I started to type.

We open in a clearing full of great stumps. A small man in a worn, turn-of-the-century suit stands atop one of them. He raises one hand in an old-fashioned oratorical gesture and begins to make a speech. His voice is hesitant at first, then builds as he gains confidence.

It didn't take long. It was all there, had been all there in the back of my head, for weeks. Now it was coming out. I sat and typed until my back got stiff. I went upstairs and made myself some tea and a sandwich, but didn't turn on the TV. Then I went back down to the office and worked until it was finished.

I went back over the text, changed a few words, printed it out, and put it in an envelope. Then I sat at my desk, my hands on my thighs. My chest hurt, and my leg. I ignored them.

I opened a new file on the computer and wrote:

Dear Mo:

I screwed up because I was afraid you'd leave me, and now you've left me. I'm not sure, but I think the guy who was so afraid died in the fire.

If you give me a chance to prove it, I will never let you down again.

I added, *Love, Sid*, then printed out the note and put it in the envelope with the treatment. I sealed it up and put it on the top of her things in the box. I put the box on her desk, turned out the light, and went upstairs.

Tomorrow, I would call Miggs and set a time for her to come over. I wouldn't be there, but the envelope would.

And then we'd see.

Afterword

This is a work of fiction that touches on some real history. The life and death of Albert (Ginger) Goodwin happened as I have related them, but the events recounted here after his funeral cortege left Cumberland are all my own invention.

And those who were horrified by television images of the Black Hole clearcut twenty years ago might want to take a drive along BC Highway 4 and try to spot that allegedly devastated zone. All there is to see is a healthy second-growth forest.

About the Author

The name I answer to is Matt Hughes. I write fantasy and suspense fiction. To keep the two genres separate, I now use my full name, Matthew Hughes, for fantasy, and the shorter form for the crime stuff. I also write media tie–ins as Hugh Matthews.

I've won the Crime Writers of Canada's Arthur Ellis Award, and have been shortlisted for the Aurora, Nebula, Philip K. Dick, and Derringer Awards.

I was born in 1949 in Liverpool, England, but my family moved to Canada when I was five. I've made my living as a writer all of my adult life, first as a journalist, then as a staff speechwriter to the Canadian Ministers of Justice and Environment, and — from 1979 until a few years back— as a freelance corporate and political speechwriter in British Columbia. I am a former director of the Federation of British Columbia Writers and I used to belong to Mensa Canada, but these days I'm conserving my energies to write fiction.

I'm a university drop–out from a working poor background. Before getting into newspapers, I worked in a factory that made school desks, drove a grocery delivery truck, was night janitor in a GM dealership, and did a short stint as an orderly in a private mental hospital. As a teenager, I served a year as a volunteer with the Company of Young Canadians (something like VISTA in the US). I've been married to a very patient woman since the late 1960s, and I have three grown sons.

In late 2007, I took up a secondary occupation — that of an unpaid housesitter — so that I can afford to keep on writing fiction yet still eat every day.

You can find me at: *http://www.matthewhughes.org*

Books by Matt Hughes

As Matt Hughes

Downshift
Old Growth
Paroxysm

As Matthew Hughes

Fools Errant
Fool Me Twice
Gullible's Travels (omnibus edition of *Fools Errant* and
    Fool Me Twice)
Black Brillion
The Gist Hunter and Other Stories
Majestrum, A Tale of Henghis Hapthorn
The Spiral Labyrinth, A Tale of Henghis Hapthorn
Hespira, A Tale of Henghis Hapthorn
The Commons
Template
The Other
To Hell and Back: The Damned Busters
To Hell and Back: Costume Not Included
To Hell and Back: Hell To Pay
Nine Tales of Henghis Hapthorn
The Meaning of Luff and Other Stories
The Compleat Guth Bandar
Devil or Angel and Other Stories

As Hugh Matthews

Song of the Serpent
Wolverine: Lifeblood